STEEL
Rush
In the Shadows
BOOK 5

Cass and Calder

a BLACK *Shadows* novel

STEEL
Rush

In the Shadows

BOOK 5

Cass and Calder

by P.T. MICHELLE

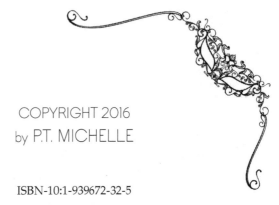

Interior designed and formatted by E.M. Tippetts Book Designs
www.emtippettsbookdesigns.com

To stay informed when the next **P.T. Michelle** book will be released,
join P.T. Michelle's free newsletter http://bit.ly/11tqAQN

STEEL
Rush
In the Shadows
BOOK 5
Cass and Calder

by P.T. MICHELLE

This is the second book in the BLACK SHADOWS duet, Cass and Calder's story. You must read GOLD SHIMMER before reading STEEL RUSH.

Cass has spent years trying to forget her past. But the thing about pasts...they always come back around, sometimes in the most unexpected ways. When Celeste goes missing, Cass discovers how intricately entangled her past and present are with Celeste's, making it impossible to walk away.

In an effort to ignore his own painful history, Calder challenges a corrupt, underground organization, but his mission gets sidelined when Cass's life becomes endangered.

The passion simmering between Calder and Cass tempts them to share their darkest secrets, but can their trust in each other help them unravel the mystery surrounding Celeste? Can they eliminate the threat to Cass before the past overshadows the present and destroys their intense connection?

Note: STEEL RUSH is meant for readers 18+ due to mature content. This is the second book in the BLACK SHADOWS duet, Cass and Calder's love story. The first book, GOLD SHIMMER, must be read before STEEL RUSH. The BLACK SHADOWS duet (books 4 and 5) can be read as a standalone story or as part of the IN THE SHADOWS series.

The Day I Stopped Being a Victim

The Past - Six Years Ago

The small needle pierces the soft inside of my forearm, its sharp point moving so fast I can't track it. As hundreds of stings flood my body at once, pushing black ink into the script on my skin, the discomfort feels necessary, cathartic even. I focus on the distracting buzzing of the tattoo machine, my lips twisting at the irony that I can't seem to escape one last infliction of pain.

"Finished," Noah announces as he pats at the excess ink on my new tattoo. He glances down at the tree branch he'd painstakingly inked to cover the scars on both my wrists a year before, then eyes the detailed raven he'd inked on the branch on my left wrist. Raising a pierced eyebrow as he lifts the cloth away from my new tattoo, he says, "This one is so simple compared to the others."

The marred skin hidden under both wrists' branch tattoos tingles and itches like it always does when my emotions are especially revved. Getting this tattoo certainly qualifies as a heightened moment. I skim my gaze over the single word *Never* he just completed, loving the fancy script with trailing lines before and after the word.

Noah is the first person I called once the deep cut I'd inflicted on my wrist during a frantic relapse had fully healed.

My cutting days are over. And I will never allow Jake Hemming to touch me ever again. The first is a promise to my big sister, Sophie, who left this world way before her time, and the second is to myself. Both are vows I never plan to break.

I meet the curious sympathy in Noah's crystal blue gaze. From that first day I laid eyes on his nude form in Freshman Art 101, I saw past the twenty-two-year-old model's floppy pitch black hair and gorgeous tattooed body and knew he modeled in the buff for more than money and potential dates. This guy ran deeper than his teasing smile; he appreciated art's simplest form, which meant he'd get my answer. "Sometimes a single word can carry the most meaning, Noah. So...*thanks*."

Barking out a laugh, he kisses my forehead as he rises from his stool. "Anytime, sweet Cass."

CHAPTER ONE

Present Day

Cass

I just lied my ass off. To the police. I bite my lip and watch the detectives drive away from the Carver's estate, my heart racing. *What have I done?*

The Carver's family lawyer and neighbor, Phillip Hemming, talks to Celeste's father in a low tone for a minute, then walks home. My fingers twitch with the need to scratch my itching wrists as I follow Celeste's younger sister, Beth, and her father into their home.

I'm torn on what I should do. When I agreed to switch places with Celeste for an evening, I never could have anticipated that she wouldn't return on time. I certainly didn't know enough yet to admit to the police that I'm *not* Celeste. Right now, saying anything could cause a scandal that might potentially destroy her father's run for Senate. Considering protecting Gregory Carver's career was the whole reason she asked me to do this, I held my silence when the police asked why they found Celeste's ID in a bloody abandoned car.

For all I knew the blood and ID had nothing to do with her. Before she left, Celeste gave me her real ID, so the ID the police discovered in that car must've been a fake, which makes me question who the car and blood belong to. Not that any of this craziness answers why I still haven't heard from Celeste. The only explanation that makes sense is that she realized she'd arrive home too late to try to slip back into her life without being noticed, so she decided to wait until tomorrow. It *is* almost two in the morning. I just wish I knew why she didn't text me her change in plans. Her lack of communication is making my stomach burn with conflict.

"This is the last thing I need right now, Celeste." Gregory rounds on me in the foyer the moment he closes the door behind us, his terse tone interrupting the tug-of-war going on in my head.

"I know, Father. I'm sorry to worry you."

Tilting his silver head, he narrows his gaze. "How *did* your ID get in that car?"

I raise my hands, truly mystified. "I have no idea."

"Someone must've lifted it at the club before we got separated earlier tonight," Beth quickly jumps in. I meet her wide-eyed green gaze over Gregory's shoulder. Apparently she had already spun her own version of our earlier whereabouts to her father and the police before my cab pulled up.

I'm pretty sure Beth wouldn't confess to her father that she had actually taken me to an exclusive underground MMA championship fight. One that got disbanded midway through due to the threat of imminent police intervention. And by the pleading look in her eyes right now, her father is clearly unaware that his youngest daughter is dating one of the guys responsible for organizing and running said illegal event.

Two brushes with law enforcement in one night is more than I signed up for when I agreed to this deal with Celeste. Now that the police are gone, a part of me feels I should tell Celeste's family the truth about my identity. But if I speak up too soon, I could blow everything for Celeste. She was adamant that no one could know about me. I can see her thinking that me telling her family the truth, even under these strained circumstances, would be a failure on my part to hold up my end of the deal. I can't allow her to back out of her promise to help my father get his business development plan approved by the city.

God, this is one big screwed up mess with no right answer. It's not like I have a manual to follow on doppelganger switch-a-roos. *Why didn't I stay in bed with Calder like he asked me to?*

"Is the club where you think you lost it?" Gregory prods, pulling my focus back to immediate issues.

I slowly nod my agreement with Beth's story version, while telling myself that Celeste will text me in the morning. It had better be first thing. I can't wait to shed her royally messed up family like an overpriced, ill-fitting sweater.

Exhaling an annoyed grunt, Gregory gestures to Marco and Anthony, who've been lurking in the hallway. "And you two, keep up with my daughters like you're supposed to or you'll be replaced. Am I clear?"

"Yes, sir," both security guards mumble. Glancing at Beth, her guard, Anthony, blows out a tired sigh and shakes his sandy-blond head. Celeste's guard, Marco, pulls his dark brows down in a death glare.

Curling my hands into fists so I don't flip Marco off, I follow Beth up the stairs and huff my agreement at her muttered comment. "Ugh, they're seeing us to our rooms? Claustrophobia is already kicking in."

Just before we reach her room, Beth speaks in a low tone meant just for my ears. "Where did you go? I assumed after all the chaos at the fight that you cabbed it like you said you were going to. I'm glad you got my message and came home."

"I took your advice about the MMA fighter."

Beth lets out a surprised squeak, then drops her voice to a hushed whisper. "I meant pick one to be your *guard*, not hook up with him in some kind of revenge 'fuck you' to Father for announcing your engagement to Ben at the cocktail party." She chuckles, then eyes me sideways. "You actually slept with Hammer?"

I shake my head. "Not Hammer, Steel. We just kind of…hung out."

"Euphemism much?" Snorting, Beth steps close. "What does he look like? Is his face as hot as that gorgeous tattooed body?"

"I wouldn't know," I say. "He took the whole 'no-taking-the-mask-off' rule seriously."

It's hard not to snicker at the look of dumbfounded surprise on Beth's face, but I manage to keep my expression perfectly composed. I'm not going to say anything that could get Calder disqualified from the MMA rematch between Steel and Hammer. I would never jeopardize all the groundwork he's laid in becoming Steel in the MMA world. I believe Beth is clueless about the illegal inner workings of the Elite Underground Club aka EUC that runs the MMA events, but I can't take the chance she might expose Calder to her boyfriend. It's the only way he'll be able to bring the whole corrupt organization down.

"Night, Beth. See you in the morning."

"Night," she says softly, probably too tired from tonight's drama to drill me for more details.

My wrists feel like they're on fire, the skin itching like mad as I stare at the phone's text screen. *Seven a.m.* I've had two hours of sleep after finally succumbing to sheer exhaustion. I stayed awake as long as I could, hoping for a call from Celeste Carver. Rubbing my left wrist along my jeans, I sit up on Celeste's bed and blink as I thumb to the "missed calls" screen.

Nothing. Not a single call or text from her.

When the phone suddenly buzzes in my hand with a text, my pulse rushes as I swipe it open. My heart quickly plummets when I see it's from Beth and not Celeste.

> *Beth: I can't believe he kept his mask on. That's so twisted, it's hot.*
> *Me: My sex life is what you're thinking about at seven in the morning?*
> *Beth: Ah, so you admit there was sex.*
> *Me: Nope.*
> *Beth: No, there was NO sex, or you're not TELLING me?*

Normally I would continue stringing Beth along, but my heart's just not in it. With no contact from Celeste in more than ten hours, the memory of lying to her family in the middle of the night burns in my stomach in the light of day. What is it about daylight that seems to strip you bare and reveal all your flaws? I squeeze the silent phone as if doing so will make it ring with news from Celeste, then finally respond to Beth.

> *Me: Get a shower.*
> *Beth: Huh? It's too early.*
> *Me: Just do it, please.*
> *Beth: Fine!*

As dread rolls through me, I walk into the bathroom,

thankful Celeste had provided a small shower kit in the drawer with a new razor, soap, and toothbrush. Turning on the shower full blast, I shiver in the cool bathroom and realize why there's a dual-sided fireplace shared between her bedroom and bath as I wait for the water to heat up. A hot shower is necessary to wake me up and give me the boost I'll need.

I can't stay quiet any longer.

CHAPTER TWO

The Observer

"*This* is the early morning news edition," a perky blonde woman with a wide smile reports behind the news desk as a red banner scrolls across the bottom of the TV screen. "Police have discovered an abandoned car on 495."

I lift the remote toward the TV, turning it up.

"Blood was found in the vehicle along with a woman's ID," the woman continues in an ominous tone. "But the police aren't releasing any details. If you have any information to share about this vehicle or the person seen driving it, call the WVTV news tip line listed in the red banner below."

"They've found you," I say conversationally as I stare at Celeste's jewelry laid out on the white towel covered in blood streaks: a pair of earrings, a bracelet and two rings.

Mementos. While the newscaster drones on, an irritating pressure pushes against my chest.

Regret.

I don't do regret. I don't feel anything. It's *her* fault I'm alone now. I squeeze the remote until the pressure in my chest eases. Setting it down on the desk, I pop open her wallet and run my fingers over the attractive picture on her gym ID card.

Regret. Regret. Regret.

The word hammers like a judge's gavel in my head over and over.

"You gave me no choice!" I rage at her smirking face and throw the wallet against the wall to stop the noise in my head. The expensive leather falls to the carpet with a soft thump, flopping open once more. *What's done can't be undone.* I stare down at Celeste's smiling face and take several breaths before returning my gaze to the TV.

"They've found you and they don't even know it yet."

CHAPTER THREE

Cass

"*What* are you doing?" Beth tugs her hand from my grasp just outside her father's office. Shaking her head at the closed door, she steps back. "Can't you hear him in there talking business? We barely scraped by last night. I'm not stepping into the viper's den. No thanks."

Just as she spins to walk away, I grip her arm. "This is *more* important than anything he could possibly be talking about in there. Trust me, Beth."

Beth shakes her head and pieces of her light brown hair fall from her hastily clipped bun, brushing the sides of her suddenly pale cheeks as she glances down in confusion at the book in my other hand. "Whatever it is, it can wait until his door is open."

Releasing her, I shift the book under my arm and

quickly knock before she can argue more.

At the same time the men's voices suddenly quiet, I turn the knob and open the door.

"Celeste—"

I pretend not to hear the sharp warning in Gregory Carver's tone as I step into the room. "I'm sorry to interrupt, but this can't wait," I say to Celeste's father before I turn to Phillip, who's sitting in a chair across from the desk, a mixture of anger and disbelief on his face. "This is a private family matter. Would you mind if we had a moment alone with our father, please?"

Phillip glances down and casually flips a piece of paper to the next one in the portfolio on his lap. "Now isn't the time for theatrics, Celeste."

His condescending manner makes me want to roll my eyes, but before I can say anything, Gregory stands behind his desk. "Phillip *is* family and you will pay him the respect he's due, Celeste. Apologize and don't come back in here again until you're called. This sudden obstinate streak of yours ends now. Am I understood?"

"I tried to tell her..." Beth's voice is quiet, but at least she followed me into the room.

Resisting the urge to step back under Gregory's hard glare, I curl my fingers around the edge of the book under my arm and speak to Beth. "Please shut the door. I don't want to disturb your mother with this."

Giving me an odd look, Beth quickly shuts the door, mumbling, "This sounds ominous."

The moment the door clicks closed, the sound of

Gregory's fist slamming down on the desk makes my heart lurch. "That's it! I'm glad your mother went to stay with her sister yesterday so she doesn't have to witness this utter lack of respect. You've just lost your credit cards. All your accounts will be frozen until you can act accordingly. No daughter of mine will completely disregard my authority—"

"That's because I'm *not* your daughter," I say in a raised voice to be heard over his tirade.

"That's a line you don't want to cross, Celeste. Maybe you should take a breath." Phillip's calm words overlay Gregory's stunned grunt of silence and Beth's quietly uttered, *oh boy.*

I shake my head and keep my voice even. "This isn't an act of defiance. I waited as long as I could, for a text or a call, but I can't any longer." Inhaling slowly through my nose, I hold Gregory's gaze. "You need to call the police, Mr. Carver. I'm truly worried something has happened to your daughter."

"You've taken this charade far enough, young lady!" Gregory quickly finds his voice, his face red with outrage.

"Stop antagonizing him, Celeste."

Celeste's father and sister's elevated voices don't faze me. I expected their resistance, but the sudden suspicion in Phillip's narrowed hazel gaze sends a chill of apprehension down my spine. I still don't know who's behind those threatening notes that showed up in Celeste's text feed last night. I'm almost certain the source was a man, but one thing is for sure: Celeste had given the sender the codename Deceiver for a reason. The culprit could be a family member, a family friend, or even her security guard.

Tamping down the tension coiling in my stomach, I put a hand on Beth's shoulder and meet her worried gaze with a sincere one. "It's the truth, Beth. I'm not Celeste."

She clamps a hand fiercely on mine and directs her anger at her father. "She's doing this because you sprang that stupid engagement on her last night."

"That's enough! Both you girls are beyond spoiled," Gregory growls, crossing his arms. "Maybe a stint of honest, hard work, where you actually have to earn your own way, will jolt you back to reality."

"I had a feeling I might need this." I sigh and pull my hand free of Beth's tight grip. Opening the high school yearbook I found on a shelf in Celeste's room, I set it on Gregory's desk and point to the senior picture of me. "That's me, Cassandra Rockwell." Thumbing to the front of the alphabet, I point to Celeste. "And that is Celeste Carver."

Beth leans over my shoulder and flips back and forth between the two pages, then skims a shocked gaze over my face. "My God...it's uncanny how much you look like her. That certainly explains a lot about last night. You definitely seemed...off."

Exhaling a long breath, I nod. "Our resemblance was the whole point. Celeste knew how important last night's party was for your career, Mr. Carver, so she asked me to 'be her' while she kept an appointment she couldn't miss."

"What appointment?" Beth and her father demand at

the same time.

"She didn't say." I shrug and slide a sidelong glance Phillip's way. He's staring at me with anger and shrewd wariness now. I'm sure he's replaying all the threatening, authoritative comments he'd said to "Celeste" last night through his mind. They were vague enough that only Celeste would truly understand the subtext, but they definitely revealed a strange power-struggle dynamic between them.

Phillip adjusts his expensive tie as he stands to glance over the yearbook photos. Sliding his finger along the page with Celeste's photo, he says, "You really have no idea where she is?"

"No," I answer honestly, keeping my expression perfectly composed.

"If you're close enough to my sister to take her place, then why has she never mentioned you?" Beth asks, crossing her arms.

I slowly shut the book. "Celeste and I weren't that close in school, but she knew I could pass for her and that's all she needed."

"Celeste is obviously off pouting somewhere, but what I want to know is…what did you get out of this stand-in game you two played?" Phillip cross-examines me like I'm in a courtroom. Setting the portfolio on the corner of the desk, he continues his suspicious line of questioning. "*Why* would Celeste let a complete stranger into her home and allow her to mingle with her family?"

I start to speak, but he overrides me, his voice darkening

to a menacing rumble. "Whatever you're holding over her, I will bury you if you try to disclose anything personal you've learned about the Carver family to the public."

"Hold that thought, Phillip..." Gregory interjects, furrowing his brow. "Rockwell sounds familiar." Opening a folder sitting on his desk, he turns the letter inside with Celeste's signature on it toward me. "Do you know a Jason Rockwell?"

I straighten my spine. "He's my father. And yes, that was my agreement with Celeste. In exchange for me being her for an evening, Celeste offered to try to help my father get his development plan in front of the right people with the city." I wave my hand. "But none of that matters right now. What does matter is that your daughter never came home. I wanted to say something last night while the police were here, but Celeste was adamant that I not tell anyone about our switch. The last thing I wanted to do was cause a scandal. She'd pushed our time to meet back until midnight, and as far as I knew, I had her real ID, so the other one the police found couldn't have been hers. But now that it has been over eight hours since she was supposed to reconnect with me, I think it's time to call the police."

Gregory shakes his head and gestures to Phillip, who's typing something on his phone. "I agree with Phillip. I'm sure this is Celeste acting out. She's done this before."

"What? Run away?" Beth cuts in, her voice tense. "That was when she was *fourteen*, Father."

"Phillip found her then. I trust him to find her now,"

Gregory says with confidence.

Beth throws her hands out, her voice elevating. "What if something really has happened to her? Are all of you forgetting they found blood along with that ID? We can't ignore the possibility!"

"I agree with Beth," I quickly add. "You need to—"

"Let's go with your theory that something has happened to Celeste, Miss Rockwell, shall we?" I don't like Phillip patronizing me, but I need them to believe me so I wait for him to continue. "How do we know *you* didn't have something to do with Celeste's disappearance, and the police caught you off guard and that's why you delayed until today to come clean?"

My stomach plummets at his unexpected attack. "I would never hurt another person—"

"But if you really believed something happened to her, you would've sounded the alarm last night," Phillip cuts me off as he slides his phone into his pocket.

"I just told you why I didn't say anything last nigh—"

"Unless..." his gaze hardens, anger firing in the hazel depths. "You're insisting we call the police to throw suspicion off you?"

I gulp back my shock at his aggressive conjecture about my motives. "Are you serious? I could've just walked out and resumed my life without saying a word to any of you. I didn't have to get involved, explain a thing, or even tell you my name. I really hope I'm wrong about this. Truly I do."

"I know Celeste wasn't thrilled by the idea of the

engagement, but she understood the commitment when she took over as Carver Enterprises' CEO," Gregory says, seguing back to his original theory as to where Celeste might be.

I glance his way, thankful he isn't accusing me, but still worried he's holding onto the belief that Celeste is pouting. She didn't sound that way to me. She seemed to accept she would have a marriage in name only.

"No more fake concern, Miss Rockwell." Phillip waves his hand dismissively. "We've let you spin your tall tale, but you and Celeste are done with this game. Where is she?"

Pressing my lips together to keep from screaming at the arrogant man, I slip my hands into my slacks pockets and exhale a calming breath. "You're choosing not to hear me, so I'll say this one more time to be perfectly clear. This is *no* game. I had nothing to do with where Celeste went, but she *never* returned." Pulling my hand out of my pocket, I set the phone Celeste gave me on the desk. "The police's tech people can start with this. Celeste cloned her phone onto this one and gave it to me to use for the evening. Hopefully it'll give them a way to trace back to her original phone and locate her. At the very least it should help them follow where she went yesterday."

When the lines around Phillip's mouth deepen, Gregory's salt and pepper brows pull together and Celeste's father shakes his head, clearly at a loss. Phillip sees Gregory's reaction, then speaks to me in a calmer tone. "Miss Rockwell, would you mind stepping outside so I can discuss this with Gregory?" The lawyer's mask is back, cool and collected.

I sigh, done with this whole crazy situation. "Look, I'm not here to argue with you. I honestly hope Celeste *is* having a bit of fun at your expense. No one should have to marry someone they don't love." When both men frown at my comment, I shrug. It felt good to get that off my chest. "I'll just call a cab. Before I go, I will leave my contact information with Beth if the police do need to get involved and want to talk to me."

As I start to leave, Phillip commands, "Please wait outside, Miss Rockwell. You too, Beth."

Beth lets out an annoyed huff, then turns and opens the door. Stepping out with us, Phillip calls Marco and Anthony over from their positions by the staircase. "Mr. Carver and I have something to discuss. Please make sure the ladies remain here until we're done."

Once he closes the door, I mutter to Beth, "So much for them listening."

"Did you really think they would believe a fraud?" she says under her breath so the guards can't hear. "Just because you look like her doesn't mean you deserve our trust."

When Beth turns her back on me, it hurts more than it should. My chest actually aches. And, yet again, I'm being treated like I'm less than nothing. I didn't expect the conversation with her family to go over well, nor did I expect to be treated like a guilty party, but Beth is acting like I'm a lowlife who actively and willingly betrayed her.

Blowing out a breath, I lean against the wall and try not to freak out at the thought Phillip will act on his earlier accusation. What if Phillip was playing me and he's actually in there right now convincing Gregory to call the police to question me in suspicion of Celeste's disappearance? God, how did this turn into such a screwed up, tangled mess?

After several minutes, the escalating angst and worry over what's being discussed behind that closed door makes me realize that calling a cab is *my* best course of action regardless what her family decides to do. They have Celeste's cloned phone. That should give them a head start. Ugh, which means now I don't have a way to call for a cab while standing here. Leaning close to Beth, I ask, "Would you mind if I borrow your phone?"

Her only answer is to glare at me over her shoulder.

A couple more minutes tick by and my stomach churns tighter. As my heart rate elevates with the continued rumble of voices in the other room, my wrists begin to sting uncontrollably. I can't make out what they're saying, which only amps my nerves.

I try to fold my arms to assuage the need to scratch, but when nausea washes over me in rolling waves of heat, I instantly start for the bathroom. Marco steps in my path, his mouth curled in a determined smirk. "You were told to wait here."

Swallowing several times to settle my angst, I move back to my position against the wall and cross my arms.

I jump when the door finally opens. Gregory dismisses the men and waves us in. Shutting the door behind us, he addresses Beth first. "Most likely your sister is doing this to prove her displeasure with me, but we're not going to wait for her to return on her own; we'll treat this as if she's gone missing."

Beth's shoulders relax and she nods, then Gregory turns to me. "In the meantime, Miss Rockwell, I'd like you to continue standing in for my daughter until we locate her. In return, I'll make sure that the paperwork Celeste put together on your father's behalf is given to the right people."

My eyes widen. At first I can't speak...I'm so shocked by his dismissal of my concerns for Celeste and his apparent disregard for the signs she seemed to be under some kind of stress. I shake my head. "I don't think that's a good idea—"

"I appreciate your discretion with this," he talks over me as he smooths his tie. "Until we have more facts, we need to keep this contained for now. I have a lot of people depending on me—"

"Are you *kidding* me?" Beth shoots a furious gaze between both men. "You're not going to call the police?"

Phillip turns to Beth, the cloned cell phone in his hand. "We've got this covered, Beth. This phone is a great place to start. And I have a friend on the force who can quietly test a sample of Celeste's hair against the blood they found in that car to rule her out. But even expedited DNA testing can take a couple of days, so in the meantime—"

"She could be lying on the side of the road somewhere," Beth says, her voice elevating.

"In the meantime," Phillip repeats as if she didn't interrupt him with her outburst. "I'm hiring people to start looking for Celeste right away. Behind the scenes we'll be doing everything we can to find her, but we're going to keep this information quiet for now. Until we hear back from my contact or my people come up with more information as to her last known location, there's no need to sound the alarm just yet—"

"She's the daughter of a U.S. Senator." Beth flings her arms wide. "By default that makes her a target. Are you both forgetting that she claimed she was being followed? And that she felt strongly enough about it to ask for a new guard?"

"Calm *down*, Beth."

"Lower your voice," Phillip commands on top of Gregory's attempt to soothe his daughter.

"She has every right to be upset," I say before I can stop myself.

As Phillip cuts a "stay the hell out of this" look my way, Gregory steps forward and clasps his youngest daughter's shoulders. "Marco and Anthony do their jobs. Their presence has prevented more annoyances than you and your sister know about. That said, you shouldn't have ditched them last night—"

"Don't you dare try to pin the blame on us!" Beth shakes free of his hold and takes a step back, pressing her lips together. "This room is littered with all kinds of agendas except the one that matters: finding Celeste. Talk about screwed up priorities. I'm out of here."

When she reaches for the doorknob, her father's tone turns harsh. "Do *not* tell your mother about this. She's too fragile right now. She went to her sister's to recuperate after last night's event took its toll. We will find Celeste, but for now no one outside of this room can learn that Miss Rockwell isn't Celeste. Is that understood, Beth?"

"You're not going to tell Celeste's *fiancé*?" Beth snorts then looks at Phillip. "Shouldn't your son be informed his *wife-to-be* is a no-show?"

"That's enough, Beth." Gregory bristles at her sarcasm, but Phillip answers anyway.

"Not even Ben and Jake," Phillip states in a firm tone. "There's no reason to worry Ben right now."

Shooting both men a fed-up look, Beth starts to leave, but her father stops her once more. "Beth, I expect you to inform Miss Rockwell what attire is expected for the upcoming events."

Huffing her annoyance, Beth leaves, shutting the door behind her with a sharp click.

Celeste and Ben's engagement might just be a business arrangement, but from what I gathered last night, Ben is secretly in love with Celeste. He would be genuinely upset if he thought something happened to her and would want to know. A tug-of-war wages in my heart. I want to speak up on Ben's behalf, but if one brother knows, then the other would too. I can't chance Jake finding out that I played Celeste at the event last night, so I brush my damp hands against my slacks and swallow the words sticking in my throat. Not that my internal turmoil changes my answer one bit. "I'm sorry, Mr. Carver, but I can't in good conscience continue on as Celeste."

While Gregory visibly tenses, Phillip runs his finger along the cell phone's dark screen, his gaze laser focused on me. "It's in your best interest to make it easier for us to find Celeste, Miss Rockwell. All we have is your word that she asked you to do this. Trust me, you don't want us going to the police with your story. If we can't locate Celeste, who do you think the police will look at first?"

I instantly tense, my chest tightening. I don't have any tangible proof, no texts or emails, to show that Celeste actually recruited me. The fact the phone's passcode happens to spell my name could be passed off as sheer coincidence. But the texts between Celeste and me on the phone should contain enough back and forth to corroborate the rest of my story. If I tip Phillip off to that fact—and he or someone in the Carver family circle had anything to do with Celeste's disappearance—he could delete those texts before the phone ever makes it to the police. I should've emailed our text conversations to myself to cover my ass, but I never once thought I would be considered a suspect. An innocent person's mind just doesn't go there. "It's *not* a story."

My elevated heart rate makes me lightheaded. Phillip's ruthlessness is sharply convincing. I have no doubt he's prepared to paint the worst scenario possible with me at the center of Celeste's disappearance if I don't agree. In this moment, I can see the source of Jake's rotten genes. Like father like son has never been so true.

"Miss Rockwell…Cassandra." Gregory steps close and clasps one of my hands, ever the suave politician. "My political rivals are already circling like sharks to chum by the news that the police showed up here last night. I have an interview here at the house at four that's been set up for weeks. Celeste asked you to be here to keep up appearances. All we're asking is for you to continue on just a little longer. Give us the time to quietly locate my daughter so that the upcoming social events over the next couple of days don't go sideways with rumors of scandal."

Gregory might be trying to sugarcoat Phillip's threat, but not being given a choice highlights a very simple truth. *I'm* the only one I can depend on to untangle me from this mess. And the best way to do that is to find Celeste. By continuing as her, I'll at least have access to her things. Maybe I can dig deeper into the information I saw on her laptop. While I waited for Beth, I took a quick glance at her laptop and saw that her last search was for "women's clinics in New Jersey, eighty miles or less." But just in case I'm unable to find Celeste, I have to do everything I can to preserve the texting history between Celeste and me.

Sliding my hand from Gregory's, I address Phillip. "I'll need the phone Celeste gave me."

The lawyer's tense expression eases, but he shakes his head. "I'll get you another one. As you pointed out, this phone could be key in helping track her down."

Well shit! I need to get the evidence that Celeste was in full agreement with this arrangement off that phone. "Celeste is supposed to contact me on that one. She may try to call."

He slides his hands casually into his pockets, tucking the phone away. "I'll have it cloned on another phone for you."

Real panic squeezes my lungs, making it hard to breathe. Holding my hand out, I try to keep the anxiety out of my voice. "Would you mind letting me borrow it? If I'm going to be here for a couple more days, I'll need to make a quick call. My family will be worried if I don't return to the Hamptons today."

Phillip looks like he's about to refuse when Gregory gestures toward me, blustering, "Take off your lawyer hat for once, Phillip. Give the girl the phone so she can call her family."

The tightness in my chest lifts with Phillip's resigned sigh. Once I get the phone, I'll pretend I'm having trouble dialing out, then I'll quickly send the copy of the texts between Celeste and me to my email account before I dial my parents.

But Phillip pulls a phone from his other pocket and hands it to me. "Here, use mine."

Beyond frustrated, I mumble my thanks and dial my parents' home phone.

Just as my parents' answering machine picks up, someone knocks lightly on the door then opens it. "I'm sorry to disturb, Mr. Carver," the house maid, Beatrice, stands in the doorway, her tight dark bun making her apologetic eyes seem even wider. "But Mr. Blake insisted on seeing Celeste. He refused to leave until I brought him to her."

Calder? I quickly hang up, my whole body tensing.

"You have some nerve barging into my home." Gregory turns the full force of his anger toward the doorway, his shoulders blocking my view.

Phillip puts a restraining hand on Gregory's arm, then steps forward. "You've disturbed a private meeting, Mr. Blake. If you don't leave of your own accord, our guards will escort you out."

"I heard the police were here last night. I'm not leaving until I talk to Celeste. I want to make sure she's all right." Calder's sharp tone is reminiscent of the street-fighter "Steel" persona he projected at the MMA match last night.

"Of all the nerve...*you* are not her guard!" Gregory blusters his annoyance, throwing his hands up. "See what I mean about stupid rumors? Where the hell *are* Marco and Anthony? I'm going to fire them for failing to do their damn jobs."

Just as Philip tells Gregory, "I sent them on an errand related to the earlier issue," I step to Phillip's left and answer the maid.

"We're almost done here, Beatrice. Can you please escort Calder to the library? I'll be there in just a couple minutes."

A look of relief washes over Beatrice's normally stoic face before she says calmly, "Come along, Mr. Blake."

The heat of Calder's gaze drills into me. Its pull is so strong, I can practically feel the pad of his thumb brushing my lips and the pressure of his fingers tilting my chin so I'll meet his gaze. I bite my lip to tamp down the warmth tingling through me and blink to avoid looking directly at him.

Once Calder turns away to follow Beatrice, I slowly release my breath and greedily drink in how his broad shoulders fill out the medium blue button down shirt that's neatly tucked into the trim waistband of his black dress pants.

The aggressive way he challenged Gregory and Phillip shows he's on edge. I don't want him to see tension on my face. Celeste's family's trust in me is on a thin thread; everything could unravel if Calder goes ballistic. He might be dressed like a businessman, but unyielding determination is heavy in his tone and tension reflects in his demeanor as he walks away. His SEAL protective hackles are definitely on full alert. The last thing he'll do is stand down.

Phillip turns to me, his face ridged as he swipes his phone from my loose grip. "He was told last night that the Carvers don't need his services. Get rid of him. The family doesn't need any more *outsiders* in this house right now."

"Maybe if he'd been allowed to do the job Celeste wanted him for, we wouldn't be having this discussion," I shoot back, narrowing my gaze.

Gregory's mouth thins to a grim line and he nods toward the door. "Go tell Mr. Blake that you're fine, then send him on his way."

I stiffen. "I'll do my best," I say, knowing Calder won't like that at all.

"Miss Rockwell," Gregory calls out when I start to turn.

"You must convince him to move on or the arrangement my daughter made with you concerning your father is off."

They don't know that Calder is the only one who saw right through my Celeste disguise the moment he laid eyes on me. And I'm certainly not going to tell them. No matter how amazing last night was with Calder, I can't let my feelings for him prevent me from helping my father see his business development dreams come true. It's the last promise I gave my sister before she died and I plan to keep it.

My chest tightens as I head down the hall to convince the man who stole my heart that I don't want him here.

CHAPTER FOUR

Cass

My heart's racing by the time I reach the library. I hover just outside the closed door, flexing my hands by my sides. Taking a deep breath, I exhale and open the door.

Calder's standing at the window, his arms crossed behind his back. As he turns, I speak before he can, adopting a formal tone. "Thank you for coming, Calder. I'm sorry my engagement announcement derailed you getting more time with my father yesterday."

A look of confusion flickers in his eyes a split-second before he starts toward me.

Panic sets in and I quickly shut the door just in case Gregory or Phillip is listening.

When Calder gets closer, his steps slow. The tension on my face is giving him pause. He's not sure who he's talking to, Celeste or Cass. Stopping a few feet away, he slides his hands in his pockets, frustration evident. "Forget about yesterday. I came as soon as I heard the police were here last night. What happened?"

The way he's staring at me with such boldness makes it hard to look away. He's looking for that spark he claims to see in my eyes. I want to tell him that I'm *me*, but maybe it's for the best if he thinks I'm Celeste. It'll be easier to get him to leave without causing a fuss.

"It was all just a misunderstanding," I say with a shrug as I step around him and walk over to the wall of leather-bound first edition books. Sliding the wooden ladder out of the way, I keep my tone casual as I turn and lean against the bookshelf, facing him. "I arrived home late last night to the police questioning my father. Apparently an ID with my name on it—fake obviously—was found in an abandoned car, along with some blood." Crossing my arms, I sigh. "Needless to say, once the police left, my father chewed me out for ditching Marco."

"You wouldn't be able to ditch me if I were your security," Calder says, moving closer. Propping his forearm on the ladder, he looks down at me. He's close enough that I can smell the musky notes of sandalwood in his aftershave. I grip the chair rail edge that separates the lower half of the bookshelves to keep from leaning closer and inhaling deeply. "So you're marrying Ben Hemmings," Calder continues. "That seemed to come out of nowhere."

My heart lurches at the hint of regret in his comment. *Did he care for Celeste more than he let on?* It's not like I can blame him. We do look like twins, but the question tears at my heart anyway. Would he reveal his unvarnished feelings about Celeste now that Cass isn't in the room? Celeste definitely thought he was hot. I lift my shoulders and glance away. "Yeah, well when the attraction isn't returned, we have to move on, Calder."

"Do you have feelings for Ben?" he asks quietly. The blunt intimacy of his question, laced with an edge of vulnerability, crushes my heart and pulls my gaze back to his.

"Ben is...my shield." I answer based on the interaction I had with Ben last night after the engagement was announced. It was obvious Ben wanted to protect Celeste. When Calder's mouth tightens, the proof his feelings run deeper for Celeste pushes a perverse part of me to find out just how much.

What Calder and I shared last night was so raw and real it's hard to imagine him being with another woman. But we also only had one night. No matter how amazing it was that doesn't change the fact that he and Celeste had spent a lot of time together prior to that. I hold Calder's gaze and continue in Celeste mode, "Ben really surprised me last night, showing me that there are definite benefits to having him by my side." My chest burns with jealousy as I watch Calder's jaw harden. Spreading my hands wide, I force a smile. "I feel protected now and less worried about stuff."

When Calder's gaze narrows, I can't stand the torture of being this close to his alluring masculine bubble. It's too tempting to want to yell at him for downplaying his "friendship" with Celeste, so I push off the bookshelf and spread my hands, adopting an upbeat tone. "Thank you so much for coming today, but as you can see, you really didn't have to. I'm all good now."

He's staring at me so intensely that it hurts to hold his gaze, so I step around him and walk toward the door. "I hope you don't think I'm being rude, but I have an appointment I need to get ready for—"

Calder grabs my hand and tugs, yanking me around to face him.

"*Don't,*" he grits out as he crowds my personal space.

"Calder!" I try to step back, but he folds his arm around my waist, pinning me to his solid frame.

He bends close, his gaze locked with mine. "I will always protect you."

"Let *go* of me." I can't keep my voice from trembling as I push against his shoulders and try to struggle from his hold. His muscular arm only cinches tighter around me. *I don't want to know the truth about your feelings for Celeste. It hurts too much.*

"Cald—"

He kisses me, his mouth dominating mine, commanding a response. My stomach flip-flops and I whimper against his mouth. My instinct is to kiss him back, but he's not fucking kissing me. Anger fuels my resistance. I dig my fingers into his short hair and tug hard.

Grunting his fury, Calder clasps the back of my head and clamps his teeth on my bottom lip. The second I gasp at the pleasure/pain, he thrusts his tongue intimately against mine, stripping away my ability to resist. I release his hair to fist the front of his shirt and kiss him back. He makes me forget who I am...who I'm supposed to be. I'm want and need...and passion.

The second I yield to him, Calder pulls back, dark fury stamped on his face. "Don't you fucking *ever* do that to me again."

The sudden reprieve from his seduction yanks me back to my senses. Shaking my head to rein in my emotions, I try to pry his hand from around my waist, but he dips his head and bites the side of my neck just below my jawline. The primal move scatters goose bumps across my skin, reminding me how much I crave his touch and aggressive branding of my body. Apparently I wasn't the only one. I immediately cease my struggles, sadness zapping my fight. Even when she's not here, Celeste still overshadows me.

As I take a couple deep breaths to hold my tears back, Calder tenses against me. Clasping my jaw, he straightens to his full six-two height and forces me to look into his stormy green eyes. "How could you make me think that the blood the police found in that car was yours? Why would you do that to me, angel?"

I never thought that by pretending to be Celeste that Calder would jump to the conclusion that the blood found in that car was mine. I'm so overwhelmed to know that knee-knocking kiss *was* meant for me that I close my eyes and lay my head against his chest as a shudder of relief runs through me.

Calder slides his thumb along my cheekbone, his touch making my eyes flutter open. "The truth, Cass," he says, cupping my jaw so I meet his gaze. "Why are you still pretending to be Celeste? What the hell is going on?"

I keep my voice low and tell him everything that transpired once I arrived back at the house last night.

Calder's jaw muscle tenses several times, but he finally cuts me off when I get to the part where Phillip and Gregory struck a deal with me. He clasps my shoulders, his tone turning cold, deadly. "Get your things. You won't stay another minute in this house of liars and cheats."

I'm surprised by his harsh statement. Celeste's father may lord his authority over his daughters, but I believe he actually does care for them. And he hasn't lied to me that I know of. I shake my head. "I can't leave."

His grip tightens on my shoulders. "The Blake family name has sway, Cass. We'll find another way to help your dad get his business development approved."

My heart trips that he would call on his family to help mine even though he's distanced himself from the Blakes, but I flatten my palm on his chest and shake my head. "You don't understand, Calder. I might be the only one who has a clue where Celeste went. I feel responsible in a way after having agreed to switch with her in the first place."

Calder's brows pull together. "Do you know where she went? Where her appointment was? Why didn't you tell her family?"

"I gave Celeste my *word*, Calder."

When I press my lips together, his frown deepens. "I know you feel an obligation, but if you really think she's missing, you have to start sharing. At least with me. I hope that I've earned some measure of trust with you last night."

He didn't give away that he knew about my arrangement with Celeste to her father or Phillip when he challenged them earlier, so I know Calder has my back even when he's worried about me.

"It's complicated," I say on a heavy sigh. "What I can say for now is that I saw a snippet of a text conversation between Celeste and someone she has labeled as Deceiver on the cloned phone she gave me. She must've been deleting any other texts before I could see them. Whoever this person is—my gut tells me it was a man—he had a strange kind of hold over Celeste, and it was something she was trying to break free of. The gist of the conversation was that he tried to control her and she told him she was going to do something. Her response pissed him off."

Calder releases me and spears a hand through his short, light brown hair. "Give me the phone and I'll have one of the guys on Bash's security team run down this Deceiver's identity."

I sigh my frustration. "I don't have the phone. Phillip took it to try to re-trace Celeste's steps from last night."

"Do you think that where Celeste went might have something to do with this Deceiver person?"

"I don't know if the two things are connected. She

was definitely antagonizing him in the texts," I say on a shrug, then inspiration strikes. "I did send a copy of their conversation to my email. Would the Security guys be able to get the Deceiver's phone number and identity from that?"

"I've sent my contact info to your phone. Forward the email to me and we'll try." When I nod, Calder's brow furrows. "Where did she go, Cass?"

I shrug. "I honestly don't know yet." There's no point in sharing my assumptions. I could be completely off-base. When I saw the search Celeste made on her laptop, my heart sank. There's usually only one reason a woman goes to that kind of clinic. It would make sense that she would want to go out of town, but I didn't have time to look up how many clinics in New Jersey fell within eighty miles before Beth texted me that she was dressed.

Celeste's diary might have more clues if I could decipher what her darkly poetic entries meant. Could the "green greed" and "black deception" she talked about in her entries be the Deceiver?

"I'm going to go through Celeste's things. Now that I'm here for at least one more night, I can really look over her room. Thankfully her laptop isn't password protected. There might be more useful stuff on there. I…"

"What?" Calder urges me to continue when I stop talking.

I smirk. "It just hit me that I never told Phillip the password for Celeste's phone. I wonder how long it'll take him to realize it?" *And when Phillip asks me for the code,*

I'll come up with an excuse to hold it so I can send those texts between Celeste and me to myself.

"Phillip," Calder snarls. "I don't like that prick."

"I agree with you on that. I'll keep in touch and send you anything else I find once I do a more thorough search on her computer's history."

Calder snorts and crosses his arms. "You really don't think I'm leaving here without you, do you?"

I gape at him. "What? You—you *can't* stay. Gregory told me he'll rescind the deal Celeste made with me about my dad if I can't get you to quietly leave."

Calder's jaw muscle twitches. "I told you I'll find another way to help your father, but if you insist on staying, then you've got yourself a new guard because there's no fucking way I'm leaving you here alone."

"You must go, Calder," I say in a quiet hiss as I grip his thick upper arm and try to tug him toward the door, but he doesn't budge.

His gaze lasers on me. "If Celeste really is missing, that means someone could've hurt her. I will *not* leave you unprotected while you're standing in for her."

The fact I might be in danger goes right over my head as true panic sets in. I can see Phillip *pointing* the police in my direction and my father's dreams for his business being snuffed out completely if his pitch gets rejected yet again. I start to argue, but Calder jerks his head once, his rumbling tone harsh. "I don't care how you sell it with Gregory, Cass, but I *will* be your shadow until you're back to being *you*."

"You can't do this! They'll call the police—"

He steps close and clasps the side of my neck. "I won't risk anything happening to you." Sliding his thumb along the front of my throat, he continues, his tone husky, "I know where you were last night and will absolutely attest to that if the police get involved."

"But we weren't together the entire time, Calder," I say, my voice shaking. "You don't know what time I left or where I went. You were asleep."

He cups my face, his hold tense as he pulls me up to my toes. "*I'm* your security for as long as you're Celeste. Go insist on it, and tell them that I'll be staying here. There are plenty of rooms in this monstrosity of a house."

He's so fierce, I know he's not going to back down. I fold my hand over his on my cheek and exhale some of the tension inside me. At least I'll have one ally in this house. "I'll talk to them."

Calder dips his head in a curt nod and his fingers flex around my jaw. "I'll wait here for you."

"What do you mean he's *staying*?" Gregory huffs his fury, his chair slamming back against the wall with his swift move to his feet.

When Phillip quickly stands from his chair in front of Gregory's desk and buttons his jacket, muttering, "We'll just see about that," I close the door and lean against it.

"He's a Navy SEAL. You won't stand a chance."

Phillip pauses for a second, but when a determined expression sets on his face and he starts toward the door once more, I hold my hand up. "I asked him to stay."

Phillip halts and both men say in unison, "*What?*"

I might be shaking on the inside, but I meet their shocked stares with confidence. "If you want me to continue to be Celeste, then Calder staying on as my guard is a condition of my agreement."

Phillip slices his hand through the air, spitting out, "Absolutely not!"

I ignore Phillip and turn to Gregory. "Your daughter might have wanted to keep things running smoothly for the sake of your career, Mr. Carver, but I refuse to put myself in harm's way. Whether you believe Celeste is just being stubborn or not, I want the one person she handpicked as my guard while I'm here."

Gregory jams his hands in his pants, his gaze sharp. "Resorting to blackmail doesn't instill trust, Miss Rockwell."

"Your lawyer seems to have no issue with that tactic," I quickly counter without sparing Phillip a glance. "Calder will be another set of eyes. Everyone benefits from that. All I've told him is that you've decided to give him a trial run for a couple of days at my request."

"You're not really considering this, are you?" Phillip asks Gregory, his tone clearly annoyed with me.

The stubbornness that flickers in Gregory's eyes knots my stomach with worry. Before Phillip can talk him into nixing Calder, I fold my arms and call their bluff. "If you don't agree to Calder, then you may as well file a missing person's report with the police today. I won't continue as Celeste without protection I can trust."

"Marco is your security," Phillip snaps.

My gaze flicks to his irritated one. "He's useless."

Gregory's jaw muscle bunches before he finally speaks. "You'll have two guards then. Everywhere you go, Marco follows."

I start to argue, but Phillip interrupts. "You seem to be forgetting that you're a guest in this house, Miss Rockwell. If Gregory insists that Marco be everywhere you and Mr. Blake are, then you have no choice but to accept."

I grudgingly nod my agreement to Gregory's terms. I don't like it, but it's better than the police hauling me away for questioning. At least Celeste's room is off-limits to Marco, which means I'll have privacy to do a more thorough search of her recent internet history.

Addressing Gregory, I ask, "Will there be an evening event tonight?"

He nods, sliding his hands into his pants pockets. "Yes, one at a hotel in Manhattan and there will be another event here tomorrow evening."

"Then I'm going to have Beatrice prepare a room for Mr. Blake. I understand these kinds of social events can run late."

Phillip's gaze narrows, but Gregory just waves dismissively, already clearing me from his presence. "Just be where we ask you to be and things should run as planned."

"About the events, Miss Rockwell," Phillip chimes in. "*All* of Celeste's social roles and responsibilities must be maintained, which includes her engagement to my son, Ben."

Even though I genuinely enjoy talking to Ben, I instantly stiffen. *What is he implying?* "It's a marriage in name only."

He offers a cold, brittle smile as he brushes lint off his suit jacket sleeve. "Be that as it may, you must conduct yourself as if you're a happily engaged couple. That includes posing for photo ops and conversing with constituents and Carver Enterprises board members in attendance about causes you plan to support and issues you want to defend as a married couple."

My eyes widen. "I—I have no idea what those are."

"Just let Ben do his doctor thing. All they need to see is you being supportive."

I frown slightly at his unspoken, yet implied—*like a good wife should.* "But as Carver Enterprises' CEO, wouldn't they expect to hear Celeste's thoughts on worthy causes and social issues?"

Phillip snorts out a laugh as he folds his arms. "Do you really think Celeste runs Carver Enterprises? She knows the role she plays."

So this is what Celeste meant by her CEO title not meaning anything. How sad that she gave up her ability to choose whom she married in exchange for a business role with no substance.

I bite back my instinctive snarky response to Phillip's dismissive comment. He apparently never witnessed

Celeste bend people to her Queen Bee will in high school. "I'll bet Celeste could easily run a business."

"Capability and willingness are two entirely different things," Gregory says on a sigh as he sits down and picks up a folder, his expression shuttered. "Don't forget the media interview is at four today. Please be dressed and in the living room ten minutes before. That will be all, Miss Rockwell."

Marco stands guard just outside the library door when I walk in and close it behind me.

Calder says goodbye to whomever he's speaking with, then slips his phone into his pants pocket. When I press my finger to my lips to let him know we have an audience, then nod to answer the question in his eyes—*Did Gregory approve him as my security?*—an arrogant smirk crooks one corner of his mouth.

Striding in my direction, he says in a low tone, "Let's go. I need to run a quick errand to rearrange my coaching schedule with some other trainers at the gym, then I'll grab some clothes." He passes me, continuing his line of thought. "Will I need a tux?" When he realizes I'm not on his heels, he quickly turns, his light brown brows pulling together.

Once he steps back into place in front of me, I speak so only he can hear. "The only way Gregory agreed to you as my guard is if Marco goes everywhere you and I do. You use the gym under your MMA persona, right?" When Calder scowls his frustration, I shoo him on. "I know you need to keep "Steel" anonymous. Go sort out your schedule."

Calder's fists clench and the vein down his neck visibly pulses. I can tell he's conflicted, but he can't commit to being here with me until he takes care of his other responsibilities. I rest my hand on his chest. "I'll be fine, Calder."

Trapping my hand with his much bigger one, he lifts my palm to his mouth and presses a warm kiss into it. "Don't go anywhere alone with any of the men connected to the Carver family...including Marco. That asshole is probably leaving snot trails on the door right now." As I snicker at his comment, he continues, "It'll probably be three before I can get back here. Keep in touch with me every hour so I know you're okay."

We turn and just before I reach the door, he tugs me back into his arms, saying gruffly against my throat, "I don't want to leave you here."

I melt into him and curl my fingers along his jaw, enjoying the smooth feel against my fingers. It's an equally arousing contrast to his evening beard that left goose bumps along my skin late last night. I inhale against his neck and savor his smell, knowing it'll be the last time I can do this until I'm no longer Celeste. Stepping back, I swallow my emotions. "Once we leave this room all eyes will be watching. You must treat me like a client under your guard and nothing more." I nod toward the closed door. "To the world out there, I'm Celeste Carver and Ben's fiancé."

Calder's expression quickly darkens. "You said the engagement was a business arrangement."

I nod. "It is, but appearances must be kept in the public eye. You can't let on that you know I'm not Celeste. The only people who know my real identity are Phillip, Gregory, and Beth. Neither Ben nor Jake will be told."

"What?" His eyes flash, taking on the unusual green hue of the sky before a tornado hits.

I take a step back and he follows me right up to the door, his words a low, harsh growl. "I *don't* share, angel. If that upstart doctor makes even one inappropriate move toward you, he won't be able to stitch himself up, let alone anyone else."

I jerk my head back and forth. "You can't touch him. Ben thinks I'm Celeste. He has every right to clasp his fiancé's hand, or wrap his arm around her waist in a social gathering like any fiancé would. I'll keep him at bay."

Calder's gaze narrows. "Let him fucking try it—"

I press my hand against his mouth to cut him off and whisper harshly, "*No, Calder.*"

Biting down on the fleshy part of my palm, he steps back, his tone suddenly professional and his expression military stoic. "If you'll see me out, Miss Carver, I'll collect my things and be back here at fifteen-hundred. Will formal attire be required for the evening events?"

If my palm didn't still throb, I would seriously question whether I dreamed Calder's display of territorial dominance. "Yes, you'll need a tux." Digging shaky fingers into my tingling skin, I uncurl my fingers and open the door.

CHAPTER FIVE

Calder

Gil's cane echoes down the hall that leads to his office, it's slow resounding thump drowning out the sound of the guys' wrestling against the mats in the gym. Or maybe that's just my guilt ratcheting. I feel bad that he has to come in and cover my shift. When I saw how he was struggling to recover from the beating he took for daring to challenge the MMA EUC group, I offered to take on a few mornings for him so he could ease back into work, but as bad as I feel over Gil, the thought of leaving Cass alone in the Carver house takes precedence. I've never been so on edge.

That whole situation at the Carver estate is one big clusterfuck.

I know Cass was trying to do the right thing for her father, but now that she could be implicated in Celeste's disappearance, I'm beyond furious. Especially after I learned that son of a bitch Phillip Hemming was the one who coerced her into continuing on as Celeste by threatening her. Gregory Carver might be complicit in keeping Celeste's disappearing act under wraps, but from what I've seen Phillip is the one pulling all the strings.

I've never despised a person quite so much, nor have I *wanted* to do permanent harm using every skill in my arsenal more than I do with that conniving bastard. I didn't like the authoritative way he spoke to "Celeste" last night at the party, but the fact he dared to put Cass in harm's way with his blackmail bullshit, puts him at the top of my target list. Once Cass is safely back to her own life, I will find a way to make the despicable man pay for all his past and present sins.

"Why are you still here brooding? Get the hell out," Gil barks, yanking me out of my musings.

I snort at his grizzled face under his ever-present cap and pretend not to notice how hard he leans on his chair's arm as he takes a seat behind his desk. Even though I want to tell him to close the gym for a couple of days, I keep my thoughts to myself. He'll just ignore me. He's as stubborn as my dad was, which is probably why they were best friends growing up.

I only learned of his existence after my father's funeral when Gil walked up and clapped me on the shoulder, saying in that gruff way of his, "I'm sorry for your loss, Calder, my boy. Your father was a hell of a man." Handing me a business card, he continued, "Anytime you want to talk…or just work out some frustration, come see me at the gym."

Gil gave me back my sanity after I returned to Manhattan as a civilian. It had been easier to push off mourning my father's death during the few years I was deployed on mission after mission, but upon returning to New York and subsequently learning in a letter from my long-dead mother's attorney that Jack Blake wasn't my biological father, I finally mourned Jack's death by taking a month long drinking binge. I may have drunkenly called Gil one night. I'm really not sure. All I know is that Gil found me at a bar and dragged me to his gym.

"Wake up!" someone yelled while spraying me with a burst of hard water in a dark alley.

"What the hell!" I stumbled to my feet, wet trash sliding underneath my shoes. Resisting the urge to shiver in the cold, I blinked the water out of my eyes and tried to make out the shadowy figure in the hat wielding a firehose. "Who the fuck are you?"

"Watch your mouth!" A hard spray sliced across my face from ear to ear, jacking my fury even more. Coughing up water, I lunged unsteadily toward the man, but he just turned the spray toward my crotch and hit it full blast.

Ooomph. *The laser accuracy sent pain from my balls straight to my brain. I grabbed my junk and fell back against the wall, bent over and moaning. "Son of a motherfucker!"*

"Your father would be appalled, Calder!"

When his familiar voice sank in, I glared at him in the darkness. "Gil?"

"*Damn straight it is.*" He slammed the hose on the asphalt and stalked toward me, all gruff and grumble. "*Now that you're somewhat aware, haul your drunk ass inside and get dried off. We need to talk.*"

An hour later, we sat at his office table, and over a pot of coffee I spilled my guts, telling Gil about the letter I received from my mother's attorney.

"*I wish she'd never told me, Gil. Honest to God, I wish I could unlearn that bit of history. But I can't help but think that things could've all turned out differently if she had just confessed to my dad.*"

"*Rebecca didn't tell your father for a reason, Calder.*"

I snapped my gaze to Gil's. "*You knew about the other guy?*" I growled out the question, full of renewed resentment.

"*I was the one who told her to never tell your father.*"

I jumped to my feet, the newly brewed coffee pot jostling in the center of the table. "*Why the hell would you do that?*"

Gil held up his work-roughened hands, unperturbed by my outburst. "*Becca came to me, distraught with guilt once she learned she was pregnant. She and Jack had tried to get pregnant for four years without success. I think she felt that since I was Jack's best friend, telling me was like confessing to him. But I knew the news would destroy Jack, so I told her she could never tell him. I wanted my best friend to have a chance at happiness and with a baby on the way, it was possible for them both to have the family they always wanted if she could get past the guilt.*" He snorts. "*I suppose I understand her reasoning for telling you once Jack died—only a mother would think her child might one day need a 'familial match' for medical reasons—but I agree, I*" *wish she had never told you at all."*

I was shaking inside, ready to explode.

Gil didn't have all the facts. My mother never got over the guilt. She kept it buried. He didn't know she committed suicide, because it was easier for the Blake family to have the outside world believe she died of a brain aneurism. Other than making Gil feel like shit—when he was obviously trying to help me— what would be the point of telling him the truth then? At the very least, I could honor my dad's wish to keep my mother's suicide quiet. Bash is the only other person who knows the truth about my mother's death, but my cousin knows first hand how to live with Blake family secrets.

I sat back down and grabbed the empty coffee mug, shaking my head to clear away the liquor-fueled fog I'd been under the past few weeks. To learn I wasn't the only one who carried the burden of the truth felt freeing somehow.

Gil poured me a fresh cup of coffee and then held my gaze. "I want to clear one thing up—"

"It's over and done." My chest might've felt lighter, but I could already feel my back muscles tightening at the subject in general. I folded my fingers tight around the ceramic and tried to suppress my resentment and anger at my mother for destroying my blissful ignorance. Even as my fingers singed, I pressed them against the coffee's heat, welcoming the pain.

"Calder, son. It's best if—"

"No more," I barked out at the same time the coffee cup shattered, sloshing steaming liquid all over my hands. "Son of a bitch!" I yelled, jumping up.

Gil threw me a towel and gruffly told me to calm down.

"Listen, I know we can't do anything about the past, but Becca told me—"

"Not another goddamn word about it, Gil," I gritted out as I wiped the coffee off my hands in fast swipes. "Or I'll walk out of here and never speak to you again."

And to his credit, Gil has never spoken about the past. Instead, he became an invaluable friend. Working out with Gil's guys gave me something to focus on other than the fact I was never really a Blake. The distraction built into something far more than a physical honing of my body. It was different than being in the military, but I became a part of a family here.

After Gil got attacked for standing up to the EUC over one of his fighters who disappeared, I had a purpose that could put my special military training to use as well. I made a plan and went undercover as Steel with the sole intent of taking down the EUC and holding them all accountable for their crimes related to MMA fighting.

What I didn't expect was to grow so close to Gil in the process. The gym and the fighters are the only family he has ever had. He treats the guys like his adopted kids, but for some reason I'm different. He treats me like the son he never had. Maybe he does so out of loyalty to Jack, or he has regrets about the advice he gave my mom all those years ago.

All I know is...seeing him lying there all beaten and bruised in that hospital bed put me on the kind of focused path I've only felt during missions. The EUC group will go down. I protect my family and those close to me with fierce conviction.

And I'm close. Once I win this last rescheduled fight, I'll get to meet the benefactors. I'll finally have names and faces to give the authorities. Now that I'll have access to the Carver's house, there's a slim chance I'll get a lead even sooner if I can get ahold of Beth's phone and swipe her boyfriend's phone number. Then I could hand the info off to Bash's team to trace. I honestly believe Beth is clueless about the depth of her boyfriend and his business partner's illegal activities.

Watching flashes of pain crease Gil's face as he slides his rolling chair toward his desk tugs me back to the here and now. As a deep hole of fury burns in my chest, I look away and try not to let myself feel. Worry for Cass is consuming me; I just can't let anything else take an emotional toll on me right now. I need to stay focused and sharp for everyone I care about.

Swallowing down my emotion, I glance Gil's way and answer his gruffness with my own. "If you wouldn't take so long to get seated I'd be out of here already."

Gil scrunches his face, his gaze suddenly narrowed on me. "Where'd you say you'll be?"

I slide my hands in my pants pockets. "At the Carver estate. I'm doing some extra security duty for Celeste Carver during her father's social events the next couple of days."

Gil tilts his head and eyes me. "She's a real beauty from what I've seen in the tabloids."

When I realize I'm nodding, I shrug. "She's also spoiled

and newly engaged."

Laughing, Gil lifts his cane toward me. "Engaged isn't married. Not yet."

I stiffen. "She's a client, Gil. Nothing more. I don't need you to find me a girlfriend."

He squints at me, then taps his barrel chest. "Hey, I introduced you to Alana. You two seemed to hit it off."

Shaking my head, I reach for the door. "Again, stop trying to play matchmaker, old man. I'm going to go over the schedule with Erik and have him run the training."

Gil tugs his hat's bill, pulling it farther down on his head. "Why am I here, then?"

"To hammer that damn cane on the floor. Why else?" I say with a wide grin.

I'm pretty sure he flipped me off as I headed out the door.

CHAPTER SIX

Cass

"*Where* are my keys?" I confront Marco in the hallway outside Celeste's bedroom after I found my purse dumped on the bed.

He pushes off the wall and jams thick fingers through his dark hair, breaking its slicked hardness into standing separate pieces and shrugs his thick shoulders. I twitch my nose and try not to breathe in the waft of strong aftershave that floats my way. "Anthony took *Celeste's* car to be processed. Everything of *hers* has been taken to comb through it for any leads we can find."

Phillip must've informed the guards since he's having them collect her belongings. Great, the man who is supposedly protecting me knows I'm an imposter. I'm so glad Calder insisted on being my security, because this guy has no reason to risk his life to save mine. And I can tell by the twitching smirk on his mouth and dislike in his eyes, he's enjoying my annoyance.

My phone is in the trunk of her car. Calder is going to flip when he doesn't hear from me. God, who knows what they'll do when they discover my phone. Will they wipe it completely? Grrr. *Wait, Marco mentioned taking everything.* I step back to the doorway of the room. Damn it! Her laptop is gone too. Even though I know Celeste's family has every right to confiscate her things, I keep my gaze from skirting to her nightstand where I replaced her diary in its hidden compartment.

"Whatever," I say, showing mild irritation as I casually step into the room and shut the door in Marco's face. The second I quietly flip the lock on the door, I head for the nightstand, my heart pumping.

I apply pressure to the drawer's fake bottom panel, but when it easily gives underneath my hand and no book slides onto the carpet, my heart sinks. *Empty.* Her diary is gone too.

Standing, I rub my temples in frustration, wondering how I'll find Celeste now. Her room was supposed to be my base of operation, but now it's devoid of all potential leads. I turn a full circle in Celeste's room, looking for other sources of information, but nothing jumps out. And now I can't even do any research via the web without a phone or a laptop, nor can I chase down leads without a car.

Feeling frustrated and trapped, I pause when I notice Celeste's gold necklace with the diamond locket, gold heart and key still on her dresser where I left it yesterday. Why did they take her diary but not the key to access it? Granted, the lock could be jimmied, but why take a chance on breaking it if the key was right here? It doesn't make any sense...unless they didn't know the key on the necklace fits the lock. Pressing my lips together, I hook the necklace around my neck once more for safekeeping.

There has to be something I can do with the last search criteria Celeste used, but I'll need access to the internet. I know Beth probably has a laptop in her room, but her reaction to my request to borrow her phone doesn't bode well for me using her computer. *Was there a laptop in the library?* I start for the bedroom door, then pause. Marco will follow me everywhere I go, and who knows what he'll report to Gregory. I need access to a computer without anyone reporting my activities.

Turning toward the bathroom, I close the door behind me and open the linen closet. Sliding back the panel on the far wall like Beth showed me last night, I step into the narrow space between the walls.

Once I close the panel, darkness consumes me. I wish I had my cell phone to light the way, but after blinking in the cramped space for a few seconds, my gaze adjusts to the darkness. I'm relieved to see bits of light coming through here and there. It's probably from cracks in walls, but I take advantage of the faint light and hold my hand out to keep from smacking my head into a beam, corner or exposed nail as I move in the direction Beth took us last night. Pressing my lips together, I silently pray I don't run into any spider webs.

After a few minutes, I finally find the narrow staircase Beth took me down and turn sideways to take each step. Just when I reach the bottom, I notice a longer stream of light and peer through a place where the doorjamb doesn't quite line up with the wall.

I can see right into the formal room from here, which makes me wonder what other parts of the house I can see from behind these walls. Instead of looking for the way we exited yesterday—via a panel that leads to a cramped coat closet next to a back door entrance—I start exploring every crack on the main floor. I discover that I can see into the small alcove in the kitchen and also Gregory's office. The last place I end up is a steep stairwell that leads down to a narrow pocket door.

Cracking it open, I realize I'm in the Carver's impressive wine cellar with a long tasting table flanked on either side by floor-to-ceiling custom wooden drawers of wine. The whole collection is probably worth more than my parents' Hamptons house. Shivering at the cooler temperature, I brush off the dust from my clothes, then turn into the small foyer and take the two-person elevator up to the main level.

Thankfully the elevator is quiet as it opens into a rarely used side hall. I glance both ways, then follow the hallway when I realize it leads to the library from the opposite direction. After a thorough search of the library, I lean against the desk, deflated. No laptop. Nor did I see a house phone anywhere during my exploration. Apparently, even in this turn of the century house, everyone uses a cell.

Beth's voice carries down the hall, and I instantly move over to the bookshelves to quickly grab a book, ready to pretend I'm choosing one to read. But when Beth asks Beatrice to prepare her a late breakfast, I put the book back. While she's eating in the dining room, her room will be empty. If I move quickly, hopefully I'll be able to access her computer and narrow down potential clinics before she gets back upstairs.

"What are you doing in my room?" Beth says in a high-pitched voice the second she opens her door.

"Shhh," I quickly say to calm her down and mime for her to shut the door. Relieved I was able to send Calder an email with the attachment of the Celeste/Deceiver text, as well as message my parents, letting them know I'm staying in town for a while before she walked in, I say, "I'm sorry. I just needed your phone for a minute."

Growling her anger, she stalks over to where I'm seated at her desk and rips her phone from my hand. "Get out of my room or I'll call the police myself."

If she had just been two minutes later, I would've had enough time to check out her boyfriend's contact information too. Frustrated, I stand and face her. "I needed access to the internet. Marco and Anthony took Celeste's laptop and other personal items in an attempt to find her."

Folding her arms, she tucks her phone against her

body. "At least *someone* is trying."

I throw my hands out, annoyed. "What do you think I've been doing while you were down there stuffing your face? And now I need your help."

Beth shakes her head and walks over to rest her hand on the doorknob. "I told you to *leave*. Get out now or I'll call Anthony to throw you out."

"Then you'll lose out on a good chance to find Celeste," I snap, finally losing my patience. "I have an idea where your sister went yesterday. Do you want to help me look for her or not?"

Beth releases the door handle, her voice dropping to a hushed tone. "You know where she is?"

I shake my head. "No, but I think I know where to start.

"Where?" Beth asks suspiciously, her gaze narrowing.

I hold my hand out for her phone. "May I?"

Huffing, she hands it to me. As I quickly pull up the search parameters, I say, "While you were getting dressed, I hopped on Celeste's laptop to see if she'd made any recent internet searches that could tell us where she might've gone yesterday." I turn the phone toward Beth and hold my breath.

Beth glances at the clinics highlighted on the screen, then lifts her gaze to mine, anger stamped on her pretty face. "No! Celeste would've told me if she were pregnant... and she would never do something like this."

"Are you sure?" I ask quietly, sympathy tightening my chest. I understand the hurt shimmering in her eyes. My older sister Sophie didn't tell me she was going to commit suicide to save our family from financial ruin either. People don't always want to be stopped or talked out of it.

"Yes!" Beth hisses, her expression adamant.

I tilt my head and hold her gaze. "She didn't tell you about me, did she?"

When Beth clamps her mouth shut, I sigh. "Look, I can't claim to know what was going on in your sister's head, but the fact she needed me to stand in for her due to an appointment she couldn't miss makes a lot more sense now. According to this search..." I pause and scroll through. "There are five places to check, but only three of them have Saturday morning hours, so we'll need to get moving if we want to get there before they close. If we can learn where Celeste went, then maybe we can figure out where she might've gone next. Will you go with me to the clinics that are open so we can find out if she visited any of them?"

"What? And smear my sister's good name in the process?" She takes her phone and shakes her head. "I don't think so!"

"Then I'll just have to do it by myself." I turn away to walk out. "Beatrice can call me a cab."

Beth grabs my arm. "Oh, no you don't. Celeste can't be seen at a women's clinic. The rumor mill would spin out of control. God, this makes me wonder what my sister was thinking when she asked you to step in. You have no idea how private she was."

I'm intimately familiar with keeping a private life private, but I shrug off her dig. "I learned a long time ago not to give a damn what people think about me, so if you want to manage your sister's precious social image, then take me and you can help make our presence there as discrete as possible. Whatever we do, we need to do it soon. The clinics will close in four hours."

When Beth glances down at her phone, her teeth worrying her bottom lip, I touch her arm. "I know you feel like you can't trust me, but I want Celeste to come home just as much as you do. I hope you'll agree that finding your sister is far more important than protecting every aspect of her reputation right now."

She pulls away from me and straightens her shoulders. Grabbing a pair of sunglasses off her dresser, she hands them to me. "We'll leave the back way so Marco and Anthony can't follow us. Once we're in the car, put the glasses on. My face isn't as well known as Celeste's, so I'll scout the places out. Got it?"

I take the glasses and nod, glad to be doing something to find Celeste.

After striking out at the three clinics with morning hours, I convinced Beth to try the other two clinics to see if someone was there who could answer questions. As we approach the forth clinic and a police car's red and blue siren lights are flashing outside, Beth hits the brakes. "Hell no!"

I gesture to the side of the road. "Pull over here and we'll wait."

"For what?" she asks as she pulls up to the curb. "The

media to show up and talk about a potential bomb threat on a clinic?"

Rolling my eyes behind the dark shades, I watch the uniform police officers standing outside the clinic talking to a woman with curly blonde hair. "We'll wait until they leave. I'll bet she's a nurse or an office manager who can answer our questions. How's the bribery fund?"

"I'm down to my last fifty." Beth grumbles as she cuts the engine. "Father is going to kill us."

Once the police officers get in their car, I push the glasses up on my head and frown at her. "You really need to stop being so afraid of your dad, Beth. He obviously cares about you."

"You just don't get how he operates," she mumbles as she watches the police car turn off its siren lights then drive away.

I snort. "He operates from a position of intimidation. Don't let him threaten you. Call him on it."

When respect reflects in Beth's gaze, I hope she's opening up to the idea I'm trustworthy. "Your dad said that Phillip found Celeste once before when she was fourteen. Do you know why she ran away?"

Beth shrugs and glances out the window. "Actually, I don't. We'd just gotten back from a week long beach trip and she took off right after dinner. My dad and Phillip went looking for her everywhere. The next day, Phillip drives up with her in the car."

A beach trip? "Was that in July?" I asked without thinking.

She looks at me funny, a slight frown marring her features. "Yeah, how'd you know that?"

"Isn't July peak vacation time? Did she have a terrible time at the beach?"

Beth slides her hand over the steering wheel. "It was weird. At first she was enjoying all the attention she was getting now that she had boobs. Scrappy didn't like it at all. He even went after a seventeen-year-old who offered to put lotion on her back, not caring that at the time he was half his size." She chuckles at the memory. "Phillip had to pull his crazed son off the guy and apologize to his parents."

"Is that why you call Jake *Scrappy*?"

"Yep, that's where the nickname came from," she says with a laugh, then sobers. "The rest of the week Celeste wore a cover-up to the beach. I was shocked. It's not like Father ordered her to. She just did it."

I really hate how Beth bows to her father. "You should stand up to your father, Beth. He might come across angry, but I believe he'll respect you more for it."

"He's *my* father. I know him far better than you."

I shrug. "What's the worst that can happen?"

Beth sighs, then tilts her head, staring at my face. "I can see slight differences now: the slant of your eyes and the arch of your eyebrows. Your smile is more genuine too."

Her last comment surprises me and I take a moment to really look at Beth. "You know you have nice bone structure. The models I work with would kill for your cheekbones and jawline."

A slight smile crooks her lips. "What do you do that you work with models?"

"When I'm not pretending to be my doppelganger I'm a fashion photographer."

Beth's eyes widen. "What an interesting profession."

I grin. "The best part is that I get to be my own boss."

Beth presses her lips together and glances out the window. "I need to go before the lady locks up and leaves."

Wondering why she had a sudden change of attitude, I pull the sunglasses back down and open my car door. Beth reaches for my arm. "What are you doing? You're supposed to stay in the car."

I easily evade her hand and slip out of the vehicle. "There aren't any patients there to see me. We'll be fine."

Beth sniffs her annoyance as she steps into place beside me at the clinic's door. As the rosy-cheeked woman in her mid-thirties approaches behind the glass door, a look of surprise on her face, Beth mutters, "It would be nice to be my own boss."

"It has its benefits," I say, then push the sunglasses up on my head so the woman can see my face. Pointing to the locked door, I nod, asking her for permission to enter.

"I'm sorry but we're closed today," she says the moment she unlocks the door and swings it open. "I'm only here because the alarm went off." Waving her hand, she hurries on. "Are you here to make another appointment, Miss Carver?"

Beth and I exchange glances and I ask, "Can we come inside for a minute?"

While the lady flips on several lights as we walk through the empty waiting room and back to her office, I whisper to Beth. "Just follow my lead. If she thinks I'm Celeste, we'll get access to her medical records."

Beth is biting hard on her bottom lip. She's stressed and worried for Celeste, so I squeeze her arm to get her to calm down. Nodding, she edges a bit closer to me.

Once we're seated in the chairs across from Nancy Westin, R.N.'s desk—at least that's what the desk nameplate says—I ask, "Is everything all right? I saw the police drive away."

Nancy waves. "Please don't worry, Miss Carver. There were no threats to the clinic. Our main computer was damaged and some filing cabinets and desks were broken into, but thankfully we don't keep money here." She turns on her computer and hits a few keys. "Fortunately the appointment calendar works just fine." Sliding her finger down the screen, she nods and smiles. "It appears you're in luck. We had a cancellation yesterday afternoon for next Thursday. It's also the last appointment of the day." Lifting her gaze to mine, she continues, "Would you be able to make that?"

Beth instantly straightens in her chair, her nostrils flaring. Clearing my throat, I say, "In light of this recent break-in and your database issue, I would like to request a copy of my records."

Nancy lifts her chin slightly. "Your information is perfectly safe. We have an off-site backup system."

"I understand that, but—"

"Do you plan to switch clinics?" she interrupts, her voice pitching slightly.

I fold my hands in my lap, adopting a calm demeanor. "I'm reserving the right, but no I haven't made that decision yet."

Exhaling obvious relief, the nurse stands. "If you'll just wait right here, I'll make a copy of your records for you."

As soon as she walks out, Beth looks at me, her expression tense. "This whole situation freaks me out. I can't believe Celeste didn't tell me." Gesturing around the office, she continues, her voice dropping, "And I can't believe Celeste would—"

Hearing footsteps coming back, I grip Beth's hand and say under my breath. "We don't know anything yet. Don't jump to conclusions."

Nancy appears in the doorway, looking pale. "I'm sorry to inform you, Miss Carver, but your record appears to be among a set of folders that were taken from the filing cabinet."

Disappointed, I hold her gaze. "Are you serious? If your computer system is down, how can I get a digital record?"

The woman tenses. "Our backups will be restored next week, and I can get you a physical copy then if you would like, Miss Carver."

I stand, frustrated that we've hit a wall. Right now all we know is that Celeste had a procedure planned, but not what kind of procedure. And I can't ask what it was or even if she went through with it since, *I'm* Celeste. "Well, I guess that answers your question as to if I'm keeping that appointment."

Nancy's shoulders slump. "I'm truly sorry, Miss Carver. This is the first time we've ever had a break-in. Would you like us to destroy your blood work as well?"

"Yes!" Beth says quickly as she rises to her feet beside me, but I grip her arm and shake my head.

"No, Ms. Westin. Please keep my blood work for now."

Relief flickers across the woman's face. "That's good then. If you decide to go through with the procedure fairly soon, we won't have to re-do the blood work."

"Wait? She didn't have the procedure done? The appointment you're referring to isn't a follow up appointment?" Beth blurts, holding the nurse's gaze.

"Um?" Nancy looks at me, confused. "You didn't tell her?"

This is how we'll get our answer. We're probably breaking the law, but Celeste's life could be on the line. We need to know everything we can, right now. *Anything* we learn could help find her. I heave an exaggerated sigh and gesture to Beth. "It's okay, this is my sister. You can tell her. Maybe hearing it from a professional, it'll sink in."

Nancy's blonde eyebrows shoot up. "This is highly unorthodox, but if you insist." Turning to Beth, she says, "No, your sister has not gone through with the procedure. She had an appointment late yesterday, but she never showed for it." Spreading her hands, she shifts her attention back to me, sympathy in her tone. "Sometimes this happens. It's the woman's choice in the end."

When Beth throws her arms around my neck and squeezes me tight, a pang hits my heart. I pat Beth's back and smile at the nurse.

A slight smile on her lips, Nancy shifts back to her professional self. "Please keep in mind the sooner you make a decision the better, Miss Carver. Now if you ladies don't mind, I need to lock this place up and try to make the last half of my son's soccer game."

"I can't believe she didn't tell me," Beth says in a quiet voice when we're a half hour away from her home. She'd been quiet the whole ride, so I used that time to borrow her phone and do some research on what is required to do a paternity test. "I don't even know who the father is," Beth continues, waving her hand in frustration. "As far as I knew, she wasn't dating anyone. Unless..."

I glance up from staring at her phone's screen, glad she and I are at least on the same wavelength in thinking about the father. In my mind, it has to be the Deceiver. "Unless, what?"

Beth glances my way, her eyes wide. "Unless Calder Blake is the father."

I quickly shake my head and try not to react to her suggestion, even though my stomach churns. "It's not Calder."

Her gaze narrows. "You don't know that for certain. Why else would she be so insistent on him as her new guard?"

"Maybe because she was serious about having a stalker, Beth," I counter. "You heard that nurse. Celeste never showed for her appointment. She certainly didn't *fly* to New Jersey and since I had her car, she must've rented one."

"Okay, so she got a rental car, but the police said the one they found was on 495. That route is way out of her way."

I shrug. "I agree it doesn't make any sense, but we also don't know what else she did last night or where she went. Maybe the rental car had a GPS in it. Hopefully the police are checking that. Whatever you do...don't say anything to your father or Phillip about her pregnancy. Not right now. There's still a chance Celeste could be found or return on her own."

She looks at me like I'm crazy. "No worries. I'm not saying a *word*. But I'm also not discounting Calder as the potential baby daddy—"

"You can nix that idea right now, Beth!" I snap, furious at the doubt she's planting in my head. "There was another man in her life, and if the blood results from the abandoned car turns out to be your sister's, then I think we should share what we know."

"What man?" Just as Beth meets my gaze, her phone rings in my hand.

As the name Brent pops up on her phone's caller ID, I shake my head. "I don't know his name."

"Then how do you know this?"

I swallow, unsure if I should say anything until I hear back from Calder on the text conversation I sent him. Phillip and his men won't find that text conversation on the phone, and I don't want Beth mentioning a possible lead to anyone, not until we have a *name* for the Deceiver. "Just trust me."

She frowns. "Saying things like that doesn't help your case," she snaps as she hits the speaker button on her steering wheel to answer the incoming call. "Hello?"

"Hey!" a deep voice booms through her car speakers.

"Hey, yourself," she answers in a chirpy tone.

"Where are you?"

"Just out running errands—"

"You don't have me on your speaker, do you, babe? You know how much I hate that."

Beth gestures for me to hand her the phone, but I'm completely frozen. *That voice.*

Rolling her eyes, she grabs the phone from my hand and puts it to her ear. "Sorry, I was just trying to be a responsible driver."

Once his voice is no longer resonating throughout the entire car, I'm finally able to tear my gaze away. I feel physically ill. He's the face I never saw, but the voice I'll never forget. Beth's boyfriend is the unknown guy who helped Jake violate me in high school.

A shudder of embarrassment rocks through me as I glance out the window. Just hearing his voice brings the shame slamming back...I rub my jacket sleeves hard along my thighs to alleviate the fire burning across my wrists and hate the sudden clawing desire for slicing pain, the need to feel a release. I close my eyes and gulp, working hard to regain control.

Beth pulls into the Carver's drive, rambling on about last night's cancelled fight. "When do you think it'll be rescheduled?" As soon as the car rolls to a halt, I fling open the door. "Hey…wait—" she calls out, but I don't stop.

My lungs burn as I run in the front door and straight up to Celeste's room.

I rip off my jacket and push my sleeves up, then close the bathroom door behind me. Yanking open the drawers, my hands shake when I find a small pair of scissors. I quickly open them and stare at the sharp blades. They would accomplish what I need.

I flick my gaze to my wrist, my palms burning and my breath heaving. I flex my hand, digging my fingernails into my palm. That pain isn't enough, but the scissors would be.

When my attention slides up my arm to the Never tattoo on my forearm, a long-forgotten conversation I had with my sister during her early rounds of chemo and radiation pops into my head.

Sophie's eyes were closed when I walked into her hospital room. She looked so broken and pale. My chest squeezing with sadness, I sat in the chair beside her bed and gingerly lifted her hand into mine, hoping I don't wake her.

The moment my hand settled over hers, Sophie's brown eyes popped open and she smiled. It wasn't a weak smile. It was wide and radiant, despite the medical procedures that were destroying her body in an attempt to heal it.

"Hey, Cassie. How's it going?"

I lightly flexed my fingers over hers. "How are you doing?"

"I'm still here," she chirped, then winked.

Her lighthearted comment made my heart ache. I folded my hand around hers, in awe of her sunny outlook. "How do you do it, Sophie? How do you sit there smiling instead of screaming at the universe for what's happening to you?"

"What good would it do to waste all that energy resenting?" she said, shrugging. "Why spend my time on anger and fury when instead I can be living my life in the most positive way that I can...even if that means all I can do right now is grin at you while lying in a hospital bed?"

When I shook my head and offered an amazed smile, she waved her free hand toward the monitors and the IV in her arm. "All this stuff is just noise I choose not to listen to." Turning her hand under mine, she clasped my fingers with surprising tightness. "No one can live your life better than you can, Cass. Never forget that even at your weakest you are still in control."

Exhaling, I slowly lower the scissors to the counter, then kiss the raven on my wrist, tears trickling down my cheeks. "I miss you so much, Sophie."

Once I take several deep breaths, the need to cut passes, but I still feel dirty. Shrugging out of my clothes, I step into the shower, hoping a good scrub under hot water will help me clear my head.

The bathroom is full of steam by the time I shut off the water. I cough at the fog curling in the air and grab the towel off the fogged glass door, my skin suddenly chilled without the hot water raining down on me. Wrapping the towel around my body, I slide the glass back and suck in a breath. Phillip is leaning casually against the doorjamb.

CHAPTER SEVEN

Cass

"**G**et out of my room!" I hiss in a low tone and step out of the shower onto the oversized plush rug. Pressing the towel tighter against my breasts, I glare at him as if I'm wearing armor and not a thin layer of cloth.

Phillip nods toward my room door. "You didn't answer when I knocked and this couldn't wait. You've already wasted precious time by disappearing for several hours. What is the unlock code for Celeste's phone?"

Finally, a chance to save the text conversations between Celeste and me. But Phillip standing here impatiently while I'm nearly naked has me so rattled I can't think of a way to get him to give me the phone. "I'll come find you *downstairs*. Now leave!"

He straightens and unfolds his arms, his hazel eyes

darkening in anger. "I don't think you heard me. Give me the unlock code *now*."

Real worry flushes my skin. Despite my bravado, I'm completely vulnerable alone in this room with him. Keeping my arms down to make sure the towel stays tucked, my voice quivers with my answer. "I need to hold the phone. I remember passwords tactilely."

Phillip walks right up to me and crowds me against the counter, his tone cold and menacing. "This isn't a game. Give me that goddamn code, right *now*."

His violation of my personal space completely strips away my ability to negotiate. I blindly reach for the scissors behind me as I babble the answer. "It—it's Cass, C.A.S.S."

"Thank you, Cassandra. See that wasn't so hard." Even though his tone loses its edge, the fearful knot in my stomach doesn't loosen. I find the scissors and curl my fingers around them. "With the exception of a combative attitude and a couple of tattoos, I can see how you passed as her." Phillip bends closer and scans my features with a critical eye, his tone shifting to one of intrigued observation. "But up close, it's the little things…like the tilt of your eyes and angle of your nose that give you away."

The hint of awareness in his tone tightens my fingers around the scissors. I can handle disdain and distrust from him, but this man's up-close and personal inspection of my face is scaring the shit out of me. "You got what you came for. You need to leave."

He turns to walk away, but pivots back, his expression all business once more. "I don't know what you think you're doing with Beth, but stop it. Celeste and Beth aren't that close. Taking off together like you did...it's out-of-character actions like that that will be noticed by the staff and those who know them. Celeste always kept her distance."

His comment about the sisters breaks my heart. I want to scream at him, "And whose fault is that?" My gut tells me he's the slimy Deceiver who slithered his way into Celeste's life. So the follow on logic means that he's probably the father of Celeste's unborn child. *Was the sex consensual or coerced? And more importantly...how long has whatever is between him and Celeste gone on?* She sounded like she *hated* the Deceiver for what he did to her. Was she speaking about the pregnancy or something more?

I straighten my spine, my fingers fisted around the scissors. "*Sisters* are always there for each other, no matter what. Don't enter this room again without my permission or I will scream at the top of my lungs until the entire household comes running."

His expression hardens. "Do as you're told. Show up at the interview to support Gregory, but stay out of the limelight. Don't let anyone get too close with a camera and definitely don't answer any questions. If you hurt Gregory's career by bringing the spotlight down on this family, I'll personally make sure that not only does your father's business suffer, but your own trite photography business is shredded beyond repair." He shakes his head, *tsking*. "The last thing you should do is bad mouth the models you photograph, *Raven*. It's just bad business."

Fury rips through me that he investigated my background and is threatening to destroy a career I've worked my ass off to build. *What other dirt has he dug up on me?* I point to the door and raise my voice. "Get the hell out!"

Once Phillip leaves, I rush over and lock the door, then shove the desk chair under the handle for good measure.

My hands are still shaking thirty minutes later as I slip on a long soft burgundy sweater, a pair of dove gray fitted dress pants and matching ballet-style flats. When a knock sounds at my door, my heart kicks into overdrive.

"Yes?" I say as I press my knee against the edge of the chair to assure it holds.

"It's me, Celeste. I'm just checking in to let you know I'm settled in my room."

Calder. His deep voice is so reassuring, I exhale a sigh of relief that he's back. I have so much to tell him. I quickly remove the chair, then unlock the door, my pulse racing.

"Can you do me a favor and escort me to the garden?" I say, meeting his questioning gaze with a calm one.

Calder pushes his wool trench coat back and slides his hands in his dress pants pockets, nodding. "Your wish is my command. Though you might want to put on a jacket. The temperature has suddenly dropped outside. They're calling for flurries."

The moment we reach the center of the garden, Calder faces me, his brows pulled together in an intense scowl. "What part of keep in touch every hour didn't register with you?"

His anger amps my own tension. "I sent you the text conversation."

Calder's green eyes narrow and his breath pushes through his nose in an annoyed grunt. "That was hours ago."

I sigh and shake my head. "My stuff was in the trunk of Celeste's car that they took to scour for clues. I stayed quiet and hoped no one would find my phone hidden in the bottom compartment before I had a chance to send you that text conversation. Now that you have it, I'll see if they've returned the car."

"I saw it parked around the side of the house. I'll get your phone for you later. I sent that text conversation on to Elijah. If anyone can find the number, he can." His jaw muscle flexes. "Gregory ripped me a new one for not following you when you left earlier. Where did you and Beth go that kept you away for hours?"

I gape. "What? You weren't even here. He can't expect you to—"

Calder touches my jaw, then realizes what he's doing and pulls his hand away. "Stay focused...where."

When I glance around to make sure no one is lurking, Calder smirks. "Marco had to go pick up another tux for tonight's event. Apparently his neck had gotten too thick for his current one."

Instead of reassuring, his comment reminds me that I don't have anything to wear. "I've been borrowing Celeste's clothes and I have no idea what I'm supposed to wear tonight. Ugh, I'm *not* wearing her underwear. And

I'll need long sleeves. Beth was supposed to tell me, but she—"

"Calm down, Cass. Where did you go?"

Nodding, I swallow my nerves and tell him where we went and what we discovered at the clinic. He cuts in, his words sharp. "This Deceiver person has to be the father. Taking that text conversation between Celeste and him into context...now it makes a lot more sense." He rubs his jaw and turns to pace in front of me. "I have a few people in mind, but hopefully Elijah can tell us who he—"

"I think it's Phillip," I interrupt, anxious to get that burden off my chest.

Calder halts, sheer dislike glittering in his gaze. "He's a total dick, I'll give him that, but that takes some major balls—"

"There are other things he said to me when he thought I was Celeste. He was controlling, authoritative...and possessive of whom she spent her time with. At the time, I thought he just wanted to control the Carver wealth, but now I'm wondering if he meant more." Calder's demeanor shifts as I talk, his hands curling into tight fists, his face turning to stone. Where anger initially lurked in his eyes, now simmering fury is roiling. My own insecurities about us begin to crowd my thoughts once more, but I push them back and finish voicing my thoughts. "I think he has used his position of power in this family to influence her, possibly for years."

"That manipulative, conniving son of a bitch!" Calder grates.

With retribution stamped on his face, he pivots and stalks back toward the house. Panicked, I run after him and jump on his back just before he enters the maze. Wrapping my arms around his neck, I try to get through to him. "*No*, Calder. We need to prove Phillip is the father first." When he keeps charging forward like a bull going after a flapping red cape, I hiss in his ear, "I said to stop!"

The moment he freezes, then shakes his head, his breathing sawing in and out, I tighten my arms around his neck and soften my tone. "I have an idea how we can prove his paternity."

Calder grips my arm and tugs me down in front of him. He doesn't meet my gaze as he tucks my pea coat's collar under my chin then buttons it with tense, precise movements. When I realize he's struggling to calm down, I grasp his hands and hold him still. Finally he meets my gaze, his own deadly calm. "I want to bury that bastard. What do you have in mind?"

His emotional response to finding out about Phillip and Celeste proves that he cared more for her than he let on, more than he ever acknowledged to me. Swallowing that bitter pill, I shove my shredded feelings aside to focus on helping Celeste.

"While I find it strangely convenient the group of folders that went missing during the break-in that damaged the computer system also happened to include Celeste's medical record, there's still a sample of her blood at the clinic. On the way back from New Jersey, I researched paternity testing. All we need is a blood or DNA sample from the prospective father. With a blood sample from the pregnant mother, a Non-Invasive Prenatal Paternity test (NIPP) can be run to prove or disprove paternity. If we can prove Phillip is the father, then the police will want to question him about Celeste's disappearance."

Calder frowns. "Phillip deserves what he gets if he turns out to be the baby's father, but Celeste truly seemed to think she had a stalker. She never indicated to me that the person was someone she knew."

I cross my arms. "And yet the person she was obviously having *some* kind of relationship with was only listed as *Deceiver* on her phone. If Celeste kept that person's identity a secret, I don't think it's a leap to consider the possibility that she could've known the person stalking her but wasn't ready to reveal who."

A corner of Calder's mouth quirks in amusement. "And here I thought Talia had the investigative mind."

I ignore the heat that floods my face and glance away. "Not wanting to be arrested as a suspect in Celeste's disappearance is highly motivating."

"I won't let that happen," he says in a serious voice. When I take an unsteady breath, Calder's tone softens. "Look at me." Just as he takes a step closer, someone calls out, "Celeste, are you out here?"

"It's Ben," I whisper to Calder, then answer Ben's call in a normal voice as I put some distance between us. "Over here."

A second later, Ben turns the corner at the end of the bushes. "There you are. Beth said you were out here." His smile fades when he addresses Calder. "You're Calder Blake, right?" he says, stopping in front of us.

As Calder slides his hands into his pockets and nods, I quickly gesture to him. "I convinced Father to let Calder shadow me as my guard for the next couple of days."

Glancing from Calder to me, Ben tucks his gray scarf inside his black coat and buttons it closed. "Do you really think it's necessary to have two guards, Celeste? I just saw Marco pull in behind me when I arrived."

I shrug. "If I had my way, Marco would be gone, so I agree with you that two guards are unnecessary, but you know how stubborn my father can be."

"Yes, I do." Ben snorts as he clasps my hand. "Let's take a walk." Folding my fingers around the crook of his arm, he tugs me back toward the center of the garden and says over his shoulder to Calder, "Celeste is in good hands now. You can wait inside."

As much as I want to look back at Calder, I can't. Not without giving away my feelings. The sound of leaves crunching not far behind us tells me what Calder thought of Ben's suggestion. When Ben stiffens and acts like he's going to turn and say something, I tighten my hold on his arm and pull him forward. "Unlike Marco, he's doing his job, Ben."

Ben folds his hand over mine and says loud enough for Calder to hear. "So long as he gives us some privacy, I won't say anything."

Instead of soothing me, his comment sets my nerves on edge. *What does he need privacy for?*

CHAPTER EIGHT

Calder

Fuck privacy. With corrupt morals and skewed agendas, every person in this goddamn house is a suspect as far as I'm concerned. Any of them could've had a hand in hurting Celeste. My stomach knots over the news of her pregnancy. She never let on, not once. I wish she had told me. I could've been there for her. Guilt and anger swirl in my thoughts.

I mentally paint a target on the back of Ben's dark head. He has no fucking clue how on edge I am right now. Crossing my hands behind my back, I curl them into fists as I follow the youngest Hemming son and Cass. If he makes even one inappropriate move on her, he'll regret it. Cass can be pissed all she wants, but I'll only stand for so much bullshit.

Once I reach the end of the maze that leads to an open circular center of the garden with low bushes and a decorative fountain, Ben meets my gaze. "You can guard from here. We're not leaving this area."

My attention drops to his hand covering hers on his arm and my desire to send him flying over the hedge ignites, but Cass shakes her head, telling me not to challenge Ben. I inhale deeply, then exhale slowly. *I can handle this. I have to.* Setting my jaw, I nod my understanding and take a position near the entrance that'll allow me a clear line of sight to all access points.

As if he's trying to torque me off, Ben leads Cass to a bench on the opposite side of the open area. My view is unobstructed, but I'm too far away to hear what's being said. I shove my hands in my pants pockets and snort my annoyance.

Ben pulls Cass down beside him on the bench and every muscle in my body seizes up when he takes her hand and rubs it briskly between his. He says something that makes her smile and their breath plumes in the air as they laugh together.

I grind my back teeth when he leans in and blows his breath across her hand between his. As much as the intimate gesture pisses me off, it's the way she looks at him that's like a kick in the balls. What is he saying to elicit such rapt attention?

Hearing her laugh at whatever he's saying grates, but the fact she doesn't appear to have her guard up at all is unacceptable. She should've put layers between them.

Real, physical layers. Like gloves. Where are the fucking gloves I insisted she put in her pockets? And why is he blowing his goddamn breath on her hands?

My shoulders tense and I ignore the cold air blowing around me as I work to gain control of my thoughts. I'm the only person Cass should trust enough to get that close to her. Hemming doesn't know that her confident smile hides a deep hurt from her past.

Watching him bend close as he whispers something in her ear, it's hard to reconcile the near impenetrable wall I had to break through to be with her the other night, and even then she didn't tell me everything. It might be irrational, but I don't give a damn that she's pretending to be someone else. She needs to employ that wall of distrust with *him*. She needs to be wary.

When Ben lifts her hand and her broad smile fades slightly, I'm instantly on alert. My gut twists as he slides a ring on her left finger. What kind of business-only marriage needs a diamond big enough for me to see from this distance? But it's the look in his eyes as he presses a lingering kiss to the ring on her finger that ignites fierce territorial instincts within me. *Fuck, he wants her.*

I stride forward without a thought, but I don't get more than three steps before my phone buzzes. I halt and keep my gaze on Hemming as I answer in a low, curt tone. "Blake."

"Elijah looked over that text conversation Cass sent you," Bash says. "We were able to retrieve a phone number, but it's a burner phone that's gone dead. No way to trace it."

I move into the entrance of the maze and turn my back to the foliage, making sure I can still see Ben and Cass as I speak to my cousin in a low rumble. "Were you able to find out anything about the rental car or the blood they found in it?"

"We were right behind the police in talking to the rental car company. A woman matching Celeste's description rented the car under the fake credit card of Selma Tobian. They didn't have any security cameras to confirm her identity."

Ben points toward the sky and gestures like he's shooting something. Whatever he says makes Cass smile. Tension tightens my shoulders. I don't like that he's trying to charm her. "Did you check the car's GPS? Did it go to New Jersey?"

"The car drove through Manhattan, then it was found abandoned on 495. Why are you asking about Jersey?"

I exhale, frustrated. Tons of women could match Celeste's general description. We need a stronger connection. "It was just a thought. What about the blood?"

Bash snorts. "We're piggy-backing off Phillip Hemming's backdoor efforts. He paid someone in the forensics lab to quietly test a sample of Celeste's hair against the blood the police found. A guy in the lab owes me a favor. He promised to pass us a copy of the results Hemming will get. We should know sometime tomorrow. What about you? Find out anything?"

"Cass discovered that Celeste had an appointment at an

abortion clinic in Jersey yesterday, but she never showed. Did your guys check the rental car's GPS's destination log?"

"He only told us where it had been and where they found it. I'll head over there now and see what the guy can pull up. Money is the only thing that is an incentive for the clerk."

"Let me know what you find out. Cass thinks the appointment is what Celeste's text conversation with the Deceiver was about. He's probably the father."

The sound of a car door shutting comes across the line. "The text definitely sounded combative, Cald," Bash says as an engine roars to life. "But I didn't get that he would hurt her."

"Under normal circumstances maybe not, but he was trying to control her and she was rebelling."

"You're thinking there might be someone with a motive now instead of a stalker?" Bash asks.

When Ben brushes a lock of hair from Cass's face, I curl my upper lip and glance away so I don't bark at him to get his fucking hands off her. "Possibly. Cass wonders if Celeste actually knew her stalker, but wasn't ready to reveal him yet. Maybe things got out of control yesterday." I nearly crush the phone when Cass tries to smooth her hair against a sudden gust of wind and Ben captures her hand and locks their fingers together. "We need to move quickly. I want to get Cass away from this whole fucked up mess."

"Agreed. Talia is really worried. She doesn't like that

she hasn't been able to talk to her."

"I'll have Cass call her. I need you to find a way to get yourself invited to tomorrow night's event at the Carver's estate. Use one of your brothers if you have to."

"Thanks," Bash mutters in a dry tone. "Just what I want to do, leverage the Blake family name."

"Damien is the best at this schmooze bullshit. Your little brother seems to have no issue with everyone wanting a piece of Blake ass...ahem, wealth."

Bash barks out a laugh. "I'll be sure to tell him you're pimping him out. What did you have in mind for tomorrow night?"

"The party will hopefully give us a chance to collect DNA samples to prove who the baby's father is. If we can get it, I'll need to hand it off to you for testing. I'm not leaving Cass until this is over."

"Got it. I'll text you once Damien comes through."

I hang up just as Cass and Ben stand and then start back toward the maze's entrance. When they pass me a few seconds later, I glance down at the engagement ring on Cass's hand, then set my jaw as I begin to follow a few feet behind.

We've only moved about twenty feet when Ben's phone rings. He stops and glances at his phone, then apologizes, "Excuse me one minute. This is a patient I need to talk to."

Once Ben returns to the center of the garden and turns his back to us while he talks to his patient, I focus a hard gaze on Cass. "What happened to keeping Ben at bay?"

She shifts so her back is to Ben and says in a low

voice, "I'm playing a part, Calder. Ben just gave Celeste a gorgeous engagement ring. She wouldn't be human if she didn't respond appropriately."

Her answer might be logical, but I don't have to fucking like it. "Don't let him manipulate your emotions."

"I'm not." She sighs and glances back toward the house, her expression wistful. "I just wish Celeste had experienced it herself. He was very sweet."

I snort my cynicism. "It's a business arrangement."

"For Phillip, I agree, but not him." She glances at Ben as he gestures animatedly while talking to his patient. "I think he truly cares for her. Women would kill to be asked like that."

I pin her with an icy stare. "She's his ticket to Carver Enterprise's deep pockets. The fact he gets to fuck her is a bonus. Don't let him fool you and sure as hell don't let him touch you."

"I'm not being manipulated," she says, her tone tensing. "I know you told me last night that you don't plan to marry, but some people actually still believe in marriage. Ben is being sincere. Maybe you need to ask yourself what you're really angry about...the fact that Ben was touching me or Celeste?"

What the hell does that mean? She's missing the point entirely. "Celeste isn't the subject of this discussion. You letting your emotions be played *is*."

Cass bristles and crosses her arms. "How quickly you forget that I had to jump on your back to keep you from going after Phillip once you found out Celeste was pregnant. So *who* is more emotionally invested?"

I set my jaw and say between clenched teeth. "I'm trying to keep you safe. You can't trust anyone. Why are you defending this guy?"

"I'm not, I just..." She sighs and trails off. I don't tell her that Ben has started back toward us. I want her to finish her thought, but she glances over her shoulder and sees him coming. Quickly turning back to me, she says in a hushed voice, "We both want the same thing...to help Celeste, so let's just focus on that, okay?"

As Cass looks up at me and I watch her pulse beating rapidly, the tension between us feels like a vacuum sucking the air from my lungs. I push my hands in my coat pockets to keep from burying them in her hair and yanking her close. I want to bite her stubborn lip and take possession of her mouth, to obliterate Ben from her thoughts.

Screw this fucked up situation.

Common sense prevails, and I give Cass a curt nod of agreement just as Ben reaches us.

"Sorry about that. Come along, *fiancé*," he says jovially, urging her back toward the house.

My gaze locks on his hand resting at the small of Cass's back and I instinctively step forward, protective hackles fully engaged. At the last second, I stop myself from grabbing his arm and let them continue on while I get my shit together.

The tension between Cass and me is shredding my control. One thing we definitely agree on, Ben wants his fiancé. The difference is...he desires *Cass*. I saw her engaging personality bleeding through when she laughed at something he said in the garden. Celeste smiles, but she rarely laughs. Cass might think I've called a truce over Ben, but for us to be effective in uncovering the truth in Celeste's life, she has to trust my instincts and keep her guard up. All the men in Celeste's life are suspects, and the only way I'll get Cass to unequivocally trust me on this is if I find a way to tear down the barrier she's built back up between us since last night. I don't know why it's suddenly there, but I want it gone. Moving forward with a determined stride, I curl my fingers around the leather choker in my slack's pocket and slide my thumb over the silver raven.

Beth pulls the French door open just as we reach the back patio. "Come inside, Celeste," she says, looking impatient. "I'm trying to coordinate what to wear for the interview."

Cass quickly shakes her head. "We're just attending, not being interviewed."

Beth rolls her eyes, her tone clipped. "You're the one who taught me that you're always being interviewed even when you don't say a word. We must be dressed appropriately."

Exhaling deeply, Cass apologizes to Ben, then trails behind Beth. I step forward to follow them inside when Ben says next to me, "I'd like a word, Blake."

Beth and Cass are standing at the entrance of the main room, apparently disagreeing about the upcoming interview. The last thing I want to do is referee their squabble, so I slide a stoic gaze Ben's way and wait for him to speak.

Ben reaches over and pulls the door closed. Folding his arms, he turns on the patio and faces me, leaning back against the doorjamb. "After the next couple of events the media attention should die down. I want you to pack your things and leave."

The desire to flatten this entitled prick resurfaces all over again, but for Cass's sake I manage to rein in my temper. Keeping my eye on the ladies through the glass, I answer in an even tone. "I will leave when Celeste decides my services are no longer necessary."

I start to reach for the doorknob, but Ben puts his arm across the doorway. "You had your chance with her at that masked party four years ago. I don't know if the rumors about you two in the kitchen are true..." When I slit my gaze, he stiffens to his six-foot height. "She's my fiancé now. I'll take care of her."

I roll my shoulders, taking advantage of the couple inches of height I have over him. "But can you protect her?" When he starts to speak, I cut him off. "You want to keep her safe, right?" The moment stubborn determination settles on Ben's face, I drop my casual tone. "I don't give two shits if my presence threatens your fragile ego, she is my priority. Don't block my way again." I return my attention to Cass and Beth in time to see sheer devastation on Cass's face as she stares at Beth. Once the ladies exit the room, I step forward aggressively.

Ben yanks his arm out of my way at the last second,

then calls after me with determined confidence. "Your presence here ends tomorrow night."

Game on, asshole. I pull my phone from my pocket and keep my gaze straight ahead so I don't turn back and smash the smugness from his face. Dialing a number, I wait impatiently for an answer.

CHAPTER NINE

Cass

"*Wait* up," I call after Celeste's sister. While Calder and Ben talk outside on the patio, I approach Beth. She's standing at the entrance of the room, her hair now down, curls bouncing against her pale blue silk blouse. I can tell that I annoyed her when I said I wasn't going to wear anything with a repeating pattern of animals or nautical symbols on it for the afternoon event.

The fact that Calder avoided answering my question about Ben flirting with "Celeste" in the garden is setting me on edge. I wanted to push him to share what's really going on in his head about her, but he'd just keep challenging me about my trust in Ben. It's not like I can tell him that Ben acting polar opposite of his prick of a brother, Jake, and his ruthless father is the whole reason I trust Ben. *Why are half-*

truths much harder than full out lies? If Calder discovered what Jake Hemming did to me in the past, I worry he wouldn't be able to keep his cool when Jake shows up at these events. As long as Jake thinks I'm Celeste, I'll be fine. I need Calder's military stoicism right now more than ever. I can barely handle myself in this screwed up situation, let alone try to keep him from losing it.

Beth turns in the doorway to face me, pulling me out of my worried thoughts about Calder. "You're here for *one* reason," she snaps in a low tone. "You will wear the most "Celeste" outfit I can find in her closet and not say a word about it."

Something else underscores the irritation in her voice. A pained tension reflects in her gaze. *Worry.* This is her way of coping with Celeste's disappearance and what she discovered about her today. I can't imagine how she must be feeling right now after learning that she didn't know her sister as well as she thought. And I have a feeling that she really wanted to. With her mother off recuperating, she must feel very alone right now. "I'm sorry, Beth. I didn't mean to offend. I'll wear whatever you think is best."

As Beth stares at me for a second, I can't let her go without asking the question that had been nagging me since I left her car. "How did you meet Brent?"

She seems surprised, but answers. "It was all very mysterious. The day before the event, I got an invitation. I'd heard rumors from friends who were invited to this exclusive MMA event and was jealous I hadn't gotten one. The fact I didn't know who sent the last minute invite made it too hard to pass up, so I went." She exhales a laugh, her gaze sparkling over the fun memory. "I lined up with a couple of my girlfriends, all of us vying for a coveted ring girl position, and yep, I got pulled out of that line too. I put up quite a fuss when the security guy put me in the hall outside the arena and shut the door behind me. But then Brent stepped out of the shadows in an Armani suit and an irresistible smirk on his face and invited me to watch the fight with him instead. We've been together ever since."

I'm relieved that she didn't meet him through Jake, but I need to give her a heads up about him. Tilting my head, I ask as innocuously as possible, "Do you feel like you know him pretty well?"

"Of course," she says, snorting. "I'm sleeping with the guy."

"You can have sex with a person and not really know him." God, that's so true. Instinctive trust and major attraction keeps bringing Calder and me together, but we've barely scratched the surface of what we know about each other.

Beth turns to fully face me. "What are you saying?"

Even though her defensive tone makes me tense, I feel like I should warn her the best way I can. "Your boyfriend is running a business that you know skirts a gray line…" I trail off and spread my hands. "I'm just saying to be careful."

"Brent's an aggressive businessman who's being proactive in building his business. He's smart to entice high paying clientele by establishing a reputation for delivering exciting bouts that the competition can't hope to match. It's just a matter of time before the state legalizes professional fights here. He's just ahead of the game." Huffing, she shakes her head and crosses her arms. "Brent told me that I shouldn't trust you. He said you're a liar only out for personal gain. I said he was wrong, that you're trying to help find Celeste. And yet here you are proving him right by trying to smear his character. You don't know a thing about him."

For Beth's sake, I wish that were true. My stomach churns with the knowledge that Brent knows who I am. But does he know I remember the part he played in violating me? The fact he had already set the stage to turn Beth against me proves he was ensuring she wouldn't believe anything I said. I grab Beth's arm before she can turn away, my heart racing. "You weren't supposed to tell anyone that I'm not Celeste."

"My sister is *missing*," she hisses. "Brent is the only one I told. He's the only person I trust right now." Jerking her arm free of my hold, she glances toward the French door. "You haven't given me any real reason to trust you. Imagine my shock to look out my bedroom window and see you launching yourself onto Calder Blake's back." Narrowing her gaze, she continues. "You will *not* ruin my sister's reputation by acting like a slut with her security guard."

Hot words crowd my throat, rushing to be free. The fiery desire to tell her that I know Calder from the past burns in my mouth, but I clamp my lips together; I can't take a chance she'll share that information with Brent or what he'll do with it. The last thing I want is for my connection to Calder to compromise his "Steel" persona in the upcoming MMA fight. The fans might not know Steel's identity, but since Brent helps run the Elite Underground Club (EUC) that recruited Steel to fight, he has to know who Steel really is. Right now Brent doesn't have a reason to distrust Calder. But what if he decides to disqualify Steel because of his association with me? I swallow back the truth. "That's not what was going on—"

"Who do you think sent Ben out there the moment he arrived?" Beth rambles on. "After everything I've learned today, I've decided that he's perfect for Celeste. When she comes back, he'll treat her fairly and look out for her."

"You don't understand. I was just trying to—"

"Save it," she says, throwing her hand up. "For all I know, you're in on my sister's rebellion and even now you're doing everything you can to stall us from finding her. As much as I dislike you being here, my sister is newly *engaged* and you will play the part until she's found. Stay away from the hired help and you'd better keep things platonic with Ben or I'll tell my father. I'm sure anything you have to wear while you're here is preferable to a Rikers' uniform. I hope that is clear enough for you."

Beth may as well have punched me in the stomach. She's treating me like I'm some kind of slutty criminal. My chest aches with the need to tell her everything, starting with Jake and Celeste's involvement in my life back in high school, Jake and Brent violating me, my sister's suicide, my cutting…all of it. I don't understand my desire to make Beth understand me. I haven't even told Talia most of the details of my past, and she's my best friend. But now that Brent has poisoned Beth against me, even if I showed her the texts between Celeste and the Deceiver, she'll probably think I faked those in some kind of twisted collusion with her sister.

Swallowing the hurt squeezing my throat, I force myself to ignore the hot tingling radiating from my wrists and nod. "Perfectly clear," I say flatly. "I'm ready for you to pick the outfits I'm expected to wear for the upcoming events now."

A flicker of remorse shines in Beth's green eyes before she tosses her hair over her shoulder and leaves the room ahead of me.

My hands are shaking by the time Beth leaves my room a half hour later. I stare at the tailored red sweater, white collared shirt, black pencil skirt and matching heels I'm supposed to wear for the interview in an hour. Then I glance over the two dresses in the closet Beth chose for tonight and tomorrow night's events and realize how very different our styles are. Squeezing my hands into tight fists, I close my eyes and fantasize that Celeste shows up right after the TV crews leave this afternoon.

The idea of just being *me* once more is so appealing, I smile.

A knock at my door yanks me from the daydream and my chest instantly squeezes as reality slams back.

"It's me." Calder's deep voice carries through the wood.

I walk over to the door, but don't open it. I'm too wound up and tense right now. I don't want to argue with him over Ben anymore or wonder what he really feels for Celeste. "I just need some downtime, Calder. I'll see you downstairs in forty-five minutes."

When I hear him walk away, I sag against the door. I don't like this tension between us, but I don't know how to stop it. Instead the distance seems to be growing. That's what happens when you keep secrets. There's so much I can't tell him right now and I know he'll keep pushing for answers.

Sighing, I walk into the bathroom and brush my hair. I've just finished touching up my makeup when another knock sounds.

"Open the door," Calder says in a matter-of-fact tone.

Great. He sounds ticked. I walk over and steel myself before I open the door. "Calder, I—"

"You need to eat," he says gruffly. His expression is hard to read as he pushes a plate of food into my left hand, but I'm surprised when he sets my cell phone in my right one at the same time, commanding, "Call Talia."

Without another word, he pulls the door shut, leaving me standing there, stunned. It's like he knew exactly what I needed, but there's no way he could know just how on edge I am. With Brent potentially lurking in the background, I'm questioning whether or not I can pull this charade off with my sanity in tact. *This isn't about you. If something has happened to Celeste, you have to follow through and help.*

Glancing down at my phone, I quickly turn it on while I carry the plate over to Celeste's desk. With my hands shaking, I sit down and press the button to dial Talia's number.

Talia answers on the second ring, and instead of fussing at me for not keeping in touch the last day and a half like I expect her to, she just says, "I'm here, Cass."

Her simple statement says so much about our friendship that I instantly tear up and start rambling, "God, I miss you so much, Talia. You have no idea. I'm sorry I've been a mess the last few months and that I never told you about my past. I promise to one day, but right now I just…things here are just so messed up.

"Beth thinks I'm an evil temptress and a liar, Celeste has gone AWOL, but I believe she's really missing, and God, I don't have any underwear. Can you believe that's all I could think about while Beth selected one of Celeste's outfits for me to wear to this stupid interview happening in less than an hour? That I want to wear my own freaking underwear underneath the 'Celeste' costume I'm expected to present to the reporters. This was just supposed to be a dinner party and that was it. None of this was supposed to happen."

"Whoa—slow down. Take a breath, Cass. Sebastian filled me in on what's going on, and while I'm sorry Celeste might be missing, you don't owe her a thing. Right now I'm more worried about *you*."

Just hearing her calm voice makes me feel better. I take a couple of breaths, then pick up a carrot from the plate and munch on it. While I eat the sandwich and vegetables Calder brought me, I fill Talia in on everything that has happened so far. I'm careful not to mention Jake or Brent because I know she'll worry, and I don't want that part getting back to Calder through Sebastian. Thankfully Brent appears to be a separate part of Beth's life, away from Carver social events. I don't think her father even knows he exists. *But if he did show up for an event, I would be completely blindsided since I never saw his face.*

The uncomfortable realization has me pulling down Celeste's sophomore class yearbook and skimming through our class page for any classmates named Brent while Talia expresses her concern. "This whole situation is so messed up, Cass. I wish you could just walk away."

"You know I can't, Talia," I say as I turn pages. "And neither could the investigator in you."

She snorts. "That's so true. And you can't pry me away from helping now that I know. Oh, by the way, Sebastian's guy, Elijah, couldn't trace who wrote the Deceiver's text to Celeste. But I did just hear Sebastian tell Calder that the abandoned rental car's GPS *was* mapped to a women's clinic in New Jersey."

"Really?" My heart constricts and I pause skimming the names and class pictures. "What was the name of the clinic?"

Paper rustles in the background. "Jersey Women's Services. Is that the same one you went to today?"

I close my eyes and inhale slowly. "Yes, that's it." I don't need blood test results to know that the blood in that car belongs to Celeste.

"Are you okay, Cass?"

Blowing out a breath to release the tension building inside me, I open my eyes and turn to the very last page of the sophomore class. *Not a single Brent in the whole bunch.* "I'm fine."

"Are you sure?"

Worry laces her voice, so I give a stronger answer. "I'm okay, Talia. I just need to get through tomorrow night. If Celeste isn't found by then, the Carver's event will be my best chance to collect a DNA sample to prove Phillip is the baby's father. My gut tells me that Phillip is the Deceiver. I think that he caught up to Celeste and that's why she never made it to the clinic for her appointment. If that is her blood they found in the car, Phillip definitely has a strong motive to want to keep her pregnancy and the baby's paternity from being revealed in the blood work results, especially considering her father just announced Celeste's engagement to his son, Ben."

"Wow, if you're right, that's all kinds of screwed up. Do you really think Phillip would hurt the woman carrying his child?"

Jake briefly pops into my head. He was pretty pissed last night, but I dismiss him as a potential threat to Celeste as I shut the yearbook. "Other than her guard, whose faults are many but he has no reason to hurt Celeste, the only other men in her life was Ben and Jake. Ben just wants to protect Celeste and Jake is in love with her. He'd never hurt Celeste." *Not like he did me.*

"The brother who's in love with her isn't the one marrying her? How did that happen?"

Another idea for finding Brent hits me just as I start to slide the yearbook back into place on the shelf. I flip it open once more to the sports section and set it down on the desk to scour the names listed under the varsity football team's photo. A dark-haired junior named Brent Taylor has a wide, smirking smile as he sits on the bleachers one row behind Jake. That's right. Jake was the only sophomore on the varsity team.

I stare intensely at Brent's dark brown eyes, floppy hair, full mouth and square jawline, searing his image in my memory.

"Earth to Cass!"

"I'm sorry, Talia." I quickly shut the book to keep my mind on the present. Returning it to the shelf, I continue, "What were you saying?"

"Never mind. I just wanted you to know we'll see you tomorrow night. Damien got us an invitation to the party at the Carver estate. Sebastian and I will take back whatever evidence you're able to collect and get the proper testing done."

"If I can get a DNA sample from Phillip, then you'll still need the blood Celeste left at the clinic to do the paternity testing."

"They can test paternity from just her blood?"

"Yes, apparently the baby's DNA does show up in the

pregnant mother's blood. I'll work on getting access to her blood after we get Phillip's DNA." Knowing that Talia and Sebastian will be at the party tomorrow lifts my spirits. "I'm so glad you're both coming, Talia. Having more allies in the crowd will be just the boost I need."

"If I could fit myself in your pocket and stay with you the whole time, I would," Talia says on a low laugh. "Between now and then, I'm going to research Phillip Hemming. Based on the way you've described him, I can't help but wonder why someone as ruthless and cunning as he is would choose to remain in the shadows to the spotlight of Gregory's political career. And how could he carry on an affair with Gregory's daughter behind his friend's back while trying to marry her off to his son? This guy is seriously bent."

"He's devious, Talia. I have no doubt that Phillip has a hidden agenda. I just don't know what his end game is…other than doing everything he can to make sure the Hemmings share in the Carver millions. I'll be interested in hearing what you can find on him."

"Just keep your head low and don't take any unnecessary risks. We'll be there to back you up tomorrow night so you can get what you need, but in the meantime, don't give Phillip an inkling that you have anything on him—"

"I'm just playing my part," I quickly say, wondering if I've been too honest with everything I told her. I don't want Talia repeating her worries to Sebastian. That would definitely get back to Calder.

Talia sighs. "Please be careful, Cass. You've never done undercover work before. Trust me. I know how exhausting it is to *always* be on guard. And when you're as emotionally entangled as you are...it's especially easy to let something slip."

Emotionally entangled is an understatement. If Talia knew how deep my ties to several players connected to this bizarre household went, she wouldn't wait for Sebastian or Calder to yank me out of here. She'd drive over and drag me away herself. "I promise not to take any risks."

"I wish the event was tonight." Talia huffs her frustration. "Then we could get this over and done with."

"That just gives you time to ferret out more of Phillip Hemming's dirty secrets. I know that man must have some."

"Ah, point taken. And now I'm off to research. Remember, head low."

"Got it," I say, letting out a low laugh.

Setting my phone down, I open my door and startle when I see Calder leaning against the wall. "Hey, I um... was just coming to look for you."

Calder pushes off the wall, lowering his arms. "Did you eat?"

His expression is blank, his eyes shuttered. He's acting like the perfect guard. It's hard to tell his mood. "Yes, thank you for the food," I say casually, then I tilt my head toward my room.

Calder follows me inside, but doesn't change his formal stance as I shut the door behind him. "I have Beth's boyfriend's full name. It's Brent Taylor."

He frowns. "Did you ask Beth for it? I told you I didn't want you involved in the EUC stuff."

I don't want him to know Brent's connection to me from my past so I lie. "I didn't ask. She just mentioned it."

The sudden tension in Calder's expression eases some. "I'll have Elijah run down his information. Thanks."

I nod, offering a half smile. "Thank you for my phone. Talia filled me in on everything you and Sebastian have learned and told me they'll be here tomorrow night."

His green gaze drills into mine. "If you weren't going to talk to me, you needed to talk to someone."

It's hard not to miss the frustration in his comment, which makes me feel awful. "Talking to Talia helped so much. I don't know how you knew I needed that, but… thank you."

A moment of silence passes and as we stare at one another, I can literally feel the crackle of attraction arcing between us. I swallow to calm my emotions, then turn and walk toward my bathroom, calling over my shoulder, "I have to be downstairs soon, but I wanted to show you something."

Calder looks perplexed as I open the linen closet, but doesn't say anything until I push on the back wall and reveal the hidden passage. "Is that what I think it is?"

I chuckle and nod. "I thought you would like to know about this. It might come in handy if you need to get from one side of the house to the other without being seen. I've been all over and there are several exits." Once I rattle off all the places I used with Beth and found on my own, I grip the closet's door handle and gesture to the passageway. "Have at it. Gregory wants Beth and me to meet him in his office before we head over as a 'family' to the main room where the interview will take place. You've got at least twenty minutes to explore before anyone notices you're not around."

Calder steps close enough that his masculine smell invades all my senses. I can't resist inhaling deeply as he slowly slides his thumb along my bottom lip. His gaze follows his finger on my mouth, which sets off a swarm of anxious anticipation in my belly. He wants to brand me again and God I want him to, but Beth's harsh judgment about me rushes through my mind and I take a step back. "Just to warn you. It's kind of a maze in there."

I agonize as I wait for him to speak. Calder's not one to hold back.

His gaze snaps to mine, but instead of anger, steely determination stares back at me. "Have you forgotten that I'm a master puzzler, angel?"

His reminder of our time together in that kitchen four years ago sends chill bumps racing across my skin and my pulse skyrockets. "No, there's just so much—"

"Stop putting up walls between us, Cass."

"Then tell me why Celeste's pregnancy upset you so much."

He frowns. "It should go without saying how fucked up that scenario is."

I fold my arms. "There's more to it than that."

"Tell me why you have this zealous faith in Ben," he counters, scowling. "You shouldn't trust *anyone* here."

"I told you…he's sincere."

Calder lets out a harsh snort.

We face off in a stalemate. When I turn to walk out, the fierceness in his tone stops me mid-stride. "I'll rip the fuckers down, Cass. Every single wall you throw up, but know this…my patience with this whole goddamn situation is wearing thin."

I compose my expression to hide how much the thought of him leaving tears me up before I turn to respond. "You're free to leave any time you want."

"Not without you." He pins me with a hard stare, then steps inside the passageway and closes the wall behind him.

CHAPTER TEN

The Observer

I stoke the fire in the fireplace, mesmerized by the flames licking away the wood a bit at a time. Once the fire flares high, I toss the bloody towel onto the smoking logs and watch it burn away to nothing. The voices on the TV snag my attention; a news anchor mentions the police finding an abandoned car late last night, then the camera switches to a brunette reporter outside. She shivers in a thin coat as she stands near the road.

"This is the stretch of road where the abandoned vehicle with blood was found," she says, sweeping her arm to indicate the traffic zooming past behind her. Facing the camera once more, she continues, "There's speculation that an ID was discovered in the car also, but the police aren't releasing a name at this time—"

"It was that senator's daughter. The dark-haired one that's always in the magazines," a stocky guy in baggy jeans and blond dreads says as he photo-bombs the journalist.

The woman quickly turns, pushing her mic toward him. "Do you mean Celeste Carver? Did you see her in that car?"

His dreads sway against his back as he shakes his head. "Nah, I just heard the cops talking about it. One of the guys said there was a lot of blood and he wasn't sure she could've walked away."

The journalist pivots back to the camera. "Was that Celeste Carver's ID found in that car? If so, hopefully the police will provide answers soon. Back to you, Stacy."

The shot cuts back to the perky reporter with a wide smile sitting behind the news desk at the TV station. "Great timing with your question, Taylor. Our crew is at the Carver estate interviewing the senator as we speak." She nods to someone outside of the camera range and says, "And we're switching over to that live feed now."

Flash bulbs highlight the Senator's silver hair as he stands in front of his fireplace in a gray three-piece business suit and a red tie.

"Why did you choose to run, sir?" A bald man in a tweed jacket asks from the small group of reporters in his living room. "You had an incredibly successful business in Carver Enterprises. Giving that up couldn't have been an easy decision."

Gregory smiles. "I wanted to give back to the people.

And honestly, I couldn't have done it without the help of my daughter, Celeste, who took over the business last year." He gestures just outside the group of journalists. "Actually both my girls and their mother have really stepped up to help me out. Their mother is feeling under the weather but...Celeste and Beth, come over here."

The camera pans to his two daughters who obediently make their way over to stand on either side of their father.

While Gregory drones on about how much Celeste supports his career, I stare at *her*.

As a quick stand-in Celeste, she'll pass. Barely.

I skim my gaze back to Gregory, narrowing it. *What game is this? Why is he pulling her into the spotlight?*

A reporter asks a question about Celeste running Carver Enterprises and Gregory puts his arm around her shoulders, bragging about his daughter.

Then a reporter from the TV station asks, "There's a rumor going around that Celeste's ID was found in an abandoned car yesterday. Care to comment on that?"

Gregory's expression falters for a split second before he shrugs. "If they did find an ID with her name on it, it's obviously a fake."

I slam my fist on the table, done with watching this bullshit. I see the differences in the fake Celeste standing right beside him. Her face has been in enough newspapers and magazines. Why can't anyone else? This is why she belonged only to me.

When Celeste and Beth walk back to their positions on the sidelines, the camera stays zoomed out. Ben moves behind Celeste and he instantly squeezes her shoulders, pulling her against his chest. Look at him, trying to comfort her. I tilt my head and watch him shift to her left and fold their fingers together as he whispers something in her ear. He's smiling too much. How can he not fucking tell he's holding an imposter's hand? She's not truly yours.

Celeste is *gone*. I turn away and press my fist against my chest, growling the pain away. *She's all mine now.*

I glance back at the TV. They are *all* pretending.

She can't *be* Celeste.

I shake my head, determined. "This must end."

CHAPTER ELEVEN

Cass

The Manhattan Crest is as grand as it is elegant. It's the perfect hotel to hold a party for the upper echelon who throw money around like it's used tissue. I try not to think about how much the black-beaded floor-length gown I'm wearing cost. Instead, for once I'm thankful for Celeste's exorbitant wardrobe. The gown, along with the matching clutch purse and strappy heels is perfect for this ritzy place.

I walk into the main floor's ballroom with Beth on one side and Gregory on the other. After quick introductions, Senator Carver's benefactor instantly sweeps him away to make the rounds with the important (read: political connections) guests at the party, leaving Beth and me standing alone.

"It's going to be a long night," Beth mumbles under her breath after smiling and nodding to a couple ladies to our right. "I'm going to get a drink."

I smile at the ladies too, then ask when Beth starts to turn away, "Do you want to put your phone in my purse?"

Beth glances down at the bright pink phone clasped in her hand and shrugs. "No, I'm good."

I sigh as she walks off. Why didn't I think to ask her to get me a drink too? Then she would've had to give me her phone. Calder told me that "Brent Taylor" was a dead end, so he still doesn't have a way to track him down. I really need to get to Beth's phone, but she hasn't let it out of her sight. Nor has she spoken to me since she helped me pick out clothes. And I seriously doubt she will the rest of the evening. Maybe I can do that later.

For now I need to find out which table is ours. I glance down at the fancy gilt-edged folded card the ladies outside the door handed me just before we walked in, saying, "Welcome, Senator. We've assigned a café table for you. The number is inside this card."

Before I can open the card, my purse vibrates with a text and I quickly pull my phone out.

> Calder: I'm here, straight ahead of you, against the far wall. Marco needed instructions on where to wait with the car. The guy never learns.

I suppress a laugh, remembering the look on Marco's

face when Gregory demanded that he stay with the car once he saw Marco's black eye. When Marco shot Calder an accusing look, I couldn't help but wonder if he tried to prevent Calder from retrieving my cell phone from Celeste's car.

> *Me: Did these instructions involve another black eye?*
> *Calder: Only if he bruises easily.*

It's hard not to snicker at his reply.

> *Me: Thank you for going the extra mile to get my phone.*
> *Calder: You seem calmer now that you've talked to Talia.*
> *Me: I am.*
> *Calder: You look beautiful. It'll be hard not to stare at you all night.*

My heart flutters at his unexpected compliment and I give a sly smile as I text him back.

> *Me: Would it make your job harder knowing I'm completely underwear free under this gorgeous dress?"*

Just as I hit send, someone touches my waist and speaks behind me. "Good evening, Celeste."

"Hey, you made it," I say to Ben, tensing when Calder snaps a deadly look his way.

A middle-aged woman in a silver gown walks up and shakes Ben's hand as another text from Calder comes through.

Calder: No, the fuck it doesn't! Keep that asshole under control so I don't have to deck him too, Raven mine.

Raven mine. He knows just what to say to evoke a memory. The sensation of him clamping his teeth on my shoulder, and staking his claim on me that night in the kitchen, rushes along my skin as if he's right here.

When Ben starts to turn to me, I quickly tuck my phone away and smile at the woman with bright pink lipstick.

"Celeste, this is Claudia Sinclair. She runs the hospital like a well-oiled machine."

The woman titters at his compliment as she shakes my hand. "It's nice to meet the girl who stole Ben's heart." Glancing at Ben, she asks, "Did you see that David is here?"

Ben grins. "He's here already."

She nods. "I saw him getting a drink earlier." Lifting her card, she continues, "I'd better go put this on my table. I'll see you two later."

Ben scans the crowd until he finds the person he's looking for. "There's David. Come on, Celeste, I'll introduce you."

"I need to set our card down so Father and Beth know where our table is." The moment I open the fancy card, a smaller white card flutters to the floor. Before I can bend to retrieve it, Ben snags it and hands it to me. "Here you go."

STOP PRETENDING.

As soon as I see the two words written in bold block letters on the back of the card, I quickly snatch it from him before he sees it. "Thanks. Why don't you go chat with your friend? I'll meet you over there in just a minute."

Once Ben strolls away to talk to a well-built bald man in his late forties, I walk over and set the card with our family name on it upright on the table. Right now a hundred eyes are on me, so I act as if nothing is amiss. Any of them could've planted that card. The last thing I want to do is acknowledge that whoever is trying to rattle me is right.

My purse buzzes with a text and I pull my phone out.

Calder: What's wrong? What did that card say?

I glance up and meet his piercing gaze across the room. He's on full alert. I can tell by the way he's holding his shoulders and the not-so-casual curl of his fingers around his phone.

Me: It could mean anything.
Calder: What does it say?

I'm caught by his stare. The man is brutally beautiful in his intensity.

Me: Stop Pretending.
Calder: Leave it on the table under the other
card. We'll have a fingerprint analysis done.

I nod and put the white card under the upright card, then walk over to Ben.

As soon as I reach Ben's side, he clasps my elbow. "Is everything all right?" His brow is furrowed and he seems on edge. When his focus flicks to Calder, I touch his shoulder to bring his attention back to me.

"Yes, everything is fine. Just working through logistics on where the car will pick us up now that the weather has turned. Can you believe it's snowing? They're expecting a couple inches tonight."

The man to Ben's left laughs. "Remember that course we did in the snow, Ben? Talk about nature adding its own layer of difficulty."

Ben grins. "David Callahan, this is my fiancé, Celeste." Ben wraps his arm around my waist and introduces me to the tan man. "Celeste, Dr. Callahan was not only my mentor in med school, he's also the one who got me into multi-gun shooting competition. The sport keeps me fit and sharp."

"It's nice to meet you, Dr. Callahan." I quickly glance at Ben in surprise as I shake the man's hand. "Shooting competition? Ben just mentioned skeet shooting."

"Call me David. Skeet shooting is an entry-level kind of sport." The lines around his eyes deepen with his laugh as he releases my hand. "What we do is run a difficult obstacle course where we test our physical endurance, scaling walls and such, while also shooting at targets using three different guns: an automatic handgun, a shotgun, and, for extra difficulty, an old-school six-shooter pistol." He turns and clasps Ben on the shoulder. "Don't let Ben's laidback attitude fool you. This young man is incredibly competitive and quite the sharp shooter. He keeps me on my toes."

I raise my eyebrows at Ben, remembering our conversation in the garden. He told me he didn't believe in hunting and never went on trips with Phillip and Jake. "Is that so?"

Ben grins and shrugs. "If I'm not going to bag a deer or turkey like my dad and Jake, then the least I can do is bring home targets with the best scores on them."

When I smile at Ben's comment, David grins. "I see you've found a keeper, Ben. Don't let this one go."

Laughing, Ben pulls me close and says in a low voice, "I don't plan to." Before I can think of a witty response, he presses a kiss to my cheek, then meets my surprised gaze, murmuring, "She's the real deal."

Even though I know I'm only playing a part, my stomach lurches at his sincere compliment. Beth is right. I am a fraud. Maybe not for the reason she thinks, but for so long I've played in a world like Celeste's through my photography business. I created scenarios just like this ostentatious hotel with its overflowing champagne and caviar, and in the heart of it all stood the handsome man fawning over the beautifully adorned girl. I secretly hoped that would one day be me. But the truth is…I never belonged in that scenario. Forcing a smile, I step out of his hold. "You two keep talking. I just need to run to the ladies' room."

As I walk out of the ballroom and head for the bathroom, I hear Calder's voice behind me, telling me to slow down, but I don't want to talk. I just want a moment to myself. Time to get out of my own head. I push open the door and shut it behind me. I'm thankful the bathroom is empty as I lean against the door and close my eyes.

"Are you alone in there?"

When the knob starts to turn, I call out quietly, "Yes, I'm alone, Calder. I'm fine. I just ate something that's not agreeing with me."

As soon as he lets go of the knob, his phone rings. "Hey, hold a sec." His voice comes close to the door once more. "Stay here. I need to take care of something."

I suddenly tense. *Does he see a threat?* When I hear his deep voice lower as he walks away from the door, I strain to listen.

"Give me a minute. I'll come to you."

That doesn't sound threatening. I came in here to wallow, but Calder's phone call grabs my attention. *Where is he going? And why is he talking so quietly?*

Cracking the door, I wait until he turns the corner, then I follow. When I see Beth's guard is now standing near the hallway to the bathrooms, I fall in line with a couple walking past, then follow the path that Calder took.

When I catch up to him, Calder's standing at the edge of the hallway that leads to the lobby. I pause behind a thick marble column. Calder is talking to a girl in her early twenties with her pitch-black hair swept up into a French twist.

I can't see his face since his back is to me, but he must make some kind of comment about the stylish black leather jacket she's wearing over an elegant floor length black dress. As soon as he tugs on the sleeve, she laughs and glances down as she covertly slides a shapely leg out of the thigh-high slit in the dress.

"*That* much thigh just put your dress in the slutty category, sister," I grumble while the girl slides her leg back under the dress.

When she steps closer and reaches up to feather her fingers along the side of Calder's hair, then down the back of his neck, I grind my teeth and turn away. Whoever she is…I don't want to know. I've got enough worries of my own right now.

Once I walk back into the ballroom, I'm no longer dwelling on myself. Calder's "mystery girl" was just the distraction I needed to bury my issues and get my head back into this event tonight.

Ben hasn't seen me yet, but Beth does. She quickly walks up to me and holds her phone out. "Would you mind holding this for a few minutes? This long skirt is going to take two hands in the bathroom."

"Of course." Clasping her phone, I watch her head toward the ballroom doorway while I quickly type in the passcode and scroll through her contacts. Once I find Brent, I click on the info button. No last name, but his phone number is listed, so I memorize it. When I realize that Beth has suddenly stopped walking and is now glancing around the room quickly, I lower the phone so she doesn't catch me looking at it. She doesn't stop looking until she finds her father, who's busy talking with a distinguished older man. *What's that about?* But when Beth looks straight ahead once more and starts forward, her stride faster, I follow her line of sight out the ballroom door.

And lock gazes with Brent.

He's dressed in a tuxedo and standing among a group of people spilling into the hall from some big event in the restaurant next door.

The phone in my hand buzzes and when I look down, Brent's name flashes on the caller ID. I panic, thinking that I accidently dialed him, but then realize the call is incoming. I jerk my attention back to Beth. He can clearly see she's heading straight for him and doesn't have her phone. My heart racing, I click the Answer button and put the phone to my ear.

Brent smiles at Beth as she weaves her way around a couple of people to get to him, while his familiar voice booms in my ear, icy and threatening. "Don't you *dare* fuck this up for me. Am I clear?"

I grip the phone tight, my pulse jacking higher. "Or what?"

People walk past in the hallway, blocking my view of Brent for a second. Then I hear Beth's whispered voice in the background. "What are you doing here?" She sounds nervous but excited. "My guard will be out here after me any second."

Brent holds my gaze above the crowd. Kissing Beth on the forehead, he answers me in a deadly tone as he wraps his arm around her waist. "You don't want to find out." Before he hangs up, I hear him say, "I wanted to surprise you, babe. Want to ditch this party and hang with me?"

I'm so focused on trying to keep Beth in my sights that I startle when Calder's annoyed voice rumbles next to me. "I told you to stay in the bathroom."

I cut a sharp gaze his way. "You weren't there when I walked out."

His face instantly hardens. "I told Anthony to watch for you."

Annoyed with myself for letting the unknown girl he just met with get to me, I say, "Anthony needs to be on *Beth* at all times. Make sure that he doesn't let her out of his sight."

Calder instantly scans the room. "Is there a problem with Beth? Where is she?"

"She's just outside the ballroom. Her guard's probably looking for her in that crowd. Please remind him to be extra diligent."

Calder stiffens. "What are you worried about?"

"Celeste, we're heading to the top floor now," Ben says before I can reply. Hooking his arm in mine, he smiles.

"There will be more schmoozing, but this time there will be dancing with an amazing view of the city. Let's go."

As Ben starts to lead me away, I hand Beth's phone to Calder. "Please make sure Anthony finds Beth and gives this back to her."

It's midnight by the time the event winds down. Ben wasn't kidding about the amazing view. The bit of snow covering the city and the lights twinkling in the night was a gorgeous sight. Ben insisted on walking me to my car, so I button my coat closed as the doorman holds open the main door for us. My feet hurt from dancing so long in shoes I've never worn before, but I did enjoy his company once I stopped worrying about Beth. Apparently she had one drink too many and asked Anthony to take her home early.

Phillip left a half hour before and Calder is somewhere behind us. He stayed in the shadows along the walls most of the night, but I could feel his heavy stare.

The hotel has laid fresh salt on the walkway, but the mixture of sleet and snow coming down has already covered it again. When Ben steps forward, then starts to slip on the ice, his tight hold on my hand yanks me off-balance. My left ankle turns and as I stumble, I hear Calder grumble, "Fuck this," and I'm immediately swept off my feet.

I let out a yelp of surprise, grabbing onto Calder's shoulders in a death grip.

"Put her down!" Ben commands as Calder settles me

against his chest.

"Follow me if you don't want to break your neck, Hemming," Calder grunts out, then utters, "dumbass" under his breath. He steps into the snow-covered grass beside the walkway and strides toward the waiting car.

Calder's arms around me are so tight I don't look up to meet his gaze. He's clearly annoyed and I'd rather not be judged right now. Despite the tension between us, he's so close I can't help but inhale his amazing smell. Closing my eyes, I take in the arousing bergamot spice and other earthy scents in his aftershave. God, this man makes me want to bury my nose against his neck. I could fall asleep breathing him in.

All too soon Calder sets me down and I re-grip his shoulder to test my weight on my left foot. While I exhale my relief that my ankle seems fine, Ben reaches us and immediately clasps my hand, his expression reflecting regret. "Are you okay?"

Once I nod, he frowns at Calder. "I'm escorting Celeste home. Ride up front."

When Calder doesn't move out of the way, but instead holds Ben's gaze with a bold challenging one, I'm suddenly anxious—both for what Ben might expect at the end of this ride and Calder's reaction. Turning to Ben, I step between them and try to diffuse the tension. "That's really not necessary, Ben. What about your car?"

"I took a cab to get here. I'll just call a car service to bring me back to the city." Ben waits for Calder to move to the front of the car, then he follows me into the backseat.

While Calder slides into the front and motions for Marco to drive, I furrow my brow at Ben. "You're going way out of your way."

Ben clasps my hand and sets it on his thigh. "You're worth it."

Usually when he says something like this, Calder is too far away to hear. Squirming in my seat, I try to ignore just how deathly quiet the car feels and turn the focus to the evening. "Tonight seemed to go well. Don't you think?"

Ben smiles and talks about the people his father told him he needed to connect with. As he segues the conversation to future events Phillip has asked that we attend, I try to disentangle my hand from his, but he just folds our fingers together. "Enough about tonight's social commitments. I hope you enjoyed meeting David. He wants me to invite you to the next competition."

"So there will be a place to observe you in your element?"

Ben shakes his head, his eyes full of devilish amusement. "Observe?" He squeezes my hand lightly, laughing, "Oh no…you're going to participate."

I let out a nervous laugh. "You're joking, right? I've never shot a gun in my life."

Calder hasn't glanced our way since we got in the car, but at my last comment he turns his head slightly to the left. He's not looking at us, but the angle is enough for me to know he's actively listening. I try to ignore the muscle jumping in his jaw, but it's all I can see as Ben continues, "Don't worry… I'm a great teacher. I won't bring you with me until you can handle all three guns with ease. How about we start tomorrow? I'll take you to the shooting range."

Calder's expression hardens and his gaze narrows.

"I don't think I'll be very good at it, Ben." Marco's watching me in the rearview mirror. I can tell by the look in his eyes, he's smirking. The asshole is enjoying my fidgety discomfort.

Ben squeezes my fingers encouragingly. "You'll do great. Don't be nervous."

"She needs a license to shoot a gun," Calder cuts in, glancing our way. "That'll take time."

"No problem." Ben flashes him a cocky look, then shifts his attention back to me. "With my connections, I can get her one by tomorrow. What do you say, Celeste?"

"Um…"

"Say you'll do it." Ben runs his thumb along mine. "It'll be my only chance to spend some time with you, since I won't be at the party."

"You won't? Why aren't you coming?" I feel myself frowning. I don't like the idea of facing another political event where every word I say is catalogued and judged. Ben is my social suit of armor. I don't have to worry about blundering when he's around.

"I promised to cover for a buddy's shift a while back before…things changed." He shakes his head and smiles. "Jake is coming to help Dad support Gregory instead. Don't worry, he'll behave. I think Dad must've threatened to cut him out of the will or something, because he has gone back to his normal smart-assy, big-brother self with me."

Ben says a couple more things, but all I can hear is *Jake is coming* reverberating in my head over and over again. Except in my head it's not an innocuous comment. It's a foreboding one.

I don't like the idea of attending this event alone, but the thought of Jake being there makes me instantly nauseous. I don't care what kind of assurances Ben gives me. The need to rub my tingling wrists is almost overwhelming. I bite the inside of my cheek to try to regain my inner calm.

While stressing about Jake, I must've agreed to the gun range, because Ben's smile suddenly widens to a pleased grin. Lifting our clasped hands, he presses a warm kiss to the heel of my palm. "We'll have a blast. I bet you'll get the swing of it quickly."

A few minutes later, Marco turns into the front gates of the Carver estate. The sleet/snow mixture might've tapered off, but the vehicle slips as we try to pull up the long drive.

"Stop the car," Calder commands, and I'm surprised that Marco instantly complies.

When Calder gets out of the vehicle and walks around the other side, I assume he's going to tell Marco to slide over so he can drive. Instead, he opens my car door and puts his hand out. "Let's go, Miss Carver."

"Are you nuts?" Ben's fingers tighten around mine. "She's *not* walking up that long driveway."

Calder's laser gaze remains on mine as he answers

Ben. "The car isn't making it up there."

"It's fine, Ben," I say and pull my hand from Ben's at the same time I place my other hand in Calder's. Before I can step onto the drive, he lifts me into his arms once more. Ben starts to open his car door, but Calder's no-nonsense comment dismisses Ben in a rough rumble as he cradles me close. "There's no need to call a service. Marco will take you home. Good night, Hemming."

Calder shuts the car door when Ben starts to argue, cutting off his words. Nodding to Marco to do as he says, he steps into the crunchy grass on the side of the drive and waits for Marco to back out before he starts walking.

My stomach winds tighter and tighter as he carries me up the drive. Now that we're alone, I expect him to say something, but the fact that he doesn't speak at all has far more impact on my psyche. It's too dark for me to see his face, and too cold for me to do anything other than cuddle close to him for warmth, but I know he's angry.

I don't argue as he walks into the house and carries me all the way upstairs. Thankfully it's really late; no one is around to witness Celeste's guard carting her up the stairs as if she were too drunk to walk on her own.

When Calder sets me in front of my door and glances down at me, the low light in the hallway highlights the muscles bunching in his jaw. He's not just angry. He's furious.

"Calder..." That's all I get out before he turns away. I watch him until he enters his room and closes the door quietly behind him, then I walk into Celeste's room and lean against the closed door, biting my lower lip. The Celeste situation aside, so much is left unsaid between us. Calder and I both have enough baggage that it's a miracle we were able to get past it to have the one night we did together.

Is that all it'll ever be? One night? As I kick off the heels and slide out of the dress, the thought makes me feel physically ill, but I don't know how to fix it right now. While I mull the rising tension, I quickly slip out of the bra and find a fitted T-shirt to sleep in. My biggest worry is that if this Celeste thing drags on, it may be too late for us to mend the damage. But Calder is so angry I doubt he'll listen to me right now.

Unless...what I have to say has nothing to do with Celeste, Ben, or this frustrating limbo situation we're in. I grab my phone from my purse, intending to send him a text with Brent's information, but the phone dies just as I start to type the text.

"Just great," I mumble. I can't let this go all night. I have to try to mend the growing chasm between us the best way I can for now.

Grabbing a soft white robe from the back of the bathroom door, I put it on and slip out of my room.

CHAPTER TWELVE

Cass

$\mathcal{M}_y$ stomach knotting, I shake out my hands, then knock quietly.

A second passes and then another. I start to turn away when I hear a light thump, then another.

Frowning, I reach for the knob. I step inside just as Calder lands from a spinning back kick. He moves so fast, then next thing I know he's turning with a gun pointed right at me, an intense look on his face.

I gasp at the same time he lowers his weapon and yanks the ear buds out of his ears. "What the fuck, Cass," he says in a low tone. "You can't sneak up on me like that."

I quickly shut the door as he sets his gun down and unstraps his phone from his arm.

He unplugs the headphones from his phone and tense

music briefly fills the room before he turns it down. I stare at his bare chest and gray lounge pants, guilt riding me. Of course he has to keep training so he's ready when the MMA match is rescheduled. He's only here because of me.

The light sheen of sweat coating his hard chest makes the Celtic tribal tattoo running across his muscular left shoulder and along his chiseled abs stand out against his skin. I don't get to admire his physique long before he turns to me with a stoic expression.

As he faces me full on, his green gaze still sharp with anger, I'm temporarily speechless. Seeking common ground, my gaze is drawn to the Latin word Solus along his rib cage. He told me it meant 'alone,' but he never explained why he had it tattooed on his body.

"Cass?"

My brain finally engages as the intense song playing on his phone registers. Linkin Park's "One Step Closer." He's definitely in a mood. I clear my throat, but my voice sounds strained when I speak. "I tried to text you a number but my phone died. I thought you'd like to have it now so maybe Elijah could start working on it for you."

"Whose number?"

"Brent's. I memorized it from Beth's phone."

Other than a spark of interest in his eyes, Calder doesn't let anything show as he gestures toward the desk. "There's a pen and paper."

I'm surprised he doesn't ask anything else, but instead walks away to lower himself to the floor near the end of his bed. I watch him effortlessly do ten push-ups before I glance away.

Taking the hint he's not in the mood to talk, I jot down Brent's number. Just as I reach for the door handle to leave, Calder's cold voice sends a chill of apprehension through my body. "You don't have anything else to say?"

I slowly turn, and he's standing near the bed, muscular arms crossed over his chest, his expression dark and brooding.

When I don't answer right away, he snaps. "*Ben.*"

Trying to ease the tightness in my shoulders, I spread my hands and exhale. "What am I supposed to do? Ben thinks I'm Celeste, and Gregory and Phillip insisted that no one else know the truth. Maybe they're worried Ben and Jake won't be able to keep Celeste's disappearance to themselves. I don't know." When Calder's expression turns darker, I sigh and lower my hands back to my side. "He's being attentive, not overly aggressive, Calder. It's not the best situation, but holding my hand is pretty innocent and tame."

At the same time the song comes to its crashing one-word ending, Calder strides forward aggressively. The intense look on his face has me instinctively backing up, but the moment my shoulder blades touch the door, he stops. Resting his hand on the solid wood above me, he steps into my personal space. "Do you think standing close like this is innocent?"

His masculine scent of sweat mixed with faint hints of his aftershave tease my senses, elevating my pulse. I refuse to look at his sculpted body. He's far too enticing.

My fingers itch to slide along his hard pectorals and trace the tattoo down his arm. My heart is beating so hard it's a wonder he can't hear it. I curl my fingers by my side and swallow as I lift my chin and hold his gaze. "I'll admit it's personal, but Ben hasn't touched me inappropriately."

Calder's jaw flexes but instead of responding, he reaches out with his left hand and lightly runs the pads of his fingers over my thumb and along my index finger. When Exile's ballad "I Want to Kiss You All Over" starts playing on his phone, my hand instinctively reacts to the song's slow seductive lyrics and Calder's light touch. Calder's love of old songs makes him even more attractive and I turn my palm toward him, needing to feel more of his touch. His breathing halts just before he touches the tips of his fingers to mine.

The electricity is instantaneous the moment our skin connects. My breath hitches and I tingle everywhere, but especially where he's touching me. "What about now?" he demands ruthlessly.

I'm afraid to look into his eyes and see judgment there, so I drop my gaze to our hands. Big mistake. At that moment, he slides the tips of his fingers between mine and then slowly glides them upward. My skin prickles when the base of our fingers lock together. "Perfect fit," he murmurs and folds his thumb around mine, pulling my hand close to his.

Desire slams into my stomach and my mind is filled with memories of the first sensual moment our bodies physically connected the other night. His simulation with our hands is masterfully brutal, hitting me in the most intimate way possible. "Does this feel tame, angel?" he asks, his voice dropping to a husky timbre.

Only Calder could turn hand holding into a carnal act. I refuse to look at him or acknowledge what he's doing. Ben has never touched me like this...certainly not with the kind of heat that would melt an icecap. Calder's barely touching me, but the connection and the angry passion in his tone is so provocative, I have to hold myself still to keep from melting against him.

Lowering his hand from the door, he brushes the tips of his fingers along the base of my spine. His touch is barely there, but the warmth from his hand feels as if my terry robe is made of tissue. I swallow the gasp of surprise when sudden heat radiates from my head to my toes.

"What? No answer?" He leans close, his warm breath caressing my ear just before he presses a feather light kiss to my cheekbone. "How about now, Raven mine?"

I'm soaking up every sensation and the want in his voice, but I do my best to hold any audible responses inside. I don't want him to know how much this is affecting me. I feel like I'm vibrating with suppressed lust. God, this is hard, but knowing he's doing this just to prove a point is the only thing keeping me from giving into his seduction.

Calder slides his thumb along the heel of my hand, then down to the center of my palm. Moving his mouth close to my jawline, he presses his finger deep into my skin, hitting all the right sensual points.

Without conscious thought, I angle my chin, giving

him better access. Accepting the fantasy, I hold my breath and wait for him to clamp down along my jawline.

To claim me all over again.

Instead of the bite I expect, Calder tugs me against his chest, his other hand sliding down the curve of my back to pull me forward until I'm thoroughly tucked against him. Pressing his erection intimately against me, he slowly turns us to the seductive song. With the warmth of his body seeping into me, I can't keep myself completely detached. I melt into his hard frame and fall into the rhythm of his movements as if we've always danced like this.

"When I dance with you…" He sounds both aroused and tortured, his chest rumbling against mine. "Our bodies move in sync naturally. Chest, hips, thighs." He slides his muscular thigh between mine, hitting my sex briefly as we turn. My body throbs and I bite my lip. I want him to connect again but this time hard enough to ease the sexual tension. Pulling me close, he husks against my temple. "*This* is sex with clothes on, Cass."

He instantly stops dancing, his voice dropping to a harsh grate as he releases me. "You smell like him. To be clear, watching another man do this with you is not something I will ever tolerate again. And knowing you didn't have any underwear on only infuriated me more, I don't give a fuck if it's because you refused to wear Celeste's."

I never would've teased Calder if I had known I would end up dancing with Ben later. I didn't even know that was part of the evening event. "You're the *only* one who knew that," I say, my face flushing. "And we didn't dance like *this*."

His eyes narrow. "While you danced to that slow song, the way he looked at you, his hand pulling you closer… that was *not* innocent."

I see his point, but I wasn't the only one getting attention tonight. Stepping close, I push my thigh through the slit in my robe and brush my knee against his. Once he glances down at the show of bare skin, I glide my right hand into his hair and trail my fingers over his ear, then down the back of his hair. Clasping his neck in perfect mimicry of the unknown girl I saw him talking with at the hotel, I ask, "Do you think this is innocent?"

Calder frowns, wariness flickering his gaze. "What do you mean?"

"I saw you talking to someone at the hotel."

He stiffens. "Alana is just a friend I've known for a while."

I don't like his answer. A part of me hoped Calder would quash my worries and tell me I was imagining an intimate familiarity between him and the mystery girl. My eyebrows pull together. "So what makes this innocent is how well you know the person?

He stares at me for a second, then nods. "Yes."

I take a step back and spread my hands wide. "Then I guess that means Ben and I are good on the innocent front, because I know more about him than I do you."

His expression hardens and he folds his arms. "I'm going to assume you're not talking about sex. To be clear…

sharing is a two-way street, angel. This isn't a game. You don't truly know him."

I don't like that he's right, but there is one truth I do know. "I know what Ben is *not*, which goes a long way. Trust me on this."

I walk away then, my back ramrod straight. Just as I reach the door, Calder says, "He wants you."

I pause, but don't look back. "He wants Celeste."

"He wants the *you* he sees in Celeste. He's going to push for more."

Does Ben really want me? *I hadn't even considered the possibility.* I was just happy that Celeste would have someone in her life who genuinely seemed to care about her. If I didn't know anything else about her, I learned she really didn't have anyone she was close to in her life.

I sense Calder directly behind me now, but I don't acknowledge that he's moved closer. Instead, I pull the door open. There's no way I'm telling him about Ben drawing slow circles in the center of my palm with his thumb during the last few minutes in the car. If what Calder just did to my hand was erotic foreplay, then Ben definitely has sex on the brain. Even though Calder's touch is the only one that arouses me, sharing that tidbit from tonight would not go over well. "I've got control over it, Calder."

When I start to walk out, he says, "Someone else knows you're not Celeste. The fact they aren't sounding the alarm about that speaks volumes about Celeste and the danger you're in."

I glance back at him, my heart stuttering. "How do you know that note wasn't related to something else or even meant for Gregory?"

"My gut...and because the only fingerprints on it were yours and Ben's."

"You already had the card analyzed?" I blink my surprise. "But you were with me the whole time."

"Alana delivered the card to Elijah for me."

"How *generous* of her." I don't bother to keep the sarcasm out of my response, but at least I know Sebastian's BLACK Securities team isn't beyond doing whatever it takes—even hacking government databases for fingerprint data—to keep me safe.

Calder's gaze sharpens. "This isn't just about Celeste anymore. Don't go anywhere without me. You can't afford to be wrong about anyone, including Ben."

He made his point, but I refuse to argue about Ben. "You'll always know where I am. Good night, Calder."

The sensation of someone's hand covering my mouth pulls me awake to total darkness. A shadowy male form hovers over me, and Calder's last comment warning me to be careful repeats over and over in my head as I scream and try to back away. He sits on the bed and clamps his hand tighter on my mouth, then leans close to my ear.

"Shhh, it's me."

Calder. My heart still pounding insanely fast, my eyes

adjust to the bit of light coming from the bathroom and Calder's features start to form in the darkness. I instantly relax and pull his hand from my mouth to my chest, whispering, "How did you get in here? I locked my door."

He turns his chin back toward the bathroom. "Through the passageway you showed me."

I blink in the darkness, glad my pulse is starting to return to normal. "What is it? Is something wrong?"

Holding my gaze, Calder slides his thumb along my skin exposed by the T-shirt's vee-neck. "Yes, something is wrong. We're broken, Cass. And I refuse to let this situation we're in ruin what we have."

I inhale slowly and fold my fingers around his hand. "We're fine, Calder."

"Liar," he says, his gaze narrowing. "You've pulled further and further away from me since I got here."

"I'm just trying to stay focused." I don't want to get into it now. I honestly don't think we can get back to *us* in the current situation. Too many secrets and past issues keep creeping up for both of us.

Calder turns his hand and clasps my wrist. When he runs his thumb along the scars, I pull away from his hold.

He doesn't speak, just recaptures my hand, but instead of touching my wrist, he presses my palm against his Solus tattoo.

"Do you want to know about this?"

He's trying to share. Hope filling my heart, I swallow and nod.

Calder quickly tugs me toward him and lifts me in his

arms.

"Where are we going?" I ask, wrapping my arms around his muscular shoulders.

"You're going to wash the smell of him off you first. It's fucking playing with my head." Setting me down in the bathroom, he flicks on the shower, then pulls my long T-shirt off in one swift movement.

He grunts when he sees that I'm underwear free— I'm sure he's still pissed about earlier tonight—but I'm surprised when he doesn't join me under the hot spray. Instead he leans a muscular shoulder against the wall and folds his arms, commanding, "Shower, then we'll talk."

I don't like that he's ordering me around in the middle of the night, but this is the first time he's offered to share something of himself. In his own gruff way, he's trying, so I won't question his timing or methods. As I slide the bar of soap along my skin, I note the tension in his jaw and inwardly squirm at the hungry way he watches my hands. I want to pull him into the shower and make him wash me, then I could run my hands along the shadow of his overnight beard. That darkness only adds to his irresistible sexiness. I would spend tons of time soaping his beautifully sculpted body. In comparison, I feel inferior, so I take extra time soaping my breasts, my stomach and between my thighs to keep his gaze distracted from my flaws.

When I pour shampoo in my hand, then start to massage the liquid into my scalp, Calder reaches down to adjust himself. Excitement slides through my veins, but I pretend I don't notice and work the suds into my hair.

I know he's watching the foamy bubbles slide down my chest, along the curves of my breasts and hips before funneling through the bit of dark hair between my legs. Even though he's standing a couple feet away, I feel the magnetic pull of desire smoldering between us. Closing my eyes, I let the pounding water wash away the last remnants of suds and fantasize what it would feel like with him in here with me.

The sensation of Calder's fingers sliding down my throat along with the water feels so real, I give into the sensual moment and hold myself perfectly still, just being in the moment. But when his fingers move with the water to my collarbone, and then slowly trail down my chest and along the curve of my breast, I'm thankful the shower is washing away the tears that well up. I love that he can't stop himself from touching me.

When the water suddenly shuts off, my eyes fly open.

Calder's holding a towel out for me, heat and want reflected in his gaze.

I wring my hair out and quickly wrap the towel around me. Just as I tuck the end between my breasts, Calder fists his hand around the knot in the towel and pulls me out of the shower.

Setting me against the wall next to the shower, he slides his hand up my chest. Tracing his finger along my collarbone, he pauses to slide his thumb up the curve of my throat. "When he moves close like this, do you want him to touch you?"

I sigh. Why won't he let the Ben thing go. "Calder… what are you doing?"

"I'm getting to know you *much* better."

I frown. "That's not what I meant and you know it."

Grunting, he clasps my hand and folds it against his ribcage. Vulnerability shines in his green gaze for a split second before it's masked behind a hard stare. "Did you ask him if he has any tattoos?"

I slide my thumb over his Solus tattoo and answer honestly. "I only want to know about yours. You said it means 'alone,' but I know there's a lot more to it than that."

Calder tugs on the end of the towel and as it falls to the floor, my skin prickles at the chill hitting me. I raise an eyebrow. "That's not an answer."

His only response is to pull my hair forward and stare at it lying against my chest. As he traces the water dripping from the damp ends along the outer curve of my breast, my gaze locks on his dog tags. The memory of how creative he'd been with them and my responses makes my cheeks flush with heat. When he touches me, I forget all my inhibitions. "You said you'd tell me."

More water falls, but this time the trickle slides along the front of my breast. When it drips off my nipple, Calder exhales through his nose, his hands moving to grip my hips. "I will, Cass, but right now *this* is what I need," he rumbles before he dips his head and touches his tongue to my nipple.

As the water transfers from the puckered pink tip to his tongue and his warm breath rushes over my chilled skin in a low growl of want, I exhale a pant of aroused anticipation.

"Tell me you're still mine," he rasps, fingers flexing along my hips.

I bite my bottom lip and dig my fingers into his short hair, giving him his answer.

Calder doesn't hesitate. He grasps my waist and sucks my nipple deep. I can't believe how his aggressive possession of such a small part of me can tug so hard on every yearning in my body. My heart races and insides tighten. As he moves to the other breast and gives it the same velvety savage attention, my skin heats and my sex throbs.

He straightens and meets my gaze, skillful fingers sliding down my belly. "Every time he touched you, I wanted to break his fucking neck."

When he folds his fingers along my entrance, his gaze narrows sharply. "You're already dripping."

I quickly shake my head. "I never said I didn't want you. I just—" I gasp and grip his biceps when he slowly dips a finger inside me.

Calder closes his eyes and inhales harshly. Then his green eyes snap to mine. "You are *mine*," he growls and adds another finger, sliding them deep inside my channel.

Stepping close, he cups the back of my neck and rasps against my cheekbone, "You can't ignore this kind of chemistry, angel." He strokes his thumb against the sensitive spot where my leg meets my body. "The feel of you soaking my hand and clenching around me is so goddamn arousing and intense." Folding the heel of his hand around my mons, he presses his chest against my shoulder and rests his forehead on the wall. "The way you taste haunts me, and all I've thought about since you left my bed is how much I want to fuck you in every way possible until the only words out of your mouth are, 'More, please.'"

I'm shaking and can barely hold myself up. "Calder—"

"*No* more holding back." His hand tightens on my body and his entire frame tenses. Exhaling deeply, his rough tone softens. "When two people connect the way we do...we fucking *own* each other, Cass."

My heart melts and I turn so my cheek touches his jaw. "More, please."

CHAPTER THIRTEEN

Cass

*C*alder's head jerks up and his green eyes meet mine for a split second before he withdraws his hand from my body. "Lay down, angel."

I glance down at the towel over the thick rug. "Here?"

He turns and hits the light switch, dousing the room in darkness. When he flicks another switch and a fire leaps to life in the dual-sided fireplace, I love the warm glowing light reflected in the room and lower myself onto the rug.

As soon as I lay back, Calder crawls over me, warm skin stretched over hard muscles and unadulterated hunger reflected in his gaze. "Lay still and don't move. Think you can do that?" he says, his voice silk and steel.

While he seeks my agreement, his necklace swings between us, ticking off our intense rhythm of desire like a metronome. I clasp the dog tags, hoping to freeze this moment in time. "I want you to share with me, Calder." Sliding my fingers along his Solus tattoo, I continue, "To truly share. Think you can do that?"

He pulls my hands above my head. As he trails his fingers up my arms and toward my wrists, it takes major effort not to yank my hands away. He holds my gaze and slowly runs his thumbs over my scars. "Only if you do, sweet Raven."

"That wasn't the deal," I say, my heart sinking at the idea of revealing my past.

Calder slides his fingers along my palms, then clasps his hands to mine in a tight hold. "A two-way street, remember?"

His expression is so intensely sincere, I nod, hoping I'll find the courage to tell him.

He smiles and dips his head to press a kiss to my shoulder. Releasing my hands, he moves lower and nips at the curve of my breast, his breath warming and arousing me at the same time. I flex my stomach when he reaches my bellybutton and lingers. "When I got home after leaving the military, I received a letter from my mother's lawyer."

"I thought you said your mother died when you were young?"

Calder clasps my hips and his fingers flex tight as he glances up at me. "She did. Let me finish, then ask, okay?"

I bite my lip and nod.

He flattens his palm on my belly and holds it there, his gaze locked on his hand. "The lawyer was instructed to only send the letter once my father passed away, but he had to wait until I returned from deployment to send it to me. In the letter, my mom informed me that Jack Blake isn't my true father. She said the only reason she told me at all was so that I would know who my biological father was in case I ever needed it for medical reasons."

Oh, God, that's why Calder distanced himself from his family. He feels like he doesn't belong, that he's not a true Blake. My eyes fill will tears when his hand shakes as he moves it to my thigh. I can't stay quiet. "I'm sorry, Calder. I had no idea—"

He grips my thigh hard and shakes his head, cutting me off. Blowing out a breath, he continues as he rubs away the bits of water still left on my skin. "She said that if Jack had learned the truth it would've destroyed him so she kept the 'incident' to herself." He snorts his anger. "Incident? Can you believe that shit? Apparently the guilt of her affair was too much. At least I learned the real reason she took her life back then." He pauses his exploration of my skin and encircles my ankle with his fingers. "So not only did I lose my father before I deployed four years ago, but when I got back, I lost everything else. Every single memory we had together as a family, every father and son moment. I lost myself and who I thought I was."

How could his mother not think how this news would impact him? Tears slide down my temples. I can't imagine how hard that must've been for him. *Is that why he started doing MMA? As some kind of punishment?* I want to ask him so much. *Who is his real father?* I'm sure he feels so much anger and resentment that I doubt he'll ever contact him, but is he curious at all about the man? Instead of voicing my thoughts, I slide my hand down his arm and set my foot on his thigh, curling my toes into the muscle to let him know I'm here. I'm listening.

Calder presses a kiss to the inside of my bent knee, then rests his lips there for a second. When he finally glances my way, he shakes his head. "Don't shed tears for me, angel. I've moved on. You wanted to know why I got this tattoo and what it means to me...and now you do."

I briefly slide my gaze to the triskele design incorporated into the Celtic tribal tattoo on his shoulder. He said he got it to represent the Irish roots of the Blake family. So he must've had the Solus done after he found out the truth about his heritage. He sees himself as truly alone in the world. My heart feels like it's crushing in my chest. I cup my hand around the tattoo on his ribs. "The blood running through your veins doesn't change the fact that you have a family who loves you, nor does it erase a lifetime of memories, Calder."

"Those memories were built on a lie."

"Do you really think your father would treat you any differently if he were still here?"

He stiffens, torture reflected in his expression. "I'll never know."

"If you let this fester, it will gnaw away at you. Find a way to discover the answer you need so you can truly move on. The Blakes didn't stop being your family because a piece of paper says otherwise."

Shrugging, he snorts. "Bash is the only one who knows the truth. And he pretty much beat the crap out of me when he found out why he hadn't heard from me in months. I know the Blakes will be there for me, but yes, to an extent, I feel...adrift. Losing your entire identity has a way of fucking with your self-worth. It isn't something you just shake off easily."

I definitely get the self-worth part. As he lifts his hand from the floor, I fold our fingers together. "That I completely understand."

Calder turns our clasped hands over and stares at the tattoo on my wrist. Sliding his thumb over my scars, he lifts his gaze to mine. "Your turn."

When I don't say anything, his fingers tighten slightly. "Why don't you tell me about the tattoo then?"

That's easier. I smile and lift my arm to stare at my other wrist with an identical tree branch tattoo minus the raven. "Finding the right artist who could cover scars wasn't easy. It takes true talent to cover them." Chuckling, I continue, "I never thought I'd find my artist in a guy who models on the side, but as you can see, Noah's incredibly talented."

Calder's gaze hardens. "How did you 'discover' his talent?"

I snicker, enjoying that he sounds jealous. "He asked me out for a beer after class and when I reached for my mug, he saw my scars and told me he could hide them in plain sight if I wanted."

"You slept with him."

I open my mouth to deny his statement, but it hits me that he jumped to that conclusion awfully fast. "You had sex with your tattoo artist, didn't you?"

When Calder's jaw tightens, swift jealousy surges through me and I pull my hand from his. Stretching my arms over my head, I sigh dreamily and force amused nonchalance. "What is it about tattoo artists? And, yes, I've seen Noah in the nude."

Calder's leaning over me before I even complete my sentence, his hands clasping my wrists tight over my head. "Stop avoiding telling me about your scars, Cass. Give me something to think about other than picturing you fucking some tatted up pretty boy."

"What's going to keep me from picturing you fucking a tatted up slutty gir—"

Calder clamps his mouth over mine, cutting off my response. His kiss is possessive and hard, hitting all the right buttons. But as much as I crave his aggression, I'm pissed too. I never slept with Noah. I valued his friendship more, but the last thing I want to think about is Calder with another woman. When I bite his lip, he grunts and settles his hips on mine, thrusting his tongue deeper.

His dog tags crushed between us and his rock hard erection pressed tightly against me are both pleasure and torture. It's not enough. I need to feel the rush of the steel dragging along my skin as he slides deep inside me. I want to know that I'm the only person he's thinking about. The only one he wants. I kiss him back and arch into him, locking my legs around his hips.

Calder groans and releases my arms to cup my face. This time his kiss is so intensely emotional, he sweeps the air right out of my lungs. My heart thunders and my body thrums for more. When I wrap my arms around his thick shoulders and respond to his passionate aggression with my own, he pulls back, his breathing uneven. "We both have past relationships. The difference is *you're* not having to watch one in the present."

I frown for a second. "You're talking about Ben? That's Celeste's relationship, not mine."

He scowls. "You're the one giving the guy a free pass."

"None of it is real, Calder."

"Your trust in him is and his desire to have you to himself is very fucking real. He told me he'll have me booted off your detail after tomorrow night."

Panic grips me. "What? He can't do that. I have an agreement with Gregory and Phillip."

"Which he knows nothing about!" Calder growls his annoyance.

"It's just one more night, Calder," I say, trying to calm my own worries too. "The blood results should be back tomorrow. And regardless, at the party, we'll get what we need to give the police another suspect to consider."

Calder sighs. "Let's agree to drop the subject, because honestly, Cass, the last thing I want to think about is you with any of those assholes, past or present."

"Ben's not an asshole."

His expression hardens. "They're all A-holes."

"Only two in my past deserve that label," I say, snorting

my disgust.

Calder stills, the heat in his gaze shifting to alert awareness. Rolling us to our sides, he cups my cheek and commands softly, "Tell me."

Did I really say that out loud? Ugh. Now that it's out there, I can't take it back. I swallow and stare at the firelight dancing across his handsome face. I'm not sure if I have it in me to tell him the whole story while remaining calm and dispassionate. I shake my head. "You said to leave the past in the past."

He inhales deeply and slides his fingers into my damp hair. Stroking my cheek with his thumb, he says, "Not this time, Raven mine. Tell me everything."

He shared. It's only fair that I share in return. Thankful that the firelight is throwing my face in the shadows, I take a deep breath and tell him what happened when I was a teen at Sherry's party. I don't go into details about the Celeste lookalike connection, nor do I tell him Jake and Brent's names. I only tell him that it happened, and that the timing of that night's event right before my sister's suicide is what drove me to cutting. I avoid talking about the fact it also impacted my sexual relationships with men later in life, but I can tell by the tightening of his grip on my hair and the muscle jumping in his jaw, he's making his own assumptions.

Once I finish, his thumb halts on my cheek. He's still holding me but his whole frame has tensed against me. "What are their names?"

He'll make me leave tonight if I tell him. I can't afford

to do that, no matter how twisted up this whole situation is. This isn't just for Celeste's sake, but also for Calder's. He's put so much work into his undercover status at the EUC, but if he finds out about Brent, I don't know what he'll do. I don't want him to mess things up. Brent doesn't come around the Carver estate, and as long as Jake doesn't know that I'm not Celeste, I can handle this. I pull his hand from my face and tuck our hands between us on the towel. "The statute of limitations ran out on what they did a long time ago, Calder."

"Names, Cass," he says again, his tone eerie-calm.

Too calm. He's also amazingly still, like a hunter waiting patiently for a deer to walk right into his crosshairs.

I shake my head and roll onto my back. "It's in the past where it belongs." Holding my wrists up, I turn them so he can see the tattoos in the firelight. "It took me a few years to get my head on straight, but I got these as a reward for swearing off cutting." When Calder raises up on his elbow and encircles my left wrist with his hand, I point to the Never script on my arm. "I got this one later, after I relapsed and accidently cut too deep." His hand cinches around my wrist and his gaze snaps to my face, full of worry, but I keep going. I need to finish so he'll understand. "The 'Never' reminds me that for my own sanity, I have to let the past go. It's also a promise to myself and my sister to never be a victim or allow myself to cut, ever again."

I capture his hand and lower it to my chest. "Peace of mind is what matters to me, Calder. I worked very hard for that." The sensation of his fingers flexing against my breast makes me instinctively arch into his palm. Calder's nostrils flare, and as he cups my breast fully, I slide my fingers into his hair and pull him close to press my lips to his jawline. "When I'm with you, that part of my past fades into the background. Help me forget it ever happened. Show me that I'm capable of being as uninhibited as I want to be."

He holds my gaze for a couple seconds, then prowls back over me, his gorgeous eyes full of banked hunger. Rubbing his nose along my cheek, he slides his fingers into my hair, then presses his forehead to mine. "If you're serious, then I'm going to ask for your complete trust. Can you do that?"

I flatten my palms along his stubbled cheeks, my stomach fluttering with excitement. "With you...always."

Worry flickers in his gaze, before he gives me a dark smile and bites my bottom lip. My skin prickles as he moves to my chin and then my throat. I start to slide my hands in his hair, but he glances up and shakes his head. "You can't touch me."

I frown. "Why not?"

"You're trusting me, remember?" he says in a silky tone. "But since you most likely won't listen," he pauses and slips off his dog tags. "I'm just going to have to improvise. Give me your hands."

The moment I lift my hands toward him, he sits up on his knees and wraps the beaded necklace around my wrists, doubling it up until I have just a little room to move. Tapping his finger on the dog tags, he flips them upward and against my palm, saying, "Keep these safe for me."

I fold my fingers over on the tags, clasping them in my right hand and tease. "They're not going anywhere."

Calder pushes my arms to the floor, softly commanding, "Keep them here. I hope the necklace will remind you to do that. Otherwise we'll have to find another way."

I smile at his low threat, wondering what other inventive ways he has in mind, but I leave my arms where he put them. "I'm good."

Calder cups the back of my neck and arches my throat as he bends to run his lips down the curved skin until he reaches my collarbone. "Did you know there is a spot here that will make you squirm?" he murmurs, his tone deceptively innocent.

"Really? Whereee—" I gasp as he locks his teeth on the edge of the bone closest to my shoulder. I'm caught like a rabbit in a wolf's maw. I can't struggle or pull away. My heart thumps hard against my chest and a shudder of anticipation thrums through me. All I can do is lay still and wait for him to release me.

Calder slowly slides his fingers over my breast, his hand massaging and weighing the plump flesh. When his palm rubs along my nipple, my stomach clenches and I take an aroused breath, waiting for him to pinch the tip. Instead, he releases my collarbone and quickly moves to capture my nipple between his teeth, clamping down with aggressive force.

Moaning deeply, I nearly come off the floor, my spine

arched in primal response. I instinctively lift my arms to clasp him close, but the necklace reminds me of my promise. I clamp my lips together and lower my arms back to the floor while shamelessly pressing my chest closer to encourage more of his rough branding. This is my kind of sex play.

Calder chuckles against my breast, then gently sucks the tip into his warm mouth once more while tweaking my other nipple with his fingers.

I sigh my pleasure and fold my foot over his muscular calf, trying to pull him to me, but he quickly grabs my thigh and clasps it tight, pushing my leg back. "None of that, sweet Raven. This is my time. You can only touch me when I give you permission to."

While I snort my disapproval of such a plan, he moves to my stomach, planting light kisses along my skin. He lingers at my belly button. Dipping his tongue inside the small crevice, he presses a soft kiss to my skin. "I feel your pulse racing, angel. It's an arousing *thump, thump, thump,* but I'm going to make it jump ten times faster."

"I know one way you can make it fuel a jet engine," I offer suggestively.

"Shhh," he says right before he bites my mons. As I let out a moaning gasp at his unparalleled talent of mixing pleasure and pain, he continues, his warm breath rushing across my sex. "I'm running this show. Not you."

"But everyone knows the show is really all about the main attraction. And that would be *me*," I tease as I lift my hands and point to my head.

Calder lets out a low laugh as he trails his fingers along my thighs. Pushing them open, he looks up at me with wicked intent. "But this is a concert, angel. Yes, there will be upbeats and downbeats, tender passages and vigorous lines, even playing with texture, but it's not really about the orchestra, though we do enjoy the beautiful sound in our ears." He slowly taps his fingers on the insides of my knees as he stares hungrily at my sex, already strategizing.

Lowering his head, he swipes his tongue along my entrance and all the way to my clit. My skin prickles from the brief tease, but my whole body clenches and heats up when he straightens and closes his eyes as a growl of pleasure rolls through him.

His green eyes snap open, full of fire and lustful determination as they collide with mine. "No, Raven mine...the attention goes to the conductor. With both hands working different aspects of the score, his direction is intentionally coordinated and emotionally tied to the outcome. He is the main attraction."

That's a tantalizing statement I can't argue with. Calder's hard chest and flexing muscles are a gorgeous sight, but his mind utterly fascinates. It's hard to believe that the same man who's trained to kill with his bare hands and who participates in violent MMA fights, also appreciates and understands the finer aspects of all types of music. Even classical. As he looks at me as if he plans to literally devour my body, every bone liquefies. *He's* the one I want to watch...the one who will entertain and enthrall. I want to get caught up in his charisma. To be fully consumed by him.

Tapping my toes three times on the carpet, I roll my hips to encourage him. "Let the concert begin, Maestro."

The carnal look in his eyes shoots right through me before he grasps my right ankle. Bending my knee fully upright, he sets my foot down, then does the same to the other foot. "Keep them here and don't move them unless I tell you to."

I take an unsteady breath and nod my agreement, my gaze greedily eating up the flickering firelight playing across his shoulder and chest muscles as he touches the sensitive insides of my thighs. Sliding his hands up to my knees, he applies pressure along the way, silently telling me to angle them wider.

When I apply pressure against his hands, his gaze seeks mine, eyebrows raised. *Trust me.* This is the most exposed I've ever allowed myself to be with anyone. It's scary and decadent and arousing all at once. Calder rests his hand on my knee and squeezes, his touch releasing the tension in my legs and I let him open me fully.

He rewards me with a pleased smile then grasps my ankle. I'm unprepared for the sensation of his mouth on the tender space right under my ankle bones. It's so sensitive, I instantly try to jerk my foot free, but Calder clasps my calf muscle tight, holding me in place. He moves up my leg, alternating with tender kisses and aggressive nips.

Desire swirls in my belly, the toes on my other foot digging into the carpet. I curl my fingers tight around the dog tags in my hand and the sensation of the tiny beads biting into the sensitive scars on my wrists is surprisingly erotic.

Calder finally makes his way to my sex, but instead of giving it attention, he slides past my wet center and reaches for the other ankle.

Are you fucking kidding me? I glare at him as he slowly lifts the other foot. *He's not possibly going to do the exact same thing to the other side. That would just be cruel.* When he pushes up to his knees and takes my leg with him, I start to exhale a sigh of relief, but end up sucking the air into my lungs in a deep groan and hike my hips off the floor as he bites down on my Achilles tendon.

Calder's only response is to flatten his palm on my stomach and push me back to the floor. "Stay put, angel," he commands, then returns to silently torturing me down the entire back of that leg.

Once he reaches the spot where my leg meets my body, he lowers my leg back to the floor and slides his hands to my ass, grabbing both muscle cheeks in a firm hold. When his thumbs tug at my opening with slow, precise pressure, I exhale slowly to remain still.

I'm shaking and barely able to keep my knees bent, let alone my feet flat on the floor, but the sensation of his breath rushing close to me but not touching is more than I can take. "Enough Calder," I snap. "Taste me before I kill you."

He glances sharply at me. "Not a word."

Clamping my lips together, I close my eyes and tug harder against the necklace, letting the metal dig into my skin ruthlessly.

The deep thrust of his tongue in my channel takes me by surprise. I nearly surge off the floor at first, but then I press against him, seeking more. Calder's big hands grasp my thighs tight and he consumes my body with merciless abandon.

When I try to put my foot on his back, he yanks it back down to the floor with a fierce growl and then punishes my clit with a sharp nip. I let out a keening cry of shock. He's not fucking around about my feet.

I rock against his mouth, taking what he's giving but wanting so much more. "God, just fuck me, Calder. This is too much," I whimper, my whole body shaking for release.

He grunts and slides two fingers deep in my channel. I gasp and clench him tight, tears of relief falling into my hair. Calder flicks my clit with his tongue and an intense orgasm rocks through me.

I just start to exhale a sigh of sheer bliss, when he pushes his thumb on my clit and lifts his head, growling, "Stay with me, angel."

"Wha—" A gasp of deep arousal cuts off my comment. His fingers are stroking my g-spot with unrelenting determination.

I tense, my body wanting to fold in half and hide from the intensity. "Cal—Calder." Hot and cold shoots from my head to my toes and prickles form on my skin. "I don't think I can take this."

Calder pauses his movements and looks up at me. "Give yourself over, Cass. This is the freedom you asked for," he says, his tone both brutal and velvet with dark promises.

I swallow and close my eyes tight. My heart is racing like crazy, but it feels like it's only speeding up. Finally I nod.

"That's my girl," Calder says. He presses a kiss to my mons at the same time he hits a spot and doesn't let up.

I arch my back and neck, my whole being centered on his masterful manipulation of my body. Panting hard, I undulate my hips with his movements as the tension coils inside me.

"You're close," he says, and a new sensation layers over the ones already in play as he slides a different finger in my ass and clamps his lips over my clit.

Calder completely consumes me with sensory overload. My body is chilled and my face is on fire. "Cald...it's too much."

"Fuck, you're beautiful like this. Let go and come all over me, Raven mine."

As soon as his mouth latches onto my clit once more, a rush of warmth and body-rocking vibrations flow through me, taking my orgasm to new heights. I hang on to a temporary plane, where want and desire coalesce with body and mind in one massive emotional wave of release, changing everything I thought I knew about my body and sex.

I lay there for a minute, completely spent and panting. Only warm droplets hitting my chest brings my gaze into focus. Calder's standing next to the sink, a smug grin on his face as he flicks more soapy water at me. "Welcome back."

I quickly stand up behind him. As I untangle my wrists from his necklace, my legs wobble and almost give out. Just as I grip the edge of the counter, Calder reaches behind him and hooks his arm around me, hauling me against his back. "Whoa, Cass. I got you."

Clasping his dog tags, I wrap my arms around his trim waist and press my face against his arm. He's so freaking hot and as his gorgeous green eyes hold mine in the mirror, my face blooms with color. My naturally dried hair is a mess of dark curls, making my face look even more heart-shaped. I look like a wild thing, but a happy one. "That was...that um..."

"Out of this world? Transcendent? Life changing?" he supplies, grinning at my reflection in the mirror.

I can't even be mad at his arrogance. He's entirely right. I smile and press my body closer. "All of the above."

Calder shuts the water off, his expression suddenly serious as he takes the hand towel off the hook and dries his hands. "All I want is your trust, Cass."

My eyes widen. "You have it. What I just told you about my past, no one knows. Not my parents, not even Talia."

I hold my hand out and uncurl my fingers, revealing his tags. "Why do you still wear these? You're no longer in the military."

Calder takes his tags and returns them to his neck. "After my father died, my unit became my family."

Yet he's no longer with his SEAL team or in the Navy

at all. "Why did you leave?"

"I went on missions non-stop for over three years. When I ended up in the hospital, recovering for three months…" He pauses and shrugs. "I realized if I kept going at that pace, I wasn't going to make it to the hospital. At some point, I had to come home."

He doesn't say "to be alone" but I see the lost look in his eyes. I slowly trace my fingers along his Solus tattoo, then slide my hand up his ribs and over his pectoral to cover his heart. "I'm sorry for all that you've lost."

He shakes his head, his hand clenching on the towel. "It's in the past, Cass."

"Grieving is a process, Calder. I miss my sister every single day, but I try to lessen the loss by recalling the special moments we had together, no matter how small." Straightening my arm in front of him, I turn my palm up toward the mirror. "Now you'll never be alone."

He looks at our reflection and his gaze follows my arm to see I've lined my tattoo up with the Solus on his waist. His throat bobs as he drops the towel to trace his finger up my forearm and along the Never script.

Turning in my arms, he captures my face and presses his lips to mine, murmuring, "Are you trying to wreck me?"

I squeeze his waist and press my naked chest to his, teasing against his lips, "I'm just kissing you."

He spears his fingers into my hair, his voice gruff. "I'm never letting you go."

"Hold tight," I whisper, loving that we've come to

an understanding about us. No matter what our past relationships were, *we're* together and that's all that matters.

Sliding a hand down my back, Calder palms my ass and pulls me fully against his erection, deepening our kiss. The moment I reach up and wrap my arms around his neck, he groans and swiftly lifts me in his arms, carrying me into the bedroom.

When he lowers me to the bed and presses a tender kiss to my forehead, whispering, "Get some sleep, angel," my heart jerks. Sitting up, I grip his hand as he starts to walk away. "Where are you going?"

Calder lifts my fingers to his mouth, his gaze full of hunger and regret. "It's almost dawn. I need to get back to my room."

I clamp my fingers around his, not wanting to let him go. "But…"

He slides a simmering gaze over my chest, then glances toward the ceiling, exhaling harshly. Returning his attention to me, he hooks his finger under my chin. "The way I want you won't be soft, angel. I'll be insatiable and relentless." My lips part on a breath of aroused excitement, and a wicked smirk crooks his lips as he runs his thumb down my chin. "I want to fuck you very much, but in my own space, not someone else's."

Without another word, he turns toward the bathroom and disappears into the linen closet.

CHAPTER FOURTEEN

Cass

*M*y phone beeping with a text wakes me just two hours after I fell into a fitful sleep. All I could think about was Calder. My head throbbing, I rub my eyes and glance outside to see early morning fog is still in the air. Grabbing my phone from the nightstand, I unplug it from a charger I found in Celeste's desk.

As I click on Talia's message, I see that Calder sent me a text an hour ago.

Talia: Go outside in twenty minutes.

I blink to wake myself up and respond to her text.

Me: What's happening in twenty minutes?

Talia: You'll have a visitor.
Me: Who's up at this ungodly hour? Do you have any news?
Talia: Ha, I'm texting you from my warm bed. You'll see. No news yet. See you tonight.

I click on Calder's message expecting something personal after last night.

Calder: Get out of going to the shooting range.

He doesn't ask. He commands. As much as I want to balk at being ordered around, it's probably for the best if I cancel. After I send him a message that I'll take care of it, I quickly jump up and finger-comb my bedhead hair, then rush into the bathroom to brush my teeth. Sliding into a pair of jeans, sneakers, and a coat, I quietly open my door and walk down the stairs. I'm thankful no one's around, but when I see Beatrice instructing a younger housemaid how to mop the front entrance hallway properly, I turn and head for the side entrance that leads into the garden.

According to my phone, I have more time than I thought, but instead of going back inside, I decide to take the long way around the massive house to get to the driveway. As I follow the stone pathway and avoid patches of ice that haven't thawed yet, I turn the corner from the back side of the house and hear people talking ahead of me near the separate garage.

Ugh, I'm a mess. What if it's someone important? I'll never hear the end of how I embarrassed Celeste from Beth.

I quickly step behind a tall juniper and Calder's voice reaches my ears. "Thanks. I owe you."

I frown and peer through the evergreen. The girl from last night, Alana, is wearing tight, ripped skinny jeans, a moto-jacket and matching boots. Her black hair is down around her shoulders, but this time the tips of her bangs are a deep red color that matches her lips. She's fucking hot as hell.

"You're welcome," she purrs. Rubbing her fingerless-gloved hands together, she lifts a perfectly sculpted eyebrow. "So...does this mean you'll reconsider?"

Calder snorts and shoves his hands in his jeans. "Of course you *would* go right for that."

She releases a low, sexy laugh as she runs her finger along his jawline. Tilting his head, she eyes him appreciatively. "Yeah, I'm thinking just the barest of profile."

Disliking her I-just-woke-up husky voice intensely, I set my jaw and glance down at my phone as it buzzes in my hand.

Talia: Are you there?

Crap. I need to get to the driveway.

Me: Coming. Got delayed.

Turning, I run back the way I came until I reach the driveway.

As I jog up, Mina steps out of her car and shuts the door. Shifting the white gift bag from one hand to the other, she pushes her blonde hair over her shoulder and smiles. "Hey, Celeste. I just thought I'd pop by and see how you're doing."

Breathing heavily, I wave to her little girl, Josi, still in her car seat. "Hey, Mina. It's good to see you."

Mina's brown eyes widen with concern and she glances around to see if anyone's about. "Are you all right, Cass?"

Swallowing, I take a breath and nod. "I'm fine. I went for a walk and lost track of time. I had to run to get back here to meet you."

Relief flickers across her face. "You've got us so worried." Glancing down at the bag in her hand, she continues, "Oh, this is for you from Talia…and me. Don't open it until you get to your room."

I take the bag from her and smile my appreciation. "Thank you for driving out here to check on me and for the gift."

She nods and starts to say something when a motorcycle cranks from the side of the house. A second later, the person zooms up the driveway.

"Who was that?"

I see the black helmet first, then the ripped jeans and moto-boots, but the vanity license plate holds my rapt attention as the bike disappears up the driveway. INKART. My gaze narrows. "*That* answers a lot."

Mina's gaze slides back to me. "You um…don't sound happy."

"I'm fine, just tired." I force a smile and lift the bag up. "Thank you again for the gift and please remind Talia not to hug me when she sees me tonight."

"Got it." Mina waggles her fingers at Josie who's getting antsy in her car seat. Opening the car door, she shakes her head. "I don't know how you're doing this, Cass. I would've given myself away so many times."

"It's not easy," I say on a sigh. "But whether Celeste is missing or just hiding out, I hope to collect evidence tonight that points away from me as the first person the police might suspect in her disappearance."

"Good luck tonight. I truly hope Celeste is all right and this is her way of getting back at her father."

As I watch her get into her car and drive away, I murmur, "Me too, Mina."

Calder's just coming down the stairs at a brisk pace when I walk in. Marco turns on his way up the steps and walks back to the main floor, his gaze watching us like a hawk. Calder immediately walks over to me in the entryway, his tense expression relaxing. "You need to inform me when you leave your room, Miss Carver."

It's not fair that he appears to have had a full night's sleep, is freshly shaven and smells like sin, while I look like I've been on an all night bender. I start to inhale his appealing scent, but the INKART license plate pops into my head. I lift the bag up. "Mina dropped off something for me." *Maybe there's a miracle facelift in it.* "If you'll excuse me, I need to get a shower. I have an engagement to keep."

He falls into step beside me, a frown creasing his brow.

"What engagement? I'm not aware of anything on your itinerary until this evening."

I glance his way as I take the steps. "Ben's taking me shooting today. He's picking me up around ten, so I want to be ready."

"Miss Carver," Marco calls out and waits for me to pause. "I was on my way to inform you that there is a breakfast meeting in the dining room in fifteen minutes to discuss tonight's event."

When he grins as if knowing I'll be rushing through a shower to make the meeting with such short notice, I press my lips together in annoyance and continue up the stairs.

Calder follows silently until I reach for my door's handle. "You said you were going to take care of it."

His tone is low but tense. I glance at him and lift my shoulders. "I decided it's best to keep things real and in the present. You should know all about that."

"Meaning?" he asks, scowling.

I step into my room and turn to face him. "Considering that you conveniently left out the part that your *old friend*, Alana, is your tattoo artist, your argument of what constitutes innocent gestures is full of shit."

"No, it was on point. My argument was about *intent* and it still stands." His green gaze sharpens. "I strongly recommend that you cancel."

"Oh well, in that case, I *intend* to learn to shoot today. And I *strongly* recommend that you stay outside the building." Shutting the door in his face, I lock it and head straight for the bathroom.

I set the bag on the counter and pull it open, hoping for something to put me in a better mood. When I pull out two sets of super sexy bras and underwear, one black and one ruby red, both made of lace and barely there scraps of silk, I let out an ironic snort and retrieve the note Talia had put in the bottom of the bag.

A couple pairs of brand new underwear for you; they're both functional and impractical. I highly recommend you enjoy the impractical part.

I quickly step into the short hallway that leads into the dining room. I'm five minutes late and I can already hear Gregory and Phillip having a debate over something, but the sight of Jake leaning against the wall partway down the hall as he talks on the phone, brings me to a fast halt. *What's he doing here?* He hasn't seen me yet. I could go back the way I came and feign feeling suddenly ill.

I straighten and start down the hall, reminding myself that he's attending the event tonight. He has a reason to be here. Presumably this breakfast is where he'll get assigned people to schmooze during the event on Gregory's behalf.

Just as I pass him, Jake hangs up and says quietly, "Morning, Celeste."

"Morning," I say over my shoulder.

"Hold up a sec."

I move closer to the wall and wait for him.

Jake pushes back his rolled up shirtsleeves, then runs

his hand in his short blond hair. "I wanted to apologize for my attitude the other night."

"It's fine, Jake." I shrug and start to walk forward when he grabs my arm and hauls me backward.

He grips my face and pushes me against the wall, sneering in a low voice, "Was this your plan all along? Did you really think all it took was this to replace her?"

My throat nearly closes in fear, but I quickly shake my head and claw at his grip. "What are you talking about? Let go of me!"

His hazel eyes constrict and his fingers squeeze tighter. "You must've hated that Dad chose Ben over me. You could've finally had me all to yourself."

How does he know I'm not Celeste? Did his father tell him? His sheer arrogance makes me abandon my pretense. I pull my face from his hold and drill him with a hard stare. "Are you *that* delusional to think I've carried a torch for you all this time? You ruined my life and destroyed my self-worth. I despise the sight of you."

"Really?" He tightens his grip on my arm, the angry slant of his mouth curving into a knowing smile as he moves closer. "That's not how you acted at the club. That wasn't you *despising* me, Cass. I know different. To be clear...*you* were just a stand-in for me, and that's all you'll ever be."

He really isn't hearing me. "And you're just a selfish, molesting prick. And that's all you'll ever be."

Jake snorts and shakes his head. "Ben is so clueless. I don't know why Gregory and Dad are asking you to continue masquerading as her. She's *never* coming back."

As pissed as I am right now, his comment stops my racing heart. *Does he know something about Celeste?* "How do you know that?"

"Because she *always* belonged to me." His tone turns sharp once more and he squeezes my arm painfully. "You need to stop this bullshit."

"What is *wrong* with you?" Beth says as she approaches. Yanking Jake's hand off my arm, she looks at him like he's lost his mind, then glances at me, concern in her gaze. "Are you okay?"

I nod and rub my arm as she cuts an angry gaze his way. "Get over losing to your brother. If I see you treating my sister disrespectfully again, you'll be banned from our house permanently."

Jake opens his mouth to say something, then shakes his head and mumbles, "Sorry," and walks away.

The second he turns into the dining room, Beth exhales and shakes her head. "I guess he's taking losing Celeste to his brother a lot harder than anyone thought. Speaking of which, Calder and Ben are in the foyer having a tense conversation as to whether or not you should go to the shooting range."

The need to claw at my wrists is worming its way through me. I blink to focus on what she just said. "Ben and Calder? *Ugh.*"

Beth nods, her curled hair bouncing against her light blue sweater. "I think you should go. Jake needs to cool off. I'll cover for you with my father and fill you in on your duties for the night when you get back."

Nodding my appreciation, I leave the hallway and head straight for the foyer.

Calder and Ben are facing off, nearly nose to nose. Ben is clearly annoyed. "You don't dictate her itinerary. The appointment is set. I've arranged everything."

Calder folds his arms, an unruffled look on his face. "Today, I do. She's not going. Cancel it."

Feeling like I might explode, I stalk right past both of them and fling open the door, calling behind me, "Let's go, Ben. Today is a *great* day to learn to shoot."

Ben steps outside, gesturing to my jeans and lightweight sweater as I head toward his Audi sitting in the drive. "The snow might be gone, but it's freezing. Don't you want to grab a coat?"

"Do you have an extra in your car?"

He flashes a wide smile and steps forward to open the car's door for me. "I have one in the backseat."

Nodding, I lean on the door and turn to see Calder standing on the other side, his jaw muscle tense. "We'll wait for you, so you can follow us there." I pull my cell phone out to show him I have it with me, then let Ben close the door behind me.

"You ah, seem to be in a mood," Ben says once he pulls onto the Parkway to head into the city.

"Do I?" I say, thrumming my fingers on my phone.

Calder: You'd better fucking have underwear on under those jeans.

I glance in the side mirror and see Calder's black Dodge Charger right behind us.

Me: Stop texting while driving.
Calder: Voice text. Answer the question.

I'm wearing my new underwear, but I shut my phone off. In the mood I'm in...I'll be tempted to antagonize him and that won't be good for anyone.

Ben looks at me, a half smile tilting his lips. "Want to talk about it?"

I rub my sore arm and shake my head. "Not really."

His dark eyebrow hikes. "You'd rather just shoot at a target instead?"

I nod, hoping shooting will release the tension. "Pretty much."

"Never say I don't provide the best entertainment," he says, chuckling.

The rest of the way there, I stay lost in my own thoughts. I never once thought Jake could hurt Celeste, but based on what he said earlier...I'm beginning to wonder. He seemed pretty certain she wasn't coming back. One thing is for sure; he was furious over Ben and Celeste's engagement. Even though he apologized to his brother later...did he do that because he'd already taken his anger out on Celeste? I still believe that Phillip is the baby's father and could have his own motive for hurting Celeste if she planned to abort his baby. But it's possible that Jake had something to do with her disappearance instead of Phillip. As far as I'm concerned, both men should be investigated.

What I don't get is why Jake didn't correct Beth for calling me her sister and defending me. If his father told him I wasn't Celeste, he would've also told Jake that Beth knows the truth too. Jake obviously knows I'm standing in until she returns, so the fact he let Beth rail at him like I really am Celeste bothers me. It doesn't make any sense. Ben is obviously still in the dark. Poor Ben. I glance his way, feeling the beginnings of guilt creep into my chest. He doesn't deserve this deception. *Should I tell him?* I bite my lip in indecision, unsure what to do.

When Ben pulls into the parking lot, I shove my conflicting thoughts to the back of my mind and eye the building. It's not as big as I expected it to be. "What's this place like on the inside? Is there plenty of room?"

"The target area obviously has depth, but there's not much room in the shooting area. Only a handful of people can shoot at a time. I had to get special permission to be able to instruct you, but since I've taught classes there in the past, they allowed it. They let me store my practice guns there, so we'll use those."

"Sounds good." Turning my phone on, I send Calder a message.

> Me: *Stay outside. You won't be allowed back there with me anyway.*
> Calder: *Not a good plan.*
> Me: *I'll be fine.*

Before he can argue, I step out of the car.

Ben comes around the backside of his car and holds his fleece jacket out for me. "Some people feel it's a little bit chilly in there, so you'll want to put this on."

Calder approaches as Ben hooks the zipper on his coat and zips it all the way to my neck. "This will keep the hot brass from flying into your cleavage." When my eyes widen, he smiles and touches my chin. "Trust me. Keep this zipped. I've seen it happen."

"I'll escort you in." Calder's tone is clipped. I don't have to look his way to know he's ticked.

Once the older man at the front desk checks Ben and me in, he holds his hand up when Calder tries to follow us toward the door. "Sorry, young man, but you'll have to wait here or outside. Only those with appointments are allowed in."

"Then make me an appointment," Calder counters, frowning.

The man shakes his silver head and points to the register book on the desk. "Sorry, but we're all booked up for the hour. And as you can see there's a group coming in right behind this one. You'll just have to do as I said and wait here."

Calder cuts an accusing gaze to Ben, beyond displeased. "We'll be out in an hour," I say to relieve the tension in the room. Once Ben passes through the door, I glance back at Calder and respond to his fierce look. "*Yes*, for Pete's sake."

Ben opens a locked cage and pulls out a gun case, then

sets a rifle and a semi-automatic handgun on the counter. "Pick your weapon, then I'll go over the safety aspects with you."

When I choose the twenty-two rifle, his eyebrow hikes. "Okay then, Annie," he says, chuckling. "Let's go over where the safety is and how to load the weapon."

After a fifteen-minute tutorial on all the safety aspects I should know about handling a rifle, Ben disappears, then returns from the main office. "Turn around for a sec."

I do as he asks and jump when he grasps my hair and pulls it away from my face in a ponytail. "What are you doing?" I ask, feeling the pull of a rubber band being wound around my hair.

"You can't wear your hair down around guns." He finishes up the ponytail and leans close, squeezing my shoulders. "There's too much chance it'll get caught on something."

Just as I turn my head to thank him for bringing me, he presses his lips to my cheek. "You're welcome. And now you can go let off some steam." Handing me a pair of safety glasses, earplugs and sound-suppressing earmuffs, Ben puts on his own safety gear, then carries both guns as he takes me into the target range area.

I'm instantly appreciative of the ear protection the moment we walk in. Several people are shooting and the sound would be deafening without it.

Setting his handgun down on the small shelf space next to mine, Ben stands behind me and shows me how to hold the weapon. "Put the butt of the rifle here against your shoulder and bend slightly like this so you can line your sights up with the target. Be prepared for the kickback as you shoot."

Once he hooks up a paper target and winds it two-thirds the length of the shooting area, he lightly lays his hand on the back of the shoulder that I have the gun resting against. "Now pull the trigger and see what you think."

I lift the rifle and rest my cheek against it, lining the sights up like he told me to. Taking a breath, I pull the trigger. The kickback is surprising and I'm glad for his hand supporting my shoulder.

"Now pull the bolt to release the casing, then put it back to load the next bullet."

The hot casing flies out and pings on the shelf in front of me as I reload. After a couple more shots, I get used to the kickback.

Nodding his approval, Ben releases his hold on my shoulder and points to the bulls-eye target. "Not bad for your first few tries. The goal is to get your shots within a four-inch grouping. If it helps, try to picture whatever is frustrating you and blow holes right through it."

This time I lean into the shot and really focus on the target. I don't feel an ounce of guilt that I'm picturing Jake's face dead center on the paper as I let loose and fire at will.

Ben grins and moves over to his station. I pause to watch him lift his gun and shoot. His movements are smooth and confident as he pops off eight rounds in a tight grouping on the target in the farthest position possible in the shooting area.

I smile and give him a thumbs up, appreciating his point-blank accuracy, then we both spend the next half hour unloading rounds into different targets.

When we've used all our ammo, I realize that my wrists don't itch and the raging tension inside me is gone. I smile at Ben as we put our gear away. "That was a blast. Seriously, thank you for bringing me."

He grins and hoops his arm around my neck as we head out of the room, but we stop short when a group of seven guys walk in with all their gun cases. Swiveling me around, he says, "That'll be crowded for a bit. Let's leave the back way and swing around."

I nod my agreement and follow him out the back exit. As we step outside, my stomach growls loudly, practically echoing in the quiet alley. My face heats.

Releasing me, Ben glances down at my belly, then meets my gaze, amused. "Are you hungry?"

I give a wry smile. "I skipped breakfast since you came early."

"Now I feel bad," he says, then his eyes light up. "Ah, there's an awesome coffee and hot chocolate stand just a couple blocks from here. They have the best scones I've ever had."

Clasping my hand, he tugs me along. "Come on. We can walk from here."

I pull back, suddenly aware we'll be leaving Calder behind. "Let's drive there."

He shakes his head and drags me forward, turning

down a connected alleyway behind another building. "Vi's Café stand is a couple blocks away if we cut through an alley or two. On the road it's five blocks. It'll be nice to have some alone time for a bit. Don't worry. We'll be back before they miss us."

As we pass a couple homeless people who've pulled old newspapers up to cover themselves from the cold, I think about my promise to Calder that I wouldn't go anywhere without him. We turn the corner and the sound of a glass bottle rolling in the alley behind us makes me jump, glancing back. When Ben's hand tightens on mine and he tugs me closer, my heart begins to race.

I don't think Ben would lead me away from protection with the intent to hurt me, but I can't say the same about others. The sound of crunching gravel around the corner has me pulling my cell phone from my back pocket and surreptitiously typing Calder a message that we went to get scones at Vi's Café stand. Hitting send, I slide the phone back into my pocket.

I'm ready for a coffee the moment we reach the stand. Ben hands me a steaming cup and then a huge blueberry scone. "Try it. You'll never eat scones anywhere else."

While we stand off to the side and use the shelter of the roof to block the cool wind, I scarf down my scone in record time.

Ben laughs and hands me his. "Are you still hungry?"

I hold my coffee cup with two hands to warm them and take a quick sip before shaking my head. "No, but you were right. It was the best scone I've ever had, and that's not just the hunger talking."

The wind ruffles his short dark hair and his eyes light with amusement. "Told you," he says after he finishes off his scone. "So, do you think you'd like to go back to the shooting range again, maybe later this week? Next time you can learn to shoot a handgun if you want."

I hesitate. It feels wrong to make future plans with him, because it'll be based on my preferences, not Celeste's. "Why don't we wait until later in the week to make an appointment?"

His expectant expression falters, but he quickly nods to hide his disappointment just as his phone rings. "Sure, we can do that. Sorry, I need to answer this," he says and pulls his phone out of his coat pocket.

Now I feel bad. He's trying to forge a connection and find a common ground with Celeste. I put my hand over his before he can answer his phone. "I really enjoyed it, Ben. Honest."

He smiles and his brown eyes warm as he lifts the cell to his ear. "Hello?"

Glancing at me, his smile broadens. "That's fantastic! Thank you so much for your help with the funding. I believe this pilot program can do a world of good for the vets." He pauses and nods. "Yes, the hospital approved space yesterday."

While Ben discusses a few more things with the person about the outreach program, the tiny hairs on my neck rise. I quickly glance around the busy street to see if anyone is staring at us, but everyone continues to bustle past, oblivious to others around them.

Ben hangs up, his eyes dancing with excitement as he clasps my shoulders. "I've been working on getting this program approved for eighteen months. I can't believe it's finally coming together."

I smile. "That's wonderful, Ben."

He yanks me into a tight hug and spins me in a circle. "You have no idea. There were times when I thought it was going to fall through."

I laugh at his exuberance and hug him back "Congratulations on the success."

"This is such great news." Setting me down, he quickly cups my cheek and presses his mouth to mine.

I'm so shocked by his unexpected kiss, I freeze, unsure how to react. Calder's tight voice right behind us jars me into action, and I pull back. "*Miss Carver*, you're being summoned home. Let's go."

Ben clasps my hand and turns to face Calder. "I'll take her."

Calder slides his phone into the pocket of his leather jacket as he tilts his chin toward his car pulled up to the curb. "Mr. Carver's instructions were quite clear. He wants his daughter home immediately. No delays."

My nerves are hopping inside me like jumping beans. I release Ben's hand. "It's okay, Ben. I should go." Shrugging out of his jacket, I hand it to him. "Thank you for taking me shooting and for the *best* scone."

As I step toward the Charger, Ben follows, tucking his jacket over his arm. "I really wish I hadn't agreed to take my friend's shift."

"You'll be missed tonight." I get in the car and push the button to roll down the window. "Now go save some lives."

Just as Ben reaches for my hand, Calder presses on the gas and pulls away from the curb.

"Calder! You could of taken the guy's hand off."

"That's the least of what I could've taken off," he snaps without glancing my way.

I close my eyes and exhale. While I wait for him to speak, my head starts to throb. I blame tension and lack of sleep, but when Calder doesn't say another word the entire time, I finally break the silence as he takes the exit. "What does Gregory want?"

"Nothing."

I gape at him. "You lied?"

He continues to stare straight ahead as he turns a corner and pulls up to the Carver estate gates. "It was either that or deck the prick."

"That wasn't what it looked like, Calder," I mutter.

"What does *not* kissing him look like?" he growls, his hands tightening on the steering wheel as we start up the long driveway toward the house.

I tense at his accusing tone. "*He* kissed me. You just happened to pull up at the worst possible time."

The car slams to a halt, furious green eyes snapping to me. "Because there would've been a better time to see him put his fucking tongue down your throat?"

"*I* didn't kiss him back," I say before I open the door

and get out. Slamming it shut, I start walking. He's angry. I get it. I wasn't happy that he met with Alana early this morning, but the difference is they *have* a history, one that she appears to want to rekindle. I have no history with Ben, nor do I plan on it. Big difference.

Calder's car idles beside me. "Get in the car, Cass," he says tightly through the open window.

I fold my arms around myself to stay warm and keep walking. "Can we not fight right now? I don't have the brain capacity for it. I need to take a nap or I won't be able to function this evening."

He rolls the car along and sighs. "Get in the car. I want to fill you in on what Bash told me."

The case will only get solved if we work it, so I open the door and get in.

Calder pushes on the gas. "Elijah was able to hack into the GPS on Phillip's car. He was on the same stretch of highway as Celeste that night."

"That's good, right? It's tangible evidence that proves he went looking for Celeste and probably found her."

Calder shakes his head. "It places him in the vicinity but not with her. He could claim an entirely different reason for being on that road at that time and say he had no knowledge of Celeste being there. I agree with you that proving he is the father would go a long way in giving the police more ways to connect him to Celeste, especially as far as motive goes."

I rub my temples, trying to ward off an impending headache. I can feel it just behind my eyes. "But will that be enough if we can't prove he's the Deceiver? The threat in his text was pretty damning."

Calder nods. "It should give the police another person of interest."

We're quiet once we reach the house. When Calder cuts the engine, I share what happened before I left the house. "Jake knows I'm not Celeste."

He cuts his gaze my way, on full alert. "What did he say?"

I can't lie to Calder, not about something this important, but I stick to the present issues. "He wasn't happy that I'm pretending to be Celeste. He thinks his father and Phillip are crazy to ask me to stand in for her."

"Did he threaten you?" he asks, his eyes narrowing.

I'm unsure how to answer. Jake grabbed me, but he didn't threaten me with violence. His way is more psychologically twisted, so I decide to hedge my response. "Beth saw him getting agitated and straightened him out."

He scans my face. "What aren't you telling me?"

I shrug and shake my head. "I thought it was strange that he didn't tell Beth he knew I wasn't Celeste after she yelled at him for giving her sister a hard time over the engagement decision. Then again, the Carver/Hemming family dynamic isn't the most normal one. I still can't figure out why Phillip would tell Jake about me, but not Ben."

Calder's jaw muscle tightens. "Are you sure Ben doesn't already know?"

I shake my head. "Why would Ben keep up the

pretense with me today? No, he doesn't know. But what I do find weird is...that for someone who seems obsessed with Celeste, Jake acted oddly calm and accepting of her disappearance."

Calder clenches his hand around his keys. "Do you think Jake is the one who hurt Celeste? All because he didn't win her in their families' antiquated engagement agreement?"

The fury simmering in his gaze reminds me that when it comes to Celeste being wronged in any way, Calder is definitely affected. "I have no idea, but I think it's a good idea to try to get Jake's DNA tonight too. Once we have both men's DNA, then Sebastian's lab person can run the paternity tests."

Calder rubs his fingers along his nose and shakes his head. "That's not going to work. According to the lab guy, he did determine that Celeste's DNA matches the blood the police retrieved, but he'll need a pure sample of her blood for the paternity test. It rained some that night, and since the car door was left open, the blood isn't the best sample to work with for determining paternity. Apparently the baby's DNA in the mother's blood is much harder to determine with a degraded sample."

"I guess that means I'll need to convince Beth to release a portion of the blood Celeste left behind at that clinic," I say, sighing at the thought.

"If it's for Celeste, she'll help."

I grimace. "Beth's pretty much in the 'don't trust Cass' camp right now, but I'll try."

When I start to get out of the car, Calder's warm hand covers mine on the seat. "Alana was only here because she was doing me a favor, Cass."

I raise my eyebrow. "She wants more, Calder. And if you can't see that, then you're blind."

When I try to slide my hand free, he applies pressure. "It only matters if it's reciprocated."

Just the feel of his hand on mine makes my pulse race. "I basically said the same thing about Ben. You didn't seem to care."

He starts to slide his thumb over my hand, but stops to turn the diamond on my finger completely around and out of sight. Intense green eyes flick back to mine. "I don't want him kissing you, let alone thinking for one fucking second that anything else is going to happen."

"He took me by surprise, Calder. I didn't encourage it."

"I laid awake last night with an erection from hell, because I couldn't stop thinking about how fucking good you taste." His hand closes fully around mine. "I want this bullshit done and over. No more guys thinking you're theirs, no more lies and subterfuge. No more pretending. Just me branding myself on every inch of you."

I'm so turned on by his seductive promise, my lips instinctively part and my breath stalls. It's not fair that he has such a strong affect over me when I don't know where we're going. Maybe one day he'll share the things he's holding back. Until then, I can deal with him keeping a few secrets, since I have some of my own, but that doesn't change the fact he obviously has commitment issues. Not that I'm ready to walk down the aisle, but knowing upfront that that particular path is one he never plans to take is a double-edged sword jammed between us. No matter which direction I turn, I'm going to get cut.

As I stare at the sinfully primal look on his face, with any other guy I would be all about a down-and-dirty fling, but with Calder I want more. Owning my body isn't the same as owning my soul. I want him to covet *both*. No...I want him to demand it.

"After this branding, then what?" I say, raising my eyebrows.

Calder starts to lift his hand to my face, but remembers where we are and lowers it back to the seat. "My life won't truly be my own until the EUC is taken down. After that, you'll have my undivided attention."

I respect his sense of duty to complete what he started, but it worries me that he'll be putting himself in harm's way. Right now, I have no place in his life that would give me the right to ask him not to continue with the EUC, and it appears he intends to keep things that way. I know he's just being honest, but it's frustrating knowing he plans to keep his distance. That's not how being in someone's life works. You don't get to opt out just because the relationship is distracting or taking up too much time. I refuse to put my feelings on hiatus for an unspecified amount of time. With Calder I *want* to try the all-in thing, but if he's going to compartmentalize us to that extreme, then I don't think he's ready for a relationship, let alone anything permanent.

Wrapping self-preservation around me like a thick winter coat, I open the car door. "Thanks for being honest. It's almost over, Calder, and then you can get back to training and the EUC. We just need to get through tonight. Now I must go take a nap before my head explodes."

"Wait—"

I shut the door and walk inside, then head straight for Celeste's bedroom.

CHAPTER FIFTEEN

Calder

*W*hat *the hell just happened?* I stare after Cass, watching her walk to the front door, my jaw tight. I'm pretty sure I just got the brush off, but for the life of me, I don't know what I said that made her fold those damn walls back around herself. Wrapping my hands around the steering wheel to keep from punching something, I mentally go over our conversation.

Does she think that training for the EUC is all I care about? Fucking hell, that couldn't be farther from the truth, but I need to get this done so I can move on.

I start to open the car door and go after her when my phone rings.

Shutting the door, I quickly answer. "How the hell do you deal with a woman's brain? I swear it's like walking in a minefield with skis on."

Bash snorts. "I take it you and Cass are having issues?"

I shake my head and stare at the front door she just closed behind her. "Maybe it's the pressure she's under pretending to be Celeste that's getting to her, but honestly, Bash, I don't have a fucking clue. All I said was that my life won't be my own until the EUC thing is done and over."

When Bash barks out a laugh, I scowl. "What's wrong with that? I'm trying to protect her. I don't want her anywhere near the gym or the EUC event. These guys are dangerous. Right now the EUC doesn't know that Cass is in my life, and I want to keep it that way. I don't want to give them any leverage over me, and I would never forgive myself if anyone hurt Cass because of this MMA stuff."

"Your intentions might be honorable, but that's not how she sees it."

I scrub my hand over my jawline. "Oh yeah? Then enlighten me, oh pussy-whipped one."

"Bite me. I'm not the one asking *you* for relationship advice."

"Why *did* you call?" I snap, annoyed that he's right.

"To let you know that Mina's coming tonight."

"I don't think that's a good idea. The Blakes have never been close with the Carvers. Too many of you suddenly showing up might look suspicious, especially with another Blake they definitely don't trust staying in their house right now."

"Mina is needed."

"And why is that?"

"Because drinking glasses are an excellent DNA source."

"Not quite seeing the connection. And napkins are just as good a source."

"I agree that napkins would be easier to swipe and conceal, except not every person uses them. But almost everyone holds a drink at some point while standing around chatting. A glass will easily fit into a woman's purse. Cass sent Talia a note that she's planning to collect two samples, hence Mina's presence."

I dig my fingers through my hair, tension riding my shoulders. "Fine, but make sure to drill everyone so they don't give Cass away, especially Damien."

"We're prepared. You don't have to worry about Damien. He has no clue she's not Celeste or what we're doing tonight. He just thinks I'm suddenly interested in politics."

I exhale my annoyance that he hasn't told his brother. I know it's because they aren't very close, but that just means Damien will be insufferably irritating. He's never forgotten that I stole "Celeste" from him at that party. "I guess we're good to go."

"Not quite. Do you want my advice or are you going to continue being an ass?"

"You're going to tell me anyway."

"Damn straight I am. Cass means the world to Talia, so listen. When you said that your life isn't your own until the EUC is taken down, you were telling Cass that she's not a priority to you."

I grip the phone tight. "That's bullshit. I never said that."

Bash chuckles. "When it comes to women, it's not always what you say, but what you don't say that matters. Trust me on this, Cald. We're both men of few words, so the ones we do say count for a fucking lot. Got it?"

Well shit. I thought she knew why I needed to keep my distance while I'm still part of the EUC, but maybe Bash's right. "I hear you," I grumble. "See you tonight."

Hanging up with Bash, I send Cass a text.

Calder: Call me when you wake up.

CHAPTER SIXTEEN

Cass

I wake with a start, wondering why Beth is leaning over me, her hand pressed to my forehead.

"Are you okay?" Her brow furrows as she pulls her hand back. "You've been asleep for hours."

"I have?" I groggily blink at the clock on the nightstand, then turn wide eyes her way. "Is it really almost five?"

Beth nods. "Calder sent me in here when you didn't respond to texts or knocking."

I quickly glance at the door. "He knocked? Man, I was out."

Holding out a small plate with a sandwich cut in fourths, she says, "I brought you something to eat since you skipped lunch. The event starts in a little over an hour. I thought I'd fill you in on the meeting this morning while

I help you get dressed."

I push back the covers and take the plate. "Thank you for the food, but I think I can put on the dress you picked out by myself."

Beth purses her lips and walks over to where I've hung the mid-thigh length black dress with a scooped neckline on the top of the wardrobe door. Lifting the long sleeve up, she raises an eyebrow. "These won't hide your tattoos."

I set the plate on the desk and walk over to lift the other sleeve up. She's right. My tattoos will show through the thin material. I'm surprised she noticed my tattoos. She must've seen them while I was trying on dresses. I release the sleeve to look at her. "Why did you pick this out if you knew that I had tattoos?"

"Because it's one of Celeste's favorites and..." She shrugs and lifts a cosmetic tin out of a small wicker basket she'd set on the desk. "Because I have this."

"What's that?"

"It's a waterproof concealer. This stuff won't come off without using baby oil and soap in the shower, so once I put it on it's not coming off no matter how much you rub it." Beth sets the tin down and pulls out the chair. "Have a seat and roll your sleeves up."

I do as she asks, my heart suddenly heavy. Beth is in a friendly, upbeat mood. Either she is in complete denial or Phillip didn't share that his lab person determined the DNA in Celeste's hair did match the blood found in that abandoned car.

While Beth taps the triangular sponge into the

concealer, I take a bite of my sandwich and casually say, "So fill me in on breakfast."

She glances up, her eyebrows pulling together. "Why did you tell Jake who you really are? I thought he was angry at Celeste about the engagement, but once we sat down for breakfast it became clear he was furious at my father and Phillip for having you fill in as Celeste. No matter how angry he was, I still can't believe he attacked a total stranger."

I swallow the bite of food and clear my throat, hoping she doesn't focus too closely on that part. "I didn't tell him. I thought Phillip did, though I couldn't figure out why he would."

"No, it wasn't his dad. I wonder who told him?" Beth snorts and shakes her head.

Marco. He had to be the one who told Jake. I scarf down the rest of the quarter piece of bread, chewing hard. That asshole knew Jake would more than likely take it out on me.

"Phillip was highly annoyed that Jake had discovered the truth." Beth's comment pulls me out of my own head and back into our conversation. "He insisted that Jake not tell Ben, saying that he'd recently discovered another place to look for Celeste buried in an old email on her computer. He's hoping one of these will lead him to her." While dabbing the makeup along the swirls on the outer edges of my Never tattoo, Beth rambles on. "Father said he was done waiting for answers. He's going to accompany Phillip tomorrow to a resort in the Catskills—that was the place Phillip hadn't checked out yet. Jake jumped up all angry, telling our fathers that they wouldn't find her, that she was gone for good. I wanted to choke him for making me think of Celeste pregnant and out there on her own, possibly hurt or worse. It took me all day to force that image out of my head. I have to believe she's all right."

"Hopefully she is. You didn't say anything about her pregnancy, did you?" I ask, worry gripping me. Phillip cannot learn that a vial of Celeste's blood exists.

Beth shakes her head as she finishes covering the Never tattoo. "No, my father and Phillip went into plan mode. They're leaving first thing tomorrow morning."

When she lifts the sponge and then adds some kind of special powder to my forearm to set the makeup, I eat another quarter of the sandwich and stare at my bare skin. It looks so weird without the Never there. *If only it were that easy to erase my past.*

"I'm done waiting too. If my father and Phillip strike out in the Catskills tomorrow, the moment they get back I'm telling them about her pregnancy and insisting that we call the police."

Beth's adamant comment snags my full attention. *I have to convince her to help us get a sample of Celeste's blood from the clinic before Phillip learns of its existence.* I could pretend to be Celeste and call the clinic myself, but I think Beth should ask. At least then, someone from Celeste's family will be giving legal permission.

"That's probably for the best." I nod my agreement. "Did Phillip say if he heard back from his lab person yet?"

"Yeah." She moves the sponge back to the tin and dabs more on the applicator. "He said that the guy ran into issues with the sample and is rerunning the test."

God, the manipulative man is flat out lying to all of them. I want so badly to tell Beth to stop believing *anything* Phillip says, but my warning will just freak her out. While there's still hope that Celeste could possibly be found and with no proof to say otherwise, I keep my thoughts to myself. Phillip's subterfuge makes me more determined than ever to get his DNA, but I still need Beth's help to get a sample of Celeste's blood.

If I tell Beth the real reason I need a sample, she probably won't be able to keep her cool in front of Phillip until the results come back. As much as I think he's a self-serving asshole, I don't want to accuse him of something that I can't prove. So what seemingly valid reason can I give her for requesting a sample of Celeste's blood?

A valid reason...ah, *that's it*. "Beth—" I instinctively pull back when she runs the sponge across my wrist.

Sincere regret shines in her green eyes as she reaches for my wrist once more. "I'm sorry. Did that hurt? Are those scars I felt under your tattoo painful?"

I stare at the makeup half-smeared over the raven and branch on my wrist and my heart twists. It's like my sister is being erased too. It's just temporary, I tell myself. *If this helps us help Celeste, then I can handle one evening without you, Sophie.*

Shaking my head, I push my hand back into her outstretched one. "Sorry. It was an instinctive reaction.

That tattoo means a lot to me. It doesn't hurt."

"The makeup won't mess up your tattoos," Beth reassures while using a softer touch with the sponge on my wrist. "You started to say something?"

As she works on my wrist, her head bent in concentration on her task, I say, "I'd like your permission to retrieve a sample of Celeste's blood from that clinic to have it tested."

Beth straightens and tilts her head. "Why?"

"I want to make sure that, beyond the pregnancy, she's fine health-wise. When she asked me to help her, she looked stressed and tired. We can test her blood to confirm that nothing else was going on with her health that might be preventing her from contacting us. For all we know, she might be in a hospital somewhere under a Jane Doe."

"That's a good idea." Beth nods, her face brightening. "As far as I know, Phillip's been concentrating on checking all Celeste's vacation and spa retreats. I'll contact the clinic when we're done and approve the release of a sample." She pauses, her brow furrowed. "Who's going to retrieve it for testing?"

I exhale a quiet sigh of relief that she agreed. "I have a friend who can get the blood tested and have the results back to us by tomorrow. Just let the clinic know that Elijah will be stopping by today for a sample."

A few minutes later, Beth drops the sponge in the tin and smiles. "And voila! All covered."

I rub my fingers along my arm, surprised that the makeup doesn't come off. "You weren't kidding about this concealer. It's there for good."

Beth quickly puts her makeup away in the basket and stands, purpose in her expression. "I'm going to call the clinic now, but...just wait here for a sec."

She leaves the room before I can ask why. A minute later she returns to my room minus the basket, but obviously something else is hidden under her sweater. Shutting the door behind her, she keeps one arm wrapped around her waist, holding whatever is hidden in place.

I stand, my eyebrow raised. "What's that?"

"I believe you truly are trying to help find my sister." Beth grips my arm and tugs me over to sit down on the end of the bed with her. Biting her bottom lip, she continues as she pulls the book out from under her sweater. "Maybe you can help me figure out what this is saying..."

My eyes widen and I instinctively reach for the book. "You've had your sister's diary this whole time?"

Beth frowns, her grip tightening on the book. "You knew about it?"

I let my hand drop to my thigh. "I stumbled across it, yes. I was upset when I couldn't find it in the spot she kept it after she disappeared. I'd hoped that it would provide some clue as to where she might've gone."

Grunting her understanding, Beth pulls a bobby pin from her jean pocket at the same time she sets the diary on her knees. "I didn't want Phillip or anyone else pawing through Celeste's most private thoughts. The diary doesn't make any sense anyway. It's like she wrote it in prose-like code or something. I had no idea my sister had such a darkly poetic mind."

"Wait, Beth…" I quickly unhook Celeste's necklace and hold out the key to her. "Use this."

"Hiding in plain sight, huh? Clever of Celeste," she mutters as she takes it. "I can't believe you had the key this entire time."

I offer a slight smile. "Looks like we were both trying to protect her secrets."

Beth opens the diary and sets it in my lap. "Were you able to decipher what she was talking about?"

I clasp the edges of the book and flip through her earlier entries. "No, but one thing I did notice." Pausing on her July entry, I set it back on Beth's lap. "After this is when something changed for Celeste."

Beth stares at the blank entry, then pages back to the previous entry where Celeste talked about going to the beach. Flipping forward to the next one, she pages forward several more…and then more until she reaches the end. "What happened at the beach?" she whispers, disillusionment in her gaze.

I lift my shoulders, then let them fall. I don't want to say anything else right now, but I also want Beth to be at least a little prepared. "I don't know, but something obviously did."

Closing the book, Beth stares off into space. "She ran away right when we got back. I just thought she was having a hormonal tantrum."

I fold my hand over hers on the diary. "You were just a kid. You can't blame yourself."

"I had no idea she has been holding so much inside, but now it makes sense why we haven't been close for a while. I just wish..." She exhales a trembling breath and meets my gaze. "That I had known. I wouldn't have been so resentful and angry that she pretty much ignored me."

I squeeze her hand. "Me too."

Beth frowns. "What do you mean?"

Damn, I didn't mean to say that out loud. I stand and put some distance between us so she doesn't see too much in my eyes. "Just that I wish I had known Celeste a little better." As much pain as I have in my past because of Celeste pointing Jake in my direction, she's also the reason I met Calder. He and I still have issues to work through, but he's too important to me not to try. I just need to know he feels the same.

The guilt on Beth's face tugs at my heart. "Regret is a wasted thought process, Beth. It'll only hold you in place." Stepping back to the bed, I clasp her hand and pull her to her feet. "I find that forward-moving thoughts like 'lesson learned' and 'move the hell on' are far more productive."

Beth squeezes my hand and her lips curve into a smile of determination. "Thanks for that. I'm going to go call the clinic now. See you downstairs."

The moment Beth shuts the door, I immediately group text Talia and Calder.

Me: Talia, the clinic will be expecting Elijah to pick up Celeste's blood sample. Please send him asap. I hope Sebastian has someone ready

to take the sample and run the paternity test.
Also have them run another test on Celeste's
general health...that's what I told Beth I needed
the sample for, but it might be helpful to know
regardless.
Talia: Will do.

When I don't hear from Calder, I scroll back and see
that he sent me a couple of texts earlier, so I reply.

Me: I just now saw your texts.

Less than a minute passes before someone knocks
lightly.

The moment I open the door, Calder takes in my
rumpled appearance. His eyes instantly zero in on my
wrists before returning to my face. "Why aren't you
dressed, Miss Carver? You need to be downstairs in twenty
minutes."

The fact that he's being so formal means he's annoyed
about something. "I was asleep until you sent Beth to
wake me," I say, hoping to defuse whatever is bothering
him. Glancing back at the clock, I see that he's right. "I'll
be ready in fifteen."

I quickly shut the door, then pull the tags off the red
underwear and bra and slip into them. Once I shimmy
into the dress and slide on the red-bottomed black pumps,
I finger-comb my hair into a semblance of tameness
and freshen my makeup before clasping Celeste's gold

necklace around my neck.

When I open the door, I expect to find Calder leaning against the wall, not standing directly in my path. "Oh, hey." I take a step back, suddenly self-conscious. Brushing my hair back from my face, I smile to try to lighten his surly mood. "I'm ready five minutes early. How's that for promptness?"

"Not quite," he says, reaching up to remove my necklace.

"Celeste always wears that chain," I whisper when he drops it into his suit jacket pocket.

"Not tonight," he rumbles and leans close to hook a choker style necklace around my neck. Straightening, he tilts my chin up and the enticing smell of his cologne makes my stomach flutter. "This is more like something Celeste would wear."

When did he have time to do this? Distracted by the soft collar's inch-wide velvet fabric, I run my fingers from the delicate chain hanging from the clasp in the back to the metal on the front of the choker. Without asking, I know it's a raven, but it's not a silver-worked one like the other necklace he gave me. This raven is covered in...pavé. My gaze cuts to his. "Is this all diamonds?"

A corner of his mouth tilts in an arrogant smirk. "Sometimes a bank account speaks louder than sentiment."

"You know I don't care about—"

He covers my lips with his thumb, his voice low and tense. "You need to hear what I have to say, Raven mine."

I nod mutely, excitement pinging through me as he

lightly traces his fingers down the front of my throat.

"Your safety is my priority. It comes first, before my own desires *or* yours. Do you understand?"

When I start to nod, he shakes his head. "Do you?"

"I understand, Calder."

His gaze sharpens. "While I'm training for this fight, you won't see me." Sliding his thumb along my jawline, he drops his hand to his side, his tone softening. "No matter how much I *want* to own your world, you're not safe in mine right now."

"When will the fight be rescheduled?" I ask, wondering how long I'll have to wait to see him again.

"It's already been rescheduled."

I'm not sure whether to cheer or cry. I don't want him fighting at all. "When is it?"

His jaw tightens. "You're not coming."

"*When,*" I demand.

"This upcoming weekend."

"But you haven't been able to train—"

"Miss Carver, your presence is requested downstairs," Marco calls from the end of the hall.

Nodding, I walk away from Calder as if we weren't just having an intense conversation and follow Marco downstairs.

"Gorgeous," Beth says the moment I walk into the room where several guests are already at the bar getting their drinks. Lowering her voice, she continues eyeing my necklace. "It really goes well with that dress. I wonder why I've never seen it on my sister before."

"It's mine." I touch the choker at the same time Calder walks in and stands next to the door. My brow puckers when I realize there's only one way he could've commissioned such an amazing piece of jewelry without leaving my side. That was the 'favor' Alana did for him. As an artist she most likely has connections in the jewelry business. I'm not quite sure how I feel about the fact his ex played a part in this gift. "It's a gift with…history."

"Expensive history apparently." Beth chuckles, then sobers as she nods toward her dad who's greeting a couple just arriving. "Father is in a mood. He sent Marco up after you." She glances at Phillip talking to Jake. "Phillip seems antsy tonight. I heard my father raising his voice at him earlier. I think he blames Phillip for convincing him not to call the police."

"He should," I mutter. With Jake and Phillip standing side-by-side chatting, it's hard to believe such malice can reside behind such handsome faces. Like father, like son. I immediately tense when an older man draws Phillip's attention and Jake glances in our direction. I don't want to have to deal with him tonight. Without Ben to keep his brother in line, I really could use my own posse. Talia and Mina can't get here soon enough.

I glance toward the doorway and my gaze snags on Sebastian's dark hair and imposing height as he walks in with Talia on his arm, her beautiful red hair flowing around an off-the-shoulder emerald green dress. I exhale the tension flowing through me and suppress the relieved smile trying to surface. "Excuse me for a minute," I tell

Beth and casually make my way toward the doorway. I reach it just as Mina walks in, escorted by her other brother and flirt extraordinaire, Damien Blake.

"Celeste, thank you for the invite." Damien's dark eyes sparkle with mischief and he immediately grabs my hand before Mina has a chance to say a word. Releasing his sister, he tucks my hand around his arm and turns to introduce me to his guests. "You know Mina, but this is my brother Sebastian who insisted on tagging along. I only let the old man because he promised to bring his gorgeous wife. Talia, this is Celeste Carver."

I shake my head that Damien ribs his brother and grin when Sebastian mutters, "Watch yourself, little brother. This *old man* can easily put you in your place."

But when Talia clasps my hand tight and says, "It's nice to meet you, Celeste," the look in her eyes says so much, it's hard not to get teary. I miss her too.

I squeeze her hand, then let go, blinking away the mist. "Welcome everyone. Why don't you grab a drink and mingle. I'm sure you'll see people you know here."

Damien lifts my left hand and taps the diamond on my finger. "I heard a terrible rumor and didn't want to believe it was true. Where is the lucky bastard? I want to clock... er, congratulate him."

I smile at Damien. I'd forgotten how much fun he could be. The man really knows how to stroke a girl's ego. "Ben had a shift he couldn't get out of tonight, so he's saving lives instead."

"Well, then. I'll have to take advantage of his absence."

Just as Damien starts to tuck my hand back around the crook of his arm, Mina grips his other hand. "Come on, Damien. Let's get our drinks."

Before he can protest, she tucks her arm tight around his and walks away.

Snickering, I stare after her petite frame next to Damien's tall height. "She's a force, isn't she?"

"She has us wrapped around her little finger, but don't tell her that," Sebastian says, his brilliant blue eyes flashing with admiration and humor. Pressing a kiss to Talia's temple, he murmurs, "I'm going to touch base with Calder."

When he walks away, I say lightly, "You two are so adorable I want to punch somebody."

Talia laughs. "I'll just file that under 'things Cass says when she's under stress.'" Flicking her amused gaze to my throat, she stares at my choker. "That's beautiful. It reminds me of the tattoo on your arm. Is that Celeste's?"

I absently touch the diamond raven, anxious that I haven't had a chance to see it myself. "Calder gave it to me tonight. He'd given me a silver and leather one, but that's not something Celeste would wear, so I guess that's why he had this one made."

Talia tilts her head. "That's quite a gesture for a temporary situation."

I stiffen, then realize she's talking about this Celeste thing, not whatever is going on between Calder and me. *God, I'm so freaking sensitive right now.* "Remember when I told you that you needed to give Sebastian a chance?"

"Yes."

"Why can't I take my own advice?"

Talia's auburn eyebrows shoot up. "Please tell me you're not letting that ridiculously impractical lingerie go to waste."

I shake my head and sigh. "It's not that simple. Calder isn't like other guys. When we're together, I feel like I'm getting pulled in deeper."

"And that's a bad thing because…?"

I glance over at Sebastian shaking Calder's hand, then nodding and walking away. "It's bad when he's made it clear he's allergic to commitment. I desperately want to take my own advice, but in this situation, it would suck." I meet her gaze and purse my lips. "And I don't even have you anymore to feed me ice cream from a big bucket when Calder leaves me a mess on the floor."

"Are you crazy? I'll use the soup spoon on you, girl." When I give her a pained look, her amused green gaze shifts to a serious one. "Sebastian says he's never seen Calder worry like he does for you. That says a lot about how he feels even if he's not saying it himself. Stubborn hearts might be the hardest to win, but that's what makes them worth going for. I should know, I'm married to the most stubborn man on the planet."

When a pinging sound comes from the silver pillbox purse on her arm, she glances down and pulls her phone out. "Mina has Jake's glass. I'm going to go get Phillip's."

She starts to walk away, but I touch her arm. "Wait, I'm supposed to be doing that."

"You're supposed to *be* Celeste." Talia shifts her gaze over my shoulder. "Sebastian's talking to Phillip, who has proven quite adept at amassing his own financial empire while hiding his business dealings. I've zeroed in on a shell company that appears to be lease properties. The properties are dormant so I almost ignored it, but my curious hackles are raised. Anyway, right now...I have a glass to recover. Go mingle and let me do my job."

Before I can argue, she walks away to deftly slip a cloth napkin from a waiter's arm at the same time she takes a flute of champagne. As she disappears between large groups of people chatting, I inwardly applaud her stealthy talent and make a mental note to ask her to teach me. Skills like that could definitely come in handy.

CHAPTER SEVENTEEN

Cass

As I make my way back through the crowded room, I'm stopped several times by people congratulating me on my engagement to Ben. I paste on a smile and nod, thanking them by name while making sure to ask for their support of my father in the fall. An hour passes before I finally reach Beth's side.

"I need a drink," I say, glancing down at hers with envy. "I'm exhausted."

Beth snickers. "I've been doing this since I was a teen. It's old hat after a while." Her amused expression suddenly shifts to a tense one. "Ugh, Jake's coming."

As soon as Jake steps into place beside us, Beth smiles at a couple passing by and says to him under her breath, "Be respectful or I'll personally kick your ass out tonight."

Jake brushes one hand through his perfectly gelled hair, then raises his highball glass in the air, ice chinking. "Hey, it's all good, Beth."

While I cynically scan his face, looking for his true intent, Beth turns to speak to a woman with a bob haircut and chic black glasses, who lightly touches her shoulder. "Good evening, Beth and Celeste. Do you remember me? I'm an old friend of your mother's. The last time I saw you, you were just starting middle school. I'm sorry your mom wasn't able to attend tonight's function."

Beth's eyes light up. "Hi, it's Sylvia, right?"

The woman nods and glances at the silver-haired man with her. "This is my husband, Richard."

Beth introduces Jake to the couple and he smiles and shakes their hands, but once Beth has their full attention, he turns and narrows his gaze on my throat. "That's not Celeste's style at all," he grates in a low tone. "Remove it."

"No."

Jake's mouth slants in a thin line as if he's trying to keep his cool. "I won't let you disrespect her. Take it off."

"Screw you," I mouth and start to walk away, but Jake touches my shoulder and pulls me back, all smiles.

"You must get to know your mother's two favorite people, Celeste," Jake says. Keeping his hand on my shoulder in a friendly manner, he gestures to the couple. "I'm not much on wine, but Richard just said he's a big enthusiast."

"Oh yes, we just spent a fortune renovating our house just to include a cellar," the man says, his expression fully animated.

While the man goes into detail about the cost and time it took to renovate, Jake nods and acts like he's just being chummy with me. When I try to pull away, he quickly moves his hand beneath my hair and slides his thumb under the velvet collar. I tense as the clasp digs into my skin, locking me in place.

Beth and Sylvia are so completely enthralled by Richard's story of discovering an old painting inside the wall during the renovation that they don't notice me elbow Jake in the ribs to make him let me go, but it's too late. The velvet gives way.

Fury and panic whip through me as I feel the raven slip free of the loose velvet. I quickly cup my hands and barely manage to capture the raven, saving it from hitting the floor. For a split second, the diamond encrusted raven is crystal clear, but it immediately blurs with the sudden mist in my eyes.

"Better," Jake mutters as he releases me and stares at my bare throat.

I hate that I have to hold my scream of anger inside. Instead, I blink back unshed tears and glare my fury at him, snatching the broken choker from his grasp. It's like he knows just what to do to destroy my inner happiness.

Turning to the couple, Jake says, "Hey, Richard, I'm sure Celeste would be happy to show you her parent's wine collection. It's quite extensive."

Richard rubs his hands together, grinning. "I would love that."

Jake glances my way, a knowing smile on his face. "Why don't you lead the way, Celeste?"

"I'll do it," Beth jumps in.

"But *Celeste* is the wine expert," Jake insists. "Richard can drill her on tannins and terrior, aroma, regions and variety to his heart's content."

Jake's trying to make me slip up. It's like he has suddenly decided to turn this into some kind of game.

When Beth tries to insist, I put my hand on her arm. "I'll be happy to show Richard the wine cellar."

"Oooh, I want to see it too," Sylvia pipes in.

"Since the elevator only holds two, why don't Celeste and I go down first and turn on the lights, and you and Richard can follow," Jake says, affably.

Beth looks at me, worry in her gaze.

I plaster on a confident smile. "Sure. Let's go talk wines." Holding my hand out to Beth, I say, "Hold this for me, please," then tuck the diamond raven and velvet ribbon into her hand.

As the four of us pass by Calder, he looks at me and instantly frowns.

We turn down the hall that leads to the elevator and I see Calder following. My wrists are stinging and itching like crazy, so I'm relieved to know he plans to follow us. When I hear Beth call his name, my insides jerk. The last thing I want is to be alone with Jake even for the minute or two it'll take for the couple to join us in the cellar.

I keep my smile steady as Jake and I step into the elevator, but the second the doors close and we start to descend, I snarl at him. "Were you born this evil or did that black hole inside you develop over time?"

Jake calmly slides his hands into his pants pockets. "I asked you to take the necklace off nicely. See what happens when you don't listen?"

"You're certifiable," I hiss, folding my arms to keep from gouging his eyes out as we step off the elevator.

He shrugs as the doors close and the elevator zips back up. "Did I tell you that Ben is coming later?"

"God, I hope he brings a muzzle for you," I snap, before walking into the dimly lit cellar room and turning on the main lights.

As the elevator begins to descend to the bottom floor once more, Jake stands in the doorway, rocking on his heels. "Yeah, after I sent him that text telling him you're not Celeste, it's amazing how quickly my brother was able to arrange to get off work. I bet he'll get here in record time."

I gape at him, my stomach twisting into knots at the thought of having to face Ben. He must feel so betrayed right now. "I can't believe you did that to your own brother. You truly are a vile person."

The elevator begins to slow to a stop and his gaze slits on me. "What made you think that you could fill her shoes for even five minutes?"

For a split-second, I'm instantly transported back to that moment when he said something similar to me in high school, and all those insecurities and nagging self-doubts rise to the surface. Except, I'm not the same person

I was back then. Everything he's done to me from the past to the present boils to the surface, but it's the way I felt when he broke Calder's necklace that makes me step right in front of him.

"Why did I step in for Celeste? Because I have something you'll never have, Jake. It's called *compassion*," I finish at the same time I grab his shoulders and knee him in the balls as hard as I can.

As Jake doubles over, grabbing his junk and wheezing his pain, Silvia and Richard step out of the elevator.

"What's wrong with Jake?" she asks, worry in her gaze as she pats him on the back.

I shake my head and mumble, "It's probably something he ate" as Richard grabs a chair from the tasting area and sets it against the wall for Jake.

Jake flops into the chair and waves the couple off, croaking, "I'm fine. Go check out the wine."

"Are you sure?" Sylvia asks as I hook my arm in hers.

"He's good," I assure her. "Come on, let me take you and Richard on a tour."

I'm thankful that I took the time to walk around the place the last time I was down here, but I'm even more grateful for my travels. That's where I learned to truly appreciate fine wine.

After I take Sylvia and Richard into the tasting room and they have pulled out every custom made drawer to inspect hundreds of bottles inside, I'm surprised but relieved to see Calder standing in the doorway as I lead the couple back to the elevator.

"Where's Jake?" Sylvia asks.

Calder pushes the elevator button and the doors slide open. "Beth took him upstairs to get some water."

"That's good. He definitely looked a bit pale." Once Sylvia and Richard get into the elevator, she smiles at me, her cheeks glowing. "Thank you for the informative tour, Celeste. I think Richard learned a thing or two he didn't know about wines."

Richard laughs, nodding his agreement. "You really know your stuff, young lady. Thank you for the tips. I certainly plan to implement them."

"You're welcome," I say. "See you upstairs."

They wave and the elevator doors close.

Sighing my relief, I walk back into the main room and start to turn off the lights. "Leave them," Calder says from directly behind me.

I let my hand drop but don't turn around. "Beth brought you down here?"

"She told me that Jake was mouthy yesterday and she was worried he was getting that way again. I came down expecting to flatten the jackass." He traces a finger along the scooped back of my dress. "Why didn't you tell me that he got aggressive with you?"

It's cool in the cellar, but my skin feels like it's on fire where his finger connects. "Beth set him straight. I thought that was the end of it. You didn't let on that you know I'm not Celeste, did you?"

His fingers slowly trail along my skin. "No, I'm not taking a chance that Beth will tell her boyfriend about us.

And not that I'm not damn proud of you for taking care of yourself, but having to help Beth get that shithead into the elevator without inflicting my own level of punishment grated. What did he say that set you off?"

If I tell him about the necklace, he'll go after Jake. We're too close to screw this up, so I tell him the other shitty thing Jake did. "He told his brother the truth about me out of spite. And now Ben's on his way over here," I say, my voice shaking.

Calder's fingers still on my back. "That's why you racked the guy...over *Ben*?"

Shit, he's taking what I said the wrong way. I try to refocus on the issue of common decency. "Ben didn't deserve to find out like that. He has done nothing wrong."

Calder turns me around and tilts my chin up. "Do you want—" he cuts himself off, his gaze dropping to my throat. "Where's your necklace?" he demands, his thumb tracing my bare skin.

He can't know what really happened to it. "The clasp came lose. I took it off so I wouldn't lose it."

He frowns. "You didn't go upstairs. Where is it?"

"I um..." I shake my head. "I asked Beth to hold it for me."

Calder's gaze narrows. "Have you changed your mind about us, Cass?"

"What are you talking about?" I ask, my stomach pitching.

"Do you fucking want to be with Ben?" he demands, slamming his hands on the wall behind me.

He's literally shaking with tension, tortured fury in his gaze. I don't know what to do other than to show him how I feel about him. I reach up and rub my fingers along the raised vein in his temple, then lightly press my lips to his jaw and whisper, "Does this feel like I want someone else, Calder?"

Big hands suddenly clasp my jaw, and he tilts my head as his warm mouth claims my lips in a hard, desperate kiss.

The fierce thrust of his tongue against mine is so brutally primal, my body clenches and throbs in response. I match his passion, spearing my fingers into his hair and pulling him closer.

"Why can't I think straight when it comes to you?" he rasps, pressing his mouth against my throat at the same time he lifts the bottom of my dress up and slides his hands up the back of my thighs to my rear. "*Now* she wears underwear..." he says in a dry tone, sliding his fingers under the lacy edge to palm my backside.

I snort. "Just for you."

He chuckles and murmurs, "You have such a beautiful ass," as he steps fully against me.

I moan at the sensation of his hard erection digging into me and press my body closer, letting him know I want him just as much.

Calder lifts me up, his voice gravelly with possessive intensity. "You should be wearing my necklace, angel," he says right before he bites down on the side of my throat.

I gasp and lock my legs around his hips as shivers

prickle my skin and a rush of heat flows from my head…
to my chest…to my sex in one long ribbon of yearning
want. Gripping his shoulders, I arch against him and soak
up every bit of the erotic pleasurable pain.

He nudges his cock against my sex, his fingers clasping
my ass in a possessive hold. "When I close my eyes," he
says, his voice rough against my jaw. "I can still taste
you on my tongue. So sweet and addicting, you should
be illegal." He slides his nose along my neck and inhales
deeply, then lets out an unsteady breath, his body tensing.
"*Fuck*, I want you so much, Cass."

Afraid he's going to pull away, I tighten my thighs
and yank him as close as our clothes will allow. "Then do
something about it! I don't give a damn where we are."

Calder buries his face against my neck as he walks us
over to the tasting table. Setting me down on the edge, he
clasps my knees and spreads them wide, growling, "Don't
move them."

I exhale softly as he tilts my chin up and trails his
fingers down my throat. His chest rising and falling, he
asks in a steely tone, "Am I going to have to solder my
gifts on you, sweet Cassandra?"

I tremble at the sensation of his other hand tracing up
my inner thigh, then brushing along the flimsy edge of my
panties. "I told you, the clasp came lo—aahh," I swallow
my gasp of excitement as he deftly slides my panties aside
and buries two fingers deep inside my channel.

His eyes glitter with territorial dominance as he
withdraws and presses deep once more. "I love how wet

you are for me." Turning his hand, he hits bone-melting places, jacking my desire even higher and his voice drops to a low, arrogant purr. "This, right here, is all that fucking matters," he says and bends close to take my bottom lip between his teeth.

I pant as he drags his teeth along the sensitive skin, the pain making me want to move against his hand. When I clench my fingers against his suit coat, he releases my lip and commands, "Show me, Cass. Fucking show me how much you want this."

The fact he's possessing my body without moving is pure torture. I quickly unbuckle his belt and unzip his pants, needing his fully engaged dominance. Grasping his hard cock through his silk boxers, I slide my thumb over the tip and use the material to tease him back. "Let me show you what *want* feels like," I say, then quickly bend to cup my mouth over his boxers.

Calder groans and palms the back of my head. He fists his hand in my hair and his hips surge forward as he buries his cock as deep as he can. "Your mouth and silk… fucking amazing."

I tighten my mouth, using my hand to slide the silky material against his sensitive skin. At the same time I push his cock through the slit in his boxers and rub my lips and tongue down his hard, warm flesh, I grasp his sac through the silk and moan.

Breathing heavily, Calder pulls me off him. Lust swirling in his gaze, he commands, "Put your hands on the table and keep those thighs spread wide."

Panting, I flatten my palms on the table and arch my back to force my legs against the edge of the table.

Calder leans close and puts one hand directly behind my back. My body is throbbing in anticipation. I lock my gaze with his.

When his cock presses against my sex and as I start to close my eyes, Calder grates out, "No, watch us."

My eyes fly open and I bite my lip at the sight of his thick cock pressing inside me.

Calder flattens his hand against my ass, his fingers flexing. "This is what being truly taken means," he says, pulling me forward at the same time he slams against me. I gasp as he fills me, stretching my body to accommodate his thick girth.

For a split second, Calder stills and a shudder rushes over him before he yanks me off the table and sets me against the ceiling-to-floor wooden drawers. With a powerful rock of his hips, he withdraws and then surges inside me, his hands locking my body to him. "Fuck, you feel so good." Pausing, he starts to pull out. "Cass, we should use…"

"Don't stop," I hiss, locking my legs around his hips. The need for release clawing in my belly, I grip a drawer's edge behind me and arch, taking him in deeper. We both moan and bottles rattle, but I don't care. Calder has me so primed my body is already tightening toward fast approaching bliss. Using the drawer's leverage, I roll my hips and encourage his rough possession.

Predatory heat flickering in his gaze, Calder presses

his chest to mine, his hard body hitting my clit with toe-curling force. My heart suspends and I cry out as I come, my insides clenching tight.

Calder exhales and rests his head on my shoulder, his arms like steel beams holding me up. When I slow my pace, he blows out a harsh breath, then begins to move once more. This time his need is fiercer, coming through in harsher, more powerful friction. My back hits the drawers hard and bottles rattle behind me, but I don't care if they all come crashing down around us.

This connection with Calder is beyond anything we've experienced before; it's a deeper, tangible melding of flesh and emotions.

As another orgasm rocks through my body, I let go of the drawer and clasp his jaw. Pulling him to me, I bite his sexy bottom lip and pant against his mouth. "How bad do you want me?"

"Bad enough to fucking crawl inside you," he rasps.

I grip his hair and tug hard, my voice husky with aroused amusement. "I don't think you can fit in there."

"When are you going to learn to never challenge me?" A darkly wicked chuckle vibrates against my jaw before he slides his hands lower. I gasp when knowing fingers spread my entrance wider, taking complete control over my body. My breath hitches with each kiss of his balls against my sensitive lips. The added stimuli revs my passion all over again. I feel raw, cracked open and exposed...fully laid out for his sensual taking. I'm so shredded by the way he makes me feel, I cling to him and absorb every bit of decadent pleasure.

We move together, faster, harder...our breathing labored. The moment I climax, my body clenching hard around his, he shudders and groans as his warmth pulses deep inside me. Slowing to a stop, he presses his forehead to mine. "Now that you've lost that challenge, sweet Raven..." He inhales deeply, then exhales a territorial grunt as he slides his fingers together, sealing my body around his cock. "You're keeping every last drop."

The sound of the elevator coming toward the cellar sets us into motion. Calder quickly sets me down and rights his clothes, while I slide my underwear in place and push my dress back down. Heart racing, I step over to the hidden door in the corner of the room and open it, pointing to the secret passageway. "Follow this and you'll exit upstairs."

Calder shakes his head. "Not until I know who's coming down here."

Sighing, I gesture to the passageway once more. "Hide in here until you know who it is, then you can go on upstairs."

Calder sets his jaw, and as he ducks into the darkness, the elevator doors open.

"Celeste?" Beth calls out. "Are you down here?"

I shoo Calder on and start to close the door, but he cups the back of my neck and pulls me forward, his low baritone a husky rumble against my temple. "Be glad you slept the day away. You won't be getting any sleep tonight, angel. I'm nowhere near done with you."

My heart speeding up once more, I huff a breath of

anticipation, then smile and shove him behind the door, calling out, "I'm in the tasting room, Beth."

High heels click lightly on the stone floor before she appears in the doorway. "What are you still doing down here? I saw Sylvia and Richard come up a while ago."

I pull open one of the wine drawers and turn a couple bottles around, facing the labels outward. "I was just putting the room back the way we found it. Richard is nice, but after inspecting the wines, he set the bottles back on the racks without making sure the labels faced outward. He touched so many, I was checking every drawer."

Beth waves toward the drawers, her tone dismissive. "If you're doing this in an attempt to avoid Jake, don't worry. He felt too sick to stick around, but you do need to come upstairs with me right away."

"What's so important?" I start to shut off the light, then pause, tensing. "Is Ben here?"

When Beth shakes her head, my shoulder muscles relax. Flipping the switch, I follow her to the elevator and step inside. "So what's up?"

While the elevator moves upward, Beth turns to me, her gaze anxious. "The police arrived five minutes ago and asked to speak with you."

CHAPTER EIGHTEEN

Calder

My phone vibrates in my pocket as I exit a closet in the hallway upstairs. I pull it out and notice I have a text from Bash, but when I see Gil's name in the ID, my chest tightens. Gil never calls. Is he having a relapse? Pausing, I quickly answer.

"Hey, Gil. Is everything all right?"

"I'm calling for a reason, Calder, and I want you to listen this time."

Gil's tone is harsh, reminding me of that night he sprayed me with the fire hose. My fingers flex on the phone. I don't like leaving Cass this long. "Can this wait until later?"

"No, it can't. I ran into Alana earlier and she told me about the gift she helped you with."

"That was supposed to be private," I say, my jaw clenching.

"Yeah well, she only told me because I asked why you two didn't work out."

I snort, annoyed with Gil's meddling. "This isn't important, Gil. I'm hanging up now."

I start to push End, but his harsh tone has my finger pausing over the button. "Calder Jackson Blake. *Listen to me*, damn your stubborn hide."

I put the phone to my ear once more. "What?"

"This is about the young woman you had the necklace made for. She's the one I asked about, right? The one you said you're guarding. If you truly care about her—"

"Gil..."

"Just shut it, kid. This is about your mom."

I stiffen and grit out, "*What?*"

"You wouldn't let me tell you in the past. Now you're going to listen, damn it. The incident your mother referred to in her letter wasn't an affair. Becca was drugged and rap—"

"Stop," I cut him off, my whole body shaking with fury. I stride forward, my steps fast and determined as I head down the hall and turn for the stairs.

Gil sighs. "That bastard runs in those circles, Calder. Keep your woman safe. I don't want history to repeat itself."

"I won't fucking let that happen," I say, hitting the End button.

Guilt and anger crush my chest. I'm furious that I let

my own pain keep me from hearing the truth, and in doing so put Cass at risk. Vengeance builds with each step I take, but right now getting to Cass is my first priority.

As I start down the stairs, Bash is halfway up, a determined look on his face.

My gaze shifts to the people standing downstairs. Everyone is quiet, all staring at the foyer. I follow their line of sight and freeze.

Two police officers flank Cass on either side. Their hands clasping her arms as they walk her toward the door, while Phillip, Gregory, and Beth stand there watching. *Is Beth crying?*

"No!" I bark out and rush forward.

Bash hooks his arm across my chest, forcing me to a halt, his words low but harsh in my ear, "Stop, Cald!"

I turn my fury on him, my tone deadly. "*Let* go."

"I won't let you fuck this up!" He grabs my arm in a tight grip and hauls me upstairs into the hall.

As soon as we're on even ground, I yank my arm free and start to go around him.

Bash grabs my hand and twists it behind my back, his words sharp but calm. "I've already called my lawyer to meet them at the station, Cald. You need to calm the hell down and think. I won't let you tip off any of those pricks down there that we're building evidence against them."

"Why the hell are they taking her?" I twist free of his hold and dig my fingers into my hair. Pacing, I inhale and exhale several times, trying to get a grip.

"I'm not sure, but we'll find out. Are you calm now?"

he asks, his arms crossed. "I normally don't have to explain strategic moves to you."

I turn to him, my whole body vibrating. "You don't understand."

Bash frowns. "Explain."

I shake my head and walk away. I know he's right and we need to stay on course, but Cass should never have had to go with the police in the first place. She's being railroaded. "They'd better not fucking charge her or I'm going to go ballistic."

"Calder...what the hell is going on with you?"

I blow out a shaky breath and turn to face him. "I just found out that my mother didn't have an affair. The guy drugged and took advantage of her. Gil has been trying to tell me, but I didn't want to hear anything about the past. He called and demanded that I hear the truth."

The brackets around Bash's mouth deepen. "I'm sorry, Calder. I know that's a harsh blow, but why did Gil choose now to make you listen?"

I clench my hand into a fist, wanting to punch something. "He knows I care about the person I'm guarding, so he called to warn me. He doesn't want anything to happen to her."

Shaking his head in confusion, Bash moves closer. "Why would he think something might happen to her?"

"Because my *father* is Phillip Hemming, that's fucking why!"

"What the *hell*, Calder," Bash's low, angry tone hangs between us. Walking away from me, he paces twice, then steps right in my face. "You're too fucking close to work this case with any kind of objectivity. How could you not tell me?"

I cross my arms and stare him down. "I didn't tell you, because it was no one's fucking business who my mother cheated on my father with."

"Except she *didn't*," Bash counters, his expression stony.

"And now that you know, I'd appreciate you keeping my sick-as-fuck family tree to yourself," I shoot back. "This is *my* case. I will see it through."

"No, you won't. You're going to go train for that fight. Cass is out of danger now. I'll take over the case."

"Out of danger?" I slice my hand toward the bottom floor. "She's going to the goddamn police station."

"Where she's no longer having to pretend to be Celeste *and* she's out of Phillip's reach."

We stand there staring each other down, a battle of wills silently raging.

Talia enters the hall and approaches. "Everyone is leaving. It's time to go."

When neither Bash nor I blink, she steps between us, her voice stronger. "My best friend is at the police station. I would like to go be with her. Point me to Celeste's room so I can get her phone. I don't believe she brought anything else with her."

I gesture to the room at the end of the hall. "I'll see you two at the station." When I start to walk away, she grabs my arm.

"I'm sorry, Calder, but until you're done with the EUC, it's too dangerous for you to be seen with Cass on a personal level."

I shake my head. "I won't let her think I abandoned her."

"Don't worry," Talia says, releasing me. "I'll tell her I wouldn't let you come. Go home. We'll keep you updated."

My gaze snaps to Bash, whose tense expression clearly says, *That was a perfect example of you* not *thinking clearly.* Pulling Talia to his side, he addresses me. "Go collect your stuff, and no matter how much you want to, do *not* engage with Phillip on your way out. As far as you're concerned, your trial guard role is over." When I curl my lip in a frustrated snarl, the tension in Bash's tone amps. "I promise you we'll make the bastard pay for every despicable thing he's done, Calder."

CHAPTER NINETEEN

Cass

This is a freaking nightmare. I rub my temples and try to ignore the two detectives hovering over me in the police interrogation room like a couple of vultures waiting for me to finally keel over.

"Why don't you run it down for us again?" the potbellied, middle-aged cop in a brown wrinkled suit jacket pulls up a chair and sits at the table across from me.

"Because all identity thieves are honest, right, Joe?" his female partner in a sharp pantsuit and a pixie cut says as she walks the floor behind him.

"Stop pacing, it's making me dizzy, Tori," he grunts, then looks at me expectantly.

I sigh, wondering if I repeat what I've already said several times after I made my one phone call to Talia, if they'd actually hear me this time. "I'm not saying a word without my lawyer. We can do this all night."

"If you're innocent, what does it matter?" Tori props her fit butt on the corner of the table in the small interrogation room, while her partner unbuttons his straining jacket and flips open his notebook and reads off the notes.

"According to our officers, an anonymous tip was called in this evening stating that you were impersonating Celeste Carver and that the real Celeste is missing." He pauses and gestures to me. "The Carver family says you claim that Celeste asked you to be her for one night and when she didn't show the next day, they asked you to continue on through tonight's event in the hopes they could locate her without a lot of media attention. Is that about right?"

I want to yell at them, "Yes, damn it!" but then after what I experienced once Beth and I walked into Gregory's office an hour ago, my response stays firmly stuck in my throat. Could I have said or done anything differently that wouldn't have landed me here in this room?

"Thank you for bringing her, Beth." Phillip said. He gestured to the cop and continued, "This police officer is following up on an anonymous tip called in earlier tonight that suggested you're impersonating Celeste."

I looked at Phillip and Gregory, unsure what was going on in their heads, but one thing was for certain, I refused to lie to the police again. "Yes, it's true," I address the uniformed police officer and tried not to get too anxious about the second officer waiting just outside the office door. "I'm not Celeste Carver. My name is Cassandra Rockwell and Celeste asked me to impersonate her for one night during her father's political event. When she didn't arrive home, I—"

"Let me stop you right there..." The police officer interrupted me and glanced down at the notepad in his hand. "Was that you the other night when the police came by asking about the abandoned vehicle they found with blood and Celeste Carver's ID in it?"

I nodded. "Yes, that was me. It was the night Celeste asked me to be her. I was out with her sister, Beth, and was supposed to meet up with her and switch places, but she didn't contact me, so I went back to her house. When I arrived, the police were here. You have to understand, Celeste was adamant that no one know I was pretending to be her, so I stayed quiet that night in the hopes she would contact me. The next morning, when I still hadn't heard from her, I told her family the truth. That's when they asked me to continue on as Celeste so they could quietly look for her while hopefully avoiding a media frenzy during Mr. Carver's events."

"Asking Miss Rockwell to stay on gave us a chance to conduct our own search for Celeste in places she might've gone," Phillip said smoothly as he walked over and opened a filing cabinet drawer. "But it also gave us time to conduct our own investigation into Miss Rockwell's story."

Investigate me? I gaped at him. "You know it's not a story," I said, my heart thumping hard as I watched him pull out a folder and the cell phone that Celeste gave me.

"We still hope to locate Celeste," he continued as if I hadn't spoken. "But now that it has been forty-eight hours, it's time to turn this over to the authorities." He hands the folder and the cell phone that Celeste gave me to the police officer. "I believe you'll find ample evidence in here to question Miss Rockwell in Celeste's disappearance, starting with the fact she made up the entire story of Celeste asking her to pretend to be her in the first place."

"What evidence?" I gestured to the phone. "There is proof on that phone that Celeste recruited me. Texts—"

"I found no such texts," Phillip stared at me with a bold, accusing gaze.

"That's a lie. If they aren't there, then you deleted them."

Gregory cleared his throat and glanced my way, frustration and betrayal in his gaze. "As Phillip mentioned, there are no texts between Celeste and Miss Rockwell on that phone. It is a clone of my daughter's phone, but we have since learned it's not hard to clone a phone if you have the right equipment. In the folder you'll not only find interviews of past classmates who state that my daughter was never friends with Miss Rockwell in high school, but actually the opposite. These classmates claimed that Miss Rockwell hated my daughter for some perceived wrong Celeste did to her in high school."

When I glanced at Beth and shook my head, she took a step away from me, her eyes wide. "Is that true, Cass?"

I gripped the back of the leather chair for support. "Your sister did play a prank on me in high school and I didn't like her for it. That is true, but I wasn't obsessed with Celeste. She came to me for help, Beth. That's the truth."

"Didn't you say that you pretended to be Celeste at a party in the past?" Phillip asked. "Did she ask you to be her back then *too?"*

"No, she didn't ask, but it's not what you think—"

"So you did it for what...kicks?" Phillip doesn't give me a chance to answer before addressing the police officer. "In the folder, there is also a copy of Miss Rockwell's medical history from a hospital stay a few years ago where she was put on suicide watch."

"That's private! How dare you dig through my medical records."

Phillip doesn't spare me a glance. "I believe that's enough to show her mental state isn't a stable one and could absolutely contribute to her becoming obsessed with Celeste. Not only does her photography business give you another data point into her obsession with an ultra rich lifestyle like Celeste had, but my son, Jake, claims Miss Rockwell hated the fact he only had eyes for Celeste and wouldn't give her the time of day back in high school."

"You knew Jake? Why did you pretend you didn't know him?" Beth looked at me as if every lie Phillip just told had spread through her mind like a disease.

Phillip pointed to the folder. "You'll find a sample of Celeste's hair in that plastic sleeve stapled to the top. Please have it tested against the blood that was found in that abandoned car. We're hoping it won't match, but at this point...we've almost exhausted all the places we can think to look and need your help."

"Why don't you tell them you've already had someone in the lab test a sample of Celeste's hair against the blood they found?"

The police officer turned his gaze on Phillip, a frown on his face. "Is that true? You can't tamper with evidence. We want *this person's name."*

When Phillip didn't speak right away, the officer demanded, *"Right now, sir."*

Once Phillip grudgingly provided the man's name, the officer snapped the folder shut and turned to me. "Based on this, we have to take you in for questioning, Miss Rockwell."

I wanted to tell him that they had it all wrong, that Phillip is the one they should be looking into, that they needed to know that Celeste was pregnant, but I didn't know for sure if Talia ever got Phillip's glass, and without his DNA, we might not have enough to build a case against him. Instead, I said, "This is insanity. I'm being framed!"

Sympathy reflected in the officer's eyes. "I'm following procedure, Miss Rockwell. A young woman is missing and you're the last person to speak with her. This is just a formality."

I tensed when he reached for my arm. "I insist on my phone call the moment we reach the station."

As the officer walked me out of the room, I glanced Beth's way, surprised that she didn't bring up the pregnancy. She looked confused and hurt and was probably wondering if I somehow manufactured the whole pregnancy scenario too. Pausing in front of her, I said, "Celeste asked for my help for a reason. You have to believe that."

"Miss Rockwell, do you know what the penalty is for impeding an investigation?" the detective's gruff voice pulls my attention back to them.

"A lot less than a murder rap, that's for sure," Tori says, snorting.

I jerk my gaze to hers. "Murder?"

She flips open a blue folder and reads the contents. "According to the lab report, based on the amount of blood found in that abandoned car, there's no way the person survived that much blood loss. So you'd better pray that the blood isn't Celeste Carver's, or you're potentially looking at a murder charge, Miss Rockwell. If you start talking now and tell us where you dumped the body, we might be able to talk the district attorney into reducing your sentence."

I'm so shocked by the proof that Celeste has been murdered, I open my mouth to speak, but nothing comes out. I try once more but a tiny woman with striking silver hair opens the door. "Not a word, Cass. Understand?" When I nod, she turns to the two detectives, her bobbed hair swinging with her movements. "I'm Felicity Danvers and you two have no right to talk to my client without her lawyer present. Get out of this room right now before I have you both written up."

Joe rolls his eyes and pushes himself to a standing position, muttering his disgust over uppity lawyers. Tori raps the edge of the folder sharply on the table and says in an ominous tone, "We'll be back, Cass. Don't think you're going anywhere."

As soon as they close the door behind them, Felicity sits down beside me and puts a petite hand over mine. "It's nice to meet you, Cass. Sebastian and Talia sent me to lift your spirits while kicking ass. Do you want me to represent you?"

"Why wouldn't I?"

She smiles and sets her briefcase down. "You're apparently very popular tonight. There's another lawyer outside, claiming he was sent to represent you."

I frown. "By whom?"

Felicity shrugs. "I have no idea. I've already talked to Sebastian and he's brought me up to speed on your investigation. He hopes to have all the evidence necessary to build a strong case against Phillip. This evidence might all be circumstantial, but it'll certainly be more compelling and easier to draw an inference of guilt than what they have on you. Right now I need to go talk to the Chief, but I wanted your permission to ask for this deal."

"What deal?" I ask, eyeing her warily.

She squeezes my hand. For a woman under five feet she has a surprisingly strong grip. "They aren't going to charge you, dear. I won't let that happen, but we need time to get the paternity tests run against the DNA samples. Would you be willing to stay here overnight? We should have the results in the morning."

My heart starts racing with worry. "You just said that they won't charge me."

"That's why this conversation is only going to happen between me and the Chief. He'll know what we're doing, but because we don't know who else in this department Phillip Hemming might have on his payroll, it's going to have to look like you're being held, pending charges. That way Phillip won't be tipped off."

Pulling out a pad and pen, she hands it to me. "For now, I need you to write down everything that happened from the moment Celeste approached you."

"There's one thing none of us knew while collecting this evidence."

Her eyebrows shoot up. "What's that?"

My hands tremble so hard I have to set the notepad and pen down. "One of the detectives just told me that the lab report on that abandoned car states that the person couldn't have survived that much blood loss." I look down at the blank pad, my voice shaking. "We know for certain that the blood is Celeste's. I can't believe she's gone."

She presses her lips together, then takes a deep breath. "Murder certainly ups the stakes, but it doesn't change the plan. We just need to provide them with compelling evidence, which is coming."

"But all of this hinges on us proving that Phillip is the baby's father." I put my hand on my chest and take several breaths, trying not to hyperventilate. "If I'm wrong and the tests prove he's not...I'm screwed."

She takes the pen and puts it in my hand. "We will know for sure tomorrow. This is just for me for now, but I think it will also help calm you down. Start writing."

CHAPTER TWENTY

Calder

I body slam Erik to the mat, shoving my shoulder into his chest. He tries to wrap his arm around my neck, but I'm relentless and don't let him get a good lock. Grabbing his arm, I roll over his body and fully extend his arm into a brutal arm bar hold.

In the distance, I hear voices followed by pain exploding in my shoulder.

My vision comes into focus. Gil is bent over me. He jabs his cane into the same spot and raises his voice. "Let him go, Calder!"

I immediately release Erik, who quickly rolls away holding his shoulder. "Sorry," I mumble while rubbing sweat off my brow.

"Take it down a few notches, dude," Erik gripes before

walking off.

I start to sit up, but Gil jams his cane right in the center of my chest, shoving me back to the mat. "Get your head on straight, Cald! You have a fight in three days and getting disqualified isn't how you win fights." Lifting his cane back to the floor, he leans on it, his lined face scrunched in lecture mode. "I know you didn't expect the bout to be rescheduled so quickly, but if you can't get back to the level of focus it'll take to beat Hammer, I will find a way to get you pulled, and the EUC will continue their shitty ways for another year."

"He'll get there," a deep voice says from behind Gil.

I jump to my feet, fists clenched. "You'd better be here to tell me Cass is at home."

Bash slides his hand into his slacks pockets and looks at Gil. "Can we have a minute?"

Gil's gaze pings from Bash to me and back. "I've got some paperwork that needs doin' anyway." As he ambles off, he waves to Erik. "The others won't be here until eight. Come do some filing for me, Erik. Nothing will make you want to finish that college degree more."

Once Erik follows Gil into his office, I face my cousin, still fuming that Cass had to spend the night in "holding". "Well?"

"I *came* to check on you. After you woke me at five ranting about Cass, and then again at six, Talia kicked me out of bed." He pauses to glance back toward Gil's office. "It appears sending me here was a smart call."

"I can't fucking believe Cass had to stay the night. Is

there any way to rush the test results?"

Bash snorts. "We are rushing them, but short of opening the lab earlier and conducting the tests myself, no. We'll have the results by ten, Cald. Calm down."

"What if neither of the assholes turns out to be Celeste's baby daddy? What happens to Cass?"

"Felicity says what they have on Cass is very circumstantial."

"Then why the hell go through this ruse?" I say, flinging my arms wide.

"Because, short of having other suspects to go after, Cass is it. And there is a wrinkle, Calder. This is going to turn into a murder investigation."

I go very still, my heart jumping to a sprinter's pace. "Did they find Celeste's body?"

Bash shakes his head. "No, the lab has already ruled that the abandoned car is a murder scene due to the amount of blood found there. Once the lab confirms that the blood is Celeste's, they will make this a murder investigation and we need to be ready for that. Cass's past ties to Celeste may be circumstantial, but the police have just enough to make her life hell while they investigate further. They could turn over every minute detail in her life. We're trying to avoid that for Cass by asking her to stay put while we get the evidence. I think giving the police another suspect will go a long way in keeping her off their radar."

I shake my head, gut twisting. "I can't believe that Celeste is dead." Curling my hands into fists, the churning in my stomach turns into burning knots. "I'm going to bury that sick fuck."

"You'll stay on course, Calder," Bash orders, his expression hard and just as angry. "The last thing I need is you being charged for murder, no matter how justified…"

Bash trails off when two police officers walk into the main door. He and I glance at each other, then walk briskly over to greet them. "What can we do for you, officers?" I ask while ripping open the Velcro fasteners on my grappling gloves.

"Is Gil around?" the tall one with a crooked nose asks.

I gesture to the closed office door. "He's in there working. I help manage the place. Is there something I can help you with?"

The younger, freckle-faced guy tilts his head. "Do you know all the guys who frequent this gym?"

I tuck my gloves under my crossed arms. "Yeah, I'm responsible for the scheduling."

The crooked nose cop pulls his phone out and turns it around. "Do you recognize this sweatshirt?"

As I stare at the bloodstained heather-gray sweatshirt with *Gil's Gym* and a pair of MMA gloves printed on the front, the guy scrolls to the next picture, saying, "This is the back." A single name is printed in the center: Rampage.

I swallow the hard rock in my throat. "That's Thomas's. The last time I saw him, he was wearing that sweatshirt. We haven't seen him in months. Where did you get this? Is he okay?"

He pulls his phone back. "We're just trying to get a name at this point. There wasn't any ID in the clothes and the body was too decomposed for a visual one."

"Thomas's dead?" Gil asks quietly from the open doorway.

As I give Gil a solemn nod, Bash steps forward, his tone all business. "Where did you find his body?"

"Some homeless dude stumbled upon it in an abandoned part of the Lower East Side."

"Which road?" Bash drills.

The young guy starts to answer, when his partner interrupts, looking at Gil. "Can you provide Thomas's full name and home address? We'll need his dental records so we can officially ID him."

While the officer follows Gil into his office, I ask the younger cop, "Where was he found? It'll help the guys here with closure if they have the full story."

He glances at his partner writing down the information from Gil and whispers, "Don't tell him I told you, but I understand the need for closure. The guy was found in a Dumpster next to the old Opera house in the Bowery."

Once the officers leave, I follow Bash out, my chest tight. First the news about Cass potentially facing a murder charge, and now this? I've never felt so powerless. I fucking want to punch a wall. Cass's face flickers through my mind. I hate that I can't be there with her right now. And Celeste...God. I clench both fists, digging my fingers into the gloves. I will find a way to completely destroy Phillip for all the misery he has caused.

"You okay, Cald?"

"I blame myself for not seeing how unhappy Celeste

was. I could've shared my thoughts on Phillip. I could've—"

"*Don't* go there." Bash scowls. "You just found out from Gil how truly despicable Phillip is. Your mom, Celeste, and now the way he has set Cass up to take the fall…they're all victims of the narcissistic son of a bitch's maneuverings. A person with sociopathic tendencies like his obviously lives in that space where he believes he'll never be caught."

I shake my head and try not to freak about Cass. If I do, I might just lose my shit. Taking a couple of deep breaths, I work to refocus on something less personal. "Okay… back to Thomas. The guys in the gym clung to the belief that Thomas had just gotten frustrated and started over somewhere else, but Gil and I knew he wasn't the type to run from a fight. Unfortunately, the location where he was dumped wasn't anywhere near any of the previous secret EUC bouts, so there's nothing in the location that directly ties it to the EUC ."

"I'm going to have my guys check out the site anyway, while I run down how Thomas died. If he was shot and bullets were recovered, we might be able to help the police connect the dots."

I nod my thanks. "Call me as soon as you get the paternity results, and Bash…make sure to check that Cass is doing okay—"

Bash puts his hand on my shoulder. "Talia's already at the station with our lawyer waiting for the lab to call. We've got it covered." When I nod and start to go back inside, his hold tightens. "I shouldn't have to tell you to watch your back, Cald. I'm sorry about your friend, but I hope this kick-in-the-gut brings things into sharp focus as to where your head needs to be. Winning this fight puts you behind the curtain. I want to know what the hell they didn't want Thomas to see back there."

CHAPTER TWENTY-ONE

Cass

"*Go* on, jump!" *Jake stands to my left, his voice carrying over the howling wind.*

I shake my head, my heart screaming inside my chest. I'm on the edge of a cliff overlooking a wide valley. I try to step back, but my feet won't move. I wobble instead and gasp as I almost pitch forward.

"You know it's for the best. It'll be quicker this way," Phillip says from my right, his hazel eyes turning toward the valley below, showing me where to go.

"No," I whisper, my voice trembling. Rocks scatter underneath my feet, tumbling down, down until they disappear into the dark cavern.

"She's gone. That means you no longer exist either," Phillip speaks calmly, his tone clear and logical.

"You're the doppelganger who was supposed to die. Not her," Jake sneers and jabs my shoulder with his knuckles.

When I cringe and try to avoid another jab, Phillip grabs my right arm and tugs, trying to send me over.

I scream with everything I've got, and then I hear Calder's voice in the distance behind me. *"Cass, I'm coming!"*

"Calder!" I yell and glance over my shoulder, trying to see him. My heart leaps and I try to pull free of Phillip's hold, but now Jake has grabbed my other arm and is pushing my shoulder forward with the flat of his other hand.

"Calder," I call out and look back once more. He's running hard, but he doesn't seem to be getting any closer.

The toe of my right shoe pushes just over the cliff, and then the left. Both men shove me at once, and I scream as I tumble forward, falling into total blackness...

"Get up, missy."

My eyes fly open to see a thick-boned woman with short dark hair standing in the doorway. Her police uniform registers and my chest suddenly feels like it's collapsing.

"Yes?"

She pulls open the door, her stoic face not giving any indication as to what she wants. "Let's go."

I sit up in the lumpy bunk bed and glance around the tiny windowless room. I must've fallen asleep around eight in the morning. I'd been too anxious to sleep in the cell last night. I wanted to be awake when the news came.

Worry fills me. *Were we wrong? Phillip wasn't the baby's father?* "Where are we going?"

"Paperwork," she grumbles.

When I see Felicity standing there smiling after we walk through another door, my eyes well with tears and I croak, "Can I go home now?"

She nods. "The police are on their way to Phillip's house as we speak. Now let's get this paperwork done and get you out of here."

As soon as we walk into the front of the police station, Talia jumps up from her chair and hugs me.

"Tell Sebastian I'll touch base with him later," Felicity says as I slip on the wool coat Talia brought for me. Squeezing my shoulder, the lawyer smiles and leaves us standing there in the busy station.

"You're free." Talia keeps her tone light as she fusses with the buttons on the coat. Making sure I'm fully buttoned up, she pulls me into a really tight hug and whispers harshly in my ear, "Don't ever worry me like that again. I think I've grown a few gray hairs the last few days." Releasing me, she hooks her arm in mine and walks me out the door. "I'm so glad we got him, Cass. Phillip is going down."

My stomach pitches as the news sinks in and the cool morning air hits my face. It's not that I didn't expect Phillip's guilt, but hearing it and knowing what that truth means about Celeste's past makes my heart ache for the loss of Celeste's and her unborn child's lives, but also for the loss of her youth and of her innocence. *Everything* that vile man stole from her.

Somewhere a bird chirps, unsure if it's spring yet. I glance up as it zooms past, its wings spread wide, and my heart squeezes. I'm free, but Celeste will never be.

I take three steps, but don't make it any farther.

My legs give out and I sit down in the middle of the sidewalk, letting the tears fall.

I cry harder than I ever have before.

All the hurt I've held back rushes out in deep, heart-wrenching sobs.

For the loss of my sister.

The loss of my own innocence.

The loss of myself for years.

For almost dying.

Every bit of pain flows with the tears dripping onto my knees as I grip my wrists.

And Talia holds me. My best friend sits beside me and folds her arms tight around me. Rocking me against her warm body, she says in my ear, "I love you, Cass. I'll always be here for you. I'm your sister and you're mine. 'Til death do us part."

When the tears dry, I gulp back a sob and snicker. "I think Sebastian might have something to say about you using that line with me."

She giggles and whispers, "Shh, it'll be our secret." Wiping the tears from my cheeks, she holds my face, her gaze searching mine. "Are you all right?"

I clasp her hands and squeeze. "I will be. There um… was more going on just now."

"I know." Sighing, she pulls me to my feet and tucks a hank of my hair behind my ear. "I also figure you'll tell me when you're ready."

"I told your mom that you're staying the week with me," Talia says once we pull away from the station in her car.

"Thank you for covering for me," I say, staring absently at Manhattan's busy traffic. Its chaotic normalcy is strangely soothing.

"Sebastian will let Calder know you're okay," she continues and I just nod my appreciation. Now that I've bawled like a baby, I feel numb and drained. I fold my arms against myself, thankful for the coat she brought. The dress' thin sleeves are pretty, but not warm at all. Talia had my back in so many ways, but especially the last twenty-four hours. I'll never be able to repay her, but I can try.

"Thank you so much for Felicity. That woman is a… power pixie."

Talia chuckles. "Sebastian calls her his pocket secret weapon."

My eyes widen. "There's no way he says that to her face."

"This is Sebastian we're talking about." She snorts. "The man never holds back. Though I'm pretty sure he's the only one who gets to call her that."

We're quiet while she maneuvers through traffic, then she says in a casual tone, "I noticed last night that your tattoos were gone. How'd you manage that feat?"

Talia's trying to draw me out, when all I want to do is crawl inside myself. She's been here for me and I need to return her friendship.

I lower my hands to my knees and turn them palms

up, staring at the bit of bare skin peeking outside of the dress and coat's sleeves. "Beth covered my tattoos for me. I miss them. I can't wait to wash the makeup away."

"Tell me what the raven means. Why do you kiss it every once in a while," she asks quietly.

"The raven represents my sister." I rub my thumb along the scarred skin that the raven and branch normally hide. How ironic that the makeup makes the scars stand out in vivid clarity in the daylight.

She raises her eyebrows. "I didn't know you have a sister."

"Had," I correct her, then continue as I lift my gaze and stare straight ahead. "When I told you what Celeste did to me back in high school, I didn't tell you the whole story." Taking a deep breath, I tell Talia everything. About Jake and Brent, my sister's death, and my past issues with cutting. I vomit it all out without stopping, like I'm telling someone else's horrible history. I'm thankful that Talia never interrupts, but once I'm done and she still doesn't speak, I glance over to see silent tears streaking down her face, her hands tight on the steering wheel.

Finally she looks at me, her eyes glassy. "Jake? Until you just retold the whole story...I didn't put two-and-two together. I'd forgotten the boy's name tied to Celeste from high school. Jake Hemming is the Jake from your story."

When I nod, she reaches for my hand and folds our fingers together. "How could you go through with helping Celeste knowing that Jake would be there?"

I shrug. "At the time I agreed to help Celeste, I didn't

know that she knew Jake on a personal level outside of high school. She'd always blown him off at school. But by the time I got detailed information from Celeste about the people in her family's life, I'd already agreed to help and was knee-deep. I had to go through with it. The *only* reason I was able to continue on as Celeste after Phillip, Gregory, and Beth discovered that I wasn't her is because Jake still believed I was, and Phillip insisted that his sons not be told." I sigh and shake my head. "Which worked up until Jake somehow found out the truth. I'm still not sure who told him, but while laying in that cell last night, I realized that Jake had to be the one who called the police with that anonymous tip."

Laughing a bit manically, I slide my hand from hers and rub my temple. "Can you imagine my horror to discover Beth's boyfriend Brent is the other boy I never saw, but the voice I'd never forget? At times, it felt like Jake and Brent were the perfect storm to test my sanity to its limit."

"There is no way you told Calder any of this, Cass."

I tense at the disapproval in her tone. "I told Calder what happened in high school, but I refused to tell him the boys' names. He would've bodily carried me out of the Carver house right then and there, and we never would've learned about Phillip, the baby or any of it."

Talia's lips press together in angry frustration, but I stand my ground. "Don't look at me like that. I did what I had to do, and because of my time in Celeste's world, hers and her baby's death will have justice."

She grudgingly nods, but then tilts her head, looking

thoughtful. "Do you think Beth told Brent about you, and since he knew Jake in high school that he's the one who told Jake?"

I shake my head. "Beth did tell Brent about me, claiming he's the only person she trusted. Even though Brent never came around the estate, I worried about the possibility he could share that information with Jake, so I asked her how she met Brent. Turns out, she met him when she attended one of the MMA events with some friends. That and the fact that Beth kept Brent a secret from her family, probably because in her heart she knew his business dealings could hurt her father's career, makes me think that the two guys aren't friends, not any more. Jake had to have found out another way."

"Well, now that you're away from the Carver estate, you need to tell Calder all of it, Cass. About Jake and Brent…everything."

"I will, but not until after the fight is over. I don't want to distract him."

"I get what you're thinking, Cass, but considering Brent is running the group Calder's trying to take down, I think he should know now. That way he has a full picture of that guy and doesn't go in blind. Oh, by the way, he's not going by Brent Taylor. That's why his name was a dead end. He's using his mother's maiden name, Tremmel."

"Ah, I see. You do make a good point about telling Calder." Glancing out the window, I look around in confusion when I don't recognize the upscale street Talia just turned down. "Where are we going?"

She takes two more turns and hits the button on her sun visor, stopping in front of a high-end apartment building. "You're staying with Sebastian and me."

"Talia..." I sigh heavily as we pull into the building's underground parking. "I know you told my mom already and I appreciate it, but I really just want to go home to my own bed."

"No arguing, Cass." She parks and cuts the engine, turning to me. "With what you've just been through, you're not spending time alone."

"But—"

Talia clasps my hand between hers. "Do it for me, Cass. You had even more going on than I could've possibly imagined. I'm freaking out more than a little here. I need to see you smile and laugh again, and know that you're okay."

"I *am* okay," I insist.

When her lips purse, her gaze full of skepticism, I glance toward the elevator. Knowing my wishes have been outvoted, I give in to my friend. "So are you going to show me this awesome place I've never seen or hold my hand all day?"

After I *ooh* and *ahh* over their apartment's amazing top floor view of Manhattan, Talia sets two duffle bags on the island in their kitchen. Pointing to the first one, she says, "I know you want to get a shower, so here's a few days worth of clothes."

I glance up at her, my eyebrow hiked high. "You planned this all along. When did you go by my apartment?"

"Yesterday," she says, giving me an unrepentant look. "I still have a key, remember?"

Gesturing to the other bag, I ask, "And what's in there?"

Talia unzips the bag and pulls out my favorite go-to camera. "I thought you might be missing this. Your phone is in this bag too."

I immediately snag the camera from her grip. "Never hold it by the lens, silly." Before she can turn away, I quickly snap four pictures in a row of her staring at me with a wide smile. She truly is a beauty, but she has never let me take her picture before without putting a hand up and fussing. Apparently life with Sebastian has made her truly comfortable in her own skin. Lowering the camera, I smile at that realization. "Thank you. I've missed this so much."

She gestures to the apartment. "Well, this neighborhood is right up your luxurious lifestyle alley. So go out and walk around, snapping pics to your heart's content.

"I'll probably go explore just to get my muse muscles working again, but I actually have another project in mind I've been planning. I want to create a photo book highlighting real life here in New York, beyond the glitz and glamor." Setting the camera down, I glance toward the bedroom she said I would be using. "But for now, I'm definitely taking you up on that shower."

Sebastian walks out of their penthouse elevator just as I rejoin Talia in the kitchen, where she'd laid out plates of meat, cheese, bread and fruit and insisted that I eat.

"Hey, jailbird," he says to me as he shrugs out of his

suit jacket and drops it on the back of a kitchen chair.

When I frown at him in the midst of taking a bite of my sandwich, he looks at Talia, all innocence. "Too soon?"

As she rolls her eyes and pinches her fingers close together while chewing on a mouthful of blueberries, I fluff my damp hair. "And just when I was about to thank you for sending Felicity, the power-pixie, my way."

Sebastian barks his laugh as he approaches Talia sitting on the stool opposite me. "That's definitely going in my arsenal for future use when Felicity is being particularly stubborn," he says before kissing his wife on the temple.

His laughter subsiding, he pushes Talia's hair over her shoulder and lightly massages the back of her neck, addressing us. "I'm sure you'll both love to hear that they expect to bring charges against Phillip Hemming for Celeste's murder."

"Justice prevails," Talia says, raising her glass of juice to me.

"I couldn't have done it without all of your help," I say, smiling my appreciation.

Sebastian nods. "Calder's been asking about you. He wants to be here, Cass."

"I know, I know. He's getting ready for the fight." I shrug off my disappointment and force an understanding expression. "I hope he hasn't lost too much time with this stuff that it hurts his training."

"Cald will get there. He's incentivized."

"In what way?" Talia asks, glancing up at Sebastian.

He leans over and takes a bite of his wife's sandwich.

"I have more research for you later if you're up for it."

When she glances at me, a torn look on her face, I yawn and stretch. "Don't mind me. After I take a quick walk to get my photography fix in, I'm going to fall into bed and sleep for a year."

Talia smiles, then says to Sebastian, "Oh, I've been meaning to ask you about this..." She brushes her hands clean on a napkin, then hops off the stool to open her purse on a shelf next to the window. Retrieving something, she hands it to Sebastian. "Do you know a jeweler who might be able to fix this?"

My heart clenches when he lifts up the pavé raven and black velvet ribbon necklace, frowning his confusion. "Whose is this?"

"It's mine," I say, glancing at Talia while I eat a strawberry. "Thank you for getting it for me. The whole jailbird thing distracted me."

Sebastian gestures toward me, his smirk telling his wife, *Justified.*

She gives him a stern look. "*She* can say it. You can't." Looking at me, she says, "Beth put it in my hand right before we left their house. She said she saw us talking and asked me if I could be sure to get it to you."

"Do you think it can be repaired?" I ask Sebastian, hoping.

"It was a gift from Calder," Talia tells him as she returns to her seat. "The second apparently, since he'd already given her a leather one with a silver raven."

Sebastian inspects the pavé raven. "This is quite the

upgrade from leather and silver."

I smile, but shake my head. "I prefer the leather one. It's something I can wear everyday. I had to leave it behind at Calder's apartment, because it's not the type of jewelry Celeste would wear. Calder gave me this one so I could wear something more in line with Celeste's style."

He tries to bend the mangled clasp back into place. "This is destroyed. What happened to it?"

I twist my lips in anger. "Jake didn't think it was Celeste's style at all."

"What?" Sebastian jerks furious blue eyes to me. "He destroyed it because it wasn't something Celeste would wear?"

"Yes, he did." I drop the strawberry back to my plate, my appetite suddenly gone. "If it can't be repaired, can you recommend someone who can replace the clasp?"

"It truly is beautiful and one of a kind," Talia says, watching her husband try once more to fix the clasp so it'll stay closed.

I smile and sigh. "For a guy with commitment issues, Calder sure gives gorgeous gifts. He'll freak out if he sees this. I would like to restore it back to its original condition so he won't have to."

Sebastian grunts and turns his attention to me. "My cousin has issues he's dealing with, but commitment to you isn't one of them."

I snort my disagreement. "He flat out said he doesn't plan to marry. I'd say that's highly commitment allergic."

Curling his fingers around the ribbon, Sebastian turns

to face me. "Calder doesn't buy gifts *once*, let alone twice. When you couldn't wear his other necklace, he replaced it with this one so you could. He's collared you, Cass. This choker is as committed as a wedding band. In his mind, you're his."

"That's a stretch," I say, trying to ignore the warm fuzzies and false hope his statement gives me. "Yes, Calder's a bit territorial, but that's not the same as...ugh, never mind." Waving to Talia as she takes a sip of her juice, I say, "Tell your husband he doesn't know what he's talking about with this 'collared' stuff."

Talia coughs and spews juice all over the granite island.

Sebastian slides my necklace in his pants pocket, then flattens his palm on the center of Talia's back as she wheezes and hacks. "Do you need me to smack you back here? Just tell me where, Little Red."

When Talia glances up at him with murderous eyes, her face turning bright red as she continues coughing, I laugh. "I think that look means you'd better let her catch her breath on her own."

I wake in the darkness to the sensation of warm fingers tracing my cheek, while a clean, masculine smell tickles my senses.

"Calder..." I inhale deeply and try to touch his face, but I'm still too groggy to make my arm work properly.

He chuckles and takes my flailing hand. "Hey,

sleepyhead," he says quietly, kissing my knuckles. "I'm relieved you're okay. What did you need to talk to me about? Your note said it was important."

I glance at the clock. Nine. I can't believe I've slept the whole day away. "Are you okay? How's training going?" I search the shadowed planes of his face, giving myself time to form the right words.

"Training is fine." His steady gaze holds mine as he presses his lips to my fingers.

"I wanted to wait until after your fight, but Talia said you need to know now." I pause, psyching myself up to tell him. "You asked me who the two boys were from high school…"

Calder stills, then he quickly pulls me upright and sits on the bed facing me, his thigh pressed to mine. "Tell me."

Exhaling slowly, I say, "It was Jake Hemming and Brent Taylor…who's apparently going by Brent Tremmel."

Calder's expression instantly shifts from tender concern to cold steel. "Why didn't you tell me before now?"

Tension makes my heart race and I curl my fingers around the covers. "Because you wouldn't let me stay, and staying was the only way to clear myself of suspicion and help Celeste. When I agreed to help Celeste, I had no idea that she knew Jake personally. And I never saw the other guy's face that night, but when I heard Beth talking to Brent on her speakerphone…I'll never forget his voice. Despite my past colliding with my present…I knew I could handle it, because Beth never brought Brent around and Jake didn't know that Celeste was actually me."

"But Jake did learn who you were," he says in a tight voice.

I reach for his hand, but he quickly stands and stares at the ceiling, his fingers digging into his scalp. "Calder, the *only* reason I'm telling you now is because of Brent's role in the EUC. Talia thought you should know."

He glances down at me, his tone hard, judging. "I told you the Hemmings were monsters."

I shake my head, surprised *that's* what he's focusing on. "Ben's not like that—"

"You *don't* get to say that any more, Cass," he grates.

"Yes, I do…" I say, pushing back the covers to stand in front of him. Tugging on his hoodie's string, I look up at him and flatten my hand on the soft fabric across his chest. "For the very reason I knew firsthand how shitty his brother *and* father could be."

His hard chest rises and falls under my hand, his breathing elevating as he looks down at me. "Well, I don't have to stand here and listen to it."

I'm surprised by the pain and anger in his eyes. When he turns to walk away, I grab his hand. "Don't leave."

He pivots back to me. "I need to stay focused, Cass. This…" He exhales deeply. "Isn't helping."

I release his hand, guilt squeezing my chest. "I'm sorry. I thought…I was just trying to—"

Calder clasps the back of my neck and presses a soft kiss to my forehead. "It's not you, angel," he whispers against my skin. "But I need to go."

And before I can say a word, he leaves me standing there in the dark.

CHAPTER TWENTY-TWO

Cass

I park at the curb outside my apartment and turn my phone on after packing my camera away for the day. I'm excited about the pictures I was able to capture for my New York city book idea; my mind is already hopping with other locations to explore tomorrow. My phone instantly buzzes with several texts from Talia.

Talia: Did you see that the Carvers are holding a private funeral for Celeste late today? It was in the morning's paper.

Talia: Where are you? I've tried to call. I just get voicemail.

Talia: Where have you been? I've been calling all day. Sebastian pinged your phone. I'm officially freaking out. I should never have let you go home yesterday!

So much for going off the grid for a bit. I sigh and hit the button to call her.

Talia picks up on the first ring. "I don't know whether to hug you or wring your neck."

"I'm fine, Talia," I say, shaking my head. "At some point you need to stop worrying about me and get your chapters done. Don't you have a deadline coming up?"

"Which I could concentrate on if you'd answer my text or better yet come back here and stay."

"I wasn't ignoring you. I had my phone turned off so I could get work done. I've been driving all over the city taking black and white pics. I'm really digging finding the best of New York's real life."

"I know Phillip is being held on charges, but please keep your phone on. I promise not to bother you too much."

"I love you too. And thanks for letting me know about the funeral. I'm sure the Carvers need closure."

"Probably. I was trying to get in touch with you for another reason too. Can you send me some of your pictures? I want to pitch your book to my editor."

My heart races. Talia's publisher is the biggest and oldest in the country. "Really? You don't have to do that, but thank you!"

"I'm just the messenger, Cass. Your work has to sell the idea."

I grin like a loon, appreciating her so much for giving me something to work *toward*. So far I've been using my creative outlet to force me out of the apartment. That way I wouldn't think about the fact I haven't heard from Calder since I saw him thirty-six hours ago. "Love you anyway.

I'll get some prints to you with a mock up of how I see the page layouts."

"Sounds good. I'll be waiting."

Hanging up, I get out of my car and start toward my apartment entrance when my steps slow. Ben is leaning against the post right outside the building, his arms crossed.

When I arrived at my apartment yesterday, my doorman told me a guy named Ben stopped by and left his number for me. I was glad I'd missed that conversation, but it looks like I can't avoid it any longer.

Stepping onto the sidewalk, I haul my camera bag onto my shoulder. "Hey, Ben."

He meets me halfway across the sidewalk, his wool jacket open, hands in his jean pockets. "Hey."

He doesn't look angry or even mad, so I put my hand out and smile. "I'm Cass."

Ben lets out a half-laugh and takes my hand. "Nice to know your real name." Releasing my hand, he looks at me with a self-deprecating smirk. "Though I'm pretty sure I knew all along you weren't Celeste. I *knew* something was different. But I didn't care. That girl I couldn't take my eyes off of four years ago at that masked party was back… and I was going to do everything in my power to keep her."

"Ben…" I say, unsure how to reply to that statement. His world has just been torn apart with his father's arrest. So far the papers haven't disclosed Celeste's pregnancy or talked about the evidence that links her death to Phillip, but still, Ben must be spinning.

"I know you were just playing a part, Cass, but I wanted you to know that I didn't believe *any* of what my father and Gregory accused you of."

As I nod my appreciation, realization dawns. "Did you send a lawyer to help me?"

"I did, but it appears your lawyer ate mine for lunch." Nodding, he gestures toward the sidewalk. "Can we take a walk?"

"Sure," I say, falling in line beside him.

Ben looks straight ahead, and says, "I'm sincerely sorry for what my father tried to do to you, Cass. I'm not sure how many of the despicable things he's being accused of are true, and honestly, I don't want to know the details. But if even part of it is, I hope he pays for it. I think Jake is in shock. He's kind of disappeared, but my mom is fully supporting my dad. She doesn't believe any of it."

"Why do you believe it?" I ask, curious as to what would make a son turn against his father.

Ben squints against the cool wind ruffling his dark hair. "Because of what he tried to do to you."

"Me?" When I gape at him, he nods.

"You were the final push I needed to accept that my father is truly a bad person. I've grown up watching him manipulate everyone around him into doing what he wants: my mother, my brother, me, Gregory. I can't tell you how many times he pitted Jake against me. I would always be second fiddle to Jake in his eyes. When I was younger, I was in awe of his powers of persuasion, but as I grew older, I came to recognize his machinations for what they really were...sheer selfishness. He doesn't care for anyone other than himself. The fact that he fully supported my request to marry Celeste, overriding Jake's assumption that he would be with her, should've been a red flag to me that more was going on. Celeste and I really seemed to click that night, so I was too happy to question it."

"I'm sorry, Ben. For all of it. No son should have to compete for his father's love or approval."

Ben shrugs. "He's the reason Jake and I aren't close like brothers should be. I don't plan to attend any of his hearings or support him. I'm beyond furious that they let him out on bail."

I instantly stop and turn to him. "What? He's out? Since when?"

He glances at his watch. "My mom called to tell me an hour ago."

And just like that, the sense of relief I'd been feeling completely evaporates and my mind starts whirling. *Does Phillip know I was the one behind the evidence against him?* "But he's been charged with murder. How is that even possible?"

"My father is one of the best lawyers in New York. He's been 'cooperating' with the police...and there's no body. No one can work the system like Phillip Hemming."

Ben is suddenly shoved away from my side, and Calder pulls me behind him, growling in a deadly tone, "Stay the fuck away from her, you Hemming piece of shit."

"Calder!" Pushing free of his hold, I dodge around him and step between he and Ben just as Ben rebalances and charges back at Calder.

Barring my hands on both guys' chests, I look at Ben and say in a calm voice, "I think it's time for you to go, Ben."

He looks down at me, still fuming at Calder's unprovoked attack, but I nod firmly. "I'm serious, Ben. Now is not a good time. Please, just leave."

I wait until Ben drives away to face Calder. "What the hell is wrong with you?"

His expression turns livid. "The moment I find out that Phillip is free, I rush over here to make sure that you're safe, only to find you chatting it up with the murderous bastard's son? How many more sick Hemming fucks are you going to hang out with?"

I step back, gutted by that slap in the face. "Why would you say something so mean?"

"So you wake the fuck up and stay away from him," he bites out.

We glare at each other for a second before he rubs his forehead and sighs. "Go pack a bag, Cass. I'll take you over to Bash and Talia's."

I turn to walk back toward my apartment, fury building in my chest that I let Sebastian's comments about Calder and me get in my head. What Calder just said was meant to hurt. Who does that to someone they care about? I'm going to take that fucking choker and wrap it around Sebastian's neck.

When Calder starts to follow me inside the main door, I turn and push him back. "*If* I decide to go to Talia and Sebastian's, I'll drive myself there. Since you're all about keeping your distance lately, you should probably get back to that."

The muscle in Calder's jaw jumps. "I'm trying to protect you."

"Oh yeah? Who's going to protect me from you?"

Calder steps back, tension etching the brackets on his face. "You're probably right. This is for the best."

I watch him walk away, his hands deep in his jean pockets. My heart slowly shreds with each step he takes. I want to call him back and demand that he tell me what's going on because the Calder I thought I knew doesn't say intentionally cruel things.

I hadn't planned on coming, but for some reason after taking three more hours of photos, my car finds its way to Trinity's cemetery. The cemetery is peaceful with just a few others paying their respects to their loved ones.

Parked outside the gates, I watch the Carvers say goodbye to their oldest daughter, while the pastor reads scripture from the Bible in his hand.

It's a small group, just the immediate family: Gregory, Nadine, and Beth, while their security guards stand discretely back.

Nadine's hair partially covers her face as she weeps

uncontrollably. Beth tries to console her mother as her father stands there stoically, his face pale and unblinking.

The pastor stops speaking and moves away to give the family some privacy. Beth lays a bouquet of pink roses on her sister's grave, and then takes the red roses her mom is holding and puts them on the grave too. Standing, she helps her mother walk inside the church, while Gregory follows slowly behind. The pastor goes in last, closing the door behind him.

I wait a few minutes, and then put on my sunglasses as I make my way through the front gate. I'm thankful that the media has respected Gregory's wishes for privacy, but the last thing I want is for anyone to see me and recognize *Celeste*.

The flowers are both beautiful and bittersweet lying against the brand new headstone. Untouched by weather and time, the stone shines. My lips tremble when I squat down and read the inscription.

May Celeste and her little angel find peace in heaven's arms.

"I'm sorry for what happened to you, Celeste. I tried my best to help."

My heart jumps when Beth speaks quietly beside me. "I had to slip out for a bit while the pastor talks with my parents. It was getting to me."

When I straighten to stand beside her, she lifts her gaze to mine. "I should never have doubted you, Cass. I'm sorry. Truly I am."

I shake my head. "I understand. Phillip was very good. It's how he got away with everything he did for so long."

"And he still might," Beth says, curling her lip in disgust. "We just learned that they released Phillip on bail. Our lawyer says bail was probably allowed because all the evidence against him is circumstantial. He says the prosecutor will need something more than just the fact that Celeste was pregnant with his baby and them driving on the same road to try to get it revoked."

My brow furrows. "But what about the diary? It shows a pattern of Celeste's dark thoughts that goes back for years, starting right after that Fourth of July vacation."

Beth blinks. "Celeste only called the person the Deceiver and other names in her diary. She never mentioned Phillip directly."

I bite my lip, wishing we could have tied the Deceiver text from that burner phone to Phillip. Unfortunately because a baby wasn't directly mentioned either, lawyers can only make assumptions that that person was talking about an unborn child. But there's a *definite* threat toward Celeste in the text…if we could only tie it to Phillip.

I sigh my frustration and look at Beth, noting the dark circles under her eyes as she quietly stares at her sister's headstone. "How are you doing, Beth?"

"My mother cries a lot, though it's getting less now. My father is devastated. Not only did he lose his daughter, but he was betrayed in the worst possible way by his best friend. He's decided not to run for the Senate and instead focus on our family. He and I are going to run Carver Enterprises together so he can spend more time with Mom."

She said all that like she was reading it off a teleprompter. I reach over and clasp her hand. "I asked how *you* were doing."

She squeezes my hand and exhales a shaky breath. "You've been more a sister to me these past few days then Celeste has been since we were kids." She glances down at the gravestone. "I don't blame her; I now know that Phillip was the one who changed her."

Looking back at me, she says, "I'd better get back inside, take care, Cass." She starts to walk away, then quickly turns back. Opening her purse, she holds out an envelope. "I've decided to pull closer to home too. I think you had fun that night we went to Brent's MMA event. Why don't you use this? I won't be going."

"Are you and Brent over?" I ask, trying to keep the relief out of my voice.

She glances down at the envelope she's holding, her lips twisted in a wry smile. "Take it and keep me from temptation."

I quickly take it before she changes her mind. "When you're ready, the right guy will come along."

She shrugs. "Honestly, Cass. I don't really care. Right now I'm just...numb."

Before she can walk away, I give her a quick hug. "Goodbye, Beth. Take care of yourself." I'm surprised at how tightly she hugs me back, so I whisper into her hair, "You will always miss Celeste, but over time the pain will fade."

Sobbing, she squeezes me once more, then hurries back into the church.

CHAPTER TWENTY-THREE

The Observer

I stand behind a tree, digging my fingers into the bark as I watch them hovering around Celeste's grave.

Gregory looks pale. Did he ever really care about her? Or is that guilt adding more lines to his face?

Nadine is sobbing. I never remember her being an emotional person.

Beth's expression is blank as she tries to console her mother.

So much grief over an empty coffin.

I know where she is…but they'll never find her.

She had to remain mine forever.

I've come full circle with my acceptance of her death.

My gaze drops to her headstone as her family walks into the church.

Now no one can try to impersonate her.

Celeste was unique. A one of a kind.

She'll remain that way, frozen in time.

Peace washes through me. "Things are as they should be." I start to walk away when someone else approaches her grave.

What's she doing here? Cass Rockwell, who all the news outlets are dubbing as Celeste's "doppelganger," bends down and stares at the inscription. When I move to another tree to get a better view, Beth joins her by the grave. I watch her straighten next to Celeste's sister and dissect their expressions. Frustration. Anger. Sympathy. *Friendship?*

My gaze sharpens. *No one* can resurrect Celeste.

I won't allow it.

Celeste must remain mine forever.

CHAPTER TWENTY-FOUR

Cass

Darkness descends on the empty graveyard. Dead leaves rustle with the cooler air swirling among the graves. A chill rushes across the back of my neck, evoking a sense that I'm not alone. The lamppost suddenly pops on, its warm glow creating long shadows off the headstones. The feeling shifts to one of being watched. I quickly glance around, looking for the source. Sighing, I touch Celeste's gravestone and say a final goodbye.

My emotions ping all over the place as I drive away from the cemetery. Celeste's death and then seeing the finality of her gravestone hit me hard. Why didn't she tell *someone*?

Life is too fucking short.

I'm suddenly angry with myself for not calling Calder

out on his bullshit earlier and demanding that he tell me what was going on. Whatever it is…it's way beyond his claim he was protecting me. My gut told me that something was eating at him, but I let him distract me. And then he just walked away.

Screw it.

No better time than the present.

I turn my car around and head in the direction of his apartment.

By the time I get close to his apartment, common sense and reasoning starts to set in. Calder's worried for my safety. That's why he has stayed away. Driving right up to his place is probably not the smartest move. I pull over to the curb and park a hundred feet away, chewing my lip as I stare up at the light on in his place.

Pressing my forehead to the steering wheel, I realize this is foolish. We'll have time to talk later.

I sit up and reach over to turn on the engine when Calder's apartment door opens. A woman steps out and turns back to say something as she tugs on a sweater over a sports bra.

My heart tightens and I immediately reach for my camera, zooming in on her face. Fucking Alana! Calder joins her at the door, shirtless, and she laughs at something he says, then leans in and kisses his jaw.

He's protecting me? But what about her? He doesn't *look* like he doesn't give a shit about the tattoo artist.

I snap the shot to remind myself why I'm never speaking to Calder again.

I glare at her as she lugs her big-ass purse and other bag onto her shoulder. I refuse to stare at how well her leather pants show off her tight ass, but I exhale a breath of relief once she drives away.

My hand shakes as I try to put the key back in the ignition. Two tries later and I still haven't managed to get the damn key in. "Fuck!" I scream and throw the keys onto the floorboard.

Leaning over, I grab my keys and get out of my car, slamming the door shut behind me.

I don't knock lightly. I take out my anger and hammer several times on his door.

He swings it open, a scowl on his face, fist raised... until he sees me and his anger shifts from shock to fury... all in an instant.

Grabbing my arm, he yanks me into his apartment and quickly shuts the door. "What the hell are you doing here?"

I yank my arm free and slap him hard. "Fuck you!"

Calder grips the back of my hair and pushes me against the wall, his hard chest trapping my arm between us. My handprint vivid against his flexing jaw, he bites out, "That'd better be a precursor for one *seriously* hot fuck, because I sure as shit didn't deserve that."

"You lying bastard!" I grit my teeth at his sheer arrogance and try to slap him again with my free hand, but he grabs my wrist and traps it against the wall.

Folding his fingers tighter in my hair, he tilts my head back, his tone hardening. "What the fuck are you talking about?"

"You pretending that keeping your distance was for *my* safety, when it was all about you screwing your ex-girlfriend."

Surprise lights in his eyes before he steps between my legs and aggressively presses his erection against my body. His soft black lounge pants accentuating his steel hardness, he tugs my hair to turn my head to the side and rasp in my ear, "Does this *feel* like I've been fucking someone else, Cass?"

I close my eyes and refuse to let the feel of him, hard and ready against me, turn me on. I try to keep it together, but my voice shakes with anger. "I know you can go all night, so that only pisses me off more."

Calder traces his thumb along the base of my hairline just behind my ear, his breath hot against my temple. "I have never wanted to fuck that sweet pussy of yours more than I do right at this moment, Cass Rockwell."

"I saw her leaving, Calder," I snap, my chest heaving with fury. "Let me *go*."

"No," he rasps, nipping at my neck.

I gasp, tears welling. Not from the pain, but because I still can't help but want him despite his betrayal. He has seriously embedded himself in my heart and screwed with my head.

He slowly plants hot kisses along my jaw, killing me with wicked intent, his mastery over my body so strong, my muscles tighten in response. Loosening his fingers on my wrist, he slides them down my arm to trace the side of my breast with his thumb. "How does it feel to see me with another person?"

His incendiary words flint over my raw nerves, sparking my fury once more.

I shove at his chest, and when he stumbles back a few steps, completely taken by surprise, I run at him like a linebacker, blind rage fueling my strength.

We land on the thick rug in his living room, but I don't stop to take pleasure in the *oomph* that rushes past his lips. When I crawl over him to hammer his chest with my fist, Calder grabs my arm and quickly flips me onto my back.

Before I can recover, he straddles my hips and grabs my arms, slamming them down to the thick pile of rug underneath me. "Look at me," he growls.

I squeeze my eyes shut and shake my head, my chest heaving.

Pulling my arms together, Calder grips both wrists with one hand, then clasps my jaw and forces my face forward, commanding, "Fucking look at me, Cass!"

When I drill my furious gaze into his intense green one, his anger evaporates. "What do you see, Raven mine?"

His dog tags sway slowly back and forth between us, reminding me of our most intimate times together. It hurts too much to be this close, to inhale his arousing scent, and yet feel so very far apart. I whimper and close my eyes.

The necklace chinks as he drops it on the carpet next to me, then slides his thumb down my chin, his fingers feathering along the front of my throat. "I will hold you like this all night if I have to." The arousing promise in his voice is like heavy silk sliding along my skin.

When his hand moves to my shirt and he tugs several buttons free, my eyes fly open in renewed anger. "You don't get to do that—" I stop speaking when my gaze locks on the black-feathered tattoo fanning over his left forearm and up his shoulder. I'd been too freaking angry to see it before. I meet his gaze. "Alana's the one who paints your Steel tattoo?" When he nods, I press my lips together. "I saw her *getting dressed*, Calder."

"It takes her hours to paint the tattoo while also covering up my real one, Cass. She gets hot, so yeah, she wears a sports bra so she can remove her shirt if she needs to while she works."

I frown, unhappy with that answer. "So you'd be okay if I spent hours with some other guy half-naked? Maybe I should ask Noah how well nude modeling pays."

Calder quickly clasps the back of my neck, tugging me partially off the floor as he bends close. "I don't give a fuck what Alana does, but unless you want a shit ton of poor saps failing art class due to swollen black eyes, don't even think about it."

"That's the biggest double-standard—" Calder kisses me with dominant aggression, thrusting his tongue past my lips in a kiss meant to completely obliterate all other thoughts.

I don't kiss him back. Instead I bite his lip hard.

He draws back, scowling. "What the hell, Cass? Steel dies when the fight is over."

"I don't do bullshit, Calder." I narrow my gaze.

"Whatever set you off at my apartment earlier had nothing to do with protecting me. That's why I came—to get you to talk. The last thing I expected to see was proof that I was right walking out your damn door!"

"You *aren't* right," he snarls. "The way I acted had every *fucking* thing to do with protecting you. From *me*." Clasping my chin, he tilts it up and clamps down on the side of my throat, hard.

He may have been trying to prove a point, but I gasp and arch into him, unable to curb my response. Calder groans and releases his hold on my throat. As he places a hot kiss on the same spot, the guttural rumble of need vibrating from his chest melts my bones. "I don't have a name worthy of you, angel. And I know it's best for you if I stay away, but I can't fucking stop wanting you."

Releasing my arms, he lowers his body to mine, the ravenous heat in his gaze combined with his hardness pressing against me sending shivers all the way to my toes. "I crave every part of you, Cass…deeply and in every dirty, filthy, decadent way possible."

I slide my fingers in his hair, then touch his jaw. "If you want all of me, then tell me the truth. Why do you think you're not worthy?"

Calder rolls off me and sits up. Facing away, he rests his elbows on his bent knees.

When he doesn't speak, but instead tilts his head back to stare at the ceiling, my heart twists and my gaze slides to the skull covering his entire back. At this moment its soulless eye sockets seem eerily appropriate for his brooding mood. Whatever is bothering him…he's tortured by it.

I rise up on my knees and slide my hands along his muscular upper back, touching the intricate wing tattoo that partially covers the skull. Its black feathers spread at an angle from the top of his right shoulder to his left side, curving around his ribs. "This wing is awesome. I'd love to photograph you like this before it's gone for good." Leaning close, I whisper in his ear, "Talk, Calder."

He exhales a harsh breath and tilts his head forward, staring straight ahead. "You can't change who you are, no matter how much you wish you can, Cass."

He sounds so disgusted, worry grips my chest. "Tell me," I say, needing to know what he's thinking.

"My mom didn't have an affair. I recently found out the truth. The 'incident' she referred to in her letter was far worse."

I squeeze his shoulders, but stay silent, letting him tell me at his own pace.

Calder silently rolls his head from one shoulder to the other. The tension in his muscles makes me want to shake the rest out of him, but I force myself to wait for him to continue.

"My mother was drugged and violated." He lifts his shoulders, then lets them fall. "She might've kept it from my father because she thought it would destroy him, but in the end it destroyed her instead."

My heart wrenches for Calder. He had to go through so much with his parents' separate deaths, then learning he wasn't a Blake…and now this? I flex my fingers against his skin, letting him know I'm here for him. "I'm sorry, Calder. To learn something like that must've devastated you."

He drops his head between his arms and stares at the carpet. "I looked up sexual assault in the hopes I could bring charges against the sick bastard, but to my disgust even if I could prove it happened, the maximum statute of limitations here in New York is five years."

Sadly, I know that timeframe by heart. I slide my fingers through his hair and over the feathered ink that curves just around the right side of his neck, hoping that my touch gives him comfort. "Please don't tell me that's why you don't feel worthy, Calder. You couldn't control the actions of that man."

"You mean the vile fucker who created me?" he snarls. "My *father*?"

Sitting up, he pulls away from my touch. "That twisted monster's blood runs through my veins. You won't feel the same. *I* don't feel the same."

"It doesn't matter to me whose DNA you have. What matters is who you are."

He shakes his head. "It matters to me, Cass. It fucking matters a lot."

My heart races and panic grips me. He sounds like he's going to walk away from us, no matter what I say. I can't let him do that. I won't! I unbutton my shirt the rest of the way, then my bra, sliding out of them. "Why are you giving this horrible man so much real estate in your head?

Why do that to yourself?" I ask as I slip off my shoes and the rest of my clothes.

"Because of you."

He says it so softly I almost don't hear it as I slip his dog tags over my head. "Me? But I just told you I don't care."

Calder grips his upper arms tight, his voice like gravel. "It matters because I'm a fucking Hemming, Cass!"

I stumble as I move to stand, floored by his unexpected answer. *He's Phillip's son? Oh my God.* I clench my hands and close my eyes, needing a second to calm the shock to my heart and process it. I open my eyes and stare at Calder sitting there, unmoving. He's so beautiful in his self-effacing torture, my heart twists with love for him. How could I not fall for such a complex man? He's everything I could hope for. But does he care for me enough that we can get past *this*? He hasn't turned around or said a word. I don't know what to do other than to shake a response out of him.

Taking a deep breath, I walk over and lean back against the wall next to his apartment door. "You're right. I think you'd better walk me out, Calder."

The skull and raven's wing flex with the sudden tensing of his back muscles.

When Calder exhales deeply and turns to get up, I say, "Unless you'd like to have all of me instead?"

His head snaps up and lust scrolls across his face as he takes in my naked state.

The fact he hasn't moved worries me, so I up the ante.

Tracing my fingers between my bare breasts, I touch the chain along the way until I reach the tags on the end. "I'll bet there's a lot more creative ways we could use this. What do you think?"

Calder is up and in front of me before I can blink. Cupping my jaw with one hand, he fists his other in my hair and yanks me close. "Don't change your mind about us, angel. Fucking ever," he husks against my lips before slanting his mouth over mine in an all-consuming, take-no-prisoners kiss of heat and want, pain and sadness, emotional desperation, and fierce dominance.

The need to possess me oozes from the tension in his hold. I know he still doesn't believe he's worthy, but all I can do is kiss him back and hold him tight, letting him know without words that—I'm his and he's mine.

When Calder effortlessly lifts me up, I wrap my arms around his neck, loving that he doesn't break our kiss as he walks us over toward his bed.

A cell phone starts ringing on the counter near us.

Calder halts and turns to stare at it, but I put my hand on his jaw. "No."

He presses his lips together and sets me down. "It's Bash. He usually texts. If he's calling, it's important."

When he reaches for the phone and clicks to answer it, I snag it from him and hover my finger over the End button, whispering, "You can call him back."

"Cald, you there?" Sebastian's voice floats between us.

I glance down at the phone by my side, my finger still over the End button, and déjà vu hits me with such clarity,

I lift an excited gaze back to Calder and put the phone to my ear. "Hey, Sebastian. Give us a couple minutes and we'll call you back."

Before he can respond, I hang up. Shoving the phone in Calder's hand, I snatch up my pants and quickly slip them on. Stepping into my shoes, I reach down and grab my bra.

"What are you doing?" he asks, frowning.

Hooking my bra on, I grab my shirt from the floor, then wave my hand in a circle. "Hurry up and get some clothes on if you want to go with me. I need to drive to the Hamptons."

As I start to button my shirt, Calder clasps my shoulders, his brow creasing. "Why do you need to go to the Hamptons right now?"

I meet his gaze, hope thrumming through me. "It's a long shot, but it's worth checking into. Do you remember that day you challenged Gregory and Phillip, demanding to talk to Celeste?"

When he nods, I take a breath. "Phillip was being a stubborn ass, refusing to give me Celeste's cell phone back so I could call my parents. Gregory told him to give me the phone, but instead of Celeste's, he handed me another phone to use."

Calder shakes his head, his fingers flexing on my shoulders. "I'm still not getting why this is a good thing."

"Because the phone he handed me isn't the one I've seen him using. What if in his desire to keep Celeste's phone out of my hands, he gave me his burner phone,

Calder? The one that he used to send all those personal texts to Celeste?"

Calder nods, understanding flickering. "We'll finally have a direct connection between that threatening text to Celeste that would lead right back to Phillip."

"Which means the prosecutor could have his bond revoked and send him back to jail to await trial."

After I button my shirt, Calder captures my hand. "Why do we need to go to the Hamptons? Can't the police just pull the phone records?"

"I think normally they could, but I never talked to my parents that day. I got their answering machine instead and was just about to leave a message when Beatrice announced your arrival. So I hung up."

"Are you saying they might have a partial recording?"

I nod. "My parents never check their voicemail. It might still be on their recorder which also logs the phone number."

Calder picks up his T-shirt from the back of the couch and pulls it on, then changes into jeans. "It's definitely worth a try."

"When you call Sebastian back, you can fill him in on our trip to the Hamptons," I say, while Calder locks his apartment door.

Once we reach my car, I start to walk around the front and a loud sound *pops*. At the same time Calder yells for me to get down, three more *pops* fire, one after the other. I barely have a chance to move before Calder's grabbing me around the waist and hauling me behind the passenger side of my car.

"Can you see where the shooter is?" I keep my head low beside Calder, while he tilts my car door's mirror to look up on the rooftop across the street. "Does anyone live in that building?

"No, it hasn't been renovated yet. It's too dark to see, but that can work to our advantage." Taking my keys, he unlocks the passenger side door and partially opens it to slide a hand inside and flip the locks. "I'm going to get in the front. You get in the back. Stay low and I'll start the car and then we're gunning it. Got it?"

Nodding, I do as he says and quietly climb in the back seat.

The moment Calder starts the engine, a couple more shots ping against the hood, but Calder quickly jumps into the front seat and jams the gas, gunning down the street as fast as my car will go.

I don't say anything until we're a couple miles away. "Holy shit, that was intense!" Thankful we got away safe, I shake my hands to alleviate the adrenaline trembles. "We need to call the police."

"*No,* Cass." Calder pulls off to a side road and turns to look at me. "I need you to drive while I call Bash and let him know we're on our way to his place."

Nodding my understanding, I climb out and start to get into the front when I see a streak of blood smeared across my leather seat.

"Were you shot?" I immediately sit down and try to see where he's wounded, but Calder just grimaces.

"If you've got a First Aid kit in the back, bring it up here. Otherwise Bash should have stuff at his place."

Panicked and unsure just how hurt he is, I retrieve my kit from my trunk. "We're going straight to the hospital," I say once I get in and close the door.

Calder shakes his head as he presses gauze to his hip. "I can't go to the hospital. Bullet wounds have to be reported, and I can't afford for this to get back to the EUC. Any whiff of police involvement in my life, especially related to something illegal, and they'll disqualify me."

I gape at him. "That's insanity, Calder. You're bleeding. You need medical attention!"

He stares at me with hard eyes. "No hospital, Cass. I'm pretty sure the bullet just grazed me and it looks worse than it actually is. Take me to Bash's place. He'll be able to assess the damage and dress it for me."

I set my jaw and drive, tension building in my shoulders as I listen to Calder talk to Sebastian. "It sounded like a handgun. Yeah, I think it's a flesh wound, but I need you to look it over." A pause. "Cass is bringing me to you now." He glances my way. "No, she doesn't."

When he hangs up, I ask, "She doesn't *what*?"

Calder sighs and leans his head back against the seat. "Agree with me."

"You're damn right I don't," I mutter, then clamp my lips shut before I'm tempted to yell at him for being so incredibly stubborn.

"Who do you think it was?"

Calder shakes his head. "Don't know, but we'll start

investigating tomorrow."

"All you're doing tomorrow is resting." When Calder lifts his head and starts to speak, I glare at him. "Don't argue or I'll drive your stubborn, bleeding ass straight to the hospital and report the gunshot wound myself."

Calder's gaze narrows for a second before pain flickers and he closes his eyes once more.

As angry as I am, my heart jerks with worry for him. I touch his thigh. "We'll be there in five minutes."

Calder just grunts and nods, keeping his hand pressed against the quickly staining gauze on his hip.

Sebastian meets us outside and pushes the remote to allow me access to the garage. Before I even shut off the engine, he's pulling open the passenger door and hauling Calder out of the car.

Talia flicks on all the lights in the kitchen, gesturing to the cleared-off island. "This is the best lighting. Get up here, Calder, so Sebastian can see."

Calder grunts as he hitches himself up onto the island and pulls his bloodied shirt off. When Talia pauses for a second to stare at his tattoo, then lifts a pair of scissors to cut his jeans, he grates, "This better just be a flesh wound."

"Shhh," she says and starts on his pants, cutting an opening for Sebastian to access his wound.

When Calder lets out a flurry of curses as Sebastian pours alcohol over his wound, his cousin frowns. "You know the drill, Cald. Grit your teeth and let me get this cleaned so I can see."

Dabbing at Calder's wound with cotton gauze, he

glances up. "You're right, the bullet grazed you. I can dress it, but it would be better if you got stitches, especially with your fight coming up."

"Would you two stop talking like that fight is still going to happen?" When the men just ignore my comment, I turn to my friend. "Talia, tell them!"

Talia hooks her arm around my shoulders and pulls me away from the kitchen. "Calder's going to be fine, Cass." Stopping, she clasps my arms. "Are you okay? You were just shot at too."

"I didn't get *hit*." My voice shakes as I look over at Sebastian and Calder talking in low voices. "We were on our way out of his apartment, planning to drive to my parents." I shake my head and exhale to calm myself. "I'm honestly not sure who the person was shooting at, me or Calder."

Talia nods. "Sebastian tried to call Calder when I couldn't get a hold of you. He said you answered his phone, so why were you going to your parents this late? Did they insist on meeting the guy who's been keeping you away from them lately?"

I snort at her teasing, then fill her in on why we were going to go to my parents' house.

She smiles when I tell her our plans. "That would be wonderful if you're right. I'd love to know too—"

"Talia," Sebastian says. "See if you can reach Elijah. The doctor we normally use won't be back in town until tomorrow morning."

"I'm fine, Bash." Calder grunts to cover a wince as he

swings his legs over the side of the island to sit up.

My heart squeezing with worry, I stare at the stretchy bandage wrapped around a thick wad of gauze taped to his side. The only reason for that bandage is to keep pressure on his wound. Which means he must still be bleeding. I immediately pull my phone out of my pocket. "You're getting those stitches. I know someone."

Calder frowns as I quickly send Sebastian's address along with my text.

Me: It's Cass. I need your help. Please bring your medical bag.

Sebastian ignores Calder's attempt to brush him off and lifts his cousin's arm over his shoulder, helping him off the island. "I'll take you to the bedroom. You need to keep pressure on that wound until Cass's friend can help."

"I told you I don't need stitches." Calder tries to sound fine, but tension laces his tone. "I wouldn't turn away a couple shots of whiskey though."

"Don't you dare give him alcohol," I say, walking toward the elevator.

"Where are you going?" Talia pauses in the process of tossing bloody gauze into the trash.

I push the elevator button. "To wait for my friend downstairs." When the door slides closed and I start to descend, I mutter, "And hope I can convince him to help."

CHAPTER TWENTY-FIVE

Calder

$\mathcal{M}y$ hip hurts like a son of a bitch, but I've had worse, and honestly I'm more worried about Cass. I don't like that she went downstairs by herself. Rationally I know that very few people know about Bash's apartment and there's security downstairs. That's partially why I told Cass to bring us here, but once she brings her friend upstairs, at least one other person will know where we are. I hate this out-of-control feeling of not knowing who the hell just tried to kill us. I hope they were after me. The thought of someone trying to hurt Cass, especially when I'm not one-hundred-percent, really fucks with my head. *I hate this shit.*

Propped up with pillows against the headboard, I snap at my cousin, who's leaning on the doorjamb after handing me a pair of his lounge pants. "I don't need a babysitter. Go downstairs with Cass."

Bash shakes his head and crosses his arms. "She's safe or I never would have let her go. Tell me as much as you can remember, starting with your address—you've got to stop this reclusive shit." Pinning me with a hard glare, he continues, "After Cass's friend gets here, my team and I will head over and see if we can find spent casings or anything else that might give us a clue as to who's after you."

Once I relay as much as I can remember, Bash's brow furrows. "Isn't your apartment in the revitalized part of the Lower East End?"

"Just...it's on the edge," I say, daring him to challenge my choice with a hard stare.

"So for all you know, the shooting could've just been random sketchy shit?" Bash frowns, then calls over his shoulder, "Talia, did any of the buildings in the revitalized part of the Lower East End pop up in your research?"

When she doesn't answer, he walks away and a couple seconds later curses as he steps back into my doorway with his phone to his ear.

"Where is she?" I ask, suddenly tense.

"Being *Talia*," he says before speaking into the phone in a clipped tone. "Theo, I need you to track Talia's cell and follow her. You're the only one she won't rip into if she sees you." He pauses and sighs. "Yeah, just...keep her safe and text me once you locate her."

When he hangs up, I chuckle, then instantly regret the

agony that shoots across my hip. "She challenges the hell out of you, doesn't she?"

Bash slips his phone in his pocket, muttering, "Every day." Glancing up at me, he snorts. "What are you chuckling about? If Cass hasn't already barreled through your bullshit, get ready for the freight train, Cald."

I smirk. "She literally sacked me in a fit of rage earlier."

Bash holds his hand to Cass' height. "Little Cass?"

"She packs a punch," I grunt. Not that I'll ever admit that my back still hurts from hitting the floor, but I'd take the hit and pain all over again just to know that Cass cares. She'll never know how much her extreme reaction meant to me, even if I'll never be worthy of her.

"Good, maybe she knocked some sense into that thick skull of yours."

I ignore his comment and focus on his earlier question, hoping to distract myself from the pain in my side. "What research of Talia's were you referring to?"

"She's working on several angles between researching both Brent and Phillip's backgrounds. I'd like to know if that building across from yours turned up in any of the paperwork."

"Did Talia uncover anything related to the Opera house and Thomas?"

"Surprisingly, one of Phillip's subsidiaries owns that Opera property."

"Phillip?" I frown my confusion.

"Yeah, that was unexpected. As for Thomas's murder, my police contact says he'll pass along the medical examiner's report on Thomas's autopsy, hopefully by tomorrow."

"Phillip doesn't strike me as a MMA enthusiast. Did Talia look to see if he has any connections with MMA fighting in New York or elsewhere?"

Sliding his hands into his pants pockets, Bash nods. "It's the first thing she did, but she couldn't find anything. At least not yet. We're still look—" He pauses, glancing into the living room. "Cass is back. I'll see if they need anything."

"I'll just wait right here," I say to the empty doorway, then glance down to see blood wicking up my bandage and grunt my annoyance. "Slowly bleeding out."

A minute later, Cass walks in and the determined look on her face puts me on instant alert. I cut my gaze to the friend walking in behind her and snarl, "What the fuck is he doing here?"

"You don't get a choice in the matter," Cass says, approaching my side of the bed.

"The hell I don't. He's not touching me." I narrow my gaze on Ben Hemming setting his medical bag on the end of the bed. I might need stitches, but the last thing I want it is to owe a fucking Hemming anything.

"Show me your wound," Ben says in a stern tone after flicking his gaze to the tattoo on my shoulder, arm, and ribs.

I consider flipping him off, but Cass glares at me, so I peel back the tape and show him my wound, then quickly push the bandage back into place to keep more blood from flowing.

Ben picks up a pair of rubber gloves and snaps them on. "Actually, you don't have a choice, so stop being an asshole and let me do my job."

"Screw you, Hemming. I know the only reason you're here." When I cut a pointed gaze to Cass, she crosses her arms and sets her jaw at a stubborn angle.

"Ben said you'd be a pain in the ass, but you're *going* to let him sew you up."

"I sure as hell would hate to disappoint," I bite out, eyeing them both.

"And surly too." Ben looks at me after threading a curved needle. "Do you want a shot to numb the area first?"

I look at Bash, who's standing in the doorway like he's ready to tackle someone if necessary. "Whiskey, straight up."

Ben shakes his head at Bash. "Alcohol will thin his blood. That's the last thing he needs right now. I recommend juice."

"What am I, five?" I growl, then grit my teeth at the pain my snappy response caused.

Setting down the needle on a sterile pad, Ben glances at Cass and Bash. "I need everyone to clear the room, please."

Cass's gaze pings nervously between Ben and me. When Bash walks away, she bends close and whispers harshly in my ear, "Behave."

Once they close the door, Ben gestures to the bed.

"Scoot down and lay on your side."

Grunting my annoyance, I do as he says.

When he rubs something that smells like astringent across my wound, I growl and jerk upright, my fist clenched and ready to punch. He quickly shoves me back down. "Lay still. I need to clean the area. Aren't you supposed to be a SEAL?"

"It's a knee-jerk reaction," I grumble and suck up the pain the second time he runs the pad across my wound.

While Ben sews my injury closed, his movements swift and professional, I set my back teeth together and stay quiet.

He's done in a matter of minutes and once he puts a clean bandage on my wound, he looks at me. "Cass says you have some kind of fight you're doing in a couple of days. Your stitches need to be kept clean and take at least a week to heal, two weeks is better based on the location. Fighting is *not* recommended."

"I'll take it under advisement," I mutter.

Ben quietly puts his bag back together and when he's done, he walks to the door. Putting his hand on the doorknob, he turns back to me, his dark eyebrows pulled together in a determined expression. "I had no idea what all Cass had been through until now. She thinks you're worth fighting for. Do right by her and help her forget or I'll fight you for her."

The fact that Cass confided in him about her past really rankles. I narrow my gaze. "Thanks for the stitches, *Hemming asshole.*"

His jaw muscle jumps as he turns the knob. "Right back at you, *brother*."

My gaze narrows to thin slits as I watch him open the door and walk out.

CHAPTER TWENTY-SIX

Cass

I let go of the tightness in my chest when Ben leaves Calder's room without them coming to blows. After he nods to Sebastian, who's on the phone in the kitchen, I walk him over to the elevator.

"Thank you so much for your help. I know Calder wasn't the easiest patient."

He twists his lips in a wry smile. "That's an understatement. I told him he definitely shouldn't fight with those stitches, but you'll probably be calling me again in a few days. Next time, I'll take a beer as payment when I'm done."

"It's a deal," I say, putting my hand out.

Ben takes my hand and nods toward the kitchen where Sebastian keeps one eye on us while carrying on a conversation. "I'm glad you have so many people watching over you, Cass. Their protectiveness eases my worry over this shooting business, not to mention my own guilt."

"Sebastian runs a security business, so I'm in good hands. And don't you dare feel guilty. You can't control your father or your brother's actions. Your friendship means too much to me to let you feel bad about that."

Ben cups his other hand over our clasped ones. "My family is just whacked, Cass. My mom is *still* in denial about my dad. Can you believe she's worried about him? She said he came home furious that his release from jail was contingent on a gun-free home. Makes me think he loves those freaking guns more than his family."

He sighs and releases my hand to slide his fingers through his dark hair. "Jake sounded pretty unstable when he called me yesterday, ranting about how he planned to destroy our father for what he did. He says he's going to take away the only thing that ever really mattered to him. Other than money, I have no idea what he was going on about."

"Do you think Jake would try to hurt your dad?" I ask, unsure how I would feel about one bad guy taking another one out.

His mouth thins as he pushes the elevator button. "After what you told me tonight, I'm so disgusted with both of them...I don't really care."

"I'm sorry, Ben."

He shrugs. "Don't ever be sorry for telling the truth. I plan to stay away from family drama and focus on building my practice. Work is the only thing that makes sense right now."

I wince. "And here I dragged you into ours."

The elevator opens and he walks in. Turning to face me, he smirks. "At least I see caring here. That's far more than I see within my own family."

I hold the sliding door to keep it from closing. "You have family here too." I glance toward Calder's room and then turn back to him. "If you want."

He snorts. "I don't see that happening. He hates the sight of me."

I shake my head. "He hates the pain and suffering your last name represents. But you just showed him today that not all Hemmings are evil. It's a start."

Ben clears his throat, his tone gruff. "Make sure he keeps those stitches dry for forty-eight hours."

I nod. "Night. And thank you again."

Once the elevator door shuts, I join Sebastian in the kitchen and glance around. "Where's Talia?"

"At your parents' house," he says, setting his phone on the counter.

"What?" My eyes widen. "When did she leave?"

"She left while you were downstairs and I was distracted with Calder." Sebastian snorts his displeasure as he opens the fridge and takes out a carton of orange juice. "You were right, by the way. A partial recording was on your parents' answering machine. That was Talia calling to ask me the Deceiver's phone number."

I pull down a glass from the cabinet and set it on the

counter for him. "Don't keep me in suspense. Does it match?"

Sebastian pours the juice, then holds the glass out to me. "Take this to Calder...along with the good news. That bastard was careful for so long, but Phillip Hemming finally screwed up. Thanks to you, he's going down."

I start to take the glass, but he holds tight. "That was a hell of a risk you took bringing Ben here. That could've gone South very quickly."

My hand is steady on the glass even though I'm shaking on the inside. Calder may never forgive me for revealing his secret to his half-brother, but Ben had to know the whole story to understand the depth of Calder's anger and self-disgust. I could only hope that learning the truth would be the push Ben needed to offer his help. "You have no idea how much Calder needed that, Sebastian."

"Actually, I do." He releases the glass and stares at the closed door. "I want Calder back. Make it happen, Cass."

My heart rams against my chest as I stand outside of Calder's door. I have no idea what kind of reception I'll get, but I take a breath and turn the knob.

Stepping inside, I smile. "I have some good news. Talia went to my parents' house and the phone number on the recording matches the Deceiver's. Hopefully that will be enough for them to revoke Phillip's bail."

Calder doesn't react other than to narrow his gaze on the glass of juice in my hand. "I see you're following doctor's orders," he says in a tight, controlled voice as I set the glass on his nightstand. "What else did my *brother* convince you to share?"

I jerk my gaze to his furious one. "He told you?"

"*Why* did you tell him?"

My chest tightens at the anger and betrayal reflected in his gaze. Sebastian was right...my risk failed. But if Calder and I are over, then there's no reason for me to hold back.

I take a breath and keep my voice strong. "I didn't just tell him the truth about you, Calder. I told him what Jake did to me too."

His mouth thins as if that answer only pisses him off more. "*Why*, Cass?"

I swing my hand toward the closed door. "Ben stood there in that lobby downstairs and had to hear all the horrible things his brother and father have done, and yet, even knowing you despise *every* Hemming, he selflessly came here and helped you anyway. That's *why*, Calder."

When he just pins me with a stoic stare, I swallow and tilt my chin up, standing my ground. "You needed to see that DNA doesn't define the person, the *heart* does. Who better to show you that than your brother?"

"He's *not* my brother," he snaps, his hand clenching on his thigh.

"He *is* and it's your loss if you choose not to acknowledge that." Lifting my shoulders, I sigh. "You may never forgive me for revealing your secret, but I did it because I was fighting for *us*, Calder. You needed to experience *good* in action so you'd realize you are worthy of your family's love, no matter whose genes you have. And so you'd accept my love, but you're apparently too freaking stubborn to acknowledge any of it."

My heart breaking, I start to walk away, but Calder's fingers suddenly clasp mine. Holding me in place, the heat of anger is gone from his voice. "Look at me."

When I lift my gaze to his, he slides his fingers between mine. "I admire that you're not afraid to go the distance, that you never let another person define your worth, and that you refused to let me hide from a past I couldn't control, but mostly…" He pulls me down to the bed beside him and thumbs the tears off my cheek. "For being the strongest fighter I know. For all those things…and not just because you're sexy as hell, I love you, Cass Rockwell, so fucking much it hurts every time I look at you."

Emotion swells in my throat and I exhale a sob of happiness as I lay my head on his hard chest. "It's about time. I love you too, you beautiful, bull-headed man."

Calder exhales and slides his fingers in my hair, pulling me close. "One day, I'll find a way to make Jake and Brent pay, Cass. I promise."

Careful to avoid his wound, I burrow my nose against his chest and breathe in his wonderful smell. "All I care about is you. The rest is just noise," I say, smiling that I finally understand the peace behind my sister's statement.

Calder presses a kiss to the top of my head and grumbles, "Ben's still a Hemming asshole."

I lift the mug of hot coffee to my lips and take a long sip.

Swallowing its warmth, I set the cup down and push my hands against my lower back, grimacing at the tightness.

Talia walks into the kitchen yawning, her hair a mess of wild red tresses. She stops when she sees me. "Good morning. What are you doing up so early?"

"You look well-tumbled. How was your evening?" I say with a wicked chuckle, remembering last night.

Sebastian had just informed me that they didn't find any bullet shells on the rooftop across from Calder's apartment, but they did get a partial shoe print and were running it down when Talia walked in. She barely got out, "Hi, Cass. Your parents said for you to call them," when her husband walked over to the entryway and scooped her up, saying gruffly over his shoulder as he carried her off to their bedroom, "Night, Cass."

Talia's cheeks turn red and she touches her hair self-consciously. "Um, good. I didn't expect you to be up."

I gesture to her couch. "The leather's soft, but it's not the most comfortable bed."

Turning to take a cup from the cabinet, she says, "Why did you sleep there?"

"That's what I want to know," Calder's deep voice resonates directly behind me at the same time his hands settle on the island, his warm body blocking me in.

A shiver rushes through me, but I calmly take another sip of my coffee. "Because I didn't want to accidently bump your wound." After I forced him to drink his juice, I told him that the only way I was sleeping with him was if he kept his hands to himself. Calder rumbled his displeasure and tucked my back against his chest. The second he slid his hand between my thighs and promptly fell asleep, I knew he'd lost more blood than he wanted to admit and needed his rest, so I quietly got up and moved to the couch.

Taking the mug from my hands, Calder sets it in the middle of the counter. "Here's a fresh cup, Talia."

"Hey—" I frown and lean to retrieve it, but big hands grip my waist and I'm quickly lifted and cradled against his muscular chest. "Put me down before you pop a stitch!" I want to struggle, but I'm afraid any excess movement will open his wound.

Talia snickers and reaches for my mug as Calder rumbles, "See you later, Talia," then he carries me into the bedroom and kicks the door shut.

The moment he sets me down, I immediately touch his bandage to see if blood is wicking into the gauze. "Have you lost your mind?"

Calder clasps my jaw and tilts my face up, his intense gaze locking with mine. "Waking up to find you gone isn't how I wanted to start my day."

I fold my fingers around his wrist. "You need to heal."

He swiftly pulls Talia's long sleep-shirt over my head and hauls me against his sleep-warmed chest before the shirt hits the floor. "The only thing I need at this moment is you, angel."

I want him so much I'm trembling inside, but the few times we've been together it has always been very physical. He *will* rip open his wound. I push against his chest and take a step back. "We can't, Calder. Not until you've healed. We're too...um vigorous."

His lips curl in a predatory smile and he steps close to slide his finger along the curve of my breast. Tracing his beaded necklace up my chest to my neck, he moves to my jawline. "While I admit you definitely bring out my primal side, I promise to be gentle."

The lethal purr in his voice shoots straight to my toes, but I shake my head. "I'm not worried about me, you obstinate man."

"*Determined*, Raven mine." He tips my chin higher while his other hand slides down the curve of my back to hook the edge of my panties. Lust flashes in his eyes and with a flick of his wrist, my underwear floats to my ankles "*Very* determined."

I'm naked and tense with want, but I shake my head. "Calder, this is a bad idea."

He glides his fingers into my hair, cupping the back of my head. "The only bad idea is making me wait, because then I won't be gentle. Take off my pants."

I exhale deeply as I tug his black silk pants down, and I can't help running my tongue along his hard cock as I straighten.

Calder's fingers tangle in my hair and he gently pulls me up and fully against him. "That's playing with fire with the way I want you right now."

I smile and slowly trail my palms over the hard slabs of muscle resting at his hips. "You need to take it easy. Do you think you can do that?"

When I trace my fingers down the side of his erection,

he exhales harshly and closes his eyes, then snaps them open. As the deep green sparks with heat, he rasps, "Lay down, Cass before I toss you down."

My limbs shake as I lie down on the bed and stare up at Calder resting his knee on the mattress, his thick cock jutting toward his defined abs.

He moves over me and I can see the mixture of pain and yearning in his face. My heart twists and I touch his biceps, then clasp his shoulders as he settles between my thighs. "Are you sure? I think we should wait."

Calder nudges my entrance, then rubs the tip of his cock against my clit. "You're soaked for me. How can you say you want to wait?"

I swallow back my whimper of want and resist the urge to clasp him against me. "Because I care about you more."

A low rumble erupts from his lips as he eases himself in my channel. "At least that's one thing we can agree on."

I arch my back and dig my fingers into his muscular shoulders, panting through the blissful, simmering burn as my body accepts his unhurried possession.

Calder dips his head and captures one of my nipples, sucking the tip in a leisurely, erotic drag. Inching deeper inside me, he moves to my other breast and grazes the tip with the sharp edge of his teeth.

I gasp and pant, my hips wanting to move, fingers flexing against him. "Calder...God, just fuck me...I can't take this."

He runs his nose up along the curve of my breast, his voice gravelly with desire. "Slow and easy...that's what you wanted," he says, pushing his hips forward another inch.

I swallow and close my eyes, unable to look at his handsome face full of concentration. His arms are straining and his whole body is taut against me. Calder groans when he finally seats himself fully inside me.

As he lowers his head to my shoulder, I slide my fingers into his hair, my heart thumping rapidly against my chest.

He rolls his hips against me once, then twice more, and the tingling building inside me blooms in my belly, shooting straight to my center. I'm not sure how much more I can take; my pulse thrums and my stomach aches from the throbbing need in my sex.

Calder lowers to his elbows. "I feel your pussy flexing around me. You're perfect, so fucking hot and tight. I love that your body is telling me what it wants. Now let me hear the words, Cass."

I clench my fingers in his hair. "Move, Calder."

He slowly pulls back, then slides inside me and we both groan.

Panting against my collarbone, he thrusts forward, his tone harsh with mounting desire. "Come for me, angel. I want to feel you telling me how much you love this."

He rolls his hips and just as I explode, he slants his mouth over mine, muffling my scream as my orgasm takes over my body. My chest heaves with the need to let out my blissful cry as vibrations rock through me, but Calder's tongue tangling with mine only jacks my heart rate higher.

While I'm quaking in post orgasmic euphoria, he

breaks our kiss and pulls my hands above my head. As he folds his fingers tight around mine, his body tightens with tension above me. Yet even with elevated breathing, he somehow manages to pull back and ease inside me with focused control of his hips.

Tears slide down my temples and I press against him, amazed that my body is already revving up again. Calder's shoulders and arm muscles flex as he dips his head and presses his jaw to mine, his words guttural with leashed hunger. "A long, slow fuck with you is going on the daily agenda. This feels so damn good I never want it to end. God, I fucking love you, Cass."

I feel both possessed and cherished, and the combination is so stimulating, I press my breasts against his hard chest and circle my hips, giving us both another wave of ecstasy. "This is making love, Calder," I say against his jaw. "But whether you fuck me hard and fast, or slow and tender, there's one thing you'll need to do the same no matter what."

"What's that?" He lifts his head to stare into my eyes, while his heart pounds hard against my chest and his hands tighten on mine.

I elevate my hips, tilting them to give him better access. "Always take me deep and brand me yours."

I don't get to finish speaking as he surges forward and thrusts impossibly deep. "Is this what you meant, angel?" His green eyes glitter with fierce need.

I swallow my gasp once the sudden pain of him hitting my womb melds into sheer pleasure. The moment

I tighten my thighs around him, an orgasm flashes over me in rapid-fire bursts of heat and tingling nerves.

"I love how orgasmic you are." Calder releases my hands to spear his fingers in my hair, twisting the locks as he burrows deeper and deeper, each hip movement measured but intense. Pinning me to the mattress, he releases a throaty moan of sheer pleasure and shudders as he comes.

I'm so turned on by the contrast of the sensual toe-curling build of his lovemaking with the forceful rush of him pulsing deep inside me that I nip at his beard-roughed jaw and inhale deeply, drawing in his arousing masculine smell.

When Calder releases my hair to trace the tips of his fingers along my face, I kiss his fingers as he slides them over my lips and whisper, "*More,* please."

Exhaling a dark chuckle, he tilts my chin up, his breath warm against the side of my throat and bites down with wicked intent.

CHAPTER TWENTY-SEVEN

Cass

I*ve* had two days of living in a blissful cocoon with Calder and spending time with my best friend, and now I'm a nervous wreck.

Calder's fight is tonight, yet all I want to do is jump on his back and tell him he can't go. I want to remind him that he's not healed enough and that he hasn't been able to train the way he should, but once Sebastian told me about Thomas, I knew the fighter's death only intensified Calder's need to find out the other major players behind the EUC beyond Brent. Learning about Thomas at least helped me accept that I couldn't change his mind, even if I didn't like it. So yeah, I've been in a funk all day.

Talia looks up from her research spread over the island. "Why don't you come help me look through this, Cass?"

I lift my gaze from the grid of photographs on my laptop screen. Talia's editor asked me to put together a mock-up book for him to evaluate, so I'd set up my workstation at the coffee table to get work done, but also to be closer to the door. "I don't have your investigative mind, Talia."

"Staring at the elevator isn't going to make them walk in any faster, you know."

I've been waiting for Calder and Sebastian to return from his apartment since five. I refused to let Calder go alone to collect his fighting gear and insisted he take Sebastian with him to his apartment. He instantly hated that idea, so the sarcastic barbs between the two alpha males was definitely high as they walked out the door. I glance at the clock. It shouldn't have taken them this long to get back.

"The sooner we find the shooter, the sooner Calder can get back to his own space," Talia says. "I swear that man prowled around here like a caged animal all day."

Even though I'm sure Talia and Sebastian are more than ready to have their apartment back to themselves, I know her comment was meant to be lighthearted, but it just jacks my anxiety more. I can't help but wonder if things will change between Calder and me once he goes back to his normal life. As much as I'd like to hope there is a future for us, he hasn't said anything about us beyond these last forty-eight hours.

That alone makes me tense, but not near as much as the fact we've had more than our share of unprotected sex the last couple of days. Calder is all I want in a life partner, but I need to know he feels the same. My cycle is like clockwork, so we should be safe, but until I know *where* we're going, I need to get home and get back on birth control.

My concentration completely blown, I cut my gaze back to Talia. "What can I help you with?"

"The shooter's partial shoe print they found turned out to be from a custom made shoe. She approaches the printer on a small desk in their kitchen, then holds up a thick stack of papers and staples it. "Elijah just sent me the list of customers who purchased from that custom shoe maker. This list goes back five years, which is the timeframe the shoe maker has been stamping this logo stamp on them. Why don't you look over the list and see if any names jump out at you. I'll have Calder do the same when he gets back."

Standing, I arch my back and then walk over to take the stack. "I can't believe it took two days to get this information."

Talia taps on the paperwork. "We had to get a judge to sign off on a court order for the shop owner to turn over his client list."

I raise an eyebrow. "Felicity convinced the judge, huh?"

"She sure did." Chuckling, Talia gestures to the stool opposite her. "Now pull up a seat and start looking."

I start at the top of the two thousand names and skim my gaze down the column of first and last names. Five hundred names and an hour later, I'm just getting through the first third of the alphabet, when my eyes feel like they're crossing. I take a break and rub my eyes. So far... nothing jumps out at me.

Leaning over, I look at the folder that Talia's flipping through. "What's that?"

She lifts the folder up. "This is on Brent. We're still trying to find out more about his financial holdings to see who else might be an investor." Gesturing to the other thick folder on the island, she says, "I swear for as deviously secretive as Phillip Hemming was, he was still easier to investigate once I dug a couple layers deeper. This Brent guy is squirrelly-secretive. Beyond changing his last name, I found where he's stashing what has to be his EUC funds, but I still haven't figured out what this Scrape Corporation does. Whatever it is...it also makes a tidy sum."

Talia's phone beeps with a message. She immediately opens it, then sends a note back. Two seconds later, the printer starts running once more.

"Who was that?"

"That was Sebastian's police contact." Talia sets her phone down and walks over to retrieve the paperwork she just printed. "And this is Thomas's autopsy report, the MMA fighter who was murdered." Scanning the pages as she walks back over to her chair, she jerks her head up, her mouth pressed together. She tosses the folder down in front of me. "The report says he was strangled to death. The killer tried to wipe away his prints, but they were able to recover one partial print and you'll never guess who it belonged to."

I glance down at the report, then look up at her. "Brent?" I blink as I pick up the page the police officer had added where he matched the print in the autopsy report and listed Brent as the suspect. "How do they already have his fingerprints?"

Talia's eyes light up. "That's a good point." She quickly flips through the background information she has on Brent. "It wasn't from a passport, because he doesn't own one."

"Has he ever been arrested before?"

"Not that showed up in anything I looked at. Unless—" Talia frowns and then thumbs several more pages, pulling out one from the back. "That's brilliant, Cass. I just didn't look back far enough. I only focused on his adult years. This one was when he was in college."

Leaning over, she grabs Phillip's folder and slides it next to Brent's. "We've been looking at these as two separate cases, when we should've been looking at them together."

I shake my head, confused. "But they are two separate cases. Phillip's is about Celeste's disappearance and murder. And Brent's is about running his illegal EUC business."

"Now that we've found a connection...we need to rethink our strategy."

"What connection?"

Talia sets the paper down and slides it across to me. "I was so busy focusing on all the money Phillip has amassed as part of Carver Enterprises. I forgot about his profession."

I pick up the page she'd taken from Brent's folder. It's a police report showing that Brent was arrested for a DUI but never charged and his attorney of record was Phillip Hemming.

My eyes widen. "If there's a connection between these two, then it's only because of Brent's friendship with Jake."

Talia shakes her head. "After you told me what Brent and Jake did to you in high school, I went back and double-checked Brent's background. Unlike Phillip and Brent's paths and business dealings crossing, there is nothing on Jake. The only connection he has to either is that he works as a lawyer at his father's firm." She points to both folders. "He has no holdings or dummy corporations in his name whatsoever."

I hold my hand up. "Wait...where did you find a connection between Phillip and Brent before now?"

She shrugs. "I didn't. When I discovered that Phillip happened to own the abandoned Opera house where Thomas's body was found left in a Dumpster, I passed it off as coincidence because Phillip owns a lot of properties. I assumed he was hoping to cash in on the revitalization project as it expanded in the Lower East End." She pauses, her brow puckering as she rests her palms on both folders. "But now, I don't think that's the case."

I pick up the stack of papers from the shoe business I was looking through earlier, my hands shaking. "If Brent killed a previous fighter for refusing to take a dive...who's to say he didn't try to again?" Setting the papers down, I quickly flip through them, then turn the page, pointing to his full name: Brent Tremmel. "Brent was the one shooting at us!"

When I pull out my phone to call Calder, Talia puts her hand over mine. "Wait, Cass." She flips the pages forward, then turns the whole thing back to me. "Or it could've been someone else."

I stare at her finger next to another name: Phillip Hemming. A comment Ben made about his father's fury over his guns being been removed from his home comes back to me and I nod. "You're right. It could've been Phillip."

Talia's face sets in determined lines. "This is what you call a pattern, where Phillip and Brent's lives have crossed in multiple paths." Lifting her hand from the paper, she nods. "Now you can call Calder."

"Call me about what?" Calder says as he and Sebastian step off the elevator.

Once we fill Sebastian and Calder in on the details, Calder's fist is clenched tight around his duffle bag's strap. "After this fight is over, beyond running an illegal business, the charges against Brent will include Thomas's murder and our attempted murders."

"But you only have a partial shoe print. It could just as easily have been Phillip," Talia reminds him. "Both men have proved they're willing to commit murder."

"We'll present both of them as suspects for the shootings against Calder and Cass. Hopefully forensics will be able to determine which one is responsible." Sebastian glances at both folders. "As for the other, it makes sense why Phillip would remain in the shadows as a silent partner with Brent in the EUC. With his strong political affiliations, he couldn't be directly tied to an illegal business like the EUC, so he used layers of shell corporations to hide the money he's gained from financing that business."

I gesture to Brent's folder. "When I tried to talk to Beth about Brent's questionable business, she defended him saying that Brent is just getting his business ready so he could quickly pivot to a legitimate business once MMA was legalized. He would already have a high-end clientele base and the reputation EUC has established for delivering great bouts. So yes, that ties in with what you're saying."

Calder narrows his gaze. "From Phillip's self-serving perspective, who better to align himself with than the people who have the political power to decide MMA's fate in New York. He made sure he was poised to benefit the moment the vote finally passed making MMA legal."

I shake my head at the intricate web of deceit Phillip had pulled people into. "I know Talia couldn't find any ties, but it's hard for me to believe that Jake isn't one of the partners."

Talia shrugs. "Unless all his money is in his father's accounts and everything is in Phillip's name, it's just not there. He lives off his law firm earnings."

Setting his duffle back down, Calder snorts and wraps his arms around my waist, pulling me close. "Jake doesn't have his father's business savvy or cunning. The guy wouldn't have a clue what to do with that kind of money, let alone know how to hide it."

"At least we have a lot more to give the police to help with the charges," Talia says as she glances at her watch. "Oh...it's getting late. We'd better go get ready."

Sebastian clasps her elbow. "About that. I was only able to get two tickets via a third party. I need Theo with me as backup, since Calder said the metal detectors would go off if we carried."

Talia stares at her husband. "I feel like I should go, Sebastian."

He shakes his head. "You're safer here."

She frowns. "I thought it was because you only have two tickets?"

The tension swelling between them is palpable and I totally understand her frustration. I want to go, but I won't push it. Calder will be distracted if I'm there and he needs to focus on the fight. While Talia and Sebastian face off in a silent contest of wills, Calder lifts his bag and tugs me toward the guest bedroom, saying, "I'm going to get ready."

As soon as he shuts the door, I sit on the bed and silently watch him change from a button down shirt and jeans to black shorts and running shoes. I study his technique as he winds black tape around his left wrist and palm, then he puts strips of tape between each finger before running the tape around his palm several times.

Once he cuts the end of the tape off, I stand and take the roll, then tape up his right hand for him using the same technique. When he moves his fighting gloves and mouth guard to an outside zip-up pocket in his duffle bag, then puts a towel and change of clothes in the main pouch, I hand him extra gauze and medical tape to keep his stitches covered and clean. As he tucks them away, I watch the raven wing and skull tattoo on his back flex and move with his muscles. The tattoo has faded a bit, looking more worn into his skin. Calder told me that's the reason he gets it done a few days early so it'll look like he's had it for a while. The tough street fighter, Steel, is transforming to life right before my eyes. As magnificent as his body is like this, I don't want to think about the fact he'll be in a ring fighting another guy who's determined to beat the shit out of him.

When he turns to face me, I take his dog tags off and slip them around his neck. My heart aches a little without them, since they've been on me the past couple of days, but they're part of his Steel persona and belong with him tonight. "For luck."

Calder winks at me, then hands me the tape to wrap up his tags. Once I'm done, I tap the tags and give a wry smile. "I like wearing them. They make me think of you."

Calder touches my neck and frowns. "I don't like seeing a bruise on you."

"Then stop biting me," I say, snickering.

He lifts his gaze to mine, regret flickering. "Is that what you want, Cass?"

I lift up on my tiptoes and whisper against his jaw. "*Never.*"

He instantly cups my face and presses his mouth against

mine in a tender, lingering kiss. Breaking our kiss, he pulls something out of his shorts pocket and moves close to hook it around my neck. When the material tightens and I realize it's a choker, my stomach does somersaults. All the doubts I felt earlier about us floats away. To Calder...I'm his.

I inhale his wonderful scent and when he lifts his head to meet my gaze, my fingers instantly move to my throat. I smile at the feel of the leather under my fingers. "I really missed this," I say, excited to have it back.

Calder's eyes shift to a deeper green as he slides his thumb along the leather band to touch the silver raven in front. "It looks perfect on you. I expect you to be wearing this and nothing else when I get back tonight."

I admire his confidence and freaking adore his swagger. Wrapping my arms around his hard waist, I lay my head on his muscular chest and listen to his heart's steady thump. After a full minute of basking in his hold, I look up at him. "You'd better come back to me, *able* to make good on that implied promise."

"Tell me you love me," he says, folding his arms around my body.

I slide my hands up his muscular back and grin. "I do."

His gaze narrows. "When I get back I'm going to make you pay for teasing me." Crushing me to him, he drops a kiss on my nose. "Be prepared to be ruthlessly provoked, then well-fucked, angel. I can't wait to watch you come apart with my necklace on." As a shiver of anticipation rushes across my skin, he moves his lips to my ear, his voice husky with heat. "This time around I will fill you up until you're overflowing."

After I snicker at the contrast of Sebastian wearing a tux as he stands beside Calder in a sweatshirt, shorts and sneakers, I walk up to Calder and kiss his jaw, then whisper in his ear, "I love you. Now go kick ass."

Talia presses her lips together and doesn't say anything when Sebastian kisses her on the temple.

Once the men leave, I sit down on the couch beside her and tuck her auburn hair behind her ear. "Why are you so upset with Sebastian? It's not like you can take out a two-hundred-pound bad guy like your man can. And with two Navy SEALs there watching over him, Calder will be much safer."

Talia lifts her shoulders. "It's not that, Cass. Of course I want Calder to be as protected as possible. It's just..." She looks away and sighs.

"What?" I poke her ribs to make her look at me.

Taking a deep breath, she exhales quickly. "I just have this feeling I should be there. I can't explain it."

I eye her, my chest tightening. "How strong is this feeling?"

She curls her fist against her stomach. "Deep in my gut." Her green eyes flick to mine. "I almost feel sick, Cass."

I exhale slowly and reach for my purse leaning against

the couch. "Sebastian is going to kill me," I mumble and lay the ticket that Beth gave me on her thigh.

Talia's eyes widen and she looks up at me. "Where'd you get this?"

"Beth gave it to me." I point to the envelope. "This event's secret location is at an old abandoned ice rink. The address is inside with your ticket."

When Talia jumps up and runs into her room to find a dress, I call out, "Please be careful!"

I wait a half hour after Talia leaves to pick up Calder's phone he'd left on the island. Flipping through his address book, I find Sebastian's number. I figure that thirty minutes is long enough that Sebastian won't send her home, but there's no way I'm letting my best friend head over to that abandoned ice rink alone, no matter how strong her gut instinct is.

> *Me: This is Cass. Talia is about ten minutes behind you. Wait for her!*
> *Sebastian: Be glad you caught me before I went inside or I'd have your hide.*
> *Me: Women's intuition. She needs to be there.*

Fifteen minutes later, I finally get a text back.

> *Sebastian: Got her. Thanks for having her back.*
> *Me: Crack open that EUC!*

Setting my phone down, I smile, admiring Talia for

sticking to her guns about her instincts. I should trust mine more. I stare at Brent and Phillip's folders, shaking my head. I just can't believe that Phillip would have a business relationship with Brent that didn't include Jake, considering that's most likely how Brent knows Phillip in the first place.

Frowning, I pull Brent's folder toward me and open it, turning to the page on financial holdings. I skim until I find the corporation Talia talked about, the one with the sum of money she couldn't identify. My gaze freezes on the company name.

ScrapE.

I jerk my head up, my heart racing. "Holy shit!"

CHAPTER TWENTY-EIGHT

Calder

"**S**teeeeel and Haaaaaammmer...round four!" the announcer calls out, his deep voice echoing over the indoor arena that has been everything from an ice rink to an indoor football stadium. From the skybox in the corner where the executive contributors are watching us fight behind the safety of privacy glass, to the graduated stadium seating, the crowd of well-dressed fans have been wild with excitement, screaming and yelling their bloodlust for the last hour.

Hammer and I have definitely given them a good fight.

When it comes to typical MMA moves, my opponent and I are evenly matched, but I also pull my interactions from other disciplines. Every time I've adapted a move, Hammer hasn't been able to get past me, not without taking several powerful hits to his ribs, chest and a few really good ones to his face.

While the ring girl waltzes around the outside of the chain link cage, I use this short time to mentally assess my damage. My jaw aches and my right side hurts like a motherfucker. I'm pretty sure my wound is bleeding into my waistband, but at least my black shorts hide it.

Despite a swelling left eye behind his white full-head cover mask and several bruised ribs, Hammer is pacing on the other side of the arena like a rabid beast. His eyes are wild, as if he's hyped up on drugs, not just fight adrenaline.

The bell rings and the ref indicates we can commence fighting. I grit my teeth against my mouthpiece, and ignore the salty sweat rolling from inside my mask and down into my eyes. I blink past the stinging, determined that this is the round Hammer will lose the fight.

Hammer runs straight at me and slams me into the cage. As he pounds his fist into my aching side, I grab him around the neck and squeeze with my bicep. He growls around his mouthpiece, "'ake a ive."

I blink as his mumbling takes form in my head. *Take a dive.*

"*Fuck* no," I reply, but just in case he didn't understand me, I knee him hard in the chest and take him down to the floor.

We each have the other locked in place on the mat, and while his face is close to mine, he spits out his mouthpiece and grates, "If you want to win, to see up into that glass box...then you have to take a dive, asshole."

I jerk my gaze to his and give him a *"what the fuck kind of fight is this?"* scowl. Then I flip him over and cinch my thighs around his chest. With cheers swarming all around us, I lean close and spit my own mouthpiece out so he hears my words clearly. "I *will* finish you," I say through clenched teeth right before I pound three hard punches to his face.

Hammer acts like he's going to tap out, but at the last second, the bastard forces me over and tries to lock me in an arm bar. The crowd goes wild all over again.

I manage to get my legs free, then curl my whole body toward my head. Flipping right out of his hold, I steam roll over his head in the process. He looks a bit dazed and twists away just as the bell pings.

I glare at Hammer from my side of the mat, wondering if I'm being played.

To win, I have to take a dive? How the fuck does that work?

This time the ring girl waltzing around the cage with the number five card held high is wearing Hammer's white mask. I skipped the tradition of putting my black carnival-style mask on one of the ring girls on my way into the fight. I wanted to stay focused and didn't need the added distraction.

When the masked blonde ring girl stops and steps up on the ladder on the platform to hand Hammer a rolled-up towel over the top of the cage, I experience a flash of regret that I didn't think to ask one of the girls to hold a towel for me. Wiping the sweat out of my eyes would be appreciated right now.

The last thing I expect is for Hammer to unroll a handgun from the towel and immediately fire it at the metal plate on the cage door. The crowd screams their surprise as the gunfire echoes in the huge building and a wave of shocked gasps follow before suddenly everyone goes quiet.

I realize Hammer has purposefully jammed the door closed and while he's distracted, I zoom across the mat, intending to take him out, but he quickly turns the weapon on me, his gaze slitted in fury. "Back the fuck off, *Steel!*"

Out of the corner of my eye, I see Sebastian shouldering his way past the frozen crowd toward the arena, while several EUC security men also move forward. A couple of the security guards are already at the cage door, trying to open it. I know none of them are carrying anything stronger than a Taser. It has always been a EUC rule for their security.

"All of you, back off!" Hammer barks, shooting a warning shot toward the ceiling.

A hush settles in the room and the men rushing forward outside the cage suddenly freeze. I stop moving, my hands up. He doesn't have to know I'm assessing the best way to take him down.

Holding up his other hand, he lifts a remote device. "This is rigged to two explosives, one is underneath this stage and the other up there inside the box with our illustrious guests. If anyone fucking moves toward this cage, I'll hit this button...and trust me, there's enough explosives under here to make sure none of you make it out alive."

"What do you want?" I grit out.

"Isn't it what you want, Steel?" he taunts, then turns to face the crowd. As they all gasp at the sight of his thumb on the remote device, Hammer's wrath booms, reverberating off the walls. "You want to see behind that glass?"

Turning, he fires five shots straight into the skybox's smoky panes and as the glass shatters and the crowd screams, six business men wearing carnival style masks are all revealed at once, ducking for cover from the bullet spray.

When the men's security guards standing outside the skybox's door renew their efforts to bust it open, Hammer chuckles, raising his voice above the din of the screaming audience. "If you open that door, the bomb up there will go off, so I suggest you *don't*."

The men immediately back off, their hands raised. Theo stands there with the guards, adopting the same backing off stance, but I see him nod to Bash, letting him know he's going to take care of that area.

My heart pounds with a different kind of adrenaline; survival. And my gaze becomes laser focused.

"You have to have a plan beyond this," I say in an even tone, trying to distract his attention back to me. Bash has managed to inch his way closer and that's when I catch a glimpse of Talia's red hair shielded behind him. *Fuck, how did she get here? That better not mean Cass is anywhere near this place, or I'm going to go ape-shit on this crazy prick.*

If Hammer had just brought a gun to the fight, I

would've jumped him already and taken my chances that I'd be faster, but a fucking bomb? I can't stop that from going off too, especially not with his finger resting on the detonator.

He turns cold eyes to me. "My plan is very clear and you're all going to play your part...total annihilation."

The second he says that, the frozen fans closest to us scream and surge toward the exit, creating mass hysteria.

"Don't do this, Jake!" a woman calls as she steps toward the cage out of the rushing crowd.

Hammer is Jake Hemming?

Both Hammer and I jerk surprised gazes to the dark-haired beauty making her way up the stairs, her curled hair bouncing in soft waves against her bare shoulders and strappy black dress.

"Celeste?" Jake says, his voice softening. "Is that really you?"

"I'm here," she says softly, her gaze staying locked on Jake.

I blink to clear the sweat from my vision, needing her to look at me so I can tell who I'm seeing. It can't possibly be Celeste, but then they never did find the body. What about the blood? My brain flashes through the facts I know to be true, yet can't deny the evidence of the woman standing before us.

She hooks her fingers on the cage fencing, pulling herself close. "Please, Jake. Please don't do this. It was a mistake to leave. I'm not dead. I'm here for you."

I edge closer to Jake as he steps toward the fencing,

sadness in his tone. "Why did you try to leave? You know you always belonged to me, not Ben. If you had stayed, I would never hurt you."

Tears shimmer in her eyes as she looks at him. "I was wrong, Jake. So very wrong."

Jake shakes his head as if clearing it. "No," he barks. His shoulders straightening, he takes a step back. Glancing my way, he tightens his hold on the gun and jabs it toward me. "Get back, asshole."

"You're dead, Celeste." Jake glares at me, refusing to look back at her. "You're an illusion. I mourned you."

Beth calls out from the ground floor, her voice steady and sure. "It's Celeste, Jake. She came home."

Celeste nods, her fingers tightening on the cage. A trembling smile curves her lips. "I came back for you, Scrappy."

The nickname pulls Jake's and my attention back to her and at that moment, my gaze locks on the familiar bruising on her neck. The moment I see Jake's finger leave the button on the remote, I spin and slam my foot into his chest with a powerful kick.

The crashing impact jolts the remote and the gun from Jake's hands. I quickly kick the gun out of his reach and smash my fist into his chest, knocking the wind out of him.

"Get the remote, Cass," I yell, glancing at her.

Cass is already hunched down, her arm stretched through the fencing, fingers straining for the remote, but the device landed an inch beyond her reach. "I can't reach it!"

"*Cass?*" Roaring his rage, Jake pounds a fist into my chest and flips me onto the mat.

Jamming a knee into my chest, he pins me with all his weight as I try to regain my breath. "Did you know that I had Cass first?" He snarls out a laugh. "Actually, I've had your little bitch twice. That second time around was hot enough to almost make me forget about Celeste." He bends close, drilling his knee into me. "How does it feel to have my sloppy seconds, Calder *fucking* Blake?"

Red flashes across my vision and I grab his shoulders, throwing him across the cage and into the fencing.

As I rush after him in a blind rage, Bash yells my name. I glance up to see him holding the wired trigger from the bomb and I vaguely register him saying, "Theo got the other one."

Before Jake can recover, I let loose on him, pummeling the jeering shit's face into a bloody mess.

For stealing Cass's innocence and trying to destroy our firsts.

For being a disgusting, molesting fucker.

For threatening to kill hundreds of innocent people.

I don't stop moving until a couple of police officers pull me off the demented bastard.

CHAPTER TWENTY-NINE

Cass

"Great news!" Talia says as I answer my phone and slip into my car.

"That was fast." I snort. "I just dropped my proposal off."

She laughs. "Not that. You're right. It'll take my editor a couple weeks to evaluate it and run it past the marketing committee. I'm calling to let you know the verdict came in. Phillip Hemming is going away for a very long time on multiple counts, with Celeste's death giving him the most jail time. Brent and Jake will be sentenced tomorrow."

After two weeks of endless police interviews, the high profile nature of multiple murders, attempted murder, and other crimes, pushed the trials against Phillip, Jake, and Brent up quickly. I'm just glad to be done testifying.

I'm so ready to put that whole part of my life behind me.

"Oh, and Sebastian got your father's proposal rescheduled to this week. He wanted to make sure that the Carver name didn't taint the project. Don't worry, I've already called your dad to let him know to get ready for it."

"Thank you, Talia. And please thank Sebastian for me too."

"I will. Now, if he would only be so accommodating with his wife. Can you believe he's ignoring my suggestion that I join BLACK security? You would think after I proved that my presence at the fight was necessary, he would agree, but he's being so stubborn."

"I saw you come out from under the fight arena with him. Did you actually help him defuse that bomb?"

"No, but *my* nail clippers did."

I snicker. "Clever. Well, I'm sure it's because Sebastian wants to keep you safe. He already doesn't like when you have to do undercover stuff for the Tribune."

"I know, but at least he can control the cases I work if I'm working for our own company. Ugh...the infuriating man."

"He'll come around," I say chuckling. "He just needs to think it's his idea."

"Hmmm, now there's a thought. Anyway, why don't you tell Calder the good news about Phillip. I think he's at his parents' house—Oh that's Sebastian calling. Got to run." She hangs up before I can ask her to have Sebastian tell his cousin.

It's not like I'm avoiding Calder. It's just that ever since that night at the fight we've both been inundated with the prosecutor's demands pertaining to the cases. And during the trial proceedings our lawyers recommended that we not speak to each other. They didn't want our testimony polluted in any way. Ironically, because he didn't have to testify, Ben had no conflict issues. He asked me to go for coffee and I met him at a local cafe. While sipping lattes, I gave him his ring back. When he asked to meet again, I begged off. I want his friendship, but I know he wants more.

As for Calder, I've been terrified at the idea of facing him after that bomb Jake dropped about us. I agonized over what Calder must be thinking, how he might be twisting what Jake said. I wanted to tell him the truth, but it would take longer than a quick whispered answer in the lobby outside the courtroom.

The day the testimony phase of the trial was over last week, I received a bouquet of roses from Calder. The note inside made me cry with relief.

> *All the firsts that matter happened between us.*
> *Give me time to get myself in order.*
> *Calder*

Before I call Calder with the news about Phillip, I decide to clear all the Celeste stuff from my life. I scroll to the email I sent myself with the Deceiver text conversation between Celeste and Phillip. I'd kept it "just in case" until the trial was over. Once I delete that, I see another email I'd sent myself. It was of the picture from Celeste's last diary entry. I'd sent it to myself intending to read it later, but the chaos that ensued afterward quickly absorbed my attention.

Settling into my seat, I skim over her moody poetic entry until I get to the last paragraph. One line jumps out at me, because even though it stays consistent in tone and mood, it addresses the reader. And Celeste never did that.

My life was colored by design. It was always your favorite.

Colored by design could be referring to all the colors she mentioned throughout her entries: black, green, red, blue. But if I remember right, the colors were always tied to somber moods or used to describe a person's attributes. So who is she talking to…it was *whose* favorite?

I shake my head and start to close the image when it hits me where I'd seen the phrase *Colored by design* before. It was the book I constantly studied in our high school library. The same book Celeste teased me for using an outdated resource. Why would she mention that old book? I can't help but think this note was meant for me.

There's only one way to find out.

CHAPTER THIRTY

The Observer

I've delayed long enough. It's time to move on, but I can't leave this dangling. I should never have let sentiment sway me in the first place.

Only fools trust others to make smart decisions.

I start to get out of my car when Cass Rockwell pulls up.

I quickly shut my car door and flip the visor down so she doesn't see me.

Tension ratchets as I reach over and pop open the glove compartment, my gaze following her into the high school.

Too late.

All I can do now is wait.

CHAPTER THIRTY-ONE

Cass

Shaking my head, I can't believe I'm standing in our high school library, looking for a book that has probably been sent to the incinerator years ago.

When my gaze lands on the familiar spine of the oversized book, I take it down, my body tense with anticipation.

I spend the next half hour flipping through every single page, unsure what I'm looking for. When I turn to the last page with no clue as to why Celeste pointed me to this book, I start to close it as I stand, but something slips out of the yellow return card pouch in the back, landing on the carpet.

My pulse thrumming, I put the book away and pick up the thin USB stick.

By the time I return to my car in the parking lot, my hands are shaking. I rub them on my jeans, then open my laptop and slide the memory stick into the slot.

I grunt my annoyance that a passcode is required, but when I see it's four digits, I immediately type in my name and my heart rate picks up when the drive opens, and a doc pops up with my name on it.

I click it.

Dear Cass,

If you're reading this letter, then I'm already dead. I debated whether or not to write this at all, but I wanted you to know the truth. I feel I owed you that much.

Phillip took everything from me. Everything.

He colored my life and changed who I became.

If you've gotten this far, I can only assume you've also read between the lines in my diary, so you know what he did. I was only fourteen! I won't go into details, but life didn't get better. It got much, much worse.

For years I suffered in silence.

Until I saw you show up at that Blake party, pretending to be me.

My heart races when I read that part. *Wait...what? She*

saw me? I never saw her there and she never mentioned it. I continue reading on, my fingers folding tight around my computer screen.

>*What better way to find out what people really think of you then to go to a masked party anonymously? I despised the Celeste people thought they knew. What did they say about her when she wasn't around? Would they even notice her absence? Or care?*
>
>*You were an unexpected surprise, but so very convincing as Celeste...you gave me hope.*
>
>*It took me years to make sure every detail would go as planned.*
>
>*You were pivotal, if I ever wanted to own myself again.*
>
>*But it would only work if you helped.*
>
>*Phillip owed me the life he stole, so I made him pay by killing his meal ticket.*
>
>*Celeste had to die.*
>
>*She had become a thorn in my side. A body to shed.*
>
>*I wanted to make sure that Phillip never did to another what he did to me. And now he's paying for my life with his own.*
>
>*This baby wasn't part of my plan—yet another of Phillip's brute force tactics to ensure his child inherited the Carver estate—but I'm going to raise my child with love so that she*

never knows what it feels like to be alone in a crowded room, or to be unable to speak the truth because the words' edges are too sharp on her tongue. She will laugh and play and be... happy. Something I never was.

I'm a ghost.

Celeste no longer exists.

But this new person thanks you for giving her a life.

I did my best to protect you from a fate I was already living. I hope you realize that now that you've walked in my shoes.

Your friend,

P.S. I'm aware that you can give this letter to the police and undo the justice I worked so hard to gain, but this is the risk I'm taking.

I stare at the letter, gutted that Celeste felt so alone that she chose such a twisted path to happiness, but also guilt-ridden by the realization that *I* helped put a man in prison for a murder he didn't commit. Shutting my laptop, I start my car and pull out of the school's parking lot, my mind in a daze.

CHAPTER THIRTY-TWO

The Observer

I glance at the car's clock, my fingers tapping rapidly on the steering wheel.

Where is she?

When Cass walks out of the main door, her steps brisk, her face pinched, I grip the steering wheel and straighten, watching her body language.

She unlocks her car and gets in, then turns to mess with something in her passenger seat. *Ah, a laptop.*

I watch her face, full of intense concentration.

She leans close like she's gripping her laptop.

What is she thinking?

What will she do? Will her new friendship impact her decision?

My gaze narrows.

I had to secretly bank five pints of blood, go to an abortion clinic, feed you texts and clues, all while you wormed your way into my family and stole my sister's affection.

Don't steal this from me too, Cass.

If you go to the police and Phillip gets out, he won't stop until he finds me.

Not ever.

Don't make me wrong about you.

Don't make me regret my trust.

I lift the handgun sitting on the passenger seat and set it in my lap, pressing my lips together.

Don't make me kill you.

Cass starts her car and I do the same. Setting the gun back in the passenger seat, I push my sunglasses tighter against my face and tug my ball cap down, following her.

Pulling the gun closer, I check to make sure the safety is Off. She'd better not go to the police.

When she pulls into the Blake estate, I exhale my relief and turn my car toward the Interstate.

It's good to know you're just as smart as you were in high school, Cass.

CHAPTER THIRTY-THREE

Cass

I *ring* the bell at the Blake family home. Calder's place isn't quite as ostentatious as the Carver's estate, but it's a good-sized estate set far back on several acres.

Calder opens the door, a beer in one hand and surprise reflected in his gaze. "Hey, Cass. Are you here to help me pack?"

"Phillip is going away for a very long time," I say, then step inside and take his beer, draining the bottle in one long gulp.

"Are you okay?" He chuckles when I hand him the empty bottle.

I shake my head and walk into the living room, apparently the only room that's not completely cleared of furniture or full of boxes.

Calder follows me into the room and I look at him, my eyebrows hiked. "Why do you have a fire going? It's sixty degrees outside."

Instead of answering, he points to my laptop tucked under my arm. "Does the beer chugging have to do with that?"

Lifting my laptop up, I open it and turn it around for him to see. "I need to show you something."

Calder takes my laptop and reads the document, his brows pulling down as he reads. When he's done, he lifts his eyes to mine. "Where'd you get this?"

I gesture to the memory stick still in the slot. "Celeste left that for me to find. An obscure clue only I would get at the end of her diary led me to it."

Calder closes my laptop, a smirk tilting his lips. "Karma has nothing on a smart, determined woman. That's one hell of a payback."

"I *told* her father she could run a company," I mutter, then shake my head. Turning to face the fire, I wrap my arms around myself, suddenly chilled. "I know Phillip has done horrible things and he absolutely deserves jail time, but he didn't murder anyone. My stomach is knotting that I played a part in putting him away for murder, Calder."

Taking the memory stick, Calder sets my laptop down on the floor, then moves to stand beside me. "If there was a way to erase Phillip from my family tree, I would, Cass. But if I did that, I never would've met you. And since I can't change the past, I absolutely want him to suffer to the full extent of the law and beyond for every bit of pain he's caused."

I glance at him as he stares at the memory stick. "I wish I'd never found her letter. I don't want this burden."

"Then I'll carry it," he says, tossing the memory stick into the fire. Turning me to face him, he takes my hand and flattens it on the scar across his hip just above his jeans' waistband. "Forensics proved Phillip was the one who shot at us that night, Cass. We were lucky it was dark, because he's a hunter who was absolutely shooting to kill."

I nod as I rub my thumb over the scar the bullet wound left behind, then cup my hand over his hip. When Calder doesn't react or touch me back, my heart constricts a little. I release him and glance around the room. A box of records and another box of books sit by the doorway. The other boxes around the edges of the room are taped closed and marked donation. The only piece of furniture left in the room is a soft leather chair. Sitting in front of the chair on the wood floor is a shoebox and a six-pack of beer.

I gesture to the shoebox. "What's in there?"

"Memories that *aren't*."

"Memories always *are*, Calder. Good or bad. They exist."

He shrugs. "Not when they weren't real."

"Let's see about that," I say, scooping up the shoebox before he can stop me. When I pull the lid off and all I see are remnants of pictures someone has snipped up with scissors, I gape. "Did you do this?"

His face hardens. "A *child* did that after his mother killed herself." He glances away, shoving his hands into his jeans. "When my father found out what I'd done to our family pictures, he was furious, but he refused to throw them away. I found them in the attic while cleaning it out this week."

I lift a handful of the colorful images showing bits of happiness: smiling faces, beach sunsets, waterslides, carnival rides, Christmas trees, a woman laughing. "There are happy times here, Calder. You just need to remember them."

He snorts. "I was about to toss that into the fire when you rang the bell. It was the last thing I had left to do."

"You're *not* done." Raising my eyebrows, I turn the box upside down, dumping the contents on the floor.

"Not playing, Cass," he says, his expression unreadable.

I drop to my knees and begin to turn the picture pieces right side up. When I find one that has Calder's face, I *coo* at the baby ones and *awww* at the little boy pictures. Apparently Calder has always been adorable.

He watches me for at least ten minutes until I look up at him and huff, "Well, come on, Master Puzzler. This will go much faster with both of us working this massive puzzle.

He frowns. "You plan to put them all back together?"

"Of course. How else am I going to get to see your family album? I'm dying to know what the deal is with the stuffed purple gorilla."

He snorts. "You mean Grape Ape."

I lift my hands. "How would I know? You have to tell me the stories."

Calder joins me on the floor. Opening two beers, he

hands me one. While we spend a couple hours putting the pictures together, he tells me stories about backpacking and beach trips. At one point while he's telling me about Menemsha beach in Chilmark in Martha's Vineyard, he closes his eyes and inhales. "I can still feel the sun on my face and smell the fresh ocean air. There's nothing quite like it."

"Sounds amazing," I say, smiling.

He looks at me and taps his beer bottle to mine. "I'll take you there one day so you can experience the beautiful sunsets. They're indescribable."

"I'd like that."

He stares off into space and a slow smile spreads across his face. I can tell he's reliving a happy memory. "What are you thinking?"

He glances my way. "I remember my mom and dad dancing in the sand. Even on the beach, people stopped to watch them. That's one thing I definitely got from my dad."

"Oh yeah, what's that?" I tease, loving that he's starting to reconnect with happy family memories.

Setting his beer down, Calder stands and picks his phone up from the fireplace mantel. Scrolling through it, he selects a song and then walks over to me, holding his hand out. "Dance with me, Cass."

I put my hand in his as Ed Sheeran's soulful ballad "Thinking Out Loud" streams from his phone. As the music comes alive and the empty room's acoustics gives the song a larger than life feel, Calder folds his arm behind my back and holds my other hand out. And then he dances with me around the empty room, directing me in big sweeping spins and turns, ballroom dancing style.

While the song's first words weave a sweet spell of togetherness around a couple who've been together forever, my heart aches for the loss of his parents. Yet I can't help but yearn for the kind of forever the lyrics describe. I let myself fall into the security and peace the words evoke for as long as it lasts while Calder holds me in his arms.

I'm enthralled with his dancing skill and adore the happiness in his face as he stares down at me right before he twirls me away from him. When he pulls me back toward his chest, I grin and relish the excitement in my belly from the quick kiss he drops on my nose before sending me away from him once more. It makes me hope that he might want the same...a permanent future together.

Once the music ends, my pulse races and I know my cheeks are glowing. My heart is so full of love for this man. "Your dad taught you how to ballroom dance?"

He laughs. "Actually, yes and no. My mother was the one who danced with me so I could learn the male parts, but my father was the expert who instructed. He drilled me until I learned every step."

"I had no idea there was such hidden talent in those toes of yours."

He yanks me close, a cocky grin flashing. "Head to toe, baby. Head to toe." Just when I think he's going to kiss me, my phone starts buzzing in my back pocket.

"Oh crap, that's my reminder that I have dinner with

Beth in a half hour." I grimace when reality hits. "How will I keep a straight face now?"

Calder clasps my shoulders. "You didn't make Celeste's decision to leave. She did. Knowing the truth doesn't change the fact that Beth lost a sister forever. Just be her friend, Cass. You're probably more a 'sister' to her than Celeste has been in a long time."

He's right. As soon as I saw Jake's nickname on Brent's shell corporation, I knew that Jake was Hammer. And once I called and told Beth what Brent did to me in the past and the other crimes he was suspected of, she was completely on board to help me get past EUC security and back me up if Jake was as off-the-rails as Ben claimed. Ever since that night, Beth has kept in touch. When I nod my agreement about Beth and start to pull away, Calder slides his hands down my arms and captures my wrists. "Thank you."

"For what?" I ask, confused.

He rubs his thumbs slowly over the fine bones of my wrists, then glances toward the pictures on the floor. "For reminding me that even in sad memories…there are good ones too."

I smile. "By my count, you still have a third of the pictures left. Your assignment is to look at every single one."

He smirks. "I have three more beers. I think I'm covered."

Before I can step away, he folds his hands around mine. "I owe Alana a favor for her part in procuring the necklace I gave you."

I tense at the mention of his ex and notice that he glances down at my bare neck. Does he wonder why I'm not wearing his leather necklace now? Talia had returned the diamond one to me in mint condition a week ago, but wearing either one of Calder's gifts without him in my life was just too painful. I'd put them away in the hopes that one day I'd never have to go a day without wearing one.

Calder's fingers tighten around mine. "Alana's creating a special portfolio of all her work and has a section on her temporary tattoos. Now that Steel is done, I agreed to model for pictures. Not of my face, just my back. You mentioned wanting to take pictures and since this will be the last time I have Steel's tattoos, do you still want to take photos?"

Jealousy surges in my chest, but I appreciate him telling me upfront about Alana, and also for remembering my wish to photograph him. I nod and try to keep my thoughts out of my response. "I would love that. Just let me know where and when."

His fingers flex around my hands. "Tomorrow at my apartment. Come around four so you'll still have daylight if you want."

When he releases my hands, I feel suddenly adrift, like I'm no longer tethered to him. The feeling is so upsetting, I swallow and glance away.

"Cass, are you okay?"

Unsure where we stand, I force a smile. Even though Calder was dealing with his own issues today, he was sweet and supportive. Yet the heat that's normally in his gaze when he looks at me was definitely subdued. I know that note he sent me said we're fine, but I can't help but wonder if what Jake said is affecting how Calder feels about us.

"I'm good. See you tomorrow," I say and walk over to pick up my laptop.

CHAPTER THIRTY-FOUR

Cass

"Come in and get set up," Calder says, pulling his apartment door open. He's bare-chested and barefooted, wearing nothing but a pair of well-worn faded blue jeans riding low on his hips.

I try not to stare at the black feathers standing out across his muscular shoulder and arm, but he's just too beautiful not to admire, at least for a second or two.

"You coming in, Cass?" he asks, his light brown eyebrows elevated.

I clear my throat, clasping my camera bag strap tight. "Um yeah, where's the best light?"

He gestures toward the window. "This is the best time of the day for it."

Even though this shoot is highly personal, I go through

the motions of setting up my tripod and adjusting for lighting like I would any other job. I even make Calder stand in a certain spot while I adjust my camera on the tripod to assure I'll have the best angle and lighting. Shooing him away, I take out my other camera and check the lens for dust, then double-check that my settings are where I want them to be. After several minutes of deep concentration, I realize Calder hasn't said a word.

I look up to see him leaning against the counter, watching me.

"What?"

He smiles. "Nothing. It's interesting to watch you in your Raven persona. You're so focused and intense. Are you ready for me?"

Unsure if that was a compliment or not, I lift my camera and gesture to the space I want him to stand in.

When Calder moves into place and reaches for the button on his pants, I lower my camera and frown. "What are you doing?"

He pauses with his pants halfway unzipped and I can see that his goody trail continues. He's completely commando under his jeans. I grit my teeth. "You didn't say you did a *nude* photo shoot with Alana."

Calder unzips his pants completely. Stripping out of his jeans, he kicks them away and narrows his gaze. "You didn't tell me you went for coffee with Ben either."

How does he know that? I hold my camera up. "I haven't fucked Ben," I say in a tight tone, snapping off a couple of test shots.

Calder folds his arms, muscles flexing against his chest. "I haven't fucked Alana either."

"I meant *ever*." I lift the camera to my face to keep him from seeing how hurt I feel, but when I peer through the viewfinder and see he's fully erect, my hands tremble. I have to grip the camera tight to keep it from shaking, but I manage to take a round of shots, keeping my attention from the waist up.

Calder lowers his arms, his green gaze peering directly at me through the lens. "Look at me, Cass."

"I am," I say, moving to take a couple of zoomed-in portrait shots. The softness in his eyes staring into my lens surprises me and I lower the camera.

"I didn't model for her in the nude." He spreads his arms, his chest and abs flexing. "This is for you and *only* you."

My throat tightens and I nod my appreciation. "Can you turn around and bend your left arm toward your head?"

Calder turns and bends his arm up, flexing his bicep and the raven's wing along with it. *Breathtaking. God, he really is a beautiful man.* I spend the next half hour taking shots of his back from every angle, making sure to capture those two perfect balls of muscle just below his waist. I want to cop a feel so bad my fingers tingle, but I force myself to stay focused on the shoot.

Raven would have kept on shooting for at least another hour, but after another flurry of shots, I set the camera down and walk up to run my hand over his tattoo. "It's truly a work of art. I'm glad Alana will have it immortalized in her portfolio so it won't disappear forever."

When my fingers trail down his spine, then lightly slide over the curve of his ass, Calder inhales deeply and glances at me over his left shoulder, his eyebrow hiked. "What about you? Is Raven going to include Steel in her book?"

His comment sparks a thought and I run my other hand over his left shoulder, then down his bicep, flexing my fingers against the tattoo on his muscles. "I've had a hard time deciding on a cover that would encompass the heart of my book without having the exact same cityscape you always see on books about New York. My book is different. It deserves a unique cover. You just gave me the perfect idea."

He turns around and spears his fingers under my hair, cupping the back of my neck. "I'm glad to be your inspiration." His cocky smile turns my heart over as his gaze searches mine. "I've missed you, Cass. Your sweet smell and the feel of you against me." Leaning close, he husks against my cheek, "But most especially your hands cupping my ass, pulling me deeper inside you."

My breath hitches at the memories and I slide my arms around his waist, looking up at him. "I've missed you too. Did you finish looking at all the pictures?"

He folds his muscular arms around me, his erection pressing against my belly. "Yes, my parents' home is now empty."

I know putting the house on the market is part of his

grieving process, but my chest still twinges. "It was your childhood home too. Do you plan to keep this apartment?"

Nodding, Calder kisses my forehead. "I'm going to need a place closer to the BLACK Security office, but yes this apartment will remain mine so I can help Gil with training as much as I can in my free time." He pauses and cups my face. "Now that you're done shooting, would you like to help me wash off the tattoo?"

I smile and press close, enjoying his warmth and the smell of spicy deodorant. I will miss the tattoo, but I'm glad that he's shedding the loner part of his life and joining Sebastian's business full time. "I would love that."

Stepping back, he gestures to my clothes, heat simmering in his gaze. "Strip, Raven mine."

He doesn't have to ask me twice. I quickly unbutton my jeans and shimmy out of them along with my underwear, then slip off my sweater and bra.

Calder chuckles as he steps toward his record player and stacks the spindle several vinyls deep. "I think that might be a record, Cass. Maybe I should've offered to shower with you before now."

"Are any of those from your dad's collection?" I ignore his teasing. I'm too excited, remembering the first time I watched him wash his Steel tattoo away. I'd wanted so badly to be the one sliding my hands over his skin, helping him shed the dark persona. Now I get to.

"A few," he says, testing the needle.

I grin and turn for the bathroom, saying over my shoulder, "Hurry up, slow poke."

Foreigner's "I Want to Know What Love Is" begins to play through the apartment speakers as Calder joins me in the small bathroom and flips on the shower.

Once he adjusts the temperature, he wraps his arms around my waist and walks us into the shower together. I know the hot water won't wash away his tattoo, so I let the steam fill my senses and relax against his hard chest, enjoying the moment of being in his arms after so long.

As we stand there in silence, Calder hasn't asked me about what Jake said, but it has to be bothering him. I know I would want to know the truth. Taking his arms, I wrap them around my breasts, then fold my hands over his. "I never told you the story about when I almost died."

He stills, tensing against me. "When was this?"

"In college. That night I went to a nightclub with my girlfriends. We were partying, doing shots, and hanging out on the dance floor having a general good time. While each of my friends hooked up with guys they met there, I wasn't interested. I did a few more shots and continued to dance." I shrug, smirking. "It's not like my hook-ups would lead to anything earth-shattering. The place was wall-to-wall packed. The last person I expected to run into on the dance floor was Jake."

Calder exhales harshly. "You don't have to tell me, Cass."

I shake my head. "No, you should know what happened. Apparently Jake had just seen Celeste kissing her boyfriend near the bar. He was pissed as hell and also high. When he saw me, it's like a switch flipped. He pushed me against the wall and said, 'I can't believe my luck. I need a release and here you are.'"

The shower washes away the tears as I recall my humiliation that night.

"He violated you on the dance floor?" Calder asks, his arms tightening around me.

"Yes and no," I say, answering honestly.

Calder turns me around, his hard gaze grilling mine. "I don't understand, Cass."

I glance away. "He dry humped me against a wall, Calder, and I didn't fight him."

His fingers tighten around my arms. "Why?"

I look down at his chest, unable to meet his gaze. "I was drunk, and because the only time I'd ever climaxed was that night with him and Brent. It wasn't what I wanted; I had no control over it back then, but since I hadn't climaxed ever again, a twisted part of me had to know that I wasn't completely dead inside."

Calder lifts my chin. "Did you come?"

I sob. "I did, which told me that I was completely fucked up! Afterward, I was so appalled and disgusted with myself that I went back to my room and cut my wrists. I hadn't done it in so long, and I was so upset. I accidently cut too deep and...I ended up in the hospital." I exhale a shaky breath, relieved to have it out there, but worried what he'll think of me.

Calder slides his hands in my wet hair and pulls me close. "That wasn't something you could control. My guess is the reason you came was because strong emotion can stimulate a physical response...and fear is a powerful emotion." Cupping my jaw, love and support reflects in his gaze. "I'm sorry for everything Jake put you through, Cass. I meant what I said when I sent you those roses. All that matters are *our* firsts." Water pings off our faces as he stares into my eyes. "Do you believe me?"

The tightness in my chest eases and I nod. "Thank you for being the amazing man you are. I love you, Calder."

Calder presses a tender kiss to my lips, then smiles. "Are you ready to wash Steel away?"

I nod and he hands me the special bottle of soap, then turns around.

Grinning, I squirt the strong citrusy soap on his shoulders and down his back, then giggle as I hand him the bottle to rub the soap against his skin and watch the ink slide away.

"Hand me the soap again. I must not have put enough on your shoulders. The feathers are being stubborn." Calder clasps my hand and pulls me in front of him, kissing my jaw. "That's because it's there to stay, angel."

"What?" I squeeze his bicep, then turn him around once more to stare at his shoulders. The skull is gone and the only bit left is the raven's wing across his shoulders and down his arm. The feather design covers most of the Celtic tattoo except for the bit on his ribs next to the words Solus.

"Why did you decide to keep the raven's wing?" I ask, stepping back under the spray with him.

He smiles and shakes his head. "It's not just a raven's

wing, Cass. It's a raven. It has always been a raven." Turning, he points to the curve where his neck and right shoulder meet and that's when I see what I haven't before…a raven's head and beak along the curve of his neck and shoulder. Apparently the whole time I thought I was seeing a raven's wing, I was actually seeing an entire raven wrapped around his shoulders.

My heart is so full of love, I can only gape at him. Calder smiles and turns me back around in his arms, pulling me fully against him. "You told me that now I'll never be alone." Folding his tattooed left arm across my chest, he continues, "And now you'll always have a raven watching over you, angel."

Deep sentiment floods through me, and I grip the feathers on his bicep wrapped around my chest. "Calder, that's the most romantic gesture. I'm just—" I swallow my emotions and try to calm my racing heart. "You know, if you need a place to crash closer to work, I could use a roommate…" I trail off and hold my breath.

"Sorry, not interested in the roommate thing," he says briskly, shaking his head.

"Oh, okay. I just thought I'd offer." I keep my tone light to cover my disappointment.

Calder chuckles as he lifts my hand and slides a gorgeous black diamond on my ring finger. "I couldn't resist. The way it shines, I immediately thought of a raven's eye. I love you, Cass. Deeply, passionately and without reservation. I want to protect you and make love to you until we're old and gray. You are *all* I want."

I turn to him and touch his jaw. "I love you very much."

"Say you'll marry me, angel. Then Ben can stop asking you out. *Hemming asshole.*"

Laughing, I clasp his neck. Calder lifts me in his arms and I wrap my legs tight around his waist.

His nostrils flare and he grips my hips as he slowly glides his cock inside me. "Is that a yes?"

When he's as deep as he can go, I gasp and flex around him, moaning.

Calder sets me against the shower wall and thrusts deep, his voice turning rough when I dig my fingers into his skin and mewl my pleasure. "I'm not hearing the right word, angel."

I lean my head back and let my body answer for me, moaning through a long wave of satisfaction as my orgasm takes over. I shudder and tremble through the tremors of happy bliss.

Calder's breathing rushes against my neck and he drives into me as if he can't get close enough. His shoulders bunching, his chest crushes mine as he roars through his own release.

We're both panting and I shiver as the warm water pounding down on us suddenly turns cold. Calder grunts and sets me down to quickly shut off the spray.

I laugh softly unable to keep my hands off his body while he rubs my skin and hair with a warm towel. When he's done and takes the towel to himself, tousling his hair into a wild array of spiky sexiness, I press a soft kiss to his lips.

"Is that your answer?" he says impatiently, then drops the towel to scoop me in his arms and carry me over to the bed.

"Hold that thought." I quickly wiggle out of his hold before he can lay me down. Walking over to my purse, I retrieve the raven leather necklace from a zipper compartment inside.

I smile and start back toward him, but pause when I'm a foot away and stare down at the leather collar in my hand. Rubbing my thumb across the teeth marks along one side, I turn glistening eyes to his. "This is the band from your hat from the party, isn't it?"

Calder nods and pulls me close. "I told you I found the perfect material for the choker." Taking the necklace, he hooks it around my neck, then lifts my chin, his intense gaze holding mine. "I never want to wake up to an empty space beside me again. I love you, Cass. No matter where we choose to live, you are my home. Marry me, angel."

Not a question, but a statement. It's so Calder.

The Lumineers' song "Ho Hey" begins to pump through the speakers. Its lyrics are so appropriate for us, I get teary. *We* belong to each other. I cup his face and whisper against his lips, "Don't sell your childhood home. Let's make it happy again with our own family."

He hooks his hands around my waist, his fingers flexing, emotion churning in his gaze. "That'd better be a yes."

Tears spilling, I throw myself against his hard frame, knocking us onto his bed. "Yes, I'll marry you, you stubborn, beautiful, complex man."

When Calder presses a kiss just above my necklace, I sigh my happiness and tease, "Sebastian says you collared me."

Lust fills his gaze and he tugs me underneath him. "If I could stamp 'property of Calder Blake' on that gorgeous forehead of yours without you wanting to kick me where it counts, I would." His attention slides to my necklace. "But since the choker isn't waterproof, I'll just have to give you a reason to keep that ring on every single day."

"It's perfect, Calder." I lift my hand up and admire the beautiful ring he'd chosen for its personal meaning, then slowly trace my fingers along the side of his face. "And I can't wait to experience the *many ways* you do that."

"I'm glad to hear it, because you're mine, Cassandra Rockwell Blake." Calder bites the heel of my hand and then my wrist. Sliding his thigh between mine, he nips at my collarbone, then clamps down on my neck as he slowly eases himself inside me. A flood of heat envelops my whole body when he releases my throat and rumbles against my cheek, "And I'm never letting you go."

I twine my fingers in his hair and tug his mouth to mine. "You'd better not. I'm yours Calder Jackson Blake. Always and only yours."

Stay tuned for BLACK PLATINUM (IN THE SHADOWS, Book 6)!

If you found **STEEL RUSH** an entertaining and enjoyable read, I hope you'll consider taking the time to leave a review and share your thoughts in the online bookstore where you purchased it. Your review could be the one to help another reader decide to read STEEL RUSH and the other books in the IN THE SHADOWS series!

To keep up-to-date when **BLACK PLATINUM** releases, join my free newsletter http://bit.ly/11tqAQN . An email will come to your inbox on the day a new book releases.

Did you love Cass and Calder's story and want more?

If you haven't read books 1-3 (**MISTER BLACK, SCARLETT RED** and **BLACKEST RED**) in the **IN THE SHADOWS** series yet, here's the series trailer for Talia and Sebastian's story. https://www.youtube.com/watch?v=9ERYQ3HU2mw

If you're interested in other contemporary romances by me, check out my **BAD IN BOOTS** series written under Patrice Michelle.

If you'd like to read another epic romance story like the IN THE SHADOWS books—the kind of love story that spans across several books—check out my **BRIGHTEST KIND OF DARKNESS** series written under P.T. Michelle. These books were written to be enjoyed equally by upper teens 16+ and adults.

Other Books by
P.T. MICHELLE

In the Shadows Series (Contemporary Romance, 18+)
Mister Black (Part 1 - Talia and Sebastian)
Scarlett Red (Part 2 - Talia and Sebastian)
Blackest Red (Part 3 - Talia and Sebastian)
Gold Shimmer (Book 4 - Cass and Calder)
Steel Rush (Book 5 - Cass and Calder)
Black Platinum (Book 6 - Talia and Sebastian) Coming 2016

**Brightest Kind of Darkness Series
(YA/New Adult Paranormal Romance, 16+)**
Ethan (Prequel)
Brightest Kind of Darkness (book 1)
Lucid (book 2)
Destiny (book 3)
Desire (book 4)
Awaken (book 5) - Coming 2016

To contact P.T. Michelle and stay up-to-date on her
latest releases:

WEBSITE
http://www.ptmichelle.com

FACEBOOK
https://www.facebook.com/PTMichelleAuthor

TWITTER
https://twitter.com/P.T.Michelle

INSTAGRAM
http://instagram.com/p.t.michelle/

GOODREADS
https://www.goodreads.com/author/
show/4862274.P_T_Michelle

PINTEREST
http://www.pinterest.com/ptmichelle/

Sign up/join P.T. Michelle's:

NEWSLETTER
(free newsletter announcing book releases and special contests)
http://bit.ly/11tqAQN

FACEBOOK READERS' GROUP
https://www.facebook.com/groups/376324052499720/

GOODREADS READERS' GROUP
https://www.goodreads.com/group/show/130689-p-t-michelle-patrice-michelle-books

ACKNOWLEDGEMENTS

To my fabulous beta readers: Joey Berube, Amy Bensette, and Magen Chambers, thank you for always going deep, giving great wish lists and feedback, and for helping me see the book through your eyes. I appreciate you reading *Steel Rush* so quickly. You ladies definitely helped make *Steel Rush* a wonderful read.

To my wonderful critique partner, Trisha Wolfe, thank you for reading *Steel Rush* so quickly, and for all the awesome brainstorming! Major hugs, girl!

To my family, thank you for understanding the time and effort each book takes. I love you all and truly appreciate your unending support.

To my amazing fans, thank you for loving my books and for truly broadening my audience with your mad love of the IN THE SHADOWS series and characters! I appreciate each and every one of you for spreading the word by posting reviews and telling all your reader friends about the series whenever you get a chance. Thank you for all the fantastic support you continually give!

ABOUT THE AUTHOR

P.T. Michelle is the *NEW YORK TIMES, USA TODAY,* and International Bestselling author of the contemporary romance series IN THE SHADOWS, the YA/New Adult crossover series BRIGHTEST KIND OF DARKNESS, and the romance series: BAD IN BOOTS, KENDRIAN VAMPIRES and SCIONS (listed under Patrice Michelle). She keeps a spiral notepad with her at all times, even on her nightstand. When P.T. isn't writing, she can usually be found reading or taking pictures of landscapes, sunsets and anything beautiful or odd in nature.

To keep up-to-date when the next
P.T. Michelle book will release,
join P.T.'s free newsletter http://bit.ly/11tqAQN

Made in the USA
Lexington, KY
22 September 2016